THE
OLIGARCH'S
DAUGHTER

THE
OLIGARCH'S
DAUGHTER

JOSEPH
FINDER

A NOVEL

HARPER

An Imprint of HarperCollins*Publishers*

HarperCollins books may be purchased for educational, business, or sales promotional use. For information, please email the Special Markets Department at SPsales@harpercollins.com.

FIRST EDITION

Designed by Nancy Singer

Library of Congress Cataloging-in-Publication Data
Names: Finder, Joseph, author.
Title: The Oligarch's Daughter: a Novel / Joseph Finder.
Description: First edition. | New York, NY: Harper, 2025.
Identifiers: LCCN 2024014724 | ISBN 9780063396012 (Print) | ISBN 9780063396036 (Trade Paperback) | ISBN 9780063396029 (Digital Edition)
Subjects: LCGFT: Thrillers (Fiction) | Novels.
Classification: LCC PS3556.I458 O45 2025 | DDC 813/.54—dc23/eng/20240401
LC record available at https://lccn.loc.gov/2024014724

24 25 26 27 28 LBC 5 4 3 2 1

For my longtime readers, with gratitude, who've stuck by me since
The Moscow Club *and allowed me to make my living as a writer.*

The Russian soul is a dark place.

—Fyodor Dostoyevsky, *The Idiot*

PART ONE

EVERYONE DIES

Present Day

1

Until that day, Grant had never killed anyone. He had thought about it before, of course, the way you imagine the worst thing you could do if you had to. You rehearse it in your dreams, in your unconscious. Inwardly, you debate.

How far would I go?

Grant's girlfriend was helping him cook dinner, the night before it happened. She was Sarah Harrison. She taught first grade in the town's elementary school and was sweet and gentle with a core of steel. He'd been attracted to her since the first time he met her, at the Starlite Diner five years ago. But there remained a distance between the two of them. Entirely his fault. He cared about her, but there was too much he couldn't tell her about himself.

Sarah was making a salad while he kept watch on a chicken roasting in the oven. The kitchen of the old farmhouse was big and comfortable and cluttered—red-and-white linoleum floor, a tin-topped dining table, wood-paneled walls. He'd restored the house himself, mostly, doing the carpentry in his boat shop. The whole kitchen smelled of roasting garlic, an aroma Grant loved.

As she chopped, Sarah told him about her day. "This girl threw up on the stairs during dismissal, and I sent her out to her mom," she said. "The mom was so pissed off she called the school to complain that her daughter had vomit on her shirt. 'Why didn't you clean her up before sending her out?' she said. So I get yelled at, and meanwhile, I had to clean up this giant pile of barf." Sarah was tall and slim and had shoulder-length chestnut-brown hair and cognac-brown eyes, and she was wearing her old UNH sweats, maroon with fraying cuffs. (It was a chilly evening.)

Grant tried not to laugh, but then she did, a rueful laugh, which made it okay.

"How was your week?" Sarah said. "Tim still refusing to pay you a deposit?" A local fisherman named Tim Ogilvy had brought in a bare-hull fiberglass boat for Grant to finish out but refused to pay until the work was done.

"Today I told him either he gives me a couple hundred bucks for materials or I'll put his boat in the yard and chain her to a tree."

"What'd he do?"

"He paid."

"Didn't that piss you off? That you had to do that?"

Grant shrugged.

"There's that shrug. Was that too feel-y a question?" she asked.

That was when his phone rang.

Later, he would wish he'd never answered the call. But it was a good friend, Lyle Boudreaux (Captain Lyle, he liked to be called), and he didn't phone very often.

Sarah nodded and smiled, silently letting him know she didn't mind if he answered it. She was peeling a cucumber.

"Captain, what's up?"

"Look, Grant, I'm not feeling so hot tonight, and I don't think I can make tomorrow morning's trip. And I was wondering if you could cover for me. Some couple from New York. I don't want to lose them as customers." Lyle had a deep-sea fishing charter business and depended on repeat business.

Meanwhile, Grant was waiting for a coat of epoxy to dry and didn't mind making a couple hundred bucks for a morning of sailing Lyle's boat. Lyle was very protective of her, a twenty-eight-foot Downeaster, but he trusted Grant. After all, Grant had built her.

"Sure," he said.

"Oh, great, thank you," Lyle said, sounding relieved.

"Okay. Be at the boat at seven?"

"Can you deal? I know it's early."

"Sure."

Grant had taken Lyle's boat out for a morning charter once before, when Lyle's second baby was born, a few months back. She was a great boat, of course, and according to the maritime forecast, tomorrow was supposed to be a clear, sunny day.

No problem, Grant told him.

HE WOKE JUST A FEW minutes before five the next morning, before his phone alarm sounded, and he turned it off before it could wake Sarah, who was staying over. It was still dark. He made coffee, dressed, and drove the ten miles to the harbor. He arrived by quarter of seven and found the *Suzanne B* docked where she always was.

There's a whole routine to starting up a boat. He pulled out the rods, set her up. Lyle kept a stack of folding chairs in the cabin so they wouldn't get wet from condensation overnight. Grant unlocked the cabin and retrieved them, set them up on the deck. He checked the engine, turned on the valves. Lyle's boat was only three years old and still looked new. He took excellent care of her, was fanatical about cleaning her, thoroughly scrubbing her down before and after each trip. *He'd want me to do the same*, Grant thought.

He gathered the cleaning solutions from the pilothouse down below, and in fifteen minutes he'd cleaned and sanitized the *Suzanne B*, first with boat soap and a long scrub brush and then with Clorox bleach; finally, he sprayed the deck with an alcohol-based product.

After checking the oil, Grant started the engine, let her warm up. The customers were scheduled to arrive by seven thirty, so there was plenty of time. He switched on the radios and talked to some of the early-bird fishermen who were out there already, to find out where the good fishing was. You'd think they wouldn't want competition, and some didn't. But a few Good Samaritans told him where they were having luck. It's a bountiful ocean.

Right at seven thirty a stout man appeared at the boat wearing a navy windbreaker and jeans and expensive-looking sneakers. He was balding, with curly black hair at the sides, and wore steel aviator-framed sunglasses. He had the air of an athlete gone to seed, soft around the middle but stocky, thick-limbed in ways that could be muscle as much as flab. He looked to be in his forties, and with his pasty complexion, he didn't look much like a sportsman.

"You're not Captain Lyle," the man said.

"My name is Grant Anderson," Grant said, "and I'm filling in for Captain Lyle, who's sick today."

"All right, Captain Grant," the man said. "My name is Frederick Newman." He had a little tic, the cheek below his left eye twitching every so often. He was studying his phone.

"We're waiting for your wife, is that right?" Grant said.

"No, my wife is not coming," said Newman. "She's under the weather. She won't be fishing with us this morning." He had the barest hint of an accent, which Grant couldn't quite place, but it made him nervous.

"So it's just you?"

"Right." Newman's cheek twitched, and he resumed studying his phone. "I'm good to go, Captain Grant."

Grant gave the man a version of Lyle's introductory spiel, Newman nodding impatiently throughout as if he'd heard it all before. Probably he had. Grant said he just wanted to make sure he had a good time. He showed the man all the gear, explained about the wire line. Newman kept nodding.

He wanted to catch striped bass, he said; bluefish was too fishy to eat. Grant told him the secret to cooking bluefish was to soak it in milk for a half hour. Newman didn't care; he wanted striper. Then he said, "Hey, how about we go shark fishing? Use the speargun?" His cheek twitched.

"We'd better not." Shark fishing destroyed a lot of equipment. Captain Lyle wouldn't be happy about it. Grant knew Lyle used a speargun recreationally for striper or bluefish or flounder fishing once in a while. It was a powerhead speargun, a .44 magnum. Good protection against sharks. When Lyle fished for tuna, he used his speargun to kill sharks that tried to steal his yellowfin.

Grant returned to the pilothouse, the enclosure that allows you to stay out of rain or direct sunlight, and took the wheel. They steamed out to a cove where there was a big drop-off. The *Suzanne B* wasn't fast, could go maybe thirteen or fourteen knots, but she was a good, sturdy boat. Mackerel swam around the edge and top of the sandbar, around thirty feet down. And striped bass loved mackerel.

Grant throttled the engine down, slowing the speed to two knots. Now they were over a school of fish, according to his fish finder. No other vessels were in view. Newman was sitting on a deck chair, examining Lyle's speargun. "I went shark hunting with this famous guy out of Miami once," he said. "That was awesome."

"Be careful with that thing," Grant said. Threaded onto the end of the speargun was a .44 magnum bang stick, a smooth stainless-steel screw-on cylinder that held a cartridge.

Newman was studying him. "You know, you look familiar," he said, setting the speargun down on the deck. "You always had a beard?"

"Oh, yeah," Grant said, attempting to sound casual, but his heart was drumming. "Long before it was cool." He was pretty sure now that Newman's very slight accent was Slavic. An eel of unease squirmed in Grant's belly. It had been years since he'd heard a Russian accent. Newman's fluent English had the flat American *a*'s of an émigré who'd spent most of his adolescence in the United States. Probably came to the U.S. as a teenager.

Frederick Newman shook his head. He was speaking to Grant in a low voice, but Grant could barely hear him over the thrum and whine of the *Suzanne B*'s engine.

"Excuse me?" Grant said.

Newman raised his voice. "You must have known this day would come, Paul," he said calmly.

Grant's stomach caved in on itself. He was looking at Newman's face, at the eyes behind those aviators. They were intent, alert, almost the eyes of someone playing a video game, neither cruel nor kind. Grant expected that tic to return, but Newman's face was absolutely placid.

"I'm afraid you've got the wrong person, Mr. Newman. I'm Grant Anderson."

"You know, Paul, everyone dies one day. With me, it's different. Clean, quick, no suffering."

Grant caught the quick flash of gunmetal. The man's right hand. Something had taken hold of Grant, something icy and willful and deliberate. His heart was racing, and he felt the first prickles of sweat on the nape of his neck. He didn't know what to do.

"You'll need to pilot the boat out another seven miles or so," Newman said, "so we're catching the Labrador Current. Best to have no body washing ashore."

"But you're making a mistake," Grant said. With a calm, slow motion, he took out his wallet and drew close to Newman. "I told you, you have the wrong man. Here, let me show you my captain's license." He opened his wallet to his driver's license and displayed it, holding it too close to Newman's face. He had no captain's license. "See, you've got me confused with someone else."

For just the briefest moment, Newman glanced down at Grant's wallet, and in that instant, Grant lunged at the man, fist balled, and batted the gun out of his hand as hard as he could. The weapon went skittering and clattering across the deck and splashed into the water.

Smoothly, with scarcely a pause, Newman picked up the speargun lying at his feet and hoisted it until it was pointing at Grant's chest. The man seemed to know what he was doing. The gun was probably five feet long, its end just a few inches from Grant's body. "You build boats for a living," Newman said. "You're very good at it. You know what I do for a living. Trust that I'm good at it, too."

Obligingly, Grant reset the wheel.

Gesturing around at the water, the wide-open vista, Newman said, "See, in my business, this is what we call a 'clean field of action.'" He glanced at something on his wrist, maybe a GPS nav device, Grant wasn't sure. "Bring us seven miles southwest, Paul."

"Berzin send you?" Grant said, sounding resigned. He watched Newman remove the cotter pin from the cartridge at the end of the bang stick, the safety. So he did know what he was doing.

"You've only made things harder on yourself, Paul," Newman said. "Messier. More painful. It didn't have to be this way."

"The currents shift a lot this time of year, you know." Grant didn't meet the man's gaze but looked elsewhere. He felt the ocean waves gently rolling the deck, smelled the diesel. He moved very slowly and carefully toward Newman.

With a sudden motion, he shoved the end of the speargun up and away from his chest and pointing into the air, to point at neither of them. His heartbeat thundered in his ears.

What followed was a blur.

They grappled over the gun, Newman yanking at the weapon, trying to gain control of it, Grant trying to grab it away from him. Grant knocked Newman to the deck, the two men struggling, fighting with each other, each of them grunting. The other man was stronger than he looked. With a guttural roar, he wrenched the speargun out of Grant's hands, and as the distal end struck the underside of Newman's jaw, there was a deafening blast. Grant's face was splashed with blood. His ears rang.

At once he saw what had happened. The .44 magnum round had torn a jagged hole in Frederick Newman's throat. Blood gouted from the wound, down Newman's chest, pooling on the lacquered wooden deck. Grant's face was beaded with blood and sweat. He squatted next to Newman and felt an artery in his bloody neck. There was no pulse, but he knew there wouldn't be one.

Grant's stomach was roiling. Something oily rose in his throat. He hadn't killed the man; the struggle over the speargun had done it. But he felt like he had just crossed some Rubicon, violated some ancient taboo, and was now on the other side of it.

Staggering to his feet, he just made it to the side of the boat and vomited.

He thought of Sarah and the little girl at her school.

Then he took the dead man's iPhone out of his back pocket. He looked at it. The phone's home screen was locked. But how to unlock it? Would face ID do it? He held the phone up to the dead man's face, but the eyes were closed, so it didn't work.

In any case, your mobile phone could be tracked, he remembered, so he had to get rid of it. Standing at the side of the boat, he dropped the phone into the ocean.

Now he was operating out of purest adrenaline. Cleaning up the puddle of blood would be easy. But what to do about the body?

The solution came to him instantly.

Returning to the wheel, he navigated over to where the sonar fish finder told him there were sharks. A whole school of them, probably tiger sharks. He throttled down to two knots.

He removed the man's wallet from his back pocket. Opening it, he found a New York State driver's license in the name of NEWMAN FREDERICK G. In the man's front pocket was a set of Porsche keys. He thought a moment. Tossing the wallet and keys overboard, he dragged the body a few feet over to the side of the boat, eased it over the edge, and tipped it headfirst into the shark-infested water with a dull splash. A cloud of dark blood instantly bloomed, and the ocean began to churn, and once again he was sick.

2

Grant tied the boat to the dock and once again scrubbed down the deck with bleach. He finished with a spray of the alcohol solution. No trace of blood, as far as he could discern. Just to be sure, he hosed down the deck again and washed it again with boat soap, and then the bleach, and then the alcohol.

If there was an investigation, the alcohol and the bleach wouldn't be suspicious, he thought. They'd be part of the close of any normal fishing excursion.

Smelling of bleach, he put away the deck chairs and locked up the pilothouse. He said hello to a fisherman on the pier he knew, then made his way to the row of parked cars. There was only one Porsche parked there, a black 911. It was a very good car, the sort of car he once used to drive but hadn't for a long time.

He unlocked his truck. On the floor in front of the passenger's seat, he set down a plastic bag containing the striped bass he'd caught. After his struggle with Newman, he'd forced himself to catch a fish, even though all he wanted to do was get home. But he had to be able to explain the time he'd spent on the water.

As he drove home, he noticed that the leaves had turned a spectacular array of colors, from brilliant red to blazing orange to bright yellow and deep russet. This was why leaf peepers drove from miles away to see New Hampshire's trees. But he wasn't enjoying the foliage. His entire body was crackling with tension.

From the truck, he called Lyle. "The guy never showed," he said. "I waited a good long time, and he never appeared. So, hope you don't mind, I took the boat out to catch some."

"No problem, but . . . that's weird," Lyle said, sneezing, sounding congested. "He even prepaid and everything. That's really bizarre. Well, sorry for the trouble."

THERE WAS A CREAKY OLD joke in the boatbuilding business: How do you make a million dollars building boats? Start with two million.

Grant Anderson was an excellent craftsman of wooden boats but not a great businessman. Which was ironic, since he used to be a finance guy. One problem was that he took only cash, and a lot of people preferred to pay with a credit card. Another was that he underpriced his work; he knew that. He felt lucky to have any work at all.

He'd arrived in Derryfield five years ago looking for a carpentry job and managed to get hired by Old Man Casey, a boatbuilder looking for an assistant. John Casey had spent his life building boats but had grown tired of sanding and painting and scraping and sweeping floors.

Grant swept and sanded and scraped and painted and, along the way, learned how to build boats. Old Man Casey wasn't much of a teacher, but he would answer questions.

Grant had invited Sarah over for dinner again, and he wished he hadn't. But he had to keep on living a normal life, as if nothing had happened. In the afternoon, he had filleted the striped bass and marinated it in olive oil and garlic and lemon juice, and now he was searing it on the charcoal grill behind the house. Fish this fresh, especially striper, was always delicious. But he had no appetite.

He kept seeing the dead man's face, the slack mouth, the ruined throat. He kept replaying that terrifying moment when the bang stick at the end of the speargun had struck Newman's jaw and fired off a round. He couldn't forget the feeling of the man's hot blood running down his fingers as he lifted the body toward the side of the boat and slid it overboard.

He was *almost* certain no one had seen him with Frederick Newman, but he couldn't be sure. There was a possibility someone had seen them together, at the marina or out on the water. He was *almost* certain no one had seen him slide the body overboard—he had been out on the water a good distance from anyone—but there was always that nagging possibility.

There was too much he didn't know, that was what was tormenting him.

Was it the traffic cam? Derryfield had recently installed its first traffic camera. Maybe an image of his face had gone out. Maybe that was how he'd been discovered after so long. After he'd been so careful. Had he been sloppy?

A lot of people were looking for him, he knew—they'd been looking for five years. But in this small town in New Hampshire, away from any big city, he was hiding in plain sight. *Live like you're supposed to be here,* he'd once read. He was Grant Anderson, carpenter and boatbuilder and good citizen of Derryfield, New Hampshire.

He flipped the fish over to get some grill marks on the other side and moved the serving platter closer. He was thinking about his go-bag, his "bug-out bag," as it was called in the books he'd read, on a shelf in the workshop. He'd have to check through it tonight, make sure everything was still good. He kept another bag in his truck; he should check that one over, too.

And he wondered if tonight would be the night he told Sarah.

And if so, how much should he tell her?

The striper had come out perfectly. Grant could tell by looking at it. Sarah had set the table and put out a salad and some boiled tiny new potatoes.

Tonight, she looked tired, but still as pretty as she'd been when he first met her at the Starlite Diner in Derryfield five years earlier. She was playing a bouncy, upbeat Taylor Swift song—"Shake It Off"—loud, on his speaker system, but Grant wasn't feeling it.

"How's Mr. Madigan's boat coming along?" They sat at the kitchen table.

Distracted, he didn't respond. She put down her knife and looked up for a moment. "Earth to Grant? You there?"

"Oh, sorry. Yeah, not sure—this last batch of epoxy isn't curing right."

"So what happens next?"

"I'll check it out again before I go to bed. May have to reapply."

"Is that going to be a problem?"

"Shouldn't be. I told Madigan November sometime. I'll make it."

"This is delicious, Grant. What did you do with this?"

"The usual. Caught it this morning, so . . ."

"Well, it's great."

He had to maintain a normal façade, keep Sarah from having suspicions, and tonight it was taking considerable effort. "Report cards coming along?"

"They're called 'progress reports,' and they're taking forever." She put butter on her potatoes. "Plus, I had an annoying email to deal with."

"Oh?"

"Atticus's mom. Remember Atticus?"

"Yeah, sure. The kid who's always wearing *Star Wars* T-shirts?"

"That could describe half the class. They all wear *Star Wars* T-shirts. Anyway, his mother is worried because he keeps telling her he doesn't want to go to school. This kid Atticus is the happiest kid, I swear. Like, the happiest kid in the class."

"So why does he not want to go to school?"

"He tells her that kids have been saying mean things to him."

"Like?"

"'Underwear Head.'"

He forced himself to smile, to push his preoccupation aside. He wasn't going to tell her yet, he'd decided. Not until he had to. Which could be any day . . . but not yet. He didn't have to do it yet.

"That's mean, I guess?" he said after a pause. "Have they been saying actual mean things to him?"

"Not in my earshot. Maybe during recess?"

He'd stopped listening. He was thinking: Had Frederick Newman sent a picture of him or a text to his colleagues? To let them know they'd finally found him? If so, both he and Sarah were dead.

That thought was terrifying. He had to get his head back into the conversation.

"Huh." He was barely paying attention to what she was saying.

"Why aren't you eating, Grant? You haven't touched your fish. It's delicious."

"Yeah, thanks. What were you saying?"

"You're not even listening to me. I mean, what is with you? You invite me over for dinner, and you're somewhere else."

"Sorry, I'm preoccupied."

"Something wrong?"

Grant shook his head.

"Why am I not surprised? You're not there. I feel like I don't even know who you are sometimes."

He took another tasteless bite of fish.

"You're doing that thing you always do—there's stuff you're not telling me, you're always preoccupied. I can't live like this."

"I know," he said quietly.

"I mean, you're a great guy and everything, but I don't know how much longer I can go on like this."

"I know," he said again. "I understand."

"But do you? I feel like I have a lot to offer."

"You do. You're incredible—"

"Oh, yeah? You never talk about your past. I don't know a damned thing about you. You never open up to me."

"I know, I—"

"I can't live like this."

"I get it."

"Something's missing," she said. "I just don't get you."

He stood up. "I want you to have something." He went to the cupboard under the kitchen sink and found, behind the Drano, a large Ziploc bag. He handed it to Sarah.

"What's this? A bunch of . . . cash?" She knew he accepted only cash for his work and kept a lot in the boat shed.

"Yes. And a burner phone."

"What the hell, Grant . . . ?"

"If anything happens to me, if I have to take off suddenly, this is how you can reach me. I've programmed in a mobile phone number for me."

"'Take off suddenly'—what's going *on*? Where are you going?"

He shook his head. "Maybe nowhere. Maybe nothing will happen." *How do you even start?* Grant wondered. The less she knew, the better. The safer, for her. "This isn't the time to get into it. I just need you to trust me for now."

"That's not good enough," Sarah said. "I want to know what you're talking about."

Grant paused. "Soon," he said.

3

For the next couple of days, he watched the clock, listened for every noise, every passing car. One day, two days . . . At the end of day three, while he was watching a forgettable show on Netflix, trying to distract himself, the doorbell rang.

He paused the show, went to the front door.

A policeman, a thickset middle-aged man in a blue uniform. Someone Grant didn't recognize.

"Are you Grant Anderson?" the cop said.

"I am," Grant said, his heart rate quickening. "What's up?"

"I'm Detective Sergeant Frank Lundberg from the police department over in Hamlin." Hamlin was the coastal town where Captain Lyle kept his boat. "I'm sorry to interrupt your evening, but mind if I ask you a couple of questions?"

"Of course," Grant said. "Is there a problem?" He felt a bead of sweat form behind his ear and slowly trickle down his neck.

"May I come in?"

Grant opened the door and showed the cop in.

Settling into the chair next to the couch, Detective Sergeant Lundberg took out a notebook. "So, I'm looking into the disappearance of a thirty-six-year-old man from New York. His car was found over by the dock in Hamlin. A Porsche Nine-eleven. Anyway, your friend Lyle Boudreaux said you were supposed to take a man named Frederick Newman out on his boat, which is harbored in Hamlin, but he never showed. That right?"

Grant's heart was jackhammering, but he kept his expression neutral. Another droplet of sweat coursed down the back of his neck. "Exactly." If the sweat started streaming down his forehead, it was all over. He inhaled and exhaled silently, trying to calm himself.

"What time was Mr. Newman supposed to meet you?" Detective Sergeant Lundberg had a comb-over, strands of gray hair inadequately covering a large bald spot.

"Seven thirty. That's when Lyle normally takes his morning group out. I waited until, I don't know, maybe eight thirty? And when he didn't appear, I took the boat out for a bit by myself. Caught some striper." He smiled casually—anyway, he hoped it looked that way.

"And you never heard from Mr. Newman, never saw him?"

"Right. He never showed. That's all I know. Sorry I can't help you."

Lundberg leaned back in his chair. He seemed to be satisfied. Grant felt a flood of relief wash over him.

"Hey, so I see you're a boatbuilder," the cop said. He pointed toward Grant's workshop, the shed to the left of the house. "How's the boat business these days?"

4

For the last five years he'd found himself always thinking ahead, always calculating the next step, never fully able to relax and enjoy his blessed life. He'd set up several motion-triggered Canary Flex cameras on the exterior of the house. He didn't like surprise visitors.

Normally, Grant found serenity in mindless tasks like painting or sanding: a chance to be in his own head and mull things over, let his mind wander. But the next morning, as he brushed on epoxy, his brain churned with fear—*What if Newman's body washed up onshore? What if there were security cameras in the harbor in Hamlin? Capturing video of Newman coming aboard the* Suzanne B?

Jesus, he didn't want to think about it.

He was startled by a knock at his workshop door.

He put down the brush, went to the door. It was Alec Wood, the deputy police chief in Derryfield, who was also a friend of his and Sarah's. Alec was tall and slim, around thirty. He was wearing his navy-blue Derryfield Police uniform.

"This an okay time?" Alec was as un-coplike as you could be, soft-spoken and informal. He was good looking, with a strong jaw and a heavy brow that gave him a vaguely threatening look.

"Sure, bud. What's up?"

Alec had once confided to Grant, after many beers, that he had originally joined the police to write a book about what it was like. He was a writer, once. But then he found he liked police work far more than writing, which was brutally solitary. He never wrote the book.

"Listen," Alec said, "the FBI called, and they're on their way here to talk to you."

"The *FBI?* Is this about that no-show passenger again?" Grant hadn't told Alec about his visit from Lundberg, but of course Alec knew about it. Lundberg would have had to get permission from the police department in Derryfield to come here and ask Grant questions in a missing-persons case.

"It is. They want to talk to you. I didn't want you to be surprised."

"Huh," Grant said. "Why the FBI?"

Alec shrugged. Nonchalantly, he said, "Dunno. It's an interstate case. There's that." He smiled, but he was looking at Grant curiously.

"Bizarre," Grant said. The word *case* terrified him. He suddenly felt cold. Goosebumps broke out all over his arms. He shook his head. "Thanks for telling me."

Alarm bells were going off in his head. He tried to look as unruffled as Alec.

Had the body turned up?

He swallowed. His mouth was dry. His stomach twisted.

They're on their way. What did that even mean?

"Sure thing," Alec said. "Listen. I don't know what's going on here, and I can tell you're not about to tell me. But I get the sense you might be in some kind of trouble, and what I want you to know is—look, we're pals. If you need some help, talk to me."

Grant nodded. The last thing he could do was tell Alec what was going on. "Thank you. But I'm okay."

AFTER ALEC LEFT, GRANT RETURNED to the workshop. He opened a closet that was neatly stacked with fiberglass cleaners and marine wax and cans of marine-grade epoxy and polyurethane sealants. At the back of the bottom shelf, behind a row of anti-fouling paints, he found the small black Under Armour gym bag containing a several-inch-thick stack of banknotes, half twenties and half fifties. Just over $48,000.

Forty-five minutes later, returning home from the town's True Value hardware store, he stopped just before the turn into his long driveway.

Alec's police cruiser was parked up by the house.

Instinct told him to hide. He quietly pulled off the road and parked the car in a copse of pines, well hidden from the main road and the house. His mind was racing. Why was Alec back already? What if he was there to arrest him? Yes, they were friends, but the law was the law, after all.

It could be worse, he thought. *Could be the Russians. They wouldn't bother with niceties.*

The truck idling, he took out his phone, opened the Canary app, and a video window opened. He was watching a live feed of the exterior of his own house, with sound. The Canary Flex cameras' resolution was good and clear, high-def video, 1080 pixels. One camera was mounted inconspicuously above the front door. It had a wide-angle lens, but Grant could see only Alec, standing on the porch, and part of the driveway.

Why was Alec there again? Waiting for him to return?

Just then, a vehicle on the main road rocketed by him. He caught a glimpse: a black SUV, a Chevy Tahoe with official U.S. government plates. Its tires squealed as it passed out of sight and then slowed. Then Grant heard the familiar crunch of gravel as it turned up his driveway. He glanced at his phone, watched Alec Wood, from his place on the porch, turn back to look at the Tahoe as it approached the house. He appeared surprised.

The Canary cameras had sound, and he was able to hear through the app as someone shouted from inside the Tahoe, "Where is Grant Anderson?"

"Who are you?" he heard Alec's voice through the Canary app.

"Is Grant Anderson at home?"

The black Tahoe pulled up and stopped beside Alec's cruiser. Grant watched as two men got out, the driver and a passenger. The driver was bullnecked and bald, maybe in his twenties; the other had graying copper hair and looked significantly older. Even through the security camera app, Grant could see the apple-shaped cicatrix under the older man's left eye.

He instantly recognized the face.

It was Berzin.

The realization filled him with terror.

Now the three men were speaking more quietly. Grant turned up the volume on his phone, watched the video, listening hard.

"I talked to you before," Alec Wood was saying. "You said you were FBI. Well, I called the FBI's Boston office, and they never heard of you. Let me see your ID."

"We're not FBI," the younger man said. "We're government intelligence."

"What are we talking about, CIA? NSA?"

Berzin said something Grant couldn't make out. He heard only "need-to-know."

"I want to see your credentials, or you're going to have to leave my town."

"Right here," the driver said, his hand out, holding some kind of paper.

In the video feed, Grant watched Alec approach the driver. He looked visibly suspicious, a hand on his weapon. "Your vehicle is a rental. I can see the barcode sticker on the windshield." Alec said something about running the license plate, then pulled out his weapon and aimed it at the two men.

There was a sudden loud *pock*. Grant watched on his phone as Alec jerked sideways and then crumpled to the driveway, blood seeping from a wound in his chest into the gravel around him.

Grant gasped, his heart racing. His fingers suddenly shaking, he fumbled with his phone, accidentally dropped it. Picked it up again, increased the volume on the video feed. He watched as Berzin looked down at Alec's body for a moment and then ran back to his own vehicle, followed by his colleague.

Grant heard the two men's voices indistinctly. He dropped his phone onto the truck's front passenger seat, shifted out of Park into Drive, and hit the gas.

5

Grant pulled the truck back onto the narrow, barely two-lane country road, taking care not to accelerate too loudly so the Russians wouldn't hear him passing.

He headed for Route 16, a north-south state highway running from New Hampshire's seacoast to the White Mountains. He chose north for no reason other than because the farther north you went, the more small or unmarked roads there were, and the easier it was to lose someone.

As he drove, he hit Sarah's number on his phone. It rang five times before she answered.

"What's up?" she said abruptly. She knew that if he called her at school, it would have to be something important.

"Where are you?" Grant asked.

"At school. Classes are over. I'm using the photocopier. Everything okay?"

"Don't go home," he said. He needed to project a tone of calm, suppress the fear in his voice. He had to keep her on board, get her to do what he asked, to understand the urgency. "I want you to call your aunt Tilda and ask if you can visit her for a while. Okay? Don't go home. Everything you need you can get later. Just do *not* go home, you hear me? Or to my house." Her apartment was on the second floor of a wooden triple-decker a few blocks from the Starlite Diner.

"What? *Why—*?" Her voice sounded frantic.

"Remember I told you one day I might have to leave suddenly? Well, this is that day. You—"

"If you don't tell me why—" She sounded panicked now.

He interrupted her, speaking as calmly as he could. "Some bad people are after me, and I don't want them going after you. If you go home, they're going to take you hostage, or worse."

"*Hostage*? What are you talking about?"

"Sarah, these are—I know this is freaking you out, but I just need you to trust me."

"Grant—"

"I know you have a bunch of questions, but this isn't the time." He found himself short of breath.

"Grant, you're scaring the hell out of me!"

"Here's what I need you to do—"

She started talking, but he cut her off. He wondered if she could hear the fear in his voice. He tried to sound firm, composed, resolved: "*Listen to me, okay? Do you have the burner phone I gave you?*"

"It's in my car."

"Good. Grab it and turn it on. From now on, I'll call you on that number. Not your iPhone. Okay? Turn off your iPhone, and keep it off. They can use it to track you down."

"*Who*, Grant? *Who's* going to track me down?"

"No one. Not if you listen to me, do what I say." In the truck's rearview mirror, he saw the black Tahoe loom into sight. He felt a jolt, a surge of adrenaline. To Sarah, he said, "Go to Tilda's. We'll talk soon. You just need to get a move on. Now!" He hit the red button to end the call.

Now he wasn't sure where he was going; he knew only that he had to escape these guys.

But he couldn't go to the police station in town. That he knew for sure. How could he explain who he was after they'd run his name through their records? Would they take him into custody? Probably.

That was obviously out.

Behind him, the Tahoe was closer. He had to outrun them, elude them. The Tahoe was fast, faster than his truck, a five-year-old Ford F-150 Raptor he'd bought used last year. But the Raptor had almost twice the horsepower of his pursuers' car. He'd bought it not for speed but to tow commercial fishing boats.

All this meant he wasn't going to be able to easily outrun his enemies.

And the guys in the Tahoe were armed, he knew. He wasn't. That was the simple, terrifying fact.

The only advantage he had was that he knew the roads around here and they didn't.

When he came upon U.S. Route 302, a spur off NH 16, he took it, heading west.

The Tahoe, wherever it was, was far behind him.

Route 302 was a two-lane road that, at this time of the year, boasted dazzling foliage. On either side were steel guardrails. He glanced in the rearview: he seemed to have lost the black Tahoe. He allowed himself a moment of relief; he let out a long breath he hadn't realized he'd been holding.

Every once in a while, a Tahoe would pass by, heading east, and his breath would catch. But it would not be a black Tahoe driven by a completely bald man. It would be a different color, with a different driver.

Now he knew which way he'd go. He'd take 302 toward the town of Hart's Location, and then take Sawyer River Road, which cut through White Mountain National Forest. There was something about the woods of New Hampshire that felt protective, safe.

He glanced in the mirror again. He was so far ahead of the Tahoe by now that they wouldn't be able to tell where he'd turned off the highway. And not being New Hampshire natives, they'd have no idea he'd driven *into* the forest. It wouldn't occur to them.

A few thousand feet later, he saw the sign for Hart's Location and abruptly took the left turn.

Now he was on Sawyer River Road, a narrow two-lane road that sliced through the Pemigewasset Wilderness recreation area. Tall old-growth trees lined both sides of the road. As he drove, he continued checking his rearview. No black Tahoes. As far as he could see, his was the only vehicle on the road.

Grant noticed there were no cars parked alongside the road. *Odd*, he thought. Hikers usually parked along this stretch of Sawyer River Road before entering the forest.

He kept going. The road twisted and degraded until it was nothing more than a wide dirt trail. And then, suddenly, he came upon a gate blocking the road. A sign on it read, ROAD CLOSED.

The road had evidently washed out.

For a moment he paused, foot on the brake, trying to decide what to do next.

If he turned around and headed back to 302, he'd either run into the oncoming Tahoe or be spotted by them. And this time, they'd use their weapons.

He was trapped.

6

The sign said the road was closed, but he could easily drive around the gate and take the degraded road, for a while, anyway. He peered ahead. In the near distance, he saw downed trees and tree limbs. But that seemed like the only feasible option: driving through the woods.

The other option, turning around and heading back to 302, would be suicide.

He pulled the truck around the gate, off road and into the forest's edge, driving over shrubs and tall grasses, until he reached the beginning of the forest: a row of trees that grew close together. Too close. There was no getting through. Directly in front of him was a cluster of small boulders blocking what seemed to be the only way to get the truck into the forest and hidden out of sight of his pursuers. The thick woods would help him conceal the vehicle, but he had to get through this perimeter.

He put the Ford into 4 Low and rolled slowly toward the smallest of the boulders. He tried crawling the truck over the boulder, but there wasn't enough traction to get him over it.

He backed down, and then put the truck back into Drive, using momentum to help carry him up and over the top of the boulder. He heard something rip off the right side of the Ford with a metallic crunch, but he kept going. He'd reached the top of the boulder and found that his tires were spinning but the truck wasn't moving forward.

Gently, slowly, he hit the gas pedal. He started to move, and soon his tires gripped and took him over the boulder.

He could see Sawyer River Road from here, which meant his truck could be seen from the road. Straight ahead of him was more stone, bordering the rocky bed of a dried-up stream. These boulders were smaller, and the truck clambered over them and into the streambed. The clamber destroyed the Ford's undercarriage, but at least the truck wouldn't be seen from the road now.

Then he heard a popping sound, and the truck engine shuddered.

Soon he was out of the streambed, but the steering wheel felt loose suddenly. It shook and vibrated. Also, the brake light on his dashboard was now illuminated. Something had happened to the brakes. Maybe a rock had snagged one of the brake lines. Maybe the truck was leaking brake fluid.

But at least now he was able to drive straight through the woods. Scraping between trees, threading the needle, he was soon deep enough into the forest that he wouldn't be spotted.

He noticed suddenly that he was going steeply downhill. He braked to slow the descent, the steering wheel continuing to wobble, but the brake light hadn't lied: something was wrong with his brakes.

The vehicle wasn't stopping. It was accelerating.

And as he jammed on the brake pedal, he realized too late that only the back brakes were dead. His front brakes were still working.

The truck lurched, and he was thrown forward against the dashboard.

He felt like he was tumbling in a giant washing machine. For a split second, he floated in midair. The truck tumbled end over end, back end over front. It was terrifying. He heard the crunch of metal and the shattering of glass, and he was thrown forward again. The world spun. He was upside down, right side up. Objects from the front seat and the back seat went flying; something hard hit him in the chest, and he was nearly deafened by the sounds of the crash.

For an instant, he must have been knocked unconscious. When he came to, he found himself hanging upside down by his seat belt. But he was alive, and he didn't think he'd broken anything. His heart pounded in his chest, and his ears rang.

It took him a minute to orient himself, to figure out where the ground was. He yanked the seat belt open and dropped down onto the Ford's ceiling. Now it felt like he'd hurt something. He pulled the handle on the nearest door. It wouldn't open. He yanked again, kicked the door with his foot, but it didn't move. He tried the passenger-side door, but that one wouldn't open, either. He smelled gasoline. The engine was still on, he fumbled for his keys in his right front pocket and remembered he didn't need a key to shut off the engine. He pressed the ignition button.

But the engine wouldn't shut off. He felt a rising panic, then realized the truck was still in Drive. Finally, he managed to pull the gear shift handle toward himself and get the vehicle into Park.

The Ford's engine shuddered and stopped. But he was stuck inside the cab, the odor of gasoline growing stronger. He had to get the hell out of there.

He kicked at the smashed front windshield again and again, leaving a jagged opening, but the shattered safety glass was held in place by a plastic film of some kind. With his bootheel, he stomped on the windshield again, tearing a larger opening. He crawled through it and tumbled to the ground.

Steam rose from the hood of the upside-down truck, then black smoke and the acrid, burnt-plastic stench of something electric.

He sprang away, running through the dense trees. Then he remembered that he had left the go-bag in the backseat of the truck's cab.

He returned to the truck, crawled in through the hole in the shattered windshield and into the cab, his feet landing on the ceiling. The smoke was now pluming from the engine, and he saw flames licking upward around the Ford's upside-down hood.

Get the hell out of here.

It's about to explode.

There it was, the black duffel bag. It lay on the ceiling's white vinyl headliner. "Come on!" he shouted to himself. Grabbing the duffel, he propelled himself back through the opening in the windshield and crawled out onto the beaten earth of the forest floor.

Was there anything else in there he needed? Nothing important. He backed away from the wreck, which was still giving off dark thick smoke, the fire under the hood growing stronger. He choked on the fumes from the burning gasoline, stronger now. His head throbbed.

He turned and ran away from the flaming carcass. When he was only a few hundred feet away, the Ford finally exploded with an immense orange flash, an ear-splitting blast, a torrent of black smoke, a great ball of fire.

PART TWO

DEEP DIVE

Six Years Earlier

7

Until the moment he laid eyes on Tatyana, Paul had been dreading the evening. His employer, Aquinnah Capital, had bought a table at the charity gala, and as one of the company's star analysts, Paul had to attend. There were enough of these kinds of obligatory functions that he'd finally bought a tuxedo from Brooks Brothers a few months earlier. But wearing the monkey suit was a hassle. He was rusty on tying bow ties. Also, enduring a long evening of speeches about whomever they were celebrating—that took patience.

Paul and a couple of fellow analysts from Aquinnah were standing around a small round table drinking and trying to talk over the crowd noise when he noticed her. She appeared to be one of the catering staff, dressed in their uniform of black trousers and white shirt. She was behind the bar, grabbing a couple of freshly poured champagne flutes from the bartender.

Paul intercepted her on her way back into the crowd of partygoers. "Those spoken for?" he asked.

She smiled as she held out the tray and let him take a few of the six flutes. Hers was a winning smile, an open face. "Enjoy." She was in her twenties, had blue eyes and long dark lashes. Dark blonde hair pulled back in a tight ponytail. A slim waist and long legs. Stiletto heels. She wasn't conventionally beautiful, but she was cute. Something about her—her gracefulness, maybe, or her self-confidence or the directness of her smile—or maybe all the above—appealed to him. She was a breath of fresh air in a stuffy room. He felt the spark of attraction.

"Champagne any good?" he asked, hoping he sounded more laid-back than he felt in the moment.

"It's not Dom Perignon, put it that way." She smiled, slightly amused. She had the barest trace of an accent that he couldn't quite place.

He grinned. "But not swill, either."

"Of course not. Not here."

He nodded, looking around the magnificent, strikingly lit Great Hall and Balcony of the Met, both crowded with people in tuxes and ball gowns, before turning back to the young woman's very attractive eyes. "So," he said. "Long night, huh?"

"Umm. It's okay, I guess?" She said this with a quizzical shrug.

This was her job, no big deal—she was used to it. She'd probably worked far more of these dull charity events than he could imagine.

"And are the guests generally well behaved tonight?" he asked.

"All but you." That open smile again. "Excuse me."

Later in the evening, on the way to the bathroom, he caught a glimpse of this same woman outside, smoking a cigarette and looking at her phone. He reversed direction and stepped outdoors—a crisp, cool fall evening—toward her.

"Could you spare a cigarette?" he asked. She looked up slowly, her face then registering recognition.

"Sure," she said, handing him her pack. She watched as he fumbled to extract a cigarette, then flicked a lighter in his direction. He leaned in, lit up—and immediately started coughing.

She smiled. "You don't smoke, do you?"

"Candidly, I do not," he managed to admit when he'd recovered. "Thought I'd be better at faking it."

She laughed. "What's your name?"

"Paul Brightman. You?"

"Tatyana Belkin."

"Pretty name. Russian?"

"Right."

"When's your night off, Tatyana?" There was something vaguely mysterious about her, more than just her Russian name and that hint of an accent. Maybe the way she held her cigarette, with one hand supporting her right elbow, like in an old black-and-white movie. With her long neck and her long waist, she was as graceful as a swan.

"My night off?"

"*Mozhet poobyedaem vmeste?*" Paul said. Meaning: "Can we have dinner together sometime?" In college, he'd taken two years of Russian.

She widened her eyes, smiled delightedly. "*Tak vy govorite po-russki?*" So you speak Russian?

"A little bit," Paul conceded in English.

He asked her for her phone number. She asked for his cell, entered the digits. She started to hand his phone back, then stopped.

"Actually, how about tonight?" she asked, placing her hand on his forearm. "I know a great place."

"Tonight? When?"

"How about now?"

"They won't fire you?"

She laughed. "I think you have the wrong idea about me. Shall we go?"

IT WASN'T UNTIL THEIR SECOND drink at the Hole in One, a dive bar in Hell's Kitchen with a good jukebox, that Paul asked her how she liked catering, and he figured out the truth. Tatyana hadn't been *working* the charity gala but, rather, attending as the guest of a friend. The white shirt he'd mistaken for cater waiter garb had been, she told him, a blouse from Nili Lotan, a designer she wore a lot.

"I'm sorry," he said. "I saw the white shirt, and I assumed . . ."

She laughed. "I guarantee you that none of the staff were wearing Nili Lotan." She seemed charmed when he admitted he didn't know anything about fashion.

She didn't seem offended; she thought it was hilarious.

"So why do you speak Russian?" she asked.

"Language requirement in college."

"But why *Russian*?"

"Well, I heard it was easier than Japanese or Chinese or Arabic. Plus, one of my friends told me it would look good on my résumé."

She looked dubious, took another sip of rosé.

Paul continued: "When you tell people in an interview you took Russian, you see, it shows you accept a challenge and you're willing to take the unconventional path." He smiled, acknowledging the bullshit. "Were you born in Russia?"

She nodded, her mouth full of pizza. She swallowed. "But I came here as a little kid, around six." She shrugged, seeming to signal that she was bored with the topic, didn't want to talk about it.

"That's why your English is so good. Do you speak Russian with your family?"

She nodded. "So where do you work? For some hedge fund?"

"Aquinnah Capital. Bernie Kovan's company."

"I don't know anything about hedge funds. Aquinnah?"

"Bernie named it after his Martha's Vineyard house."

"You like the work?"

"I do."

"You like the money, too," she said with a knowing smile. "It's how you men keep score."

"Not me. To me, it means safety. I grew up with a lot of financial insecurity." He was by now mildly drunk. "My dad lost job after job. We didn't have much money."

"So now you're careful with money, right?"

"I make good money, but I'm pretty frugal, yeah. So I never have to worry about it."

"Did you deliver papers as a kid? Riding around the neighborhood, tossing the paper onto the porch, all that?"

"I mowed lawns. Made a business of it. Hired my friends as subcontractors. I got the business and a piece of each job."

"How old were you?"

"Fourteen, fifteen. Another round?"

8

Researching the pluses and minuses of the various companies that Aquinnah Capital was considering investing in was one of Paul's strengths and, he admitted to himself, a source of pride. He knew how to dig deep.

So it was second nature for him to google "Tatyana Belkin" the morning after their first date—and it surprised him to come up empty. She didn't pop up in any web searches; there was a concert pianist in Australia with the same name, but she looked nothing like the lovely woman he'd shared cocktails with the night before.

She'd told him she was a photographer, that was her main thing; the fact that she had no web presence just added to her mystery. His mother had been a painter. In the few memories he had of his mother, she was either lost in a painting or sitting down at the supper table with paint-splotched hands.

The next day was Saturday. In the afternoon, he texted her. *Great to meet you, Tatyana. Any chance for dinner Sun. night?* Saturday night seemed too soon, too presumptuous. Sunday night was already pretty aggressive. He wasn't exactly playing it cool.

Three gray dots bubbled for almost a minute, but her reply was brief. *Can't Sunday—family dinner. How's Monday?*

Family dinner? Did that mean her family lived close by? Monday was a work night, but he'd gladly sacrifice a few hours of sleep to see her again. On Tuesday morning, he'd be guzzling coffee and Red Bull, and that was okay.

He answered right away: *Monday's great.*

He thought quickly about where they might go. Right away he ruled out the over-the-top, pricey restaurants in the class of Daniel and Per Se and Jean-Georges. She was a (no doubt struggling) photographer, and he worked at a hedge fund, so that would be just showing off his relative wealth to her. He had colleagues who liked to do that, thinking that displaying their wealth made them more attractive. He could tell she wasn't into that scene, anyway.

She lived in the East Village, so he suggested a place around there, an intimate, unpretentious French bistro.

She replied: *Hmmm . . . Let's go to Axepert.*

He replied: *Sure.*

Then he looked it up. It was a bar in Tribeca where you could throw axes. He was beginning to like her more and more.

AXEPERT WAS ALSO VIKING-THEMED, AN industrial space with skulls and roses on the walls and a neon sign that read, I'M A FIGHTER & A LOVER. Their Manhattans were served in skull glasses.

She turned out to be good at the axe throwing—better at it, in fact, than Paul was. She had great form and several times hit the bull's-eye.

"You've done this before," Paul said.

She shrugged, smiled. "Practice makes perfect." She wore straight dark jeans and white Golden Goose sneakers—he recognized the big gold star—and a loose-fitting ecru sweatshirt with an Isabel Marant logo on the front. Her blonde hair was down.

She wanted to keep score. It occurred to him only after they arrived that maybe it wasn't such a good idea to combine axe throwing with alcohol consumption, but he kept his opinion to himself.

She won.

Later, while they snacked on flatbread pizzas and a second round of Manhattans, he asked, "How was your family dinner last night?"

Another shrug. "Like always. Every Sunday night we have dinner."

"Wow, that's—wow. Every Sunday night. I can't imagine."

"You're not close with your family?"

"I don't have a family. No brothers or sisters, and my mom's dead."

"And your father?"

"He's crazy."

"Literally crazy?"

"He rejects modern society. He lives in the woods somewhere."

"You don't know where?"

"I haven't talked to him in like twenty years."

"And I thought my family was strange." She laughed. "A great Russian writer once said that all unhappy families are different in their own way."

"I even read that one. I remember something about railroad tracks."

"Spoiler alert."

"So is yours one of those unhappy families?"

She shook her head. "I was kidding. I'd say it's complicated." She fell silent, and he couldn't decide whether to pursue the subject. Instead, he said, "So you're a photographer?"

She nodded. Gave a little embarrassed smile.

"You don't have a website."

"I *know*." She moaned. "I need to put one up, like, *yesterday*."

"Love to see your work."

"I'm having a show in a couple months, at the Argold Gallery."

"Really?" So she was serious, not a dilettante. "What do you take pictures of?"

She looked kind of uncomfortable. "I—I guess you'd call me a street photographer."

"Like Cartier-Bresson or Robert Frank? Or Weegee?"

"Oh," she said with a relieved smile. "You know photography?"

"Some. What kind of stuff do you do?"

"You just have to see it. I'm not good at describing it."

"Try."

"I'm so not good at that."

"My mother was an artist. A painter. I know how hard it is to articulate what you're trying to do in your art. So try me."

"She was? What kind of art?"

"Now, that's hard to describe, too. She painted the woods, the trees around our house in Washington State. But not in a photorealist way. In between abstraction and representation. She incorporated real twigs and grasses and flowers into her work. Fairy roses that bled pink. Strokes of bright colors. They were bold and happy paintings. Colorful and joyous, very emotional. Which was weird."

"Why?"

"Because she led an unhappy life. Oppressed and stressed by my father. A very unhappy woman. Anyway." Paul realized he was getting too deep too fast, and he changed direction. "Back to your work."

"Is she still painting, your mother?"

"No, she died when I was a teenager."

"That's terrible! What happened?"

Paul shrugged. "Long story. For another occasion. Let's just say, it was not a happy time. Anyway—"

"You know painting, too!"

"Just my mom's. But *your* stuff—what are they pictures of?"

She tossed her head back, smoothed out her hair, then shook her head. A delaying tactic while she thought. "So it's ordinary people—no, that's not right, I mean the sort of people you don't notice on the street. People you don't look at."

"Portraits?"

"Sort of. Usually in broad daylight." She gave a little twist of a shy smile. "I'm a happy person, so I shoot unhappy scenes."

"Are they unhappy, really?"

"No, not really. I mean, they're glimpses of people who live hard lives. And I like to think I take their pictures with empathy. I get to know them. So it's different from a lot of other photographers who sort of condescend to their subjects. I feel like I get them."

Later that evening, the moment came when they left the bar. They kissed on the street. "I'd invite you over for a nightcap if my place weren't such a mess," he said.

"So come to mine," she said.

9

Her apartment was in the East Village, a fourth-floor walk-up in a rundown-looking redbrick building on East Seventh Street, off St. Mark's Place. Kind of a funky neighborhood and perfect for an artist or photographer. It was between a vintage clothing shop and a smokes-and-beer convenience store.

As she unlocked the door, Paul heard a canine whining. When the door opened, a little dog came up to them, standing on two legs, pawing the air with the other two. A tiny, ugly dog that looked like a mix of bulldog and Chihuahua.

"This is Pushkin. He's a rescue." She picked the dog up and massaged his erect ears. "Oh, Aleksandr Sergeyevich! Pushok! You sweet beautiful thing," she said. "He was in a kill shelter in Alabama, and nobody wanted him, and he was just days away from being killed."

"You love dogs, huh?"

"I do. How about you?"

"For sure."

"Do you have one?"

"I can't. I'm always at work. It would be cruel."

Her apartment wasn't big—maybe eight hundred square feet—but comfortable and nicely decorated, with an artist's touch. The walls were painted in an earth tone, the color of a clay pot. The furniture was a mix of rummage sale items, the kind of things you find discarded in alleys, that all seemed to work together. As for the utilities, there were old-fashioned radiators that had been painted over a thousand times and a window air-conditioning unit. The floor was that kind of parquet you see in lots of New York City apartments, quite scuffed. Tatyana switched on a series of lamps until the lighting was perfect.

"How long have you had Pushkin?"

"About two years, I think? I'll get us some drinks. Scotch okay?"

"That'd be great."

While she poured drinks, Paul looked at the black-framed photographs lining the walls in the living room and kitchen. Color photos of old ladies. When he looked closer, he saw that the women looked foreign, appeared to be Russian, because most of them wore headscarves, babushkas. He looked at one portrait of a very wrinkled woman with a sweet smile and light in her eyes. She was missing some front teeth, and some of them were gold. Some of the women had sunken mouths and stern or wary expressions. One of them was walking her dog in a park; another was cutting up beets. Another was sitting at a table outside a metro entrance selling cucumbers and parsley, smiling broadly with steel teeth.

"These are terrific," Paul said.

"Oh, that's my old stuff. My new stuff is totally different. You'll see at the gallery. I mean, if you go." She handed him a Scotch on the rocks, poured a white wine for herself.

"What makes these pictures so . . . painterly? Is that the word?"

"So many things. It's the lens you choose, the focal distance. The time of day when you capture the picture. The light. And I spend a lot of time editing my pictures. And I have a great printing guy. He's expensive, but really good."

"They're really intense. What makes them so intense?"

"Because I'm not staring at my subjects. I mean, I the photographer. I get to know them until I feel an intimacy with them, even though they're strangers. I establish a connection, a—"

"Rapport."

"Yeah. Like any good portrait painter would—like Francis Bacon or Lucian Freud. But painters have it easier. They can work for hours, days, weeks, to get under their subject's skin. We have a split second."

"Did you take these in Moscow?"

She nodded. "My dad goes back to Russia every once in a while, and sometimes I go with him. My mom lives there."

He took a sip of Scotch, felt the pleasant burn. "Aren't there tribes in Africa or wherever that think that if you take their picture, you're stealing their soul, their spirit?"

The dog settled at Tatyana's feet. "I think so. I mean, I've read some critics, like Susan Sontag, who say that photography is an aggressive act.

You know, you *take* pictures. You're exploiting your subjects. It's voyeuristic. But I feel like I'm looking at them with compassion. With empathy. It's like a caress. A way of touching someone. The best portraits come out of love. I mean, Walker Evans used to sneak pictures on the subway with his camera hidden in his coat. But I always ask permission. I talk to them first. I get to know them. I love these *babushki*, these grannies. I treasure them."

He felt a swell of affection for her. They stepped toward each other at the same time. He closed his eyes and inhaled the lavender scent of her hair, then leaned in and kissed her, his arms sliding low around her narrow waist. She pressed against him, and he felt her heartbeat through her breasts. He was aware of the hard, quick thudding of his own heart. As he kissed her, he slid one hand down around the curve of her buttocks. She slipped her tongue into his mouth, gently first, then with a powerful urgency. She clearly didn't abide by some antiquated three-date rule.

Then she pulled away, murmuring, "Let's go to the bedroom."

Light filtered in across the airshaft and into the darkened bedroom. Paul took her in his arms and whispered, "Tatyana," just to hear the sound of her name. He loved that name. His arms around her waist, he slid his hands under her sweatshirt, felt her warm skin.

She helped him pull the sweatshirt over her head and unfastened her bra, stepping away briefly before pressing himself against her as the bra fell to the floor. She was perfect, silky and strong, and he actually shivered at how wondrous she felt to him now. He slipped his hand across the front of her lace panties, as her hips shifted to make room, heard her moan with pleasure as his fingers slipped inside her.

Outside the bedroom door, the dog whined.

THEY LAY, AFTERWARD, ON HER bed. She didn't pull a sheet up to cover herself. She traced a pattern in his chest hair with her index finger.

"What did you mean when you said you lost everything?" she said.

"My dad . . . Well, after Vietnam, he graduated from MIT, taught at Caltech—he was an early computer genius. The world could have been his oyster, you know? But he despised the culture of the modern university and inevitably picked fights with his department chairmen. Lost job after job that way. Eventually, he wound up at Western Washington

University, in Bellingham, where he managed to get fired again—this was when I was little—and this time, something happened with him. Something snapped in his brain. He moved out of the house and into a hovel in the woods, the North Cascades. Leaving my mom and me without any income."

"So how'd you guys survive?"

"Mom took a job as a receptionist in a dentist's office, and we scraped by. Even working as hard as she did, she never stopped making art. Every spare minute she could find, she'd paint. She used to put things in her paintings, like burlap and string and flowers. Glitter."

"So, like, collage? Mixed media?"

"Some of that, yeah. I don't really know what 'school' her work might have been classified as—abstract and expressive, I guess? All I know is, she was really gifted." He didn't want to talk about his mother. Her long, slow death had overwritten his earlier memories of her. When he thought of her, he saw her in her terrible cancer-ridden last days, her scraggly white hair sticking up from her nearly bald head, her bruised eyes. "You told me you left Russia when you were six?"

He could see surprise, or maybe a little disappointment, that he was changing the subject so pointedly—but also an innate awareness not to crowd him if talking about his mother was too painful. She nodded gently. "Yes. We'd been in Moscow."

"Do you remember what it was like?"

Now it was Paul who noticed a shift in her. Like a veil had come down over her face.

"Not really," she said. "Little things, I guess. We had a dog, I remember that. Big white fluffy dog. A Samoyed named Zeus."

"Always wanted a dog, but my dad was opposed." Paul didn't particularly want to think about his father, either.

"My papa used to tell me about how bad Moscow was before I was born. He'd go to banquets at work, and everyone was stealing bottles of wine and hunks of cheese. Famous people, powerful people—it made no difference. There wasn't enough food. Like, it was a big deal when bananas suddenly showed up in the market one year. I remember hearing about that."

He was looking at her face, wondering why, when he first met her, he'd thought she wasn't "conventionally beautiful." Deep blue eyes. Arched brows. Lying there immodestly, her breasts on display, she was gorgeous. A painting.

"And then we moved to America. And then I met you at a fund-raiser for liver cancer, and you stole three glasses of champagne from me. And here we are." She leaned over, kissed his forehead. "You said you don't have brothers and sisters?"

"Nope. Just me."

"Was that lonely?"

"Sometimes."

"You said your father lives in the woods somewhere. Like, in a tent?"

"No, a sort of lean-to. We used to visit Dad at this shack he lived in. Totally off the grid. He'd become a survivalist. No running water, no electricity, of course no telephone."

"So was he really crazy?"

"Boy, that's hard to say. It was like he was too brilliant to live in the world. He'd issue manifestos, just like—remember the Unabomber from a few decades ago, Ted Kaczynski? You're too young. But like him. My dad is like the Unabomber without the bombs."

She didn't seem to remember the Unabomber.

"My father believed that privacy was disappearing. Thought technology was a more powerful force than our desire for freedom."

"Huh."

"Dad would say you can no longer remain anonymous unless you opt out of society altogether. You're born, you get a Social Security number or an ID number, you carry around a tracking device called a cell phone, you leave an enormous digital footprint every day. Surveillance cameras record nearly our every movement, our faces in facial recognition software. We have little boxes in the home that are constantly listening to us. And there's nothing to be done about it—the genie is out of the bottle. There's no such thing as privacy anymore. All you can do is drop out. Opt out. So, that's what he did. He dropped out."

"He had a point, don't you think?"

"Yeah. Maybe. But he wouldn't listen to anyone else. And when my mom found a lump in her breast, she . . . Well, she died of cancer when I was a teenager."

He looked up and was surprised to see that Tatyana had tears in her eyes.

"I'm so sorry," she said.

"So am I," he said quietly. He found himself lost in thought for a moment, remembering his mother's last days, in Bellingham, when her body was ravaged with cancer. He remembered her when his father left, after days of loud arguments. She sat on the landing of the staircase weeping inconsolably, though Paul tried to console her, putting his arms around her. He tried to think of happier images, remembered her making dinner, usually meatloaf or Shake 'N Bake chicken, with paint-spattered hands. His childhood was blotted out by his father's rages and his mother's meek attempts to mollify him.

They were both silent for a long time. "Would you mind," she said, "if I took your picture?"

"Now?"

"If it's okay."

"Naked?"

"I like your body, but I don't want to do Mapplethorpe." She got out of bed and retrieved a camera from a side table, a serious-looking Canon digital with a big lens. "Can you turn to your side?"

"With or without the sheet?" Paul asked.

"The sheet over your lower half."

He turned in the bed and pulled the sheet down to around his waist. "Like this?"

"Shh," she said.

He heard the shutter click multiple times. She tugged at the sheet, pulled it down a little, but not all the way. The shutter clicked some more.

"There," she said. "Thank you."

"Is my butt going into your gallery show?" Paul asked.

"Don't flatter yourself," she said.

10

Paul Brightman was sixteen years old when he lost his mother. He learned this news from his father, who was still living in a hut in the woods but temporarily staying at the house in Bellingham. Even though he mostly wasn't there, his influence over Paul's mother remained strong. When she discovered a lump, he convinced her not to go to the hospital. He hated industrialized medicine. When you're a hammer, he said, everything's a nail. He had his natural cures. Snakeroot and saw palmetto and aloe vera and ginkgo and garlic. Meanwhile, her tumor got bigger and bigger, until it was too late.

Paul had last seen his mother the night before she died, at home, before Stan Brightman reluctantly called for an ambulance. She'd looked terrible—her white hair sticking up wildly from her skull, her eyes dark and sunken, her thin mouth a rictus of pain. She didn't look like Marjorie Brightman any longer. To Paul, she appeared already dead, even though he'd never seen a dead body before. That was what death looked like, he was sure.

At around nine in the evening, Paul had gone into her bedroom and found her mumbling, calling out faintly in pain, "Help me!" To his father, he said, "She needs to go to the hospital, now!"

"They're just going to kill her," Stan had said. He had a full beard and was unwashed and smelled bad.

"She's already dying," Paul said, weeping. "She should be comfortable now. Call the ambulance!"

To Paul's surprise, his father had picked up the phone and punched in 9-1-1. Stan took the one extra seat in the ambulance, even though Paul had wanted to. His father told him to stay at home.

"She's gone," he said on the phone a few hours later, in a tone Paul rarely heard from him, soft and sad. Paul was already crying when the phone rang, because he knew.

He heard his father come home after midnight, but he didn't come out to see him. At breakfast, Stan was all business. He told Paul that he was going to sell the house and that Paul would move with him to the hut in the woods, off the grid.

Paul's reply was quick and firm. "I'm not living that way," he said. "I won't go."

"I'm not asking you. I'm telling you."

"I'm not living like a crazy person in the woods. I won't do it. I want to go to school. I don't want to live like some freak."

They argued back and forth like this for a few minutes until, finally, in great exasperation, Stan Brightman called his brother Thomas, who lived on Cape Cod with his two kids.

A few days after Marjorie Brightman's funeral, Paul got on an Amtrak train, alone. It crossed the country in four days, taking him to Boston, where he caught the bus down to the Cape and out to the town of Wellfleet.

Thomas Brightman looked a lot like his brother at a slightly younger age, except clean-shaven. Paul had met him a few times when he and Paul's cousins came to visit them in Bellingham. Now he hugged Paul for a long time, and Paul noticed how good that felt. His father never hugged him, not even when his mother died. Paul got into the backseat of his uncle's Jeep Explorer with his two cousins, Jason and Alex, who were thirteen and eleven, and the three of them immediately agreed to play *The Legend of Zelda: Ocarina of Time* when they got home.

"This is your new home," Uncle Thomas said. "And your new family. You'll share a room with Jason, okay?"

Jason pouted long enough for Paul to see it, which was probably his intention.

"Okay," Paul said uncertainly.

After getting over his initial resentment at the near stranger invading his personal space, Jason became friends with Paul, as much as a thirteen-year-old could be friends with a sixteen-year-old. Paul became the elder brother. Uncle Thomas was divorced, apparently amicably, and went out with women from time to time.

And for the next two years, Paul shared a room with Cousin Jason and gradually became a full-fledged member of the family. It was not without fights. His cousins didn't always like sharing their things with

Paul. But Uncle Thomas was always there to mediate fights and to hug Paul, to remind his sons that he was a member of the family, too.

Thomas Brightman built and repaired boats. His two sons had no interest in what their father did, but Paul was intrigued. He liked to watch his uncle plane and sand and paint, the radio playing softly in the background. Whenever Thomas did something menial and uncomplicated, like sanding or painting, he used to disappear into his head, go all Zen. Paul had liked watching his uncle build duck trap wherries, dories, and sharpies, cutting marine plywood on the CNC, a computerized saw. There were always multiple copies of *WoodenBoat* magazine lying on the coffee table near the TV. Paul's two cousins loved sailing, though, and after a few lessons from Jason in Wellfleet Harbor, Paul learned to sail and got good at it.

Paul had thought about what his life would have been like without the kindness of Thomas Brightman, his thoroughly uncrazy Uncle Thomas. He couldn't imagine what might have happened—he'd have been sent, maybe, to a foster home, tossed into the maw of the social services bureaucracy, where he'd surely have been lost. His life would have become a nightmare because his own father was crazy. Uncle Thomas had saved his life.

So it was monumentally unfair that Thomas, who'd later moved to Westchester, should have had a stroke at the age of fifty-five that rendered him speechless. Ever since then, Uncle Thomas had lived in a nursing home in New Rochelle, where Jason and Alex had placed him. Paul visited him there every couple of months. He wasn't sure if Thomas understood him when he spoke, but he behaved as if he did. And Paul believed he did. The staff at the nursing home made their rounds a couple of times a day, and there was such turnover that most of them barely knew Thomas. So it was all the more important to Paul to make time to see him.

Two days after he stayed over at Tatyana's, he did so again. The nursing home smelled faintly of excrement and cleaning fluid, as it always did. Thomas looked pallid and weak, though they put him in a wheelchair and wheeled him to the courtyard every morning when it wasn't raining. Thomas's room smelled urinous.

"How are you this morning?" Paul asked that day.

Thomas didn't reply. He looked at Paul warily, his mouth frozen in a grimace.

"You look good. Jason and Alex seem to be doing fine," Paul said. Empty words that might be reassuring to Thomas nevertheless. He paused. "Hey, I met a new girl. Her name's Tatyana. She's Russian American."

Thomas blinked a few times.

"And she's beautiful, and smart."

Uncle Thomas looked into Paul's eyes.

It made Paul physically ill to see his beloved uncle reduced to such terrible circumstances while still relatively young. That and the odor in the room made him want to leave quickly, but he spent a good half hour talking to Uncle Thomas, hoping against hope that his words were registering, though Thomas gave no sign of comprehension. Finally, after about half an hour, he gave his uncle a kiss on the cheek. He thought he noticed what might have been the very faint beginnings of a smile.

On his way out, he glanced at the chart outside the neighboring room. The room's inhabitant was a man a few years younger than Paul. He'd been in a coma for five years. A nightmare for this young guy and for his family. There were still worse fates than Thomas's stroke.

11

Paul met his friend Rick Jacobson for drinks after work. Rick worked at a nonprofit that helped educate women, mostly in sub-Saharan Africa, about HIV/AIDS prevention. He had worked at nonprofits for years. That was who he was. In college, at Reed, where Paul and Rick were class-mates, Rick had spent every spare minute volunteering for community organizations. He and his wife, Mary Louise, had three kids and lived in Rutherford, New Jersey. Rick had gained weight since college, like a lot of men, but he wore it well: he had a big frame and a strong jaw line.

"I want to hear about her," he said when Paul brought him up to speed on Tatyana.

"Well, she's beautiful and smart and talented," Paul began.

"Good start. Not bad. What's her name?"

"Tatyana."

"Nice. How long have you been seeing her?"

"A month or so. But she feels . . . I don't know, Rick. She's just . . ."

Rick raised his beer glass in a mock toast. "Happy for you, pal. But isn't that how you felt about Serena just last year?"

"For about a minute. Until we realized we had just about nothing in common. Nothing to talk about."

"No comment," Rick said with a wry smile.

"Anyway . . . Do you realize how hard it is to have a relationship in my line of work?"

"Come on. You'll be rich someday. A lot richer than me. A lot of women find that attractive."

"And those aren't the ones I'm interested in," Paul said. "Dude, my job gets in the way of my personal life. I'm already stressed at work, and I'm too exhausted to put in the energy a relationship requires. What limited time I have, I want to spend it with a woman who understands how busy I am. Which is not a lot of women."

"They want some degree of commitment. Not unreasonable."

"I've got friends at Aquinnah who are downright calculating and businesslike about their social lives. They want to control every variable. Each woman, they take to the same restaurant close to their apartment. It's, like, a routine."

Rick smiled. "I'm getting the warm and fuzzies just listening to this. Anyway, so tell me. What does this Tatyana do?"

"She's a photographer."

"She *supports* herself as a photographer?"

"I think so, yeah." Paul had been wondering how she paid her rent. Living in New York City was expensive no matter what part of town you were in.

"She any good?"

"Really good. I want you and Mary Louise to meet her. A double date or whatever."

"Great—let's do it, then. I want to meet this mystery woman. Next couple of weeks, maybe? If you two're still together?"

12

Paul's workspace at Aquinnah Capital wasn't an office but a cubicle in the bullpen. A nice cubicle, as those things go. Low walls topped with glass. The concept was called "seated privacy." It was better than the no-walls, open-plan office, but not as good as a real office. Only the senior guys had real offices. Paul was one of fifteen employees who interacted in one large space.

His friend Michael Rodriguez, a fellow analyst, was standing at the edge of Paul's cubicle. Mike had jet-black hair, heavy black brows, and a blindingly bright smile and was growing an ill-advised mustache.

It was eight forty-five in the morning, a few weeks after he'd met Tatyana. Trading didn't start till nine thirty.

"Hey, you see what's going on with Cavalier? It's, like, unbelievable!"

"Saw that, yeah," Paul said with a straight face. "Bonkers."

But nothing about the Cavalier situation was unbelievable to him. Cavalier was a real estate firm whose stock Bernie Kovan, their boss, had wanted him to load up on, so of course he had. Pretty soon, Aquinnah owned almost 5 percent of the company, and Bernie was talking about getting a board seat. He wanted Paul to keep buying shares.

But Paul had begun feeling that something was rotten at Cavalier. He'd noticed a line item on their budget for legal expenses that was ridiculously high. Tens of millions of dollars. Paul had made calls to the company, but no one would talk. But instead of giving up, he'd dug in. Talked to a lot of former Cavalier employees. And in the process, he'd discovered that the CEO was known to have an "active" social life. Turned out he'd had a number of children by different women, some of them employees. He had forced those employees to sign nondisclosure agreements and paid them off handsomely to silence them. And the company had hushed it up. These women amounted to a giant ticking time bomb: potentially massive lawsuits for sexual harassment. And when the lawsuits started, Aquinnah Capital's investors would have grounds to sue Aquinnah for failing to do adequate due diligence, especially if Aquinnah were named in the press.

Paul did this research privately—for Bernie, without telling his colleagues—and a couple of weeks ago, he had advised Bernie to sell all of Aquinnah's shares in Cavalier. Bernie pushed back hard, but he relented when Paul explained the potential liability. He reluctantly agreed to selling the shares, and Paul did so.

Shortly after Aquinnah offloaded its Cavalier holdings, a huge investment management company, WhiteRock Real Estate Investment Trust, announced that it was acquiring Cavalier. Cavalier's share price shot up from ten bucks to almost twenty-five.

Bernie was furious at Paul. "Look how much money you made me leave on the table!" he shouted. "Free money! Left there on the sidewalk! And thanks to you, we just walked right by!"

But Paul knew now that he'd done the right thing by pushing for Aquinnah to get out of Cavalier stock: at seven o'clock that morning, the news of the CEO's personal life had broken on Bloomberg.

In pre-market trading, Cavalier stock dropped from twenty-five to eight. Rumors swirled that WhiteRock was going to call off its acquisition of the company because of "irregularities" and "undisclosed liabilities" found in the financials: Cavalier's legal department, it seemed, had been spending millions defending lawsuits and making payoffs.

The exchange soon announced that trading in Cavalier had just been halted. The company had put out a press release saying there had been allegations in the press that morning and that it would put out a full statement later today.

"Man, good thing we got out of it, huh? Who called that one?" Mike said.

"Bernie, who else?" Paul said. He saw no reason to grab credit.

"Phew. Hey, what's going on with that chick?"

"We're seeing each other."

"Good for you, dude. But when can you possibly go out? She's a waitress, right? Probably works most nights?"

"She's—no, she's a photographer, actually."

"*Brightman! Brightman!*" A shout came from the other side of the bullpen. It was Bernie Kovan. He was ebullient.

Bernie had the body of a lumbering bear with a monk's bald spot. His neatly trimmed beard was gray, matching what little hair he had. He rushed over to Paul, who was just standing up. "I was so pissed off at you!" Bernie threw his arms around Paul, hugged him. "Thank you. Thank you. You saved our asses."

There was a smattering of applause around the room. Mike Rodriguez was looking at Paul with a big, bright smile, shaking his head in admiration.

13

That evening, Tatyana wanted to try a new Persian restaurant in Brooklyn that served street food. Getting to deepest Bushwick wasn't an easy subway ride from Lower Manhattan, so Paul called an Uber to pick them up on East Seventh.

The Uber was a worn Toyota Camry that smelled pungently of the Little Trees air freshener dangling from the rearview mirror (Royal Pine scent). The Little Tree was there, Paul assumed, to mask the odor of the driver's cigarettes, smoked between customers.

Paul and Tatyana exchanged a glance about the smell.

"When I met you, you were smoking," Paul said to her. "But I haven't seen you smoke since."

"Mostly I vape, when I do," Tatyana replied. "I'm a light smoker anyway. I only smoke when I'm nervous or stressed out."

Her hair was in a bun this evening, and she was wearing heavily smudged eyeshadow that he knew women called "smoky eye."

"So how was your day?" he asked her.

"Not stressful. Good."

"What'd you do?"

"Went out to Brownsville to do some shooting." She paused, pantomimed clicking photos on a camera. "Two treks to Brooklyn today."

"Brownsville? Isn't that kind of a tough neighborhood? Carrying a fancy camera and all?"

"I'm fine," she said. "Don't worry about me, Pasha."

"Pasha?"

"That's the Russian nickname for 'Paul.'"

"Pasha? I like that. Makes me sound like a high-ranking officer in the Ottoman Empire." He was pleased, kind of thrilled. She had a term of endearment for him.

"You'll always be a high-ranking officer in the Ottoman Empire to me," Tatyana said, leaning over and giving him a kiss.

The Uber drove through a derelict area of old warehouses and pulled up in front of a graffiti-covered building.

Pasha, he thought as they stepped out of the car. *I like it.* "What's the nickname for Tatyana?"

"Tanya."

"I think I like 'Tatyana' better. How 'bout you?"

She smiled.

The restaurant was hip and funky, the kind of place people like to post pics of on Instagram. Fortunately, Tatyana didn't do that. Her Insta feed, which she'd just started, was all art photography. No food.

The place was loud, voices bouncing off the white subway tiles, and Paul found it hard to hear her. They both had saffron martinis.

"You see Grandpa over there?" she said and pointed with her chin.

Paul turned and saw, amid all the hipsters, a very old man at a table with what looked like his family. Maybe he was Iranian.

"Yeah?"

It was so loud, she leaned in close, which was nice. "I'd like to shoot him. He has an interesting face. There's something uneasy about it, about him. Do you see it?"

Paul shrugged. "So you like 'the olds'?"

She grinned. "I do, it's true. But only the ones with interesting faces. They don't all have interesting faces. But my *babushka*—my grandmother—now *she* had a face!"

"So what'd you find today?"

"Oh, a guy covered in tattoos, even his face. A kid on a fire escape."

"Who are your favorites?"

"Favorites?"

"Photographers, I mean."

"Oh, boy, so many!"

"Name one."

"August Sander. From the nineteen twenties and thirties. In terms of photographers working today, Katy Grannan."

"Sorry, I don't know her."

"She's amazing. And of course, Robert Frank was a god. There's a reason Bruce Springsteen looks at Robert Frank photographs to get song ideas."

"How do you know when you make it?"

"Make it?"

"As a photographer, I mean."

She heaved a sigh, shook her head. Her lip curled. "It's like a tree falling in the woods."

"How so?"

"You can be a great photographer, you can do original stuff, but no one notices unless, you know, the *New York Times* or *ARTNews* decides you're good."

They ordered charcoal-grilled kebabs with tamarind squid ink sauce, crisp octopus tentacles in garlic chili and tahini, and caramelized trumpet mushroom kebabs over coconut-creamed lentils.

"What got you into photography in the first place?" Paul asked.

She thought a long time. "It was after my parents' divorce. We had moved to America—Papa had, leaving Mama and Babushka and Dedushka behind. When Dedushka died, back in Moscow, I was gutted, I was bereft. But I had these photos of him, and they gave me comfort . . ."

"How old were you when that happened?"

"Six or seven, I think. I discovered a box of family photographs that Mama had packed in with my things. Pictures of her and my grandparents and aunts and uncles, and I just became obsessed with them. Whenever I was sad, I would pull out some of the pictures and look at them, and of course, they just made me sadder. I realized one day that this was all I had of Dedushka. Pictures. And suddenly they were everything, this old roll of photographs of my mama, my *dedushka*. I think that, on some level, deep down, I realized the perishability of the past. That the only way to preserve the past, really, was photographs. I think that's when I decided I wanted to take pictures. Papa gave me a camera, a Canon digital SLR, and I started taking pictures all the time. Later, when I was around ten, Papa gave me a book of photographs that had a picture of this little naked girl in Vietnam running from a napalm attack on her village. It brought tears to my eyes. That little girl was around my age, and you can see the pain and the terror in her face. And that was when I realized how photography can move you. Until I saw that terrible picture, I didn't know it could do that." There was a long silence. "So how was *your* day?"

He grinned. "Pretty great, actually."

"Yeah? How so?"

He gave her a simplified version of what had happened at work, and about Bernie singling him out.

Her face lit up. "That's so fantastic!"

"It's boring to you, isn't it?"

"It's not boring, not at all—I mean, I don't know anything about investments or finance. But I'm very happy for you and your good day." She caught him frowning. "What is it, Pasha?"

"Oh, it's—I don't know, I'm just thinking you must date far more interesting people. Artists and such. I'm just a money guy."

"Don't be silly. It's great to be with someone who appreciates photography," she said. "Oh, this is too hot for me."

He passed her a small dish of yogurt. "Try some of this."

She spooned some yogurt. "I've never had a boyfriend who really knew anything about my photography. Or even cared. Or bothered to learn. And by the way, my last boyfriend was a painter. A very talented one."

"Ahh . . . how nice . . ."

"He had interest from David Zwirner, about representation—do you know who that is?"

"Big-shot agent, I'm guessing?"

"Art dealer. Gallery owner. This guy—Sebastian his name was—he was about to blow up. But he was a party boy, too. And between the cocaine and the infidelity and the flakiness, he'd never show up where he was supposed to; he always had some excuse. In the end, he screwed up everything in his life. Including our relationship. I didn't feel safe or wanted or loved. He broke my heart."

She scooped up more yogurt and some fava beans with Barbari, the Persian flatbread with sesame and nigella seeds in its crust.

Paul waited, wondering, *Why is she telling me this?*

She went on, "We'll always care for each other. But I learned that I need someone sane, someone grounded and kind."

He felt himself relax. He nodded, put his hand atop hers.

"You know what they say: Never sleep with anyone crazier than you," Tatyana said. "Of course, you might think that's a low bar in my case." A rueful smile. "I usually win in the crazy Olympics, Pasha."

14

It was a busy morning, but most mornings were busy. At eight o'clock was the morning meeting, where Paul had to briefly, *briefly* summarize what was going on with the companies he covered. To talk about what had changed. (If all twelve people at the meeting got into the weeds, the meeting could go on forever.) He kept it crisp and dry. A few people kicked the tires, but that was okay. They all got paid on the whole portfolio's performance, so everyone had a stake. It was a fast-moving meeting, and you had to pay attention.

After work, he met Rick and his wife, Mary Louise, for a drink at the Campbell Apartment in Grand Central Station. Rick had just gotten a promotion, to running his small nonprofit office, the Lamson Foundation. Instead of champagne, they toasted his promotion with glasses of Brooklyn Lager, which Rick was partial to.

Rick was also partial to WrestleMania, his secret vice, which he proceeded to talk about at length instead of his promotion.

"Oh, Lord, not this again," Mary Louise said. She put her hands over her ears theatrically. She was thin to the point of skinny and had black hair with gray salted in, a button nose, and a generous mouth that was usually smiling. She crossed her eyes comically, a cute habit she had.

Rick said, "Tonight we're also celebrating Mary Louise."

"Why's that?" Paul said.

"You know her podcast?" Mary Louise had a podcast about middle-class people who'd become fentanyl victims. "It just got picked up by Pushkin Industries."

"That's fantastic," Paul said. He knew that Pushkin Industries was some kind of big podcasting enterprise.

Mary Louise shrugged, smiled modestly.

"Oh, and one more thing to toast," Rick said. "Paul has a new girlfriend."

"*Okay,*" Mary Louise said. The way she said it implied great skepticism. "How long have you been going out?"

"Couple months," Paul said.

"Who is she, what does she do?" said Mary Louise. "Come on, let's have the full debrief."

Paul told them the story of how he and Tatyana had met. "She's a really talented photographer," he said. "Very smart and very emotionally intuitive."

"Meaning nice boobs," Rick said, ribbing his old friend.

Mary Louise smacked Rick's shoulder, and Paul said, "I love spending time with her."

"She must be beautiful," Mary Louise said. "All the women you go out with are beautiful."

Paul hesitated for a moment. "Well, *I* think so," he said. "More important, she has a sense of humor, she's empathic, she's interesting."

"Wow," Mary Louise said. "What's wrong with her?"

Paul shook his head: *nothing.*

"What do her parents do?" she asked.

"I have no idea," Paul admitted. "I know they're Russian, and they're a close family."

"I can see the stars in your eyes," Mary Louise said. Putting her hand over her husband's, she said, "He's in love." Then, turning back to Paul: "Does that mean you're going to cancel your Tinder account?"

"Already have," Paul said. "Anyway, I look forward to introducing you guys to her. She's something special. I could marry her."

"Oh, please," Mary Louise said with the knowing smile of the long married. "Couple months? You hardly know her."

PART THREE

RED
FRED

Present Day

15

He needed, first of all, to disappear into the wilderness. To lose his pursuers. When they stopped where the road ended and found his burned-out hulk of a truck, they would know to look in the forest. So he had to immediately get off the well-marked trail that led into the woods.

Some people were intimidated by being in a dense forest, let alone getting lost in one, but he wasn't.

In no small part, he grudgingly admitted, because of his crazy father.

Stan Brightman had believed civilization was on the verge of collapse—after which, in the anarchy that would surely follow, we would all have to learn to live off the land, like human beings used to do. So he would take his son on excursions into the woods outside Bellingham, from time to time, where they'd have to forage for edible plants and eat whatever animals they caught, which was mostly squirrels and chipmunks.

These weren't trips Paul remembered fondly. He did not like squirrel meat. Not because of its gamey taste, but simply because he couldn't get it out of his mind that he was eating a rodent.

Around the campfire at night, instead of making s'mores, he'd listen to his father rant about how human beings were ruining the planet. Life was better in the Late Stone Age, ten thousand years ago, before the invention of modern agriculture—which he said was "the worst mistake in human history." A catastrophe, he explained, forefinger crooked as if he were passing along great wisdom. When humans started growing grain, Stan insisted, that led to greed, to class divisions, to the tax man and the birth of the state and eventually even war. He said that humans were a lot healthier back in the days of hunting and gathering, when we chased wild animals and foraged for plants. It was a matter of plain facts: We were less sick, lived longer. Back in the day, humans spent twelve hours a week getting food. Now everyone worked forty hours a week at least.

He had a point, sort of. (His son had, at one point, worked closer to eighty.)

The two hadn't spoken in years.

THE UNDERGROWTH WAS THICK IN some parts, with hobblebush, a scraggly shrub notorious for tripping hikers, making it difficult to move fast, let alone run. It grew knee-high. Paul waded through it, loped from clearing to clearing, his go-bag slung over one shoulder like a backpack. It was a clear, bright, chilly October day, and the canopy was increasingly dense, which made it cool. He was wearing the steel-toe work boots he always wore, jeans, and a barn coat—his habitual New Hampshire fall outfit.

The trees were mostly spruce and fir, with some hemlock and yellow birch mixed in. Here and there, pale green lichen clung to branches and grew like fur on tree trunks. Hikers called this "old man's beard." Paul moved as quickly as he could. Still, he knew that if the hobblebush slowed him down, it would also slow down his pursuers.

From the pine needles to the oak leaves, the forest was green. The fallen leaves were orange and gold. Spruce trees, their branches heavy with cones, gave off a pine fragrance. In places, the light was dappled.

When he was far enough away from his truck that he could no longer see it, he stopped and unzipped his go-bag. Inside, he found several disposable phones, fully charged. He switched one on.

Three bars, a decent signal. He took his iPhone out of his pocket and examined it for a second. He had heard of people being tracked via their phones, though he didn't know how this worked. The important thing was that his phone could give up his location if it remained on. He switched it off. Can you be tracked by an iPhone that was off? That he wasn't sure of. Maybe so. He couldn't remove the battery; that required some kind of proprietary hex screw.

So he picked up a large rock from the ground, placed the iPhone against a rock outcropping, and brought the rock down, smashing the device. Its screen spiderwebbed. He smashed it again, and this time the screen shattered and the phone's electronic guts spilled out. The thing was dead. They wouldn't track him this way anymore.

On one of the disposable phones, he dialed the number of a friend, Louis Westing, who lived in Lincoln. The number was written on a scrap of paper in the go-bag on which he'd jotted down possible useful contacts. Lou was a small-town lawyer with his own firm. They'd met at a Christmas party at Sarah's apartment and got to talking about baseball. Lou had handed "Grant" his business card and told him to call if he ever had any legal questions.

A woman's voice answered the phone: "Westing and Associates."

Paul asked for Lou, gave his name as "Grant Anderson."

Lou picked up a minute later. "Grant, how goes it?" he said in a boisterous voice.

"Lou, I'm sorry to just call you out of the blue, but I really need your help. I'll be in your neck of the woods soon."

"You'll be in Lincoln?"

"I will be," Paul said. "Tomorrow or the next day. And I'll explain."

"Come by the office soon's you get to town. We can have lunch."

Paul turned off the phone, to conserve the battery, and continued scrambling through the underbrush. He needed to walk west to reach the town of Lincoln.

From his go-bag, he retrieved a simple button compass. He remembered his father's chant *Red Fred in the shed!*—meaning you turned the bezel on the compass until the red needle, "Red Fred," aligned with the hollow arrow on the body of the compass, the "shed."

So he had been walking north, he found. The wrong direction. Instead, he wanted to go west, through the forest and to the town of Lincoln. It was a good thing he'd checked. He reoriented, adjusted his direction.

The land was gradually uphill for the first couple of hours, then it dipped down into a valley. After that, the terrain seemed to get steeper and rockier. At one point, he was finding it hard to keep from leaning forward. It's an instinct to lean into a hill. Instead, you want to stay upright as much as possible—or so he'd been taught by Stanley Brightman. In some of the steeper climbs, he had to make sure he had a good foothold and a good handhold. Once he passed close to Signal Ridge Trail, as it was marked, he turned away from it, heading deeper into the woods.

As he advanced, he listened for the sounds of other humans in the forest. The map told him that the town of Lincoln was some twenty miles away. He could do twenty miles in one day on an established forest path. But there was no trail cut here. Maybe he could do eight miles a day in these dense woods, at the most. That meant two and a half days of hiking, if all went well. He could make it without food, but water was more important. Stan Brightman used to say that you could survive for three minutes without air, three weeks without food, but only three days without water—the Rule of Threes.

After walking for three hours, he grew thirsty and was getting cold. The temperature had been dropping. His steel-toe boots were colder than the afternoon air, and his toes were losing feeling. For climbing in cold weather, steel-toe boots were exactly the wrong thing to wear. The steel transferred the cold to his feet. He shouldn't have worn these damn boots, but then again, he hadn't expected to have to run. He was shivering. He needed to stop and warm himself up. Change his damp socks to limit frostbite. Maybe make a fire. He remembered his father's saying: *Fire is the difference between eating lunch and being lunch.*

He shivered, but he knew that was a good thing, shivering. As long as you have sugar in your system, you can shiver indefinitely. But once your glucose stores break down, all shivering stops . . . and then you go hypothermic and you die.

He was hungry. And he was parched. He had drained the water bottle he'd packed. He'd passed several slow-trickling, nearly stagnant streams and decided not to risk drinking from them. Slow-moving or standing water was likely to contain parasites like giardia, which could give you a fatal gastrointestinal illness. *Eighty or 90 percent of the drinkable water in the world,* Stan Brightman liked to declare, *is contaminated with giardia.*

It was supremely annoying, Paul thought, to have his father in his head after all these years.

After a half hour of intensifying thirst, he saw another slow-moving stream and finally decided he would take the risk. He had to; he was so dehydrated he could barely swallow. If he got sick, he got sick. No water, and he would die. Plus, giardia took two weeks to appear.

Two weeks was a long time from now.

In his bag were some Aquatabs, which would purify water, but they took thirty minutes to work, and he could no longer wait. He took out an aluminum cup from his bag and drank deeply from the stream. The water was clear and cold and tasted slatey.

It was nearly three thirty. The sun would set in a few hours.

He had to keep moving, keep climbing.

The trail got steeper, rockier, more barren. He thought momentarily about turning himself in to the FBI, but then he flashed on images from long before, images that had been burned onto his brain. The spatter of blood on the walls and the carpet. That terrible coppery smell.

And he knew he could never turn himself in.

A few minutes later, he saw a sign: EL CAPITAN, 3,540 FEET. He was nearing the peak. It wasn't a mountain so much as a rock dome. Pulling out his map, he saw that El Capitan was a good bit north of where he'd wanted to go. He'd been walking not west but northwest. Hours out of the way. The wrong way.

Pulling out the compass, he realized that its needle pointed west no matter which way he turned it. It was broken.

For most of the day, he'd been heading in the wrong direction.

16

But how could a compass malfunction? He had kept it in his go duffel, in a plastic Ziploc bag that also held several burner phones. And . . . of course there was a magnet in each of those phones, in its speaker. That magnet alone was probably enough to have changed the polarity of the compass. That had to be it. He had known this but hadn't remembered, hadn't thought about it, when he shoved the compass into the bag with the burner phones. When he'd checked out his equipment yesterday, the compass's needle seemed to be moving okay, but he hadn't bothered to check how accurate it was.

He had no other compass. Now he'd have to rely on his own sense of where the sun was in the sky. He wanted to go west, which meant following the sun as it set. The sun would soon be setting, and he could reliably point himself to the west.

He didn't trust his sense of direction during the day, though. In effect, he was wandering aimlessly through an immense forest. Without water or food. People got lost in forests. He'd read in the *Union-Leader* about one case: a couple, lost, was found starved to death in the woods. Apparently, without knowing it, they'd been walking in a big circle for days.

Then he half-remembered a trick his father had once shown him. He tried to recall how it worked. You laid your watch horizontally and pointed the hour hand toward the sun. And then? He couldn't bring the next step to mind.

He was exhausted, but he knew he couldn't stop here. Not at such a high point, where he could be seen from a great distance. Where he was exposed. He had to continue. But downhill, he was finding, was more difficult—treacherous, even, in places with loose soil and rocks that came away if he tried to use them as a foothold.

And he found himself increasingly losing feeling in his fingers and toes. His feet felt like they were carved out of wood or stone. Plus, the knuckles of his toes hurt badly, and when he stopped to take off one boot, he found huge blisters there.

He knew he had to stop and build a fire to warm up. If he was going to do it at all, he had to do it now. In a few hours it would be dark, and a fire would serve as a beacon, a flashing neon sign for his pursuers.

His father had indoctrinated in him the technique of making a fire in the wilderness. *Build the smallest fire you need, and don't build it at the foot of a rock face*—which projects the firelight, acts like a movie screen, makes the fire, the light signature, detectable from a great distance. No, you want to build it in thicker vegetation.

You also want to make sure your fire isn't easily detected by any searchers after you're done. You must leave no trace. Paul recalled something called an H-fire, where you inscribe a big *H* into the ground, pull back the flaps of earth, and scoop dirt out of the middle. When you put your fire out, the flaps lie down like doors to cover evidence of the fire.

Paul took his fixed-blade knife and carved an *H* into the moss and dirt of the forest floor, then peeled back flaps of sod. He had two knives in his bag. One was a fixed-blade Gerber knife. The blade was made of carbon steel, not stainless, so it was easier to sharpen on a rock, if need be. The other was a multi-tool.

Now he needed fuel. He gathered some dead pieces of birch tree and peeled off the bark. With the Gerber knife, he scraped at the bark until he had a small pile of paper-thin shavings. Birch bark contained an oil that made it light quickly, he remembered. The shavings crumbled in his hand like stale cigar wrapper. To that pile he added a handful of brown pine needles. Then a couple of handfuls of small twigs of varying sizes. With the fuel gathered, he searched for a flame. None of that rub-two-sticks-together bullshit. That was a skill he'd never mastered. He'd freeze to death rubbing sticks together. They'd find him entombed in a block of ice like some cartoon character.

Rummaging through his go-bag, he found the lighter and pulled it out. Flicked it a few times.

Nothing happened. No flame.

He realized at once what must have taken place. The lighter's ignition lever had been compressed against something else in the bag, and all the butane must have gassed off.

Shit. This goddamned go-bag.

He'd never trusted lighters, anyway. When they got cold, they wouldn't spark a flame.

But he wasn't out of options, and he wasn't yet reduced to rubbing two sticks together. He rooted around in the bag until he found a flint and an old metal Band-Aid box. The box was full of cotton balls slathered with Vaseline. He rubbed the flint against the spine of the knife, but nothing happened. He could almost hear his father's voice: *You're doing it wrong.* He'd say, *You're doing it wrong, let me show you* or *You're doing it wrong, let me explain.*

Eventually, muscle memory kicked in, and it came back to him how to hold the knife, how to rub the flint against the knife's spine so that it crisply generated a spark. He did it again, and this time, a nice fat spark landed on the Vaseline-buttered cotton ball, the cotton ignited, and its flame caught the birch bark, and soon he had a crackling fire going.

He sat on a downed tree trunk before the fire. Now it was a matter of keeping it burning. He held his frost-nipped fingers close to the flames. As they warmed up, they throbbed with pain. He removed his boots, pulled off his damp socks, and placed them on the ground close to the fire, so they'd dry out, if only a little. He inched his feet closer to the fire. His toes felt like razor blades were slicing them. He rummaged through his bag until he found a second pair of socks, which he put on.

He was also almost faint from hunger. He had skipped lunch and had barely had anything for breakfast. He took a protein bar out of his bag, unwrapped it, and ate half of it. In his state of ravenous hunger, the bar tasted deliriously good. Then he stopped, realizing that this half of a protein bar was all he had to eat so long as he remained in the forest. He'd meant to add some more bars to the go-bag but had never gotten around to it. He'd better save the rest of the bar for later. He'd never been much good at foraging in the wild for food. Too many berries that looked edible turned out to be poisonous. And he wasn't going to try to trap squirrels. No squirrel meat for him, thanks.

As he warmed himself by the fire, he debated his next move. He looked at his watch. Sunset was roughly twenty minutes away, which meant he had to find a place to rest for the night. He was bone-tired and nearly fell asleep sitting up. He was experiencing an adrenaline crash, he knew: the deep fatigue caused by the hours of adrenaline rush suddenly coming to an end. His body had been running on adrenaline so long that it couldn't produce any more and had just stopped.

Also, he knew, it was dangerous to move through the woods in the dark—there was always the risk of a tree branch poking you in the eye—and using a flashlight was out of the question. That would attract attention from quite a ways off.

The shadows had grown long. He desperately needed a rest, if only a brief one, but he didn't know if he had time to take one. In any case, it wasn't safe to sleep for the night. He'd wake up with frostbitten toes and fingers, worse than he had already. He would also be giving up his head start. He remembered his father's stern admonition: *Don't sleep. Power through.* Stan used to boast that he once went for five days without sleep. "Not till the fifth day did I start hallucinating," he'd say.

Fuck Stan Brightman, Paul thought coldly. As far as he was concerned, Stan was always hallucinating.

17

He warmed himself by the fire for a good half hour. Then it was time to move, to find someplace to crash for a few hours at least. He smothered the fire and laid down the flaps of earth to conceal any traces of it.

And he thought about how he'd gotten to this point.

One lunch hour, a little over five years ago, he'd walked to the Strand in Manhattan, the bookstore that advertises "eighteen miles of books." He found the right section, pulled out several paperbacks with titles like *How to Change Your Identity* and *How to Disappear Forever* and *How to Disappear and Never Be Found* and *How to Disappear: Erase Your Digital Footprint, Leave False Trails, and Vanish Without a Trace*.

He studied the books. At the East Fifty-Eighth Street branch of the New York Public Library, he spent a couple of lunch hours using a computer. He found some interesting websites that offered help on what was called "starting from scratch." Disappearing and starting a new life under a new name, a new identity.

It was a lot.

Apparently, thousands of people tried to disappear each year. There are all kinds of reasons for people to seek to start over. Your debts pile up. Your marriage is a disaster. You're an embezzler. Or you're a bail jumper, a Ponzi schemer, an insurance scammer. Or you're trying to escape a stalker.

But it wasn't so easy anymore. Paul had once read a great old thriller, *The Day of the Jackal*, in which a professional assassin goes into a graveyard, copies down the name of someone who died as an infant, gets a birth certificate under that name, and is on his way. No longer possible. Not since 9/11.

Now, in the internet era, there were all sorts of problems with trying to disappear. Facial recognition, in the form of CCTV cameras, was all over cities and towns in the United States. You really couldn't go to a big city to hide, as you might have done in the pre-internet old days. Now, everywhere you went, you left behind digital breadcrumbs:

IP addresses, social media, electronic bank transactions, traces of your mobile phone.

The question was, how could he get a new identity? He needed a new Social Security number, that was the thing. It always came down to that. But how to get one?

According to the spy novels he'd read and TV shows and movies he'd seen, the best way to disappear was to fake your own death. "Burnt beyond recognition" in a car wreck or something like that.

But, in reality, faking your death—even assuming he could pull it off—turned out to be a very bad idea, according to his research. It was the best way to attract a lot of unwanted law enforcement and media attention. Or so the books he'd read had told him.

Whereas, if you just disappeared, the only person looking for you would be whoever you were running from.

So he hadn't faked his death. But he had created a new identity. Moved to a new place where he could disappear into woodworking. But that took considerable preparation. To create a false identity, and make it your own, the books said, you had to build it piece by piece.

First was the decision about where to move. It had to be within the United States, because he didn't have a passport in another name. And he'd need to go to a small town, one where he was unlikely to run into anyone from his past life. Not to a resort or anywhere that had a lot of tourists visiting. He loved boats and the water, but that was known, so, not to a town on the ocean. Just not too far from the water, either.

He chose New Hampshire because he had no known connections to it. He'd driven through the state several times as a kid and had enjoyed the skiing—though, later, he found that the skiing was a lot better in Colorado or Utah. He wanted a place that was as opposite to New York City as you could get. A small town but not too small. Somewhere he could plausibly move to without attracting too much attention. Somewhere he could get a job that would pay him off the books. That was crucial. Something involving boats would be appealing.

A combination of a Google search—again, always on a computer at the public library—and a real estate web search targeted the town of Derryfield, New Hampshire. Population: 1,602.

It seemed the perfect place to hide.

18

After a mere five minutes of walking, his feet tingling with little star-bursts of pain, he came upon a boulder field. A pile of giant boulders, one on top of another, formed a cleft between them that was a sort of cave. He peered into this space to make sure it wasn't already a home to, say, a porcupine. Animals loved caves. This one seemed to be un-occupied. But it was too shallow to serve as shelter, maybe four feet long by a few feet wide.

The old skills were starting to come back now. He looked around for something that could serve as a pole and found a long dead tree branch that was perfect. When leaned against a ridge in the top boulder, it made an excellent tent pole. Over the next ten minutes, he dragged smaller dead tree branches and limbs to the site and leaned them against the tent pole. As the sky grew deep orange and the sun dipped below the horizon, he created a rudimentary tent whose porous walls were made of sticks and branches and dead leaves and pine boughs. A sort of wolf's den. He then laid down pine boughs as a kind of bed, but mostly as insulation from the cold ground.

He clambered inside. He had no sleeping bag—*a sleeping bag is a body bag,* his father used to say, meaning that a sleeping bag would trap you, immobilize your arms, if someone or something came after you. *A sleeping bag is a bear's taco.* Instead, he'd brought along what Stan Brightman called a ranger roll: a fleece blanket rolled up with a poncho, a poncho liner, and a tarpaulin. He laid down the poncho liner to use as ground cover and then covered himself with the ranger roll. He remembered that he also had, in the go-bag, a space blanket, an emergency Mylar blanket in a foil pouch. He laid the space blanket over the ranger roll.

For a long time, he lay there just listening to the sounds of the woods, to the rustle of leaves in the wind, to a distant owl's hoot, to water flowing somewhere nearby.

But there were no human sounds, as far as he could ascertain. No footfalls, no crackling of human feet on dry leaves and twigs, no voices.

He was exhausted. The snap of a twig jolted him several times. He froze, listened with ferocious intensity, but each time, it was a false alarm. Not somebody close by. Just the nocturnal sounds of the forest.

It puzzled him that he still hadn't heard the sounds of his pursuers. Did that mean they hadn't bothered to come after him in the woods? Or had they gone in the wrong direction? Not for a second did he believe the Russians had given up searching for him. But if so, where the hell were they? Were they moving through the night, using flashlights because they didn't care if they were detected? If so, they might be just minutes away.

The thought did not allow him to relax. Once, in front of Paul's mother, his father had used the expression "asshole-puckering" to describe the terror he had sometimes felt in Nam. Paul's mother had objected to the language. But to Paul, it was evocative.

The ground was frigid, the cold radiating from the boulders' surfaces. His butt was frozen. He felt a stone or pebble underneath the tarpaulin ground cover, fished around to remove it.

It took a few hours, but eventually he did drift off to sleep, reminding himself that it must be only a brief nap.

Suddenly, he was jolted awake. Glancing at his watch, he saw that he'd been asleep for three hours, far longer than he had wanted. What woke him was an electronic sound, like nothing found in nature. A jumble of electronic beeps, text message sounds. He knew what it was: electronic devices hitting a pocket of signal and suddenly coming online. When you're climbing over peaks, after a long period of no phone reception, you sometimes randomly hit signals coming out of cell towers—and suddenly, all your devices come to life.

Not his. He hadn't moved.

He felt a sudden chill as he realized the sound had to have come from some other electronic devices nearby, maybe devices belonging to his pursuers. He went still, listened. He didn't know how far electronic sounds traveled in the forest. But he knew that whoever it was must be close by. How close, he didn't know.

All that mattered was that he was about to be discovered.

The pucker factor was high.

He had no choice but to remain in place, to keep as still as humanly possible. Not knowing how far away this person or persons might be, he couldn't risk getting up and contending with the branches that served as his tent walls, the noise they'd make. He remembered giving his phone number to his friend in Lincoln, Lou Westing. What if Lou were to call him back, the ringing sound filling the forest? He reassured himself that he'd turned the burner phone off.

When he constructed it, he had thought his lean-to of twigs and dead branches looked like a natural structure and would probably attract no attention. But now he was having second thoughts. Would it really, though? Would it look like a deadfall, a natural pileup of forest debris—or like something constructed by a human and, therefore, worthy of a closer look?

If the shelter did pass muster, he would be okay so long as he remained silent, didn't cough or sneeze.

He willed himself not to cough, which of course only made his throat tickle.

Then he heard the crunch of shoes on dead leaves.

They were nearby.

PART FOUR

POCKET CHANGE

Six Years Earlier

19

They'd been going out a few months, and he felt he was really getting to know Tatyana. You could be married for thirty years and not really know your spouse, he'd been told. But he was coming to know her pretty well. He'd learned that she liked bananas slightly underripe. That she liked real half-and-half in her coffee, that she snored softly, that she ate desserts, that she worked out like a fiend at a boxing gym. That she loved sushi but hated Indian food. That she was *extremely* ticklish. That she always had music on. She liked to listen to Lizzo and Saweetie and Kendrick Lamar. When she was in a romantic mood, she played Jon Batiste or John Legend. Her cheer-herself-up guilty pleasures were Olivia Rodrigo and Taylor Swift.

Paul and Tatyana were meeting Paul's friends for dinner at Sansovino, a rooftop Italian restaurant in Chelsea that had small plates and an extensive wine list. The reservation was for eight. They got there a few minutes late. The other couples were already there and had introduced themselves.

Paul's friend Rick and Rick's wife, Mary Louise, still hadn't met Tatyana. Paul, a little anxious, introduced her to them. Their opinion was important to him.

But their immediate reaction was enthusiastic. "So you're the famous Tatyana!" Mary Louise said. "Paul says you're Russian?"

"Russian American, really. I was born in Moscow."

"So your parents immigrated here?" Rick said.

"Right."

"I know a lot of Russians who come here have a hard time finding jobs," Mary Louise said. "Was it tough for your parents making the transition? I know a neurosurgeon in Russia who immigrated here and had to drive a taxi."

"True," Tatyana said. "It's very sad."

"What do your parents do?"

She hesitated for a long moment. "My father is in business. My stepmother is a housewife." Paul and Rick watched silently as Mary Louise turned up the klieg lights on Tatyana. Tatyana had told Paul that her father was a "small businessman," but she hadn't elaborated.

"I think it's so cool that you're a photographer," Mary Louise said. "You're an artist. You must have a day job, right?"

"Come on," Rick said quietly to his wife.

Mary Louise persisted, "Do you sell your photographs?"

Tatyana hesitated. "Not yet. I'm still making a name for myself."

Paul put in, "She has a gallery show of her work coming up in a few weeks at Argold."

"Wonderful," Mary Louise said. "So your parents must help out with the rent, right? Thank God for parents." She said it like a joke, but there was a bite to her voice. Paul was shocked. He interrupted with "Uh, Tatyana, why don't you sit there?"

Mary Louise said, "I'd love to sit with Tatyana, Paul, okay?"

Tatyana flashed Paul a "help me" look, but it was too late; Mary Louise had already seated herself next to Tatyana. Paul sat on Mary Louise's other side to try to tamp down the interrogation.

ONE OF THE COUPLES AT the table was Tatyana's shy friend Andrea, along with the guy she'd just started seeing, a very opinionated man named Arthur.

Tatyana introduced everyone.

Arthur was an architect and a self-proclaimed foodie, and he held strong views on just about everything. He had round black-framed architect's glasses and a goatee and wore a crisp white shirt under a black blazer. Arthur believed that white truffles were superior to black, that homemade pasta was indistinguishable from dried and boxed, that truffle oil was entirely synthetic. At dessert, when he and several others, including Paul and Tatyana, had ordered the panna cotta, Arthur put down his spoon and said, "Mexican vanilla. Clearly."

"Isn't most of the world's vanilla from Madagascar?" Paul asked.

"This is delicious," said Andrea.

"I think vanilla is an underrated flavor," Tatyana said. "If someone's boring? They're vanilla, right? Why not *beige*?"

"And the thing about Madagascar vanilla . . ." Arthur began.

"What about Madagascar vanilla?" prompted Rick, who caught Paul's eye, letting him know that he was having fun, triggering the guy.

"Vanilla is worth more by weight than silver," Arthur went on. "Eighty percent of the world's supply of vanilla beans is grown in Madagascar, which is one of the poorest countries in the world."

"One of the five poorest countries," Mary Louise said. "The poverty there is awful."

"Well, it's delicious," Tatyana said.

"Vanilla is an orchid, actually," Arthur said, settling back in his chair. "Each flower has to be pollinated by hand. On the very morning that it blooms. That's why it's so expensive. It's a huge pain in the ass to grow."

"Pollinated by hand?" Tatyana said. "All of the plants?"

Arthur nodded.

"So how much do the farmers who grow vanilla make?" Rick asked. At Reed College, he'd been big in Occupy Portland.

"Seventeen cents an hour," Arthur said. "*Seventeen cents.*"

"That's unbelievable," Tatyana said. "Should we be boycotting vanilla?"

AFTER DINNER, WHEN EVERYONE WAS breaking up to go home, Tatyana excused herself to go to the bathroom. Mary Louise said to Paul, "She's lovely."

"You did kind of put her through enhanced interrogation," Paul said.

Mary Louise drew close to him and said in a low voice, "So she met you at one of those fancy fund-raisers you go to, huh?"

"That's right."

"Well, I guess she knew you had money," she said lightly, almost as if she were joking, but she wasn't.

"Mary Louise, come on," said Rick.

"Mary Louise, that's not fair," Paul protested.

"A lot of Russian women search for rich American men to marry, you know," Mary Louise said. "It's a thing. She's an artist, she has no money, she meets a guy who works at a hedge fund—"

"There were far, far richer people at that event than me," Paul objected. "Anyway, *I* approached *her*, not the other way around."

"I don't want you getting mixed up with a gold digger, is all. I'm just looking out for you, Paul."

"It's not like that, Mary Louise. Cut it out." He looked around for Tatyana, but couldn't find her. "Where'd she go?"

"She went to the bathroom," Rick put in.

Then Paul glimpsed Tatyana standing outside the restaurant, vaping.

20

Paul and Tatyana got home to her apartment slightly buzzed from a lot of wine at dinner. He noticed that she seemed more subdued than usual, and he had a good idea why. She'd gotten the subtext of Mary Louise's questioning instantly and was, understandably, offended.

"Hey, come here," he said, taking her in his arms. "I'm sorry Mary Louise waterboarded you."

"Like I'm interested in your money?" she said softly. "You see how modestly I live. I don't care about money and fancy things."

"It was wrong of her to imply that—wrong and unkind and, frankly, unlike her. She knows how serious I am about you, and I guess she was feeling protective. But she shouldn't have done that. It's no one's business how you pay your rent." He was curious, mildly curious, about that but didn't want to ask her.

"It's no big deal," she said. "My parents help out. I bet I'm not the only twenty-six-year-old in Manhattan whose parents chip in on the rent."

"I've never met your parents. Why do you never invite me to Sunday dinners?"

"I don't know. It feels like a big step, Pasha."

"But your parents—are you embarrassed about me?"

She gasped. "How can you even ask that? Of course not!"

"You're not embarrassed about your family, are you?"

"Paul!"

"I didn't think so. I know how close you are to them. It's just a little . . . strange, that's all."

"My father's giving a party next Saturday," she said. "It's their tenth anniversary, him and my stepmother. If you want to go, I'm sure he'd love to have you."

"Of course I would."

"You can meet Papa and Polina. And they'd love to meet you.

They've been hearing me talk about you for so many months." She bit her lower lip.

"Why do you look so uncomfortable?"

She pulled away. "Because I don't know what you'll think about my parents."

"What do you mean?"

"They're . . . a lot."

"Hey, I'm the Unabomber's son. I know from crazy. Don't worry about it."

"Do you love me?" she asked.

Why was she asking? "I do love you," he said. "For sure."

It was the easiest question he'd ever answered.

THE NEXT MORNING, PAUL HAD the best day he'd ever had at Aquinnah.

It began when he arrived at his cubicle in the bullpen. Michael Rodriguez stood there waiting for him.

"You check your Bloomberg?"

"Not yet. Why?"

"Look at Robust Robot." Six months ago, Robust Robot was a tiny artificial intelligence start-up out of MIT, in Cambridge, run by a professor and his student with no employees, when Paul got Bernie's approval to invest a couple of million dollars of the firm's money for 20 percent of the company.

Now Paul looked at his newsfeed. After heated bidding among three tech giants, Microsoft had just acquired Robust Robot for a billion dollars.

The math was easy. Paul had just made Aquinnah two hundred million dollars.

He let out a whoop.

That two hundred million went into the bonus pool, which meant he'd be getting a tiny fraction of it himself, but it would still be a lot. True, he'd made a number of bets that hadn't panned out, but this one more than made up for them.

He looked up and saw Bernie Kovan heading his way with a bottle of Cristal, a grin on his face.

ON THE FOLLOWING SATURDAY, TATYANA woke up seeming out of sorts.
They went over to his apartment, in Hudson Yards, on the West Side. He
needed to check the mail, clean his refrigerator of old take-out cartons;
he barely spent time there anymore. The place had one bedroom, one
bath, and a "gourmet kitchen" he never used, except to store takeout in
his fridge. Hardwood floors, white walls, perfectly characterless. Generic
furniture ordered from a catalogue without trying it out, because he
didn't have time.

This was the thing. He didn't have time. He worked a bazillion hours
a week, rarely saw people. He could afford a nice place, but he didn't
want the hassle of living in a 150-year-old building where things broke
down, the AC didn't work, and his mail was stolen. So he lived on the
seventh floor of a luxury building, with an elevator, a washer-dryer in
the unit, and a doorman. A perfectly fine place. Every apartment looked
like every other. Very adult. Best of all, he didn't have to worry about
anything. He was all about efficiency, optimizing his precious and very
limited spare time.

It couldn't have been more different from Tatyana's funky rental.

She'd asked him, a few months ago, to move in with her, even though
her place was smaller than his. It was a big step when he agreed. But he
realized that her apartment, modest though it was, was at least *interesting*
compared to his well-manicured, generic place.

All day, while he puttered around, Tatyana seemed nervous, out
of sorts. In the late afternoon, they returned to her apartment. Around
six p.m., she started getting ready for her father's party while wearing a
fluffy white bathrobe. Paul liked watching her apply her makeup, a whole
choreographed routine. An eyelash curler that looked like the kind of
implement they give you at French restaurants for escargots. Sponges
and pots of lotion. Concealer, mascara, a highlighter stick.

He wanted to tell her she was beautiful without makeup, but this
didn't seem to be the time. She might interpret it as a criticism of her
skills with the makeup brush. But he wondered why she took such care
with her appearance for a family party.

As she dressed, Paul admired her lithe body. Her shoulders were
small and round and glossy, as if she polished them. She had tiny feet
and wore a ring on the second toe of her right foot. She slipped into

something black and satiny that was low-cut and showed off her beautiful shoulders. She didn't look like a cater waiter tonight.

THEIR UBER WAS A WHITE Tesla, immaculate. Tatyana was nibbling on a thumbnail.

"Where're we going?" Paul asked.

She sighed, ducked her head, mournful. "You'll see. My parents are very different from me. They live very differently."

She'd told him only that her parents lived way uptown, that her father worked in sales.

The Uber was traveling up Madison Avenue.

"Beautiful buildings," he said when they'd hit East Sixty-Ninth Street and pulled up in front of two elegant neoclassical town houses. They were obviously built around the same time by the same architect.

"This is where they live?"

She nodded.

He hadn't been expecting Brighton Beach, Little Odessa in southern Brooklyn, where so many Russian émigrés lived, but *this* . . . this was something else.

"They're connected," Tatyana explained.

"Not sure I'm understanding you, Tatyana. You said your parents lived uptown. You didn't say they had two . . ." He trailed off as she sighed again. He heard kind of a tremolo, a nervous sigh, escape her body.

"You'll see, Pasha," she said, but he already understood.

21

Tatyana's father's home was two Upper East Side town houses put together. Paul had never seen such a thing, only heard about it.

In front of the left town house, a couple of burly security guards in ill-fitting black suits and a woman with a clipboard were gathered at the entrance.

Inside the house, once you got past security, it was as if you'd just entered the Hall of Mirrors at Versailles. Gold leaf everywhere. The walls, mirrors, tables, chairs—all dripped with gold. The chandeliers were crystal, and the floors were marble tile. In the foyer was a giant fountain with a bronze sculpture of a nude woman with water spewing out of her mouth and, strangely, her nipples, too.

The rooms were crowded and loud. Interspersed throughout the crowd were hatchet-faced men in better-fitting black suits with curly earpieces. A proliferation of beautiful women. He recognized a number of people. Not just Wall Street titans but Manhattan VIPs—a couple of movie stars, disappointingly short; a former mayor, also short; a network news anchor. Michael Bublé was going to sing later on, Paul overheard someone say.

He was holding Tatyana's hand as they entered. He was in a state of shock, of utter disbelief.

How long had he known the woman? Seven months, maybe longer? And the whole time, she was keeping a secret from him. Her father wasn't just not poor; he was *rich*. And not just rich, but fabulously so. He was next-level rich.

Tatyana lived like an artist, in a grungy building, in a modest apartment, and her father was . . . had to be . . . a Russian oligarch.

Her parents had "chipped in." *I'll say.*

All those Sunday night dinners she went to, to which he was never invited: now he knew why. She was a billionaire's daughter, and she hadn't wanted him to know.

His mind raced. The most she'd said about her parents was that they were "a lot." Everyone's parents were a lot.

He and Tatyana had, he thought, shared everything with each other, held nothing back.

He didn't know what to feel. Hurt? Angry?

Tatyana, he noticed, wasn't looking at him. Waiters and waitresses were passing out flutes of champagne: Dom Perignon. Tatyana took a long sip, then Paul did, too.

"Want to get something to eat?" she asked him.

"Okay."

"Hope you're hungry."

They passed a glass case, built into the wall like for a museum exhibit, with some jeweled object inside lit by a spotlight, but she didn't stop to explain what it was.

Tables were heaped with food, including gigantic bowls of glossy black caviar and lobster meat. Men wearing blazers and gold chains were pouring themselves shots of Stoli from the bar. Paul, who was hungry, heaped some caviar on toast points, for himself and Tatyana. "It's beluga," Tatyana said.

"I thought beluga was illegal to import."

She shrugged and gulped hers down. "Wouldn't stop my father if it were."

Paul had a bite, then remembered he didn't love caviar, no matter how much he tried. Fish eggs, after all. He disposed of the toast-and-caviar in a napkin, crumpled it up, and put it on the nearest table.

"So I guess I should just show you this crazy place, gold toilets and all, right? You want to start with the pool?"

"There's a pool?"

Tatyana took him by the hand and led him down a broad staircase. He suddenly smelled chlorine. An Olympic-size pool was down there, crowded with half-naked people splashing and laughing. It was loud. Everywhere, bottles of Dom Perignon and vodka. A young woman in a swimsuit hooted as she leapt into the pool. A man threw a fully dressed woman into the water. She screamed as she splashed down.

"Is this typical?" Paul asked.

"I guess so. Sometimes. I don't know." Tatyana looked around, shook her head disapprovingly.

"Tatyana, sweetie, you never told me about . . . about all this."

She looked uncomfortable. "Let me introduce you to my father."

22

Arkady Galkin was a big, bald man around seventy with a great big potbelly and large, prominent ears with floppy lobes. He appeared to be deep in conversation with a red-haired, pale-skinned, hatchet-faced man wearing an earpiece. The man had a scar under his left eye.

Tatyana went right up to her father and interrupted him. "Pápachka," she said, "this is my friend Paul Brightman."

Galkin's eyebrows were like gray caterpillars and seemed to move independently of each other. They shot up when she said "friend."

"So you're my daughter's latest victim," he said. He didn't smile.

"I'm Paul Brightman," Paul said with a grin.

"I'm Arkady Galkin. I own the joint. I know I don't look like it, but appearances can be deceiving."

"It's a beautiful home," Paul said. He didn't know what else to say.

"So you work in finance, Mister Paul Brightman?" He had a thick Russian accent but seemed to speak English reasonably well.

"Right," Paul said. So that was as much as Tatyana had told her father. Just to let him know his daughter wasn't going out with some bum. "Finance" sounded serious and could mean anything.

"So, Paul Brightman," Galkin said, "how you like working for Bernie Kovan?"

So he'd done his research. "He's great," Paul said. "He's a mensch. Bernie's not a psychopath like some other hedge fund managers."

Galkin laughed. "So you are born in California. How you end up in New York?"

"Did an internship at Morgan Stanley my junior year in college, and then they offered me a job. One of our clients was Aquinnah Capital." He paused and shrugged. "Well, I guess Bernie thought I was good, because he hired me."

"He is good man?"

"He is."

"Aquinnah Capital is good firm?"

"I'd say so."

"Three billion under management."

"Thereabouts. How do you know so much about my business?"

"It's my business, too, Mr. Brightman."

"Hedge funds?"

"Well, I like to do a little investing from time to time."

"Probably more than a little," Paul said with a crooked smile, looking around at the digs.

"I noticed you don't like caviar," Galkin said. "What do you like?"

So Galkin had seen him getting rid of his toast point. At least he hadn't wiped out his mouth with the napkin.

"Actually, I could go for a good burger right about now, to be honest," Paul said.

Galkin stared at him for a long time, a stern glower, and then abruptly burst out laughing as if he couldn't maintain a straight face. He laughed so hard his belly shook. Then he said to Tatyana, "May I borrow your boyfriend for moment?"

Tatyana shrugged as her father gripped Paul's shoulder and said, "Come with me."

Paul walked along with Galkin. The crowd parted around them like the Red Sea. Galkin said nothing until they reached the swinging doors to an institutional-size kitchen bustling with cooks and servers. Inside the kitchen, in the damp warm air and amid the clamor, Galkin stopped and put an arm around Paul's shoulders. "Out there is not real food," he said.

He spoke in Russian to a short, round old lady who was stirring something in a pot on a large professional gas stove. She answered him, and then Galkin said something else, and then the old lady replied. Paul didn't understand much of the conversation, of course, but he could tell by the woman's tone and word choice that she wasn't speaking respectfully. There was something a little snippy about the way she spoke to Arkady Galkin.

Galkin laughed, removed his arm from Paul's shoulders.

The cook stopped stirring whatever she was stirring and left the stove.

"There is nothing like American hamburger," Galkin said. "Nobody makes them as good as America. I think you grew up poor, yes?"

"I don't know about poor," Paul said, "but we struggled for money. My dad was constantly out of a job. How about you?"

"Six in a room in Moscow. Yes. One unreliable bathroom. If we were lucky, we got macaroni and cheese for dinner. Is different from American 'mac and cheese.' Not like Kraft. Macaroni with butter and green, moldy cheese. If we were very lucky, we would eat macaroni with butter and sugar for dessert. Mmm."

Paul didn't know how to reply. Was Galkin nostalgic for the foods of his deprived childhood? "I think you win," Paul said.

"I am sorry we don't have hamburger in house tonight. But I think you will like what Oksana gives us."

The old lady had returned carrying two plates. On each was a sandwich of some kind made of dark bread. Paul and Galkin took the sandwiches, and then Galkin said something to the cook, nodding. Oksana said something snippy again and poked Galkin in the belly. Galkin roared with laughter.

Paul took a bite. The sandwich was delicious. It was pastrami, probably from one of the few remaining great delis in Manhattan.

"You like pastrami?" said Galkin.

"Very much. I'd forgotten how much I like it."

But the bread, a sourdough black bread, was the best bread Paul had ever eaten, full stop. It was dense and moist, had the tang of vinegar, and he could taste a blend of flavors, coffee and caraway and molasses.

"And Oksana's black bread—it is better than what you can buy in Mother Russia."

"Fantastic," Paul said, mouth full. "Truly excellent."

"Yes?"

"Best I've ever had."

"Now, finish your sandwich, and then we go out there and watch my poor guests eat fish eggs and soufflé."

Paul nodded, chewing.

"You are very different from Tatyana's usual boyfriends. Crazy artists or rich playboys. Very fancy." Galkin flicked a forefinger against his nose. "You say 'hoity-toity,' yes?"

Paul smiled.

"WHERE DID HE TAKE YOU?" Tatyana asked a little later.

"The kitchen. For a sandwich."

She laughed. "He likes you, I think."

"I guess. We definitely had a moment."

She spied a woman she knew and waved, extending her arm and flapping her fingers down. "Meet Polina, my father's wife," she said.

Paul turned. Polina was a few inches shorter than Tatyana, had a long neck and prominent cheekbones, great arched eyebrows and large, liquid eyes. A sharp chin, full sexy lips, and a tangled mane of brown hair down to her shoulders. She was cool. She was hot. She was wearing an emerald-green mini dress with ruffles at the hem and sheer sleeves. The dress's plunging neckline showed off her tanned breasts and a glittering emerald necklace. She wore an immense ring with a diamond the size of a jawbreaker.

"Polina, this is Paul Brightman."

"*Very* nice to meet you, Paul," Polina said in a thick Russian accent, taking his hand in a two-handed clasp. "What a handsome man! How you and Tatyana meet?"

"At a gala at the Met," Tatyana said with a smile. "He thought I was a waitress. A 'cater waiter,' he said."

"Oh, yes?" Polina said, amused.

"I let him believe it." Tatyana snaked her arm possessively around Paul's waist.

"They must have very pretty waitresses at the Met," Polina said.

"None as pretty as Tatyana," said Paul. He could smell Polina's perfume, something peppery and spicy.

"Or as smart." Polina touched an index finger to her temple. "Or as . . . complicated."

Tatyana took Polina's elbow and kissed her cheek. They spoke briefly in Russian.

"She says you're cuter than the last one," Tatyana said to Paul, adding "which isn't saying much."

Polina said something else in Russian, shaking her head. Paul picked up some of the words. His Russian was starting to come back.

"She asks if you have a job, because the last one didn't." Tatyana said, then replied to her stepmother, saying something in Russian that sounded an awful lot like "hedge fund." Turning back to Paul, she said, "My father doesn't like lazy men."

Polina kept speaking quickly in Russian.

Tatyana nodded, smiled politely. "*Nyet, nyet.*"

"Now what did she say?" His college Russian didn't get him very far, but it had sounded to him like a compliment. He got the word *krasivyy,* or "handsome."

"She says, 'Don't trust him. He's too good-looking.'"

Paul smiled, shook his head, couldn't stop a blush from appearing.

Then Polina spoke in English. "Be careful, Mr. Paul. Remember what Pushkin tells us. 'The less we love a woman, the more she likes us.'"

A waitress came and handed him a fresh flute of champagne, took away the old one.

"Okay, Polina," Tatyana said. "That's enough. We have to leave, *sestrichka.*" She kissed her stepmother on both cheeks.

As they left, Paul said, "*Spasibo.*" Russian for "thank you."

"*Pozhaluista,*" Polina said. "But why you leave before Michael Bublé sings?"

23

In their Uber back to Tatyana's apartment, they sat in silence for several minutes. Paul struggled with his seat belt, trying to find the buckle, which was buried deep between the seat and the seat back.

Finally, Tatyana said, "You're not going to say anything, Pasha?"

He didn't look at her. "It's an amazing house. Never seen anything like it."

"That's not what I mean."

"Did you not trust me?" he said.

"Of course I trust you. What are you talking about?"

"You obviously didn't trust me enough to tell me how rich you are. And you use a different surname, 'Belkin.' Is that a fake name? A cover name?"

"It's my mother's last name."

"Which you use so nobody will know you're Arkady Galkin's daughter." He'd heard the name 'Arkady Galkin' before, he thought. He was one of those Russian oligarchs who lived in the U.S. and owned a famously big yacht and lots of real estate.

"Obviously."

"Especially your artist friends."

"Yes! I admit it. I didn't want to be known as his daughter. I wanted to have my own life. Is that so hard to understand?"

"Does your dad not give you money?"

"Of course he does! I have trust funds and real estate and offshore entities and all that."

"Yet you live in a—"

"I love my apartment! Where am I supposed to live, in some duplex in a skyscraper like all the other Russian kids?"

"But—"

"Don't you get it, Pasha? I need to establish a separate identity. I'm trying to make it as an artist, as a photographer, and I want to have a separate profile in the world."

"Are you estranged from your parents?"

"Me? No, not at all. My family is my"—she put a hand atop her breasts—"My hearth. My safe harbor. You asked me once if I was a daddy's girl, and I said yes. My *pápachka* is the smartest man I know. And deep down, the kindest."

"What about me?"

"You know what I mean. I didn't want you seeing how my parents live. I mean, all that glitz—that's not who I am. You know that by now."

Paul was silent, processing everything Tatyana was telling him, everything that was now upside down. "And I'm surrounded by twelve-thousand-dollar suits and I'm wearing khakis from, like, J.Crew."

Paul thought: *To your father, I'm a flea. A poor, insignificant flea.* "You come from that kind of money . . ." he said. ". . . I mean, given what you're used to, being with me is a huge comedown for you."

"Huh? No, Pasha—it's nothing, I don't care at all. It doesn't *matter* to me."

"I'm not in that league, you know that."

"Nobody is."

A long pause. That was an understatement. "How did he get so rich? Do you mind my asking?"

"He's in finance. The finance world. I don't really know what. It's not my world. I'm kind of clueless."

He would be googling "Arkady Galkin" in a matter of minutes.

"He liked you," she said.

"Well, he sure did his research on me." He laughed, then smiled. "But—yeah. He gave me, I don't know, a warm vibe or something."

"You're both up-by-your-bootstraps guys."

AT TATYANA'S APARTMENT, WHILE THEY undressed, Paul asked, "Who's the red-haired guy with the earpiece who was always talking to your father?"

"Oh, that's Andrei Berzin. He's my papa's chief of security. His right-hand man. Sometimes I don't know who's really in charge," she joked, "Berzin or Papa."

Bernie Kovan didn't have a chief of security, but then, he wasn't a Russian oligarch. "He has enemies, huh?" Paul said.

She shrugged. "He thinks so."

"Who?"

She shrugged again. She didn't want to answer, or maybe she didn't know. "Berzin also does intelligence work for Papa."

"Intelligence?"

"Research, you might say."

"Is that how your father knew so much about me?"

"No doubt. It's a sign of respect that he had Berzin check you out."

"Can't say that I feel flattered, exactly. What's his story, this Berzin?"

"Papa hired him away from the FSB, the Russian security service. He was a colonel. He's Siberian—grew up outside Irkutsk. Anyway, he's an asshole. A terrible person. But he's been loyal to my *pápachka* for a long time. So I'm . . . polite to him. He's going to be very suspicious of you for a while."

"Who is? *Tvoi otyets*? Your father?"

"No, I mean Berzin. Berzin will be suspicious. Nothing personal."

PAUL SHOWERED AND CAME TO bed naked, and found Tatyana already there. Instead of her lace teddy, she was wearing a T-shirt and sweatpants, an unmissable signal that she didn't want to play around.

"Pasha, can we talk about something?"

"Of course."

"I know it's not cool to talk about your exes, but I need to tell you about an old boyfriend."

"Why?"

"Just listen. So Charles Helmworth was, *is*, this Social Register type, you know? Belongs to the New York Athletic Club and the Metropolitan and this yacht club and that yacht club, and he's a member of the Brook." Paul knew this was often considered the most exclusive gentleman's club in New York.

"Very fancy," Paul said. A *different kind of rich*, he thought. *Inherited*.

"Not what you'd think. He was always just barely scraping by. His grandmother paid for all his club memberships, but he was still desperate for cash. His family had gone broke. They had the prestige but not the fortune."

"So why didn't he, I don't know, *work*?"

"He was lazy. My father called him a 'layabout.'" She laughed. "He must have looked that word up. He also called him 'Astor,' though he wasn't an Astor. Pápachka kept saying, 'Who was the last person in that family who did a lick of work? His great-great-grandfather?'"

Paul smiled, then laughed.

"Charlie wanted us to live in keeping with my wealth. Which I paid for. Wherever we went, he wanted to stay at the Mandarin or the Four Seasons, in a suite. He wanted to go on these big, lavish vacations—a safari in South Africa, or stay in the South of France or a private island in the Caribbean. The swankiest ski resorts. He insisted on Courchevel, in the French Alps, or Verbier. He said because the skiing was better. But I knew it was really because of the scene. He kept asking me to marry him, and I kept saying no."

Paul noticed that she was no longer smiling. She'd grown pensive. "Is this the artist with the coke problem?"

She shook her head. "Before him. Anyway, Charlie became insatiable. He wanted to go to the fanciest restaurants, the—"

"He was a gold digger."

She paused. "My friends warned me, and I should have listened."

"What happened?"

She paused even longer. Her eyes filled with tears. "My papa put a P.I. on him and caught him cheating."

Was she sad or was she angry? He couldn't tell.

"I went into therapy. I—how could I trust anyone again? I just became really wary of everybody. Do men just want me for my money? What about friends who take advantage of me because they know I'm rich?"

"Do you think I love you for your money?"

"No, but I'm getting the feeling you're going to break up with me because of it."

Paul felt stung. "Seriously, Tatyana?"

"I know you don't like that I kept it from you."

"That's true. I don't."

"I wanted to know you loved me for me."

"I get that now. Obviously I do."

"Are we okay?"

"Of course we are."

"I know you want to be the big breadwinner in the relationship. Isn't that the conventional thing?"

He smiled. He didn't want to admit to her that that was exactly how he thought: the conventional, patriarchal mode. "It'll take some getting used to. I know you don't like spending money on anything."

"But that's not true! I'll spend money on clothes—have you taken a look at my closet? My clothes aren't from, you know, a vintage clothing store."

"I did notice that," he admitted.

"So let me ask you something."

"Yes?"

"As long as our relationship isn't the traditional patriarchal . . . thing."

"Yes?"

"You're the first guy I've ever met who bothers to understand me. Who appreciates my work. Who isn't after me because I'm rich. You're a regular guy, and you seem really grounded and *real*. And we love each other."

He nodded. "Yes," he said. They'd been seeing each other for eight months, had lived together for two. Every once in a while, they'd make flip references to marriage, jokes about the "institution of marriage," punch lines.

"When Charles Helmworth asked me to marry him," she said, "it made me start thinking about the idea of marriage. What it means, and am I ready for it. I feel like I've been adulting recently."

He rolled his eyes. "That's why you've been thinking about marriage? *Adulting?*"

She nodded, then said, with a catch in her throat, "That and . . . I love you. The person I am with you is the person I want to be. And that person wants to build a life with you. And I kinda think you might feel the way I do."

He realized she wasn't joking. His throat went dry. He began to think about what it would mean to lose her, about how much she meant to him. The fact was, he was in his thirties and had shopped around enough to know what he was looking for, what he wanted. And what he wanted was Tatyana. She was a happy, sparkling presence. She lit him up. She loosened him up, straitlaced workaholic that, he had to confess privately, he was. His heart lifted when he thought about her. She was everything: she was smart and talented and kind and fun, the whole package. To him, the world was an obstacle course; to her, it was a playground. He was a better person when he was with her. She brought out the colors in the world.

His heart was pounding. "Same," he croaked out. He swallowed. "You said you wanted to ask me something?"

"Well, this isn't very traditional, I guess, but . . . Pasha, will you marry me?"

24

Paul met Rick Jacobson for an after-work drink at a bar off Times Square. It was crowded, and there was no room at the bar, so they were forced to sit next to a table of rowdy guys in their early twenties. Paul and Rick hadn't seen each other in a few months. The longer Paul went out with Tatyana, the more time they spent together, the less he saw his old friends.

"Been a long time," Rick said.

"I know. Sorry about that. Been crazy at work."

"I thought you were pissed off at us because of Mary Louise."

"What do you mean?"

"The way she was interrogating Tatyana at that dinner at Sansovino."

"She might have come on a little strong."

"Ya think? I was waiting for her to take out the rack or the thumb screws or the iron maiden."

"No, I know she was sort of vetting Tatyana. It was a little . . . *aggressive*, maybe."

"We like Tatyana," Rick said. "We both do. A lot. Honestly, she's terrific."

"Good," Paul said, "because I'm going to marry her."

Rick's face lit up. "If we were at a tonier place, I'd order champagne. If we're lucky they might have André Cold Duck here." He got up, gave Paul a bear hug. "Congratulations. I'm so happy for you." When they sat back down, Rick said, "I kind of thought you were allergic to marriage. You've avoided it for a long time."

"Not that long. But Tatyana's much more interesting than other women I've been with."

"How's the sex?"

He smiled. He wasn't going to elaborate. Even with a best friend.

"That's great, because right now it's as good as it's gonna get."

Paul was silent for a long time. The guys at the table next to them roared, laughing over some joke one of them had told. Then Paul said, "I'm going to tell you something about her that's kind of . . . well, unusual."

"She's divorced."

Paul shook his head. "Her last name," he began. "She uses her mother's last name. Her real name is 'Galkin.' 'Tatyana Galkin.'"

"Okay . . ." Rick didn't immediately get it, seemed to be waiting for the big reveal.

"You might have heard of Arkady Galkin."

Rick shrugged.

"He's a Russian oligarch. A mega-billionaire." Paul had done his googling. The man had houses around the world. His yacht was immense.

Rick's eyes widened. "Jesus."

"So when Mary Louise thought Tatyana was dating me for my money . . ."

Rick shook his head, snorted a laugh. "My God, man!"

Paul was expecting Rick to say something crass about the money he was marrying into. But instead, he said, "Have you met him?"

"Just once."

"What's he like?"

"I like him," Paul said. "He seems to be what Bernie Kovan would call a mensch. A good guy."

"So how does he feel about you marrying his daughter?"

"We haven't told him yet. Or her family. She's invited me to go to a family dinner Sunday night. That's where we're going to let everyone know."

"I wonder how he'll take it. I mean, you're well paid for your age, but you're not rich. By his standards, you're probably, like, a hobo. And you're an American. You're an outsider. He's never going to trust you. You know?"

Paul looked at him for a moment. "I don't know about that. We'll see."

"Listen, uh . . . be careful, man. These Russian oligarchs are bad guys."

"Or he might end up being perfectly nice."

"Yeah," Rick said. "Right. Maybe. Just be careful."

25

Paul was thinking about the Galkin family dinner they were going to. They were planning to announce their engagement, and he wondered how it would go over, what the reaction would be. Besides polite congratulations, would her father be pleased—or not? He seemed friendly enough, but he'd met Paul exactly once. And what about her brother?

"You said tonight is a special occasion of some sort," Paul said to Tatyana. "I mean, besides telling your family we're getting married."

"It's an old Russian holiday called Maslenitsa."

"Which is?"

"It means something like 'Butter Week.' Or 'Pancake Week.' It's hard to explain. A spring festival. It's just a lot of food. Oksana, who made you the pastrami—she's cooking tonight, and I thought you'd enjoy it."

"I love Russian food. Especially hers."

They lapsed into silence. Then she said, abruptly, "I should warn you that my brother, Niko, can be difficult."

"How so?"

"He can be an asshole to my boyfriends. He's just very protective of me."

"Maybe he'll be different to a fiancé."

"Doubt it. He'll be even worse."

THERE WAS NO SECURITY IN front of the double town house this time. They went to a room on the first floor, next to the kitchen, that Paul hadn't seen the last time. Ten people were already crowded around a dining table meant for eight.

Tatyana's brother called out to her, "Always late, always making a grand entrance."

Everyone laughed. She grinned and bowed.

Her father emerged from the kitchen. He was wearing jeans and a blue-and-white fleece that emphasized his large belly. He announced something in Russian, and then Oksana came out, stout and cross-looking in a faded housedress under a white apron, with a platter full of thin pancakes or crêpes. Her famous blini.

"What did he say?" Paul asked Tatyana.

"Oh, he . . ." She shook her head. "Just about the holiday. Maslenitsa. We say goodbye to winter and welcome spring and the, uh, fruit-bearing powers of nature. The renewal of its life force. Like that. And he says Oksana's blini are the best in the world."

Tatyana directed Paul to sit next to her, so she could be his tour guide for the food. On her other side sat Niko, her brother. He worked for their father, Tatyana had said, but she hadn't explained what he did. Niko was a couple of years younger than her and spoke English without an accent. He and Tatyana exchanged words in Russian.

Paul turned to Tatyana and furrowed his brow. She looked irritated, shook her head, sighed. "What'd he say?" Paul persisted.

"Just that it's a family dinner, and why is an outsider here."

"Oh. That's a little awkward. What did you tell him?"

"Just that I consider you a member of the family."

"I take it that didn't satisfy him."

Quietly, she muttered, "I told you he can be an asshole."

Paul leaned past Tatyana and extended a hand to Niko to shake, which he ignored. "I'm Paul," he said.

Niko nodded, looked bored, and didn't bother to introduce himself.

The blini were served with trout roe, shining orange beads, and sour cream plus vodka in carafes. This was followed by a traditional Russian cabbage soup called shchi, and Russian pierogis filled with meat. It was delicious—everything except the trout roe. The soup was cabbage soup, which didn't sound good but was in fact zesty and delicious and had an appealing amber color. The pierogis were half-moon-shaped savory dumplings, steamed and then pan-fried, and were extraordinary. All with Oksana's sourdough black bread, which Paul already loved.

Toasts followed, and voices grew louder. Most of the conversation around the table was in Russian. During a pause in the toasts, Niko poured out a shot of vodka for Paul and one for himself. Handing Paul the shot glass, he said, "You work for some hedge fund?" He made it sound exceedingly boring.

"Yeah," Paul said. "Aquinnah Capital."

Hoisting his glass high, Niko said, "To the almighty dollar," and downed the shot.

"How do you like working for your dad?" Paul asked.

Niko narrowed his eyes hostilely, pretended he hadn't heard the question. "You make good coin, eh?"

"Not by your standards, I'm sure."

"No?" He lowered his voice, turned his head. He poured out two more shots, handed one to Paul. Without looking at him, he said, "Then it's good you found yourself a rich girl, yes?"

Did he have to explain that he'd asked her out not knowing who her father was? That seemed too defensive. With a bland smile, he finally said, "Well, rich in the things that matter."

Tatyana, who didn't seem to have heard the exchange, tapped Paul on his shoulder and said, "Now?"

Paul held her gaze a moment and then nodded, feeling a tightness in his belly, apprehension despite the number of vodka shots he'd just imbibed.

Tatyana clinked on a glass with a spoon and said, in English, "Excuse me. Excuse me! I have something I want to say. *Izvinitye!*"

The room quieted down. She looked around the table, smiled hesitantly. "Paul and I are so happy to let you know that we are engaged to be married."

There were gasps and exclamations of delight and a smattering of applause.

Arkady Galkin was beaming. He rose and held up his little vodka glass and said, "Wonderful, wonderful news! *Za vashe schastye!*"

"He says, 'To your happiness,'" Tatyana explained to Paul.

Everyone except Niko drank a toast. Paul kissed Tatyana and hugged her. Arkady came lumbering over to his daughter and hugged and kissed her. Then he said to Paul, "Welcome to the family," and gave him a big, damp bear hug. He said something quick and cutting to Niko and made a knife-slicing gesture. Niko bowed his head, apparently chastised.

Polina rushed over from her side of the table, squealing, and gave Tatyana a big hug, then Paul. Niko said something to Tatyana in Russian; he didn't sound pleased. Tatyana replied in Russian, then turned to Paul. "He says, Where's the ring?"

"Tell him it's coming."

She nodded. She already had the ring. On his lunch break, Paul had picked out an engagement ring at a wholesaler in the Diamond District whose owner was a friend of Bernie Kovan's. Given the wholesale price, he was able to buy a bigger diamond—three carats, good color and clarity and all that—than he ordinarily might have. Tatyana had exclaimed over it, said she loved it. But for this dinner, she had chosen to leave it at home, so as not to spoil the surprise.

Then Niko said something in Russian to Arkady, who shook his head dismissively as he returned to his seat at the head of the table. Paul heard Niko say a Russian word that sounded exactly like *gigolo*. Then another word: *zhopa*. At Reed, Paul and his Russian-language classmates had made a point of learning Russian obscenities, and he knew that *zhopa* meant "asshole."

Niko appeared to be drunk by now. He said to Tatyana, "*Yemu ne ty nuzhna, yemu tvoi den'gi nuzhny.*" Paul was fairly sure it meant something like "He doesn't want you, he wants your money."

His father called out from the head of the table, "*Khvatit! Zatknis!*"

Paul knew that meant "Enough! Shut up!"

Then came yet more vodka. Paul was now blearily drunk. He'd learned that Russians don't sip their vodka. They knock it back.

Then more blini, served with berries and condensed milk, for dessert, followed by cognac.

The family began to get up from the table after dessert and stand around talking. The room grew louder. Paul remained seated.

Polina had been watching him throughout dinner, Paul had noticed, and now she came up to him and gave him a kiss on both cheeks. "You are doing okay?"

"I'm great, how about you?"

"You are surrounded by Galkins. Maybe you are bored or restless? Over your head?"

He shook his head. "Not at all."

"Maybe you feel like you're auditioning for a part you're not sure you want."

Before Paul could reply—he didn't know what to say—Arkady Galkin put a hand on his shoulder. "Has Tatyana shown you the egg?" he asked.

Paul could smell the liquor on Galkin's breath. "Not yet."

Tatyana said something in Russian, quickly, and her father said something back, and they both laughed. Then Galkin said, "Come."

Paul nodded. He leaned over to Niko and quietly, in Russian, said, "*Ya ponemayu.*" I understand. Meaning: "I understood all your nasty comments in Russian."

Niko's slack-jawed look was worth whatever trouble Paul had just caused.

Then Paul got up, unsteadily, and followed Galkin out of the dining room.

26

Arkady Galkin led Paul to the built-in illuminated glass museum display case in the hallway that Paul had seen the last time he'd visited the town house. A spotlight shone on a large gold egg encrusted with sapphires and diamonds. The egg was being pulled by a chariot and an angel. Inside the open egg you could see a miniature clock.

"This," Arkady said, tapping on the glass, "is most famous Fabergé egg. *Cherub with Chariot*. I buy from guy who buy it from industrialist Armand Hammer for a million bucks. Money went right to Kremlin. See, Fabergé made fifty jeweled eggs for last two czars of Romanov dynasty. All worth tens of millions of dollars now, at least. Eight of them once believed missing. But this is one of the eight. And I have it." He smiled like the proverbial cat that ate the canary. "And people complain about price of eggs. They have no idea." He laughed, and Paul smiled.

"Please come with me," Galkin said, and he ushered Paul into his study and offered him a cigar.

Paul didn't smoke, and he particularly didn't smoke cigars, but he thought the right thing to do was to accept the offering and fake his way through it. So he took the cigar, clipped its end, and lit it using Arkady's gold lighter. He sucked in, brought the cigar to life, and puffed out without inhaling.

He looked around the room. It was a two-story library with walls paneled in rich mahogany and lined with old books in Russian. Paul wondered if Arkady had actually read any of the books. The two men sat down in high-backed green tufted-leather easy chairs.

Wreathed in smoke, Arkady said, "So you are marrying my daughter. I am very happy for you both."

"We're both happy, too." *And relieved*, Paul wanted to say. "Happy to join the family."

On Arkady's desk, atop a pile of papers, was a briefcase. It was made of elegant cinnamon burnished leather, with the manufacturer's name,

Berluti, on the brass clasp. Paul rarely noticed briefcases, but this was the most beautiful one he'd ever seen.

"You understand, please, that you will need to sign prenup."

No surprise. Paul nodded, said nothing.

"You studied Russian in college?"

"Just for two years."

"Enough to understand, I see. Please, pay no attention to my son. Everything will be okay."

Paul nodded, smiled politely. Niko was going to be a problem, he knew.

"Tatyana tell me you are good investment adviser. She say you make two hundred million at work in one week. This is true?"

"Months ago," Paul said, shaking his head. "And for the firm. Not for myself."

Arkady emitted little smoke rings into the air. "But you get piece of this."

"Sure. I mean, it gets figured into my bonus at the end of the year. You know . . ."

"You outperform benchmark all the time, yes?"

"Well, yeah, I guess I do, come to think of it," he said modestly.

"I want to invest with you," Arkady said. "Just small amount."

Surprised, Paul said all he could think of at the time, which was "We have a five-million-dollar minimum."

Arkady snorted. "How you say the money you find in your pockets or under cushions of couch?"

"Spare change. Pocket change."

"Yes, pocket change," Arkady said with a smile. "I have for you *fifty* million."

Paul tried to look cool. "For how long?"

Arkady played with his cigar, looked up at the chandelier. "Until you double it."

"We might do a couple percent in a month, if we have a great quarter. You know how it goes."

"There is Yiddish saying, '*Der Mensch tracht, un Gott lacht.*'"

Paul cocked an eyebrow.

Galkin translated: "Man plans, God laughs."

"Isn't that a hip-hop album?"

Galkin ignored Paul's crack. "You may have every plan in world, and nothing goes like plan," he translated. "Life unpredictable."

"Well, be that as it may, you're just going to have to trust me. Give us some time. Are you talking about investing in the fund or . . . ?"

"No, you. *You* manage it. My people will contact you in morning. We have deal, yes?"

Perspiration broke out on Paul's forehead. He swallowed. He offered a hand to Galkin. "We'll see what we can do."

As he left Arkady's office and walked back to find Tatyana, Paul felt an immediate flush of regret. What a mistake he'd made, agreeing to invest any money at all for Tatyana's father—his future father-in-law! Even "pocket change" of fifty million. He should have politely, respectfully refused. Because even if fifty million was genuinely insignificant to the old Russian, Paul had a feeling he would care very much if he lost any of it.

27

Stuffed with blini, drunk on vodka, Tatyana and Paul collapsed into the bed as soon as they got back to her apartment. Quickly, Tatyana was asleep, and Paul soon after.

They awoke in the middle of the night. Paul felt logy, his mind thick and slow. He got up to use the bathroom, and when he returned to the bed he saw that Tatyana was awake now, too.

"What did you and Papa talk about?" she asked.

"Ugh," Paul said, making a guttural sound. "I was drunk, and I agreed to invest some money for him."

"Really? He must really admire you. Trust you. He's very particular about where he puts his money."

"I must have been out of my mind."

"Why do you say that? He knows how well you do."

"It's a roll of the dice, Tatyana. The market could drop, you know? And he's not going to be happy about losing money."

"He's a grown-up. He'll understand."

"I doubt it."

"Well, then. If you feel that way, then let me speak to him. I'll just tell him it's a mistake, that *I* don't want his future son-in-law investing his money. That it's . . . awkward."

Paul shook his head. "No, *milaya*. Thank you, but that's okay," he said.

I don't shy from challenges, he told himself. *Especially from my future father-in-law. Or maybe I'm still drunk.*

"You sure?"

He nodded, looked down for a moment, then looked up with a half smile. "He wants me to sign a prenup."

She groaned. "Not my idea."

"No doubt."

"I don't know about this stuff. I'm the oldest in the family. The first to get married, the first to have to deal with all this. What did you tell him?"

"I didn't say anything. He didn't *ask*; he told me. Like, it wasn't up for debate."

"Did it bother you?"

Paul shrugged. "I expected it. He's a wealthy man, and he wants to protect his daughter's assets. They'll send me the document, we'll see what it says. I'm sure it'll be fine."

"He didn't mention our engagement?"

"He said he was very happy. What did Polina say to you?"

"Oh, she was thrilled. She was already talking about where the wedding should be."

"Uh-oh."

"She wants it to be in Tuscany, at my father's villa near Florence. She wants an over-the-top wedding. A showcase. Something that will show up his oligarch friends."

Paul hadn't even thought about that—competitive weddings in the oligarch world. "Is that what you want?"

"No way. I couldn't care less about all that shit, Pasha."

"Good."

"Polina is . . ." She paused, looked up at Paul with an almost helpless shrug.

"She seems nice," Paul said. "Is she not nice?"

"She competes with me, have you noticed?"

Actually, Paul had noted that Tatyana took particular care with her makeup and her outfits when she was going over to her father's house. He suspected that on some deep, psychic level, she was competing with her dad's young wife, too.

"She competes with me for my father's attention."

"Maybe you should feel flattered that she's so jealous of you," he said. "But you seem to get along."

"We get along okay," she replied. "I mean, she doesn't treat me like a stepdaughter. Or a daughter at all. If Polina tried to treat me like a daughter—I mean, she's only a couple years older than me—things would go badly. So we're like sisters, and most of the time we get along well. We go shopping together."

"What was their wedding like?"

"Unbelievable. It was in Moscow, at the Barvikha. Elton John performed."

"You're kidding me."

She shook her head. "They had a ten-tier floating cake, and she wore a seventy-carat engagement ring."

"*Seventy* carats? Did you want a bigger diamond than the one I gave you?"

"No! The one I have now is perfect. I wouldn't want it any bigger. It would be too heavy."

Ten million bucks at least for a seventy-carat diamond ring. Maybe more. He had no idea. He was glad Tatyana didn't want something as big as her stepmother's. Or even close. He was doing well, and banking a lot, but he didn't have that kind of money.

He wondered, for the first time—but not for the last—what he'd gotten himself into.

28

It was Monday, and Paul was starting the week hungover. He popped a handful of Advil. There was nothing he could do about the circles under his eyes. His head pounded.

He'd begun to wonder if Galkin had been drunk, too, when he offered to invest fifty million dollars with Aquinnah. But the morning after the meeting in the Russian's study, Bernie Kovan knocked on Paul's office door.

Fifty million bucks had shown up in Aquinnah Capital's Partners Fund Number Three. Attention: Paul Brightman.

What the hell was this?

Paul explained that Tatyana's father, his future father-in-law, wanted to invest with him. But the fund wouldn't be open for a while, and there was a waiting list of investors who wanted in. Because Paul was a star, Bernie was willing to make an accommodation.

"So you're marrying into the Galkin fortune," Bernie said. "Mazel tov." He wasn't smiling.

Paul nodded.

"I wonder what you're stepping into."

Paul tried to grin, but it came out looking more like a grimace. "He's a good guy," he said.

"Uh-huh," Bernie said as he turned to leave.

BUT HOW PAUL WOULD INVEST the money, he had no clue.

Until a weather report gave him an idea.

It was a news dispatch on Bloomberg Radio about a cyclone forming in the Indian Ocean near eastern Africa. Ordinarily, it was the sort of news he didn't pay attention to, as it involved a part of the world he knew little about. But then he remembered how, at dinner a few weeks ago, that know-it-all Arthur had gone on and on about vanilla beans, and it made him think.

He did some quick research, then he stopped by the office of one of his senior colleagues, Pete Ambrosino. Pete, who was in his forties, beefy with a chafed face and little wire-rimmed glasses, was a good-natured, fairly nerdy commodities trader. That meant he bought and sold things like lumber and gold and sugar and uranium and pork bellies—real stuff, unlike stocks, which were basically financial promises. As far as Paul understood commodities, you were buying and selling these concrete objects based on what you expected their price to do. Will the price of oil go up next March or go down? That sort of thing.

"Got a minute?" Paul asked Pete. His headache had finally disappeared.

"I'm just going cross-eyed staring at gold futures, so, yeah, I have a minute," Pete said. "I have an hour. I have hours."

"Ever trade vanilla futures?"

"Vanilla?" Pete cocked his head. "No such thing."

"You can't buy futures in vanilla beans the way you can with, like, silver?"

Pete shook his head. "Market's too small." He tapped at his keyboard. "The global market for vanilla is . . . around a billion dollars. Way too small for futures."

"So if you're convinced the price of vanilla beans is going to go up, how do you make money on it?"

Pete closed his eyes, tipped his head back, and bared his teeth. That was what he did when he was thinking hard. "Who uses vanilla beans? Like, Häagen-Dazs?"

"They're owned by General Mills," Paul said. "The price of vanilla beans, up or down, is barely going to move General Mills stock at all. Then there's the Nestlé corporation, but that's probably too big, too. Same issue—vanilla's not going to move the needle much. All right, so who does General Mills buy vanilla from?"

Pete's fingers danced over the keyboard like a concert pianist playing "Flight of the Bumblebee." "They buy it from a company called Beatrice Cade Extracts and Flavors," he said, "and that's a publicly held company. Then there's the Nelson-Holcroft Vanilla Corporation. They've got to be big into vanilla beans."

"Sounds like it," Paul said. "I mean, turns out vanilla is in, like, everything. It's in pharmaceuticals, perfumes, cosmetics, baked goods, beverages, chocolate, baby food, whiskeys—all over the place."

"And what makes you think the price of vanilla beans is going to go up?"

"Bad weather coming in Madagascar, which produces eighty percent of the world's supply of vanilla."

"If you know that, so does everyone else on the Street. Right?"

Maybe, Paul thought. But not everyone's thinking about vanilla beans. Too small a market. The more he thought about it, the better he liked his idea.

HE NEXT WENT TO BERNIE Kovan's office. Bernie was stalking around the room with Bluetooth earbuds in, talking on the phone. He held his index finger up in the air, telling Paul to wait a moment. Paul settled into one of the visitor chairs in front of Bernie's messy desk.

Bernie Kovan spent a lot of money on his suits, got them tailored on Savile Row, in London, but somehow, on him, they looked like cheap knockoffs. He wore frayed Lands' End button-down shirts and unfashionably wide ties. He hadn't gotten the memo about shoes, either: he wore wide-toed Clarks Wallabees with his fine suits. He claimed they were much more comfortable than bespoke leather dress shoes.

Finally, Bernie ended his call, turned to Paul. "What's up?" Bernie liked Paul just on general principles, but he particularly valued him because of how he'd saved his ass on the Cavalier deal.

"I have a plan I want to run by you."

"Go."

Paul started explaining his idea about vanilla beans.

When he'd finished, Bernie laughed. He leaned back in his chair, looked up at the ceiling for a few seconds. "This is a total crapshoot, you know."

"Maybe."

"Fifty million bucks is bupkis for this guy."

"I know, but it's what I have to work with."

"If you double his money, will he invest with us? I mean, serious money?"

"He didn't say so, but it does feel like I'm being auditioned here."

"Huh." Bernie looked off into the distance. "Well, let's kick the tires a little bit . . . So you want to buy put options on companies that buy a lot of vanilla, that *depend* on vanilla. Beatrice Cade and Nelson-Holcroft and Nestlé. Figuring that when the price of vanilla shoots up, their stock will take a hit." By "put options," Bernie meant buying the right to sell the stock at a certain price by a certain time. If the share price goes down and you have the right to sell its stock at a higher price, you can make serious money.

Paul nodded. "Vanilla goes into a whole bunch of Nestlé products. If they can't get vanilla, all those products are delayed, maybe even for several quarters. That definitely tanks their stock. Or they switch to artificial vanilla flavoring, which is different, and word gets out and they still take a hit."

"Well, at least you're spreading the risk around. Okay. But won't you need boots on the ground in Madagascar to make this work?"

"Probably," Paul said. "I'll go myself."

"That's just not going to happen. You're too valuable here. Send an associate and an analyst. Send Chris and John."

"You don't mind?"

"Not at all. Why not? Chris speaks French, and you'll want a French speaker."

Chris Langley was an associate at the firm. He'd gone to Exeter; done a school year abroad in France, where he became fluent in French; and then graduated from Stanford Phi Beta Kappa, where he'd played football. He was twenty-seven and just out of the Harvard Business School. John Kapinos was twenty-three and a summa cum laude graduate of Williams College, a newly hired analyst.

Bernie continued: "They'll both enjoy the trip. It'll be an adventure. But I'll tell you something. I don't want them walking around Madagascar with five million dollars in cash without any security. Call Smith Brandon or Kroll and ask them to send a couple of French-speaking ex–Special Forces brutes to accompany them."

"That'll cut into our profit—"

"I don't care," Bernie insisted. "They *have* to have security. That's nonnegotiable."

"Got it."

"Spend a couple hundred grand to protect five million in cash?

Worth it. But are they going to know how the vanilla bean market over there works?"

"I've done a little research, and I'm going to make a few calls. The thumbnail goes like this: the farmers sell their beans, cured black vanilla beans, to 'collectors,' who sell to exporters, who in turn sell to big flavor companies, who make vanilla extract out of the beans and sell that to Mars and Nestlé and Unilever."

"But you want our boys to buy directly from the farmers?"

"No, from the *collectors*. The middlemen. Fifty million is going to buy a sizable chunk of the market."

"Know what? Throw in another fifty from the firm."

"Terrific."

"Maybe bring in some other investors. You're probably going to be able to corner the market."

"Yeah? Great." Paul hadn't expected Bernie to invest in this gambit, but that was a good sign. It showed his confidence in its working. "With a hundred million bucks, we'll corner the market for sure."

"I like the sound of it," Bernie said. "But once you buy a hundred million bucks' worth of beans, what do you do with it all? I mean, that's an awfully big pile of vanilla beans."

"That's the tricky part. They have to put the beans in containers and store them somewhere safe. That means they need refrigerated containers. Climate-controlled, to protect the beans. Dehumidifiers and air conditioners and such."

"That gonna be a problem?"

"Nah," Paul said. "That part of the world, climate-controlled containers are everywhere. Our guys will be able to lease them. Or outfit them, if they have to. Load 'em up, then move 'em out of Madagascar and away from the path of the storm. Maybe a few thousand miles north, into warehouses in Mombasa."

Bernie placed his hands flat on the glass top of his desk to signify that he was done and it was time for Paul to leave. "This is going to be fun, Paul. I like it."

29

The two twenty-something employees of Aquinnah Capital, Chris Langley and John Kapinos, flew out of Kennedy Airport directly to Antananarivo, Madagascar.

Chris Langley called Paul early the next day from his room at a boutique hotel in the capital city. Between him and John and the two security officers, they had bought out the entire small hotel. The weather was warm and humid. In Madagascar, it was the wet season.

THE NEXT FEW WEEKS WERE anxious ones as Paul watched the satellite weather service get the weather in Madagascar just about right. The cyclone hit the country, causing landslides and flooding and wiping out the entire new crop of vanilla. The price of vanilla beans shot up to nearly $700 a kilo. As expected, the share price of Nestlé dropped suddenly, from $118 to $95. Those October puts were now each worth over $25 per share. That $5 million was suddenly worth $55 million.

Paul sold the vanilla beans a few weeks later for $680 per kilo.

Within three weeks, he had turned $100 million into just over $500 million. He knew of bigger trades before. Much bigger. A hedge fund manager named Bill Ackman had once turned $27 million into $2.6 billion in a little over a month, the single best trade of all time.

But this one wasn't too shabby.

So why wasn't everybody doing this? Maybe not everyone wanted to take a chance on the vicissitudes of weather on the other side of the planet. Also, not everyone knew how thinly traded vanilla beans really were, how small the market. It was all a black box to most people.

It was a bet, but a bet he had won.

ARKADY GALKIN'S OFFICE WAS LOCATED on the fortieth floor of a modern skyscraper on Fifth Avenue, at the southeast corner of Central Park. The interior had the look of a private equity firm, or a hedge fund, or any other kind of mahogany-wainscoted long-established financial office.

Paul waited for ten minutes on a couch behind a glass coffee table on which the *Financial Times* and the *Wall Street Journal* had been arranged, a folded statement for Arkady Galkin's account in his breast pocket. Finally, a pretty black-haired woman with brown eyes—Galkin seemed to surround himself with attractive women—emerged to escort him to Galkin's office. She asked if he wanted coffee or tea or water, and Paul said no.

Galkin's office was, no surprise, enormous and grandiose. Glass walls on two sides, a long walk to a long glass desk that was bare except for a landline phone and a three-array monitor.

Galkin was wearing an expensive-looking gray pinstriped suit with a blue open-collar shirt. He embraced Paul and said, "Why do I owe pleasure to see you this morning?"

Paul handed him the statement.

For once, Galkin was stunned into silence. He finally said, "Paul Brightman. Appearances can be deceiving. Tell me how you do this."

Paul laughed. "I don't know that I could do this again," he said. "There was a lot of luck."

"Then I would like some of your luck," Galkin said. "Come work for me."

"Thank you, but no," Paul said. "I like my job."

"You haven't heard my offer yet."

WHEN PAUL TOLD TATYANA ABOUT her father's job offer that evening, she looked up from her iPad, where she was editing a photo. Her eyes widened. "What did you say?"

"Haven't responded yet."

"What are you going to do?"

"I like working at Aquinnah Capital. I like working for Bernie. He's a decent guy, and he supports me. It's a good job."

Paul didn't even tell her what kind of a deal her father had offered. It was admittedly pretty spectacular. Paul could easily double or triple his income, and that was just to start. He'd be jumping several rungs up the career ladder. He'd be Galkin's head of all U.S. equities, a major promotion.

Tatyana nodded, rueful. "I get why working for my father wouldn't appeal to you, sure. But I have to tell you, I'm actually shocked Papa made you the offer."

"Why's that?"

"Business is one thing he's unsentimental about. So he must actually think you're hot shit."

Paul just smiled.

"Are you?"

"Am I what?"

"Hot shit."

Teasingly, he shrugged. "Why don't you come find out?"

30

Tatyana's gallery opening was on a Saturday night in May. She had to be there early to oversee the setup and make sure everything was hung in the right place. "You don't have to be there until eight, Pasha," she said.

"You sure you don't want me to help?"

"You'd just be in the way, to be honest."

The Argold Gallery was on Twentieth Street between Tenth and Eleventh Avenues, on the third floor of an old warehouse. The walls were white and sparsely hung with Tatyana's photographs in black frames. A lot of white space between them.

They were not what he expected. The shots of the Russian ladies he'd seen at her place, the *babushki*, were excellent and moving, but these photos blew him away.

They were brightly colored portraits of what Paul thought of as street people, maybe homeless, standing in the glaring midday sun against white backgrounds that, upon closer examination, turned out to be the white walls of buildings. Sometimes the subjects looked directly at you; sometimes they looked away or inward. Their faces were weathered. The stark sun emphasized their physical imperfections, their wrinkles and scars, making them look both vulnerable and hardened. The portraits were powerful, original, beautiful, and sad all at the same time.

A few guests were at the gallery when he arrived, not many. A few limos idled outside. One of them was a silver Maybach Landaulet with its retractable roof open and Niko sitting in the back, smoking, chatting with his driver, a handsome guy with long black hair and blue eyes. Next to Niko was a woman whose face Paul couldn't make out.

He found Tatyana inside, talking to the gallerist, a thin man in his late thirties with enormous black-framed glasses that dominated his pallid face. Tatyana was wearing a sharply tailored black suit with no shirt underneath. Her shoes were simple black suede pumps with a high heel. Her makeup looked minimal but no doubt had involved a lot of work: natural lipstick, cat's-eye black eyeliner with rounded corners, perfect brows. She looked nervous.

"These are great!" Paul said. "Just fantastic."

She hugged and kissed him. Then she introduced him to the gallerist and excused herself to speak to someone who'd just arrived.

"You know her work, of course," the gallerist said.

"Of course," Paul said. "But not these."

"I call them street portraits," he said. "It's a procession of humanity, a danse macabre of the marginalized and the powerless." He lowered his voice. "A critic from *Artforum* is here."

"Oh, good," Paul said. Gesturing to the pictures on the wall, he added, "They're very different from her Moscow portraits."

The gallerist cocked his head uncertainly.

"The old Russian ladies."

"Ah, yes. Her early work. I think she's developing her own voice, her own style," he said. "I mean, you look at Annie Leibovitz or Richard Avedon or Yousuf Karsh—you can tell their style at once, right? Same is true for Tatyana Belkin." He walked Paul over to a photograph of a strange-looking guy, shirtless and heavily tattooed, including on his face, with a strong overhead sun bleaching out part of his forehead. "Now, that's a Tatyana Belkin. You can tell from a mile away."

"Interesting, you know, it doesn't look posed," Paul said.

"Exactly. Though of course it is."

"It's like he's proud of his warrior attire—his Iron Cross belt, his pierced nipple, the war paint on his neck. He's a book you want to read."

"Photographing in bright light, taking pictures midday in the hot sun—that's typically advised against," the gallerist said. "It can create a hazy, washed-out look. Even lens flare and color distortion. But for her, it works." He looked over his shoulder, probably for the critic from *Artforum*.

"There's a contrast between the bright, sunny midday light and her subjects," Paul said, thinking out loud.

In fifteen minutes, the place was packed with an affluent crowd, nearly everyone holding wineglasses. He heard the name "Diane Arbus" a lot, floating out of the hubbub. No surprise. Arbus did strange and powerful black-and-white portraits of people on the fringes, circus freaks, the mentally ill. But Tatyana's photographs were very different. They were in color and bright, and they seemed to have been taken with compassion, not condescension or voyeurism, just as she'd said. He heard Russian being spoken, which wasn't a surprise, either.

Tatyana was soon surrounded by admirers. One of them, a sixty-something-year-old man, was telling her that her images captured people at their truest.

Paul overheard two women next to him talking to each other and looking at Tatyana. "She's wearing an Azzedine Alaïa," the first woman said. "Think that's Rent the Runway?"

"Please," replied the second woman. "She's a Galkin. She *owns* the runway."

Tatyana's brother turned up at Paul's side in front of a large picture of a Black man in a black hat and black leather jacket, an oxygen tube under his nose. The subject's face was deeply lined from life on the streets, illuminated by a glaring noontime sun.

"Bizarre stuff, huh?" Niko said. His long, dirty-blond hair, combed straight back, was either unwashed or had a lot of product in it.

"This one?"

"The whole show. Weird, don't you think?" Niko was accompanied by a beautiful girl in a short black dress and a low-cut spangly top whom he didn't introduce and who stood by him and said nothing. He always seemed to be with a different woman, Paul had noticed.

"Actually, no, Niko. Her work is terrific," he said. "This guy here shows vulnerability and, I don't know, bravado? It's surprisingly intimate."

Niko's eyebrows shot up. "Gotta wonder how she got this fancy gallery interested in her stuff, huh?" He chuckled.

Paul smiled. Niko was playing his mind games, trying to provoke Paul into saying something critical of Tatyana.

Paul looked around, saw Tatyana's father enter, with his redhead security chief, Berzin, at his elbow. Behind them followed Polina and a couple of bullnecked security thugs. Paul wondered if Arkady had to take his security people with him everywhere he went. That could not be fun.

As usual, Polina was subtly competing with her stepdaughter, who was only a few years younger. They were both fashionistas, though their styles were very different. Tatyana countered Polina's gold and glitz by dressing herself in clothes that weren't flashy. She had a super-hip, Brooklyn vibe, whereas her stepmother simply and crassly dressed to show off her figure and beauty and wealth. Even their manicures competed. Polina's nails were long and glossy, different colors each time Paul saw her—hot pink, classic red, salmon, that sort of thing—while Tatyana wore her nails short with pearl polish in an understated, natural shade. She looked subtle and hip where her stepmother went for a big, brassy look. Tonight, Polina was wearing a dramatic black fishnet dress with long fringe at the bottom. Very eye-catching, perhaps meant to steal attention from Tatyana at her opening. Smoky-eye makeup with tiny crystals on the lids. Very high heels with sparkles all over the spikes, and red soles.

Arkady hugged his daughter long and hard. While they were embracing, Polina gasped and took Tatyana's hand. "Your ring!" she exclaimed. She faltered: "It's—the diamond is so cute! I think the smaller stones are very chic now." Then she eyed Tatyana from head to toe and said with a smile, "I've said this before—I'd never be able to pull off that outfit."

"Thank you, I guess," said Tatyana.

Polina turned to Paul. "Women, in our twenties we dress for men, in our thirties we dress for other women. Who do you think is more judgmental, men or women?"

"Women can be judgmental about a twenty-six-year-old, too," said Tatyana. "Believe me."

"Your pictures are surprisingly good," Polina said. "Especially for a hobby." She gave Tatyana a hug. "Good for you. I'm glad you're having fun."

Tatyana gave Paul a knowing smile and moved on through the crowd.

Arkady put a meaty hand on Paul's shoulder. "We're going to make some money with you on the board," he said.

"The board?"

"You maybe say 'on board.' Anyway, is very exciting."

"I appreciate the offer, and I'll let you know soon," Paul said.

Galkin lowered his voice. "Maybe you will let me buy my daughter a bigger diamond. Bump her up."

Paul didn't have a chance to reply. The gallerist with the big black-framed glasses immediately glommed onto Arkady. Paul wondered if Galkin was a major customer.

Paul caught Tatyana's eye in the crowd, excused himself, and crossed over to where she was standing, in front of a large photograph of a man wearing white curlers in his hair and smoking a joint. Next to her were her friend Vera and Vera's husband, Brent. Tatyana and he had seen them at dinner a few weeks ago. They were laughing about something. But when Paul approached, Tatyana turned away from them, looked at him, threw out her arms, and said, openly vulnerable, "Do you really like them?"

"I think they're knockouts," he said, hugging her. "Portraits of our time."

"Oh, thank you, Pasha!"

He tried his Russian. "*Ochen interestnyie fotografiyi.*" Very interesting pictures. It wasn't hard to remember: *Interestnyie* sounded like "interesting," and *fotografiyi* was obviously "photographs."

"*Otlichno!*" she replied. Excellent. "Terrific." Then she switched back to English. "I love them," she said, meaning the subjects, not the photos themselves. "They're my people." Then she whispered nervously, "The critic from *Artforum* is here!"

Just behind them, a buxom middle-aged woman came up to Arkady. "Wonderful show," she said. "Congratulations."

"Is my daughter show, not mine," Arkady said. "Tell her."

"Well, let me congratulate the gallery owner," the woman said, leaning over and giving him a kiss.

Paul realized then that Tatyana's photographs were here, at this prestigious gallery, only because of her father. That Niko, with all his mind games, knew it. That Tatyana, as a result, would never really feel any sense of validation as a photographer. And his heart broke for her.

31

That night, in the middle of the night, Tatyana cried out in her sleep, saying things Paul didn't understand, in a high voice. He was pretty sure she was speaking Russian. He had noticed this happened with her from time to time. He went to comfort her, wiping away tears, and she just clutched him, pulled him to her firmly.

In the morning, he asked her what she'd been dreaming about that was so upsetting.

"It's a dream I have so often. I'm going somewhere with my brother and my parents, and I turn around, and my parents are gone."

"Did that ever happen to you?"

"Once, they took me to the zoo in Vienna when I was little, and I got lost. I guess I must have seen some ice cream, and my papa said I couldn't have any until after lunch, and I wandered off in search of the ice cream, and he and Mama were looking at the monkeys, and they lost track of me."

"Whatever happened?"

"A security guard saw me and asked me where my parents were, and I told him I didn't know. He bought me an ice cream. Eventually, my parents went to Security, and the guard who was with me got a call and—but think of how scary it must have been for them! To think you lost your child in a foreign city."

"Did your dad leave you when you were young?"

She looked sad. She paused a moment. "He was gone a lot. Long periods of time. My mama would tell me when he was coming back, and he'd call me on the phone, but I was still afraid he wasn't coming back. I have dreams where I'm in an airport. I tell my parents to wait a moment, I want to buy something from a shop, and when I come back from the shop, they're not there. I keep looking and looking, and there's no trace of them. I ask people, and they shake their heads. I call out for them—Mama! Papa!—but they're gone, and somehow I know they're gone forever. They've deliberately left me, and they're never coming back. I yell for them, but no sound comes out of my mouth. I try so hard to scream, and all I can do is make a high, squeaking sound. Like my voice has been taken away."

"You ever talk to a therapist about it?"

"Of course. I've had lots of therapists. And they all tell me I have abandonment issues. Separation anxiety."

"Oh, that's a big help," he said sarcastically.

"Yeah, brilliant insight. Thank you very much." She added, dryly, "So don't abandon me."

"I won't," he said.

32

Bad news traveled fast at Aquinnah, as it did in the whole financial world. The worse the news, the faster it sped through the circuits. And this news was very bad.

Aquinnah's fixed-income division had invested a huge sum—10 percent of the firm's assets—in Argentinian debt. The news was all over the *Wall Street Journal* online and Bloomberg and everywhere else: Argentina had defaulted.

While Paul had been having fun with Madagascan vanilla, Aquinnah's fixed-income division had lost their shirts. To be specific, they'd lost over four hundred million dollars, or 10 percent of all the assets under management. That erased all gains elsewhere at Aquinnah.

It was a disaster. There was no more cash to deploy in the firm. Nothing more to invest, which meant that Paul's team couldn't buy stocks. All activity was frozen. And no one would get bonuses.

Everyone, even those who had had nothing to do with the bond guys' fuckup, was affected. People were leaving the firm in droves. Over the course of one day, Paul realized there was no future for him at Aquinnah.

THAT SAME AFTERNOON, HE GOT a call from a recruiter. He got such calls from time to time. Headhunters are much reviled in the industry, but they're used by everybody, and this time, Paul decided to take the call. He was interested in what they had to say.

Everyone on the Street knew what had happened at Aquinnah. They all smelled blood in the water. The headhunter was calling on behalf of the largest hedge fund in the world, Bridgeport Associates, headquartered in Stamford, Connecticut. It was founded and run by Steve D'Orazio and worth twenty-five billion dollars. In 2008, when just about every hedge fund tanked, Bridgeport was up 10 percent. D'Orazio had self-published a book of advice and investing philosophy. He called it *Wisdom*.

Bridgeport Associates was famous for having an abusive and cruel workplace. Thirty percent of all new employees left within a year. Paul had always sworn he'd never take a job there.

"Tell me what you have in mind," he said to the headhunter.

TATYANA WAS AT HOME FEEDING Pushkin, who was a picky eater, easily distractible. When Paul arrived home, the dog trotted to the front door to greet him, jumping up, paws in the air. This was a first.

Paul liked dogs, as much as a non–dog owner could, but he'd found his approaches to Pushkin mostly thwarted. He would lean down to pet the little creature, but Pushkin would scuttle away. Pushkin was a one-person dog.

"You're home early," Tatyana said, kissing him. "I need your help."

"I need a drink," Paul said.

"First, can you plunge the toilet?"

She had a balky toilet that was prone to overflowing. Since moving into her apartment, Paul had plunged it a number of times. It was one of the things he didn't like about living in Tatyana's apartment, besides the fact that it was too small: there wasn't even room for his clothes, which he piled in neat stacks on the floor.

When he returned from plunging the toilet, Tatyana handed him a drink and thanked him. She'd poured him some Four Roses over ice. She had bought bourbon for him after he moved in. She'd poured herself a glass of Whispering Angel rosé.

They sat at her old enamel-top kitchen table, and Paul told her what had happened at Aquinnah. It took some explaining; she didn't understand what "fixed-income" meant or how debt worked, but when he told her he wouldn't be getting a bonus (the biggest part of his annual income, normally) and had no chance of being promoted, then she got it.

He told her about the call from the headhunter.

"Sounds like a good job," she said. "Are you going to take it?"

"Let me tell you about Steve D'Orazio," he said. "He was fired from his first job for punching his boss in the face when he was drunk."

"Oh."

"He's a world-class asshole. He has a philosophy he calls radical honesty. Which means that he and all other supervisors and officers of the company feel free to be abusive to their underlings. When you go into work each morning at Bridgeport, you have to lock up your personal cell phone. All employees are under surveillance at all times. D'Orazio's famous for saying, 'If you're not worried, you need to worry.'"

"You wouldn't work there, would you?"

He gave her a look.

"Good," she said. "And my father's offer?"

"You want me to work for your father, don't you?"

"Me? Don't misunderstand me, Pasha. I want to support you. I want you to do whatever you want."

"You don't care?"

"I mean, it would be nice, but it's your decision. Really."

THE NEXT MORNING, THE WHOLE office was visibly demoralized. People were gathered in clumps, talking nervously about what was going to happen. Michael Rodriguez clapped Paul on the back and said, "Adios, bud."

"You're leaving?"

"Got a job at Baupost, in Boston. Less money, but still . . ."

"Congrats. That's a great place."

"How about you? Are you staying?"

Paul shook his head.

"Have you told Karp yet?" Karp was their immediate boss; he generally stayed out of the way, in his office. "Or Bernie?"

"I have some emails to write," Paul said. He emailed Karp, then sent an email to Bernie, thanking him for everything.

Twenty seconds later, his email notification chimed. It was Bernie, asking him to come to his office right away.

Paul was expecting Bernie to try to talk him out of his decision to work for Arkady, so he arrived at Bernie's office armed with arguments. Instead, Bernie, who was slumped in his chair, looking haggard, not like his usual energetic self, said, "I get it."

"About leaving?"

"I'd do the same thing, if I was you."

"Thanks for understanding."

"I'm sure you have your choice of firms. You want me to put in a good word, just tell me."

"Thanks, but I think I know where I'm going."

"Boris Badenov?"

"Who?"

"You probably never saw *Rocky and Bullwinkle*."

"Before my time."

"Boris Badenov was the bad guy. I think he was supposed to be Russian. Called himself the world's greatest no-goodnik. Had a pencil-thin mustache. Spoke in a bad Russian accent."

Paul shook his head slowly.

"Let's grab a steak, okay?" Bernie said.

THEY WENT OUT FOR A drink and a steak at Bernie's favorite Irish pub in Manhattan. O'Malley's was the real thing. It offered bangers and mash and shepherd's pie, decent steaks, and Irish lamb stew. The stained-glass windows in the main room added an ecclesiastical note. Bernie had frequented O'Malley's since he was a young trader and just liked the place. The roar of traffic from the street was, thankfully, remote.

They started with black-and-tans, Guinness layered on top of Bass Ale.

"What kind of shop does Galkin run?" Bernie asked. "It's not a hedge fund."

"It's an investment fund. I think it just manages his money, his real estate portfolio, and so on. Sort of a glorified family office."

"How much they run?"

"I don't know."

"What's he worth, Galkin?"

Paul told Bernie the figure he'd heard. It was a lot.

"And do you know where it's from, all his money?"

Paul didn't reply. He took a long sip, set down the pint glass, shrugged.

Bernie answered his own question: "Who the hell knows, right? You know, there's rumors about Galkin. That he got his start by blowing up the competition with a car bomb."

"Seriously?" Paul asked.

"That his adversaries have an unfortunate way of dying."

"You don't really believe those rumors, do you?"

"That's the trouble. It's like you're walking through a cave where you just don't know what's around the corner. You don't want to put yourself in that position, Paul."

The steaks arrived sizzling on aluminum platters, medium rare, which was how both men liked them. They tucked into their food, and Bernie continued as if in the middle of a thought. "You know what *tsuris* means?" he said.

"Come on, Bernie," Paul said through a mouthful of rib-eye. He'd been around Bernie long enough. It was a Yiddish word that meant "trouble."

"Well, working for immediate family, that's the definition of tsuris. You're going to work for your father-in-law?"

Paul shrugged, gave a crooked smile.

"Plus, look, we got a good thing going, you and me."

"I know," Paul admitted. "I feel bad about that."

"These Russian guys, these oligarchs, whatever you want to call them—you don't know whether they're criminals. You don't know whose side they're on."

"Whose *side*? Bernie, this isn't the Cold War. It's not like the capitalists versus the communists. These guys are all on the side of capitalism. They're on the side of making money, which is our side, right?"

"I don't think it works that way," Bernie said, and he deposited another big chunk of prime beef into his mouth. There was silence as he chewed, then swallowed. "I need you, man. Like, when you dug down deep into Cavalier Enterprises and saved me from a lot of legal *mishegas*. And shame. You were a goddamned hero."

"Thank you. That means a lot."

"Maybe we could work out a partnership stake. I mean, it'll be tight in the short run, but five years from now, you'll be raking it in."

"I've decided," Paul said.

"But, candidly, Paul, I think you're making a mistake."

"I appreciate that, but I don't agree," said Paul.

Bernie nodded. "I hate to see you go, but that's not it. I'm telling you as your friend. This is a mistake. Don't make it."

PART FIVE

EVASION SKILLS

Present Day

33

He saw a faint flicker of light through the branches that served as the walls of his improvised wolf's den. Probably from someone's flashlight.

More footsteps.

Then voices, faint at first. It was three in the morning: these weren't hikers. As the voices grew steadily louder, Paul realized it was several people speaking in what he immediately recognized as Russian. Probably the two who'd come by his house and killed Alec Wood. The big, buff young bald guy and the gray-and-copper-haired Berzin. The two who were chasing him, maybe others as well.

He slowly sat up, his body tensing. He had seen Berzin's thug shoot Alec, a police officer who wasn't their target, point blank. They would do whatever it took to eliminate him. After five years, they had finally located him, and they would stop at nothing to get rid of him, Paul was quite certain.

He heard one of the men say, in English, "The nearest town . . ." At least, he thought that was what the man had said.

The other man replied, but Paul couldn't make it out.

He was glad he'd taken precautions in building the fire and putting it out. From a few feet away, you couldn't see any evidence of his ever having been here.

One of the men, probably Berzin, continued, saying something about "Grant Anderson."

The other one: Something about "the forest." Something about "running."

Maybe they had determined that Paul was heading toward Lincoln. How else could they have come so close?

Then the voices grew steadily fainter.

They were passing by.

He waited, listened. Now he could barely hear them.

For another five minutes, Paul sat in the shelter his father had taught him to build, his heart clamoring. When he could no longer hear the two men, he carefully got up and pushed aside the branches, slid down from the boulders, and stepped onto the forest floor. In the distance, he saw the glint of a flashlight. They had walked close to him but hadn't seen him, so they'd kept on moving through the woods.

It was too dark to walk through the trees without a flashlight, so he returned to the wolf's den and decided to try to lie down a little longer, until the sun came up.

He tried to sleep, but his mind kept racing. He was haunted by an image, a still frame of Frederick Newman on the fishing boat at the moment the bullet struck his neck. The man had come to kill him, Paul knew, but, still, he'd never killed anyone before.

He wondered where Sarah was, whether she'd left Derryfield already. He hoped she had. If so, she was probably okay.

But what if she hadn't left town yet and they'd gotten to her? He couldn't allow himself to consider that possibility. It was too terrible to think about.

He wondered if she had called him on the burner phone whose number he'd given her. Maybe she'd left a message.

He took out the disposable cell phone and switched it on. There were no bars, no reception here. He wanted to call Sarah and check in with her, make sure she was okay.

He reminded himself that if he had no phone signal, neither did his pursuers.

But they might well have satellite phones. That was more than a possibility.

Soon, despite the churning thoughts and images, and a growling stomach, he fell asleep again.

He was awakened sometime later by a drop of water on his face, then another one, then a series of spatters coming in through the branches. *Just what I need.* It was still dark, but now it was raining.

34

He had left his Paul Brightman life behind. Everything he read on the dark web had told him that you must never look back. You have to assume that the world you've left behind is dead. People who can't let go of the past will eventually get caught. Some people resort to drink and to making calls to loved ones they miss. Those are the ones who always get found out.

Grant Anderson, as Paul imagined him, had worked for years for a nonprofit in someplace like Uganda, never had credit cards before, never needed any. But what could he *do*? What skills did he have?

To be blunt about it, not many. Paul Brightman could pick a stock or structure an investment, sure. But that wasn't who Grant Anderson was. Grant Anderson worked with his hands, didn't wear Armani suits or Hermès ties, didn't fly business class. Had never been on a private plane.

Paul was going to have to live plainly and modestly. No more high-end restaurants or private cars. That life was done. He bought a prepaid MasterCard that he could use when he absolutely had to use a credit card. He found an ad on Craigslist for a boatbuilder's assistant. The pay was bad, but at least he'd be paid in cash. The bureaucrats were relentless. If he filed taxes, his new identity would be unraveled, he'd be discovered, and the Russians would track him down.

He also had to be careful taking out a bank account in Grant's name. No interest-bearing accounts. He had to make sure never to earn any interest, anything that would require an IRS 1099 form. That was going to be tricky.

But he could do it.

On his second morning in Derryfield, five years ago, he sat at the counter of the Starlite Diner inhaling the tantalizing aromas of coffee and maple syrup and bacon, and ordered breakfast. Two eggs over hard, bacon, wheat toast, and coffee.

"Okay, honey," said the waitress, a tall, slender woman with short black hair and heavy eye shadow. "Coming right up." She poured coffee into a mug.

"Thanks, Fran," Grant said. Her name was engraved on a black plastic nameplate on her pale-blue uniform.

The short-order cook was fast. Fran brought Grant's plate of food not more than three minutes later. The diner was mostly empty, five or six people eating at tables. It was six thirty in the morning. Fran looked around but didn't move from where she was standing across the counter from him.

"Visiting?" she asked.

Grant finished chewing a mouthful of egg. He shook his head until he was able to speak. "Just moved here."

"Oh, yeah?" She sounded genuinely delighted. "Welcome."

"Thanks."

"What brings you to town?"

He paused for just a moment. "A job," he said.

The Starlite Diner was slowly filling up.

"What's your job?" Fran asked.

"Helping out John Casey, the boatbuilder."

"Oh, yeah? He comes in here pretty often. Dinner, mostly." She turned, glass coffee carafe in hand, and greeted a woman who had just sat down at the counter next to him, the only available place left. "Morning, Sarah. You waiting for a table or . . . ?"

"This is fine," the woman named Sarah said. She was graceful and tall and pretty, with cognac-brown eyes and long brown hair. She looked to be in her late twenties. She smelled of woodsmoke and was wearing a pale-blue fleece and jeans.

"Usual?" Fran said, pouring coffee into a mug.

Sarah nodded.

"Meet the latest resident of Derryfield," Fran said to Sarah.

Grant offered the young woman his hand. "I'm Grant," he said.

PAUL SHIVERED AS HE PULLED his poncho and the poncho liner over himself, for it wasn't just raining, it was cold as well. And it was still too dark to navigate through the woods. He sat with the poncho's hood over his head. At least he was dry. His stomach growled audibly. He was ravenously hungry and felt lightheaded. He still had half a protein bar left, which had to last him until he got to Lincoln. That was thirty-six hours, a day and a half away—if he was lucky.

He allowed himself a quarter of the bar now, leaving just a quarter. It barely satiated the hunger, and on top of it, he was awfully thirsty, too. The more you eat, he remembered, the more water your body requires.

He gathered the tarpaulin and the poncho liner and the fleece blanket, rolled them together with the tarp on the outside to deflect the rain. Over that, he put the Mylar space blanket. He thought about collecting some rain to drink, but all he had in his bag was an aluminum cup, and that wouldn't collect much.

After another hour or so of rain, the sun came up and the sky lightened from pitch black to steel gray. It was a few minutes after six in the morning. But the rain continued, coming down even harder, a driven rain, drumming with the kind of force that can't last long.

He pulled out his map, but without knowing what direction he was moving in, it was useless. He wondered which way the Russians had gone. They'd hiked past him; were they now ahead of him in the forest? But what did "ahead" mean? Had they gone farther west? Or were they moving in another direction? That he couldn't tell. Presumably they had been following signs of disturbance in the forest, like crushed leaves and broken branches, signs that he had come this way. But he'd been careful not to leave traces, or at least to leave as few as possible. So how had they managed to get so close?

It was still raining hard. He was tempted to stay in his wolf den until it stopped, but then he remembered his father's words: *Rain is the perfect cover. Rain is your friend.* It obscures your tracks, he'd say, it muffles the noise you make, and it obscures the vision of anyone who's chasing you. These were things Stan remembered from his army days that he wanted Paul to learn. To a fourteen-year-old kid, it was a game. Evasion skills! Who would a fourteen-year-old possibly be evading?

So while it was raining was the ideal time to move through the forest.

He couldn't locate west: the rainclouds in the sky obscured the sun. Periodically, he checked his burner phone, but there was still no reception. He wanted to call Sarah but couldn't.

The rain was coming down forcefully, and the blisters on his toes hurt, and it was cold. At least it wasn't snowing; it wasn't quite that cold. He kept himself going by imagining the wonderful fire he'd soon warm himself by. Until he realized that, of course, in the pouring rain, he wasn't going to be able to make any kind of fire; that was just a fantasy. Plus, his lighter was dead.

As the rain let up, he was surprised to come upon a low, crumbling brick wall. A little farther along, he saw a pile of red bricks that looked like they had once been part of a chimney. These were clearly from the foundation of ruined houses from an old, abandoned town, a ghost town, probably from the nineteenth century. He wondered what had become of the town, what had happened to its residents, why and how it had been deserted. Probably an old logging town. Who knew? It was a reminder that the White Mountain Forest he was navigating was clear-cut and burned to the ground a century ago. People had built a town here and lived in it before abandoning it to nature.

He passed a tiny stream; it was somewhat engorged because of the rain. Flowing water was at least safer to drink than standing. He took out the aluminum cup from his bag and knelt beside the stream and scooped up some water. He swigged it down gratefully, scooped up another cupful and drank that down, too.

Then he tilted his head and listened. After a while, he thought he heard faint voices. He focused his attention, tried to determine whether they were coming closer or moving farther away. They weren't getting quieter. They were coming this way.

He picked up a roughly ten-inch stick and drove it into the ground. Another trick to determine direction. But the sky was too cloudy: the stick didn't cast a shadow. Now what? You were supposed to put a pebble at the tip of the shadow the stick cast, wait until the shadow had discernibly moved, then place another pebble at the tip of the shadow, that much he remembered. But then what? That he didn't remember. And without a shadow, the trick wouldn't work anyway.

There was another way to tell direction, using a leaf floating in a puddle of water. But he didn't remember how.

Let's see. Moss grows on the north side of the tree, or is that one of those rules that doesn't always hold true? Or he could find Polaris, the

North Star, on the handle of the Little Dipper, but he'd have to wait until dark to do that. And when the skies were clear again.

Finding north, his father would say, was one of the most important skills to master, along with purifying water and making a fire. It was important, surely, but he hadn't paid much attention, and as a result, he'd screwed it up. *You're doing it wrong.*

Still no cell signal out here, so he couldn't use the phone's GPS. All he could do was keep moving and hope that he was moving west. Later, when he saw the sun dipping in the west, he could follow that.

The faint voices—were they hikers?—faded as the Russians seemed to move off in another direction.

He had to keep going. He had no way to determine how far he'd gone, in terms of miles. There were no landmarks to help him gauge distance. He knew how much time had passed only because of his watch.

A few minutes later, he heard a helicopter overhead.

PART SIX

MISFIT TOYS

Five Years Earlier

35

When Paul arrived for his first day of work at the new firm, he half-expected to be met by Arkady Galkin himself. Instead, when he introduced himself to the icily beautiful receptionist, she smiled stiffly, nodded, and said, "Let me get Mr. Frost." Paul had no idea who "Mr. Frost" was. He hadn't been given an org chart nor told who his colleagues and bosses would be. He knew only that the company was called AGF Limited, a generic-sounding name that stood for Arkady Galkin Finance.

Two minutes later, a tall, bald man appeared in the lobby. He was wearing an expensive suit and dark horn-rimmed glasses. He had a strong brow and a weak mouth, a tall dome of a head and large ears. With a solemn expression, he said, "Mr. Brightman?"

"Paul," he said, stepping forward and offering his hand. "Nice to meet you." He had worn a jacket and tie, not sure what the dress code would be. You could always take off your tie.

"Paul, then. I've heard much about you. Your reputation precedes you. It's marvelous to have you here."

"Thank you. I look forward to it."

Mr. Frost had a very slight foreign accent, probably Russian, though his surname wasn't Russian. He had the broad shoulders of an athlete and moved smoothly, like a cat. Walking quickly and fluidly down a plush hall, he brought Paul to his new office.

Paul was introduced to his new administrative assistant, Margo Whitworth, whom he shared with a colleague, Chad Forrester. Margo was an attractive dark-skinned woman with short black hair, shaved on the sides; she was quick-witted and seemed pleasant. Paul liked her at once. Her desk was outside his and Chad's offices.

Paul's office wasn't very big but had a postcard view of the city. On top of a mahogany desk was a three-panel monitor array, a phone, and nothing else. An armoire stood on the left of the room. The desk faced away from the million-dollar view. His first real office.

The entire firm was sumptuous. Cherrywood and granite, subtle lighting, two terraces, a full gym with locker rooms and showers. The break room was outrageous. An automatic German coffee machine that dispensed espressos and cappuccinos. A juice refrigerator with some thirty kinds of juice. A breakfast spread of half-bagels with cream cheese and lox and mini-omelets of various kinds. Fruit bowls (raspberries and fresh-cut pineapple, strawberries, mango, and papaya). The breakfast was cleared away at eleven, when lunch was served. It was like a continuous buffet at the Four Seasons.

Mr. Frost brought Paul to the morning meeting, which was already under way in a conference room filled with twelve people, only two of whom were women. Arkady wasn't there. The uniform here for the men seemed to be dress shirt, no jacket or tie. Most of the men wore leather sneakers.

During a pause, Mr. Frost introduced Paul to the group. "He comes to us from Aquinnah Capital," he said. "He'll be portfolio manager for U.S. equities."

Paul was introduced quickly to his colleagues—"Ivan Matlovsky, real estate; Chad Forrester, emerging markets; Jake Larsen, venture capital," and so on, and finally to Nikolai Galkin. Niko was identified as being in "Special Projects," which probably meant a sinecure: he got paid to do nothing. Paul couldn't help but wonder if any of them knew about his relationship with the boss's daughter, but no one said anything.

Mr. Frost brought him next to the large corner office of the boss, Arkady Galkin. (Frost's office, he saw, was right next door.) Galkin lumbered around from behind his desk. He was wearing a finely cut navy-blue suit and light-blue tie. He broke into rapid-fire Russian, and Mr. Frost replied in Russian just as fluent, sounding like a native.

"I warn you, Paul speaks Russian," Galkin said in English to Frost.

"Barely," Paul said.

Mr. Frost excused himself.

Galkin gave Paul a bear hug. "Welcome to family," he said.

Paul smiled. He thought he'd joined the family when he got engaged to Tatyana.

"You see the break room?" Galkin asked.

"Very impressive."

"Impressive? You will gain twenty pounds working here, if you're not careful. Tatyana doesn't want husband with *dad bod* before he's dad." He said "dad bod" with a delighted twist, like it was a phrase he'd just learned and was happy to have a chance to use.

They both laughed, Paul probably for different reasons. He was amused to be lectured on this topic by a man with a protuberant potbelly.

"Many perks working for my firm. Best health insurance plan. Breakfast and lunch every day by private chef. But as far as company is concerned, you are not son-in-law. I show you no favor. Neither does anyone here. I suggest you do not tell people about marriage to my daughter."

"I understand. But word will get around," Paul said. "Gossip spreads fast."

Galkin shrugged. "You are an employee like anyone else, new hire. You report to senior managing director, Eugene Frost."

"Understood. Is that originally his name?"

"He was born 'Yevgenii Morozov.' You know what means *moroz*?"

Paul recognized the word. It meant "frost." Frost had Anglicized his name.

"He's Russian-born but has spent nearly all his life here. I trust him—" Galkin waved an index finger back and forth, searching for a word.

"Implicitly," Paul suggested.

"Yes. Implicitly. Mr. Frost speaks for me. He is senior managing director," Galkin repeated. "Usually, I am not here."

"Okay."

A long pause. Galkin smiled, looked at Paul for an uncomfortably long time, as if he were deciding what to say. Finally, he nodded and spoke. "I was little surprised you accepted job offer."

"Why?"

"Because I am what sometimes called *oligarch*. Oligarchs have bad image in America. All of these stereotypes in this country about Russians. *Russophobia*, is called."

"I'm marrying a Russian woman, don't forget."

"Yes. Is true. But you were at very white-shoe firm, and we are not so white-shoe."

"I wasn't exactly at Goldman Sachs."

"Please. Aquinnah? Named after Bernie Kovan's house on Martha's Vineyard? I call this white-shoe."

Paul chuckled. "Okay—fair."

Galkin clapped his hands together, signaling that the conversation was over. "Now," he said as he steered Paul toward the door, "if only you can get my daughter to move out of shithole in East Village."

36

At lunchtime, Paul ambled to the break room to check out the spread. A few other employees were there already. Chad Forrester, several years older than Paul, balding with short, pale-blond hair and vague eyes, said hello.

"We're neighbors, right?" Paul said to him. "We share an admin?"

Chad nodded. "Welcome to the Island of Misfit Toys," he said.

"Jake Larsen," said another new colleague he'd been introduced to at the meeting. Jake was a tall guy with longish brown hair parted in the center. He gave Paul his hand. "Nice to meet you, Paul." They shook. "Don't listen to anything Chad tells you." The men laughed politely.

All the guys seemed to dress alike—chinos, open-collar shirts, leather sneakers. It was a private equity uniform. Galkin and Mr. Frost dressed more formally, but maybe that was a signifier that they were the bosses.

"Seems like not a lot of women work here, is that right?" Paul asked. "I saw only two at the morning meeting."

"Wasn't it that way at Aquinnah?" Larsen asked.

"Same," he admitted.

"So we're not all that different from other investment firms in that sense," said Larsen. "Just sexist in the usual way, I guess." He paused. "But we're different in other ways. You'll see. I gotta get back to my desk." Larsen waved and left.

"What did he mean?" Paul asked Chad.

Chad's smile faded somewhat. "Wanna grab a drink later? I can give you the lay of the land, if you want?"

"Sounds good," Paul said. It made sense to meet his colleagues informally outside work if possible. Why not the first day? "Thanks, Chad. I look forward to it." He plucked a grape from the fruit tray. "Is the food always this good?"

"They don't stint on meals."

"The boss man himself warned me I'd gain weight here if I weren't careful."

"Who, Frost?"

"Arkady."

"Galkin did?" Forrester chuckled.

"Yeah, and that from a guy with Dunlap's disease." He regretted saying it even as it escaped his mouth—a feeble old joke, referring to a condition in which the victim's gut "done laps" over his belt, and Arkady had been nothing but welcoming. Whom was he trying to impress here?

Forrester winced, shook his head. "The walls have ears."

THERE WERE PEOPLE LIKE THAT in every office, Paul decided. *The walls have ears* . . . Which was another way of saying "Beware, people gossip."

He spent the afternoon getting up to speed, studying the portfolio, noting what he wanted to trim, what he wanted to add. He began to figure things out. Galkin's firm had an asset value of around five billion dollars. Of that, about two billion was in U.S.-based stocks. That chunk was his responsibility. He wondered what had happened to the last guy in his job.

Chad stopped by his office at 7:30 p.m., just as Paul was starting to lose steam. "Time to knock off," he announced. He was wearing a navy quilted vest over his blue button-down shirt and a Yankees cap to conceal his balding pate. He wore trendy, chunky black-framed glasses. His Stan Smiths were pristine.

"Good idea," Paul told Chad. He texted Tatyana: *Home late tonight. Drinks with new colleague.*

The two men walked to the elevator, took it down to the lobby. Chad was about Paul's height, maybe a little thinner. He had a particular bar in mind, a few blocks away. They talked as they walked.

"So you do emerging markets, right?" Paul asked. "What are you working on?"

"I invest in the new chip plant in India, solar power in Brazil, mining deals in Africa. You know. So . . . head of U.S. stocks, huh? Impressive. That a big jump for you?"

"Admittedly, yes," Paul said.

They had arrived at a grand old bar, which had that iconic old New York look—tin ceiling, beautiful mahogany bar, beveled mirror behind it, old-style urinals in the men's room dating from 1910.

They settled in at a beat-up-looking table.

"Welcome aboard," Chad said.

"Great to be here—excited to learn my way around." Paul clinked Chad's beer bottle as a toast, took a sip. He noticed Chad's watch, a Patek Philippe that must have cost tens of thousands of dollars. A lot of Galkin's senior employees wore expensive watches, he'd observed, but that wasn't much different from Bernie's shop.

"What are our colleagues like? Finance bros?"

Chad shook his head. "It's not bro-y at all. You're working with smart people, quants, mental athletes. If you don't put up numbers, you're out. Up or out."

Paul nodded. "About as expected."

"You gotta skate to where the puck is going. This isn't some white-shoe private equity fund where the most important thing is to join the right country club and talk college football, be a bro. People who work for Galkin are far more analytical. And more socially awkward."

Paul smiled, sipped his beer. They talked for another five minutes or so. The waiter brought a second round. As Chad finished his first beer and went on to his second, he got a little looser. He started telling jokes. Most of them weren't very funny. "Hey," he said after a while, "someone just sent me a Russian oligarch Advent calendar. Every time you open a window, an oligarch falls out."

Paul laughed politely. He'd already heard that one. "You warned me 'the walls have ears.' Are we discouraged from making jokes about our boss?"

"Off campus is safe, but definitely watch it in the office." Chad was seated at a right angle to Paul. His eyes slid to the side to meet Paul's. "So you're married to the boss's daughter."

There it was.

"Ummmm . . . well, not married, technically—we're engaged. Who told you?"

"Everyone knows."

Paul's eyebrows shot up. He shouldn't have been surprised, but it was still kind of annoying. "Arkady wants me to keep it on the DL. Plus, I'm going to be treated like everyone else, so."

"Well, good luck with that. Like that'll happen. You're the boss's son-in-law. He'll never fire you."

Paul shook his head, didn't know what to say. Was that true? How would he know? "Why are we the Island of Misfit Toys anyway? How so? If we're all 'mental athletes'?"

"Everyone here screwed up in some way in their old job."

"Really? What'd you do?"

"What'd I do? At my last job, we were taking a company public, and I decided to skim off a little cream for one of my clients."

"How?"

"I arranged for him to invest in a pre-IPO funding round. Then I did a sort of end run. Arranged for him to evade the lockup and sell his shares immediately post-IPO. Made a shitload of money for the client."

"But broke the rules in the process. You get fired?"

"Oh, yeah. And no one would hire me. But Galkin didn't mind."

"Was he the client?"

Chad gave a slow smile but didn't answer.

"All the other hires did something similar?"

"Ones that I know about, yeah. Jake did a penny stock trade on the side without telling his firm. His firm found out and fired him."

"For doing a deal in penny stocks?"

"A deal based on inside information he got working for the firm. Totally illegal."

All these screwups, Paul noticed, were ethical ones. Everyone here was ethically challenged. They hadn't lost money, though. Galkin wouldn't hire anyone who'd lost money. He would just hire cheats, apparently. *Everyone except me*, Paul thought. He hadn't fucked up. The opposite: He'd pulled off something impressive. And he hadn't done it by cheating.

"I thought I was dead meat," said Chad. "I got no callbacks. I didn't know what the hell I was going to do. And then Galkin hired me."

"So what's the catch?"

"You keep your mouth shut. And don't fuck up again."

"I see."

"Galkin's a fascinating guy," Chad said. "What's he like at home, among family?"

"I like him." Paul didn't know what else to say. "How is he as a boss?"

Chad shook his head. "Pretty much invisible. We never deal with him directly. We deal with Mr. Permafrost. Who's Russian, in case you hadn't guessed."

"I did."

"He's a ballbuster. You'll see."

"He was awfully welcoming to me."

"But you're not a normal employee, are you?"

Paul didn't answer, not sure how to reply. Did he really have a special cachet because his father-in-law was the boss? Probably so. But he didn't want to say it.

"I don't know yet," he said. "I really don't."

37

A few days later, Paul got a call at work from one of Galkin's secretaries, Maddy, asking him to come by the boss's office at one o'clock. When he arrived, he saw that it wasn't just Galkin; there was a second man, a tall, barrel-chested, silver-haired man who looked like he'd once played football, a long time ago.

Galkin didn't introduce the second man. He waited until Paul had sat down in one of the visitor's chairs in front of his desk, and then he said, abruptly, "Do you know what is wealth?"

This sounded like a trick question in a college philosophy course, so Paul said, with an indulgent smile, "Why don't you tell me."

"This word, *wealth*. You know I am not the native speaker, so I look up English words. I look up *wealth*. Long time ago, it doesn't mean 'money.' It means, how you say, 'well-being.' 'Happiness.' But a man's ultimate wealth is family, no?"

"Wealth is also money," Paul pointed out.

Galkin shook his head. "Money is moat." Paul must have looked confused, because Galkin said, "Do you say 'moat'? Around castle? Money is this moat. To protect yourself and your family from unpredictable and hostile world. Money protects your family, your wealth. You understand me?" He tapped a fist against his heart.

Now Paul understood. Galkin was talking about the prenup.

Then, without further explanation, Arkady introduced the silver-haired ex–football player. "William Dowling," he said. "My lawyer. Bill, this is Mr. Brightman. My future son-in-law. Pavel. That's his name in Russian."

"Pavel," the lawyer said, with a crusher of a handshake.

"Paul, actually."

"Paul, then. That's how I had it." Dowling lifted a silver metal attaché case and placed it gingerly on the glass desktop and popped it open. He pulled out three sets of documents in blueback folders and handed one to Paul. "This is a standard prenuptial agreement between husband and wife."

"Should I run this by my lawyer?" Paul asked.

The lawyer replied: "You're free to choose to have a lawyer."

"Will you excuse me for a moment?" Paul said. He didn't have a lawyer, really. He thought of a smart college friend who'd gone to Columbia Law. Brad Sarkisian had represented a mutual friend in a costly divorce. He and Paul weren't particularly close, but it was the first name he thought of. Paul did a quick search on his phone and found the name of Brad's law firm. He stepped out of the office and placed a call.

"Bradley Sarkisian's office, this is Meryl."

"This is an old friend of Brad's from college. Paul Brightman. I need to talk to him."

"Will he know what this is in reference to?"

"Just tell him it's Paul Brightman and it's important."

A few seconds went by, and then Sarkisian came on the line, loud and firm. "Brightman! How the hell are you?"

"Hey, Brad. Thanks for taking my call."

"Is there something I can help with? Everything okay?"

"Well, it's good news, really, but I need some advice. I'm marrying a woman named Tatyana Galkin." He paused, waiting for a grunt of recognition or at least congratulations, but none came. "Her father wants me to sign a prenup." He looked back at Galkin's office, saw Arkady deep in conversation with Dowling.

"Okay," Brad said. "Is she related to Arkady Galkin?"

"His daughter, right."

"One of those Russian oligarchs. So his lawyer is Bill Dowling, probably."

"Right."

"Tiny firm, but they do most of the high-net-worth divorces in Manhattan. Dowling's good. Anyway, email it to me, and I'll try to take a look at it this morning. Don't sign anything until I give you a call."

"Okay. Thanks, Brad." He pressed the End button and returned to Galkin's office.

"Can you email me a copy?" Paul said to the lawyer.

"Of course."

Paul gave Dowling his email address, then said, "Let's take a look." He opened the blue folder. The document was eighty-five pages long. On the first page, it read:

PRENUPTIAL AGREEMENT

THIS AGREEMENT is made this ___ day of ____ . . . by and between Paul A. Brightman of New York, New York, and Tatyana Arkadiyevna Galkina of New York, New York . . .

He skimmed the document at high speed. Eighty-five pages of fairly dense prose, written in high legalese (*Each party shall, upon the request of the other, execute, acknowledge and deliver any instruments that may be reasonably required to carry the intention of this Agreement into effect, including written consents to the election by the other of them to waive any qualified joint or survivor annuity . . .*) with Galkin and his lawyer breathing down his neck.

The basic point seemed to be: *What's mine is mine—when we got married—and what's yours is yours.* That seemed fair to him. Though he wasn't going to admit it.

One page stated the couple's assets. Tatyana had less than Paul had expected. There was a trust fund, worth a few million dollars. Then he came upon this sentence: "She is the beneficiary of substantial trusts significantly in excess of two hundred million dollars."

There was a place where Paul was supposed to state his assets. That was easy. He had some money saved up in a retirement account and a decent chunk of money invested. Less than Tatyana had. A lot less.

This felt to Paul like one of those hinge moments in your life, that this decision would have enormous repercussions, whichever way he went. Well, he'd known Tatyana was wealthy, by virtue of her being Arkady Galkin's daughter, but he wasn't interested in her wealth. If he signed this contract, and if he and Tatyana were later to divorce, he wouldn't see a penny. That seemed fair to him. Let her see that he was marrying her for *her*, not for her father's money.

"These are pretty tough terms," he said to Galkin, who smiled.

"Only if you get divorced."

"Well, let me ask you something. Would you have signed such an agreement before your first marriage?

Galkin shrugged. "I would never sign such a thing."

Paul laughed.

"But you are in different situation," Galkin went on. "My advice to you: don't get divorced."

38

The toilet was clogged again.

Paul arrived home, kissed Tatyana, and grabbed the plunger.

She was at the kitchen table working on her laptop, editing photos, and vaping. "Thank you," she said. She closed her laptop. Took a puff off her vape pen.

"What's wrong? You're vaping."

"Papa told me his lawyer gave you a prenup to sign today."

"He did."

"And he said you gave it to your lawyer."

"Right, but . . ."

"Oh, Pasha, I hate this so much. A prenup is like—"

"Tatyana—"

"It's like planning for a divorce before you're even married!"

"I made a few minor changes, but I'm going to sign it, *dushen'kaya*." He'd begun to use the occasional Russian term of endearment.

"You are? But what about your lawyer?"

He had called Brad Sarkisian back and told him what he was going to do, and Brad had let him know in no uncertain terms that he was out of his mind. "Do you realize how much you could get out of this deal?" he'd said.

"I know," Paul had said. "But I'm not planning to divorce her."

"That's what everyone says, Paul. Until they do, and they always live to regret it." Brad had about a hundred changes—redlines, he called them—he wanted to make.

Now Paul said to Tatyana, "My lawyer thinks I'm crazy. But I'm going to sign it pretty much as is."

"You *are*?"

"I want you to know I'm not interested in your money, okay? I want you to know that."

She threw her arms around him and hugged him for a long time.

He could feel her tears on his neck. "I was dreading your reaction!" she said. "I was so depressed—I thought this would break us apart."

While they embraced, he said, "No, of course not. But I think it's time to look for another apartment. With room for both of us. Deal?"

39

The first month working for Arkady Galkin's firm wasn't much different from his job at Aquinnah. He worked long hours, which Tatyana didn't love, but now she couldn't complain, since it was her father's firm.

On his way to work one day, his phone rang, and he was surprised to see it was Bernie Kovan calling.

"How goes it, Brightman?"

"Going well, thanks."

"Would you have time for a drink after work?"

"Uh, sure. That would be great. Tomorrow?"

"Sooner the better."

What did Bernie want? Maybe to try to hire him back? "Okay, excellent. O'Malley's?"

"Where else?" Bernie said. "I have a friend I want you to meet."

He was curious as to why Bernie wanted a drink and who the friend was—he knew it couldn't be just a social meetup—but work got so busy that he filed it away and forgot.

Shortly before noon, Mr. Frost knocked on the doorjamb of his office. "Oh, Paul," he said. "Load up on StratforTech. Up to fifty million dollars' worth."

"Why's that?"

"StratforTech," Mr. Frost repeated. "You know StratforTech?"

"Sure." StratforTech was a start-up cybersecurity software company. "But what's the reason, what's the occasion?"

"Just buy it."

"Can you forward me the research?"

"This comes directly from the boss. Fifty million dollars in StratforTech."

"I don't"—Paul's cheeks were starting to get hot—"I need to see the research, know the logic. If I'm in charge of U.S. stocks, that means I'm responsible for the entire portfolio. And I don't buy or sell stocks without having a good reason."

Mr. Frost gave him a poisonous look. "You don't need 'logic.'" He made dainty air quotes with his fingers. "Mr. Galkin is asking you to buy it. That's your 'logic.'"

"I'm sorry," Paul said. "If Mr. Galkin wants to explain, I'm happy to hear it."

Looking furious but contained, Frost left the office, leaving Paul wondering why the senior managing director had made the request in person and not by text or email. And why he was so hot to acquire shares in this little start-up.

Strange.

LATE IN THE AFTERNOON, PAUL spotted Jake Larsen shrugging into his black peacoat, about to leave the office for the day, and decided to ask him out for a drink.

"I don't drink alcohol," Larsen said. "But I'd love to grab a ginger ale with you, sure."

They rode the elevator together in silence. Larsen was lean, tall, vaguely athletic. Basically, like most of the guys in Midtown financial offices. Except he also looked unusually nervous. People got on and off the elevator, and the two of them stared straight ahead, saying nothing.

In the lobby, Paul said, "Well, depending on your time constraints, we could just pop into that pizza place next door. Would that be okay?"

"Perfect."

The pizzeria smelled great, and Paul was hungry, but Larsen said he was meeting a friend for dinner, which sounded like a girlfriend, but Paul didn't probe. So he ordered just a Coke Zero, Larsen a ginger ale. They took their paper cups to the only vacant table. Paul cleared away someone's pizza crusts and then returned to the table.

"So you've been here like a couple weeks already, right?" Larsen said.

"That's right."

"You—enjoying yourself?"

Paul shrugged. "Sure. It's a lot like my last job, only a lot more responsibility."

Larsen asked him about Aquinnah, and Paul filled him in. As he spoke, he remembered he'd agreed to have a drink with Bernie the next day, and he wondered what the agenda really was.

"Can I ask you something?" Paul said.

"Uh, sure."

"Mr. Frost wants me to buy fifty million dollars' worth of a stock that, frankly, looks like a loser."

"He didn't tell you why?"

"Nope."

"Did he ask you to or tell you to?"

"It was an order from the top, Frost said."

"Did you execute the trade?"

"Not yet. So I might already have screwed up."

Larsen laughed, but there was a strain there. He took a sip of ginger ale. "Look, most of your dealings here will be just like the last place you worked. They'll make sense. Then, every once in a while, they'll ask you to do something, and there'll be a reason for it, but they won't tell you."

"Like, what do you mean?"

Larsen looked around, took another sip, and said, "Between you and me, okay?" He made a zipping motion with two fingers across his lips.

"Okay."

"Mr. Frost ordered me to buy up a bunch of real estate in New Mexico today that makes no sense at all. I mean, it's so remote, you couldn't find the location on the map. And when I pressed for an explanation, he said that the government is going to be opening a new drone-testing facility there. Only nobody knows that yet."

"What did you say?"

Larsen shook his head. "I've got a plan, but I can't tell you yet. I'm trying to do the right thing, but it's hard."

"Do they have inside information?"

Larsen shook his head. "I can't tell you any more. I've already told you too much. You won't say a word to anybody about this conversation, will you?"

"Of course not, I told you. I promise—"

"I need to get going." Larsen drained the last of his ginger ale and stood up. "I have to trust you," he said, mostly to himself. Then he walked out the door.

40

O'Malley's Saloon was on West Forty-Eighth Street between Fifth and Sixth, across from Rockefeller Center. Above it was a red neon sign for a psychic. Right outside the bar was a Sabrett hot dog stand, and Paul was beyond starved. He bought a hot dog and wolfed it down, in the process spilling orange onion sauce down the front of his white shirt. He grabbed some napkins from the vendor and did his best to mop up the spill.

Inside it was dark, so dark he could barely find Bernie. Eventually, he located him sitting at one of the dark wooden booths with another guy. Bernie was wearing a red paisley bow tie and a yellow button-down shirt and looked like a J. Press mannequin with a potbelly. Across from him sat an older-looking man with a gray crewcut, large ears, and reddened cheeks and nose, like they'd been scrubbed raw. His crewcut was not at all cool. He wore a nondescript suit and tie.

Bernie introduced him as Mark Addison, a classmate from UPenn. Bernie glanced at the stain on Paul's shirt but didn't say anything. As Addison ordered a bourbon and soda and Paul ordered Scotch rocks, Bernie said, "I'm not staying. Mark wants to have a little chat with you." He stood up. "You ever decide you want to come back home, you just shoot me an email."

"Thank you, Bernie."

While they waited for their drinks, the two men chatted awkwardly about the Knicks. Then Addison told Paul he worked for a division of the FBI.

Paul looked at Bernie, then at Addison, his eyes widening. "What the hell . . . ?" he said.

Their drinks arrived. Addison nodded thanks at the server and took a long sip of his bourbon. Paul swallowed some Scotch. When the server had moved on, Addison said, "You're marrying into the Galkin family."

"And you, what—want to offer your congratulations?"

Addison ignored the comment. "Do you know anything about Russian oligarchs?"

"Is he an oligarch?" he asked, smiling. "There's some dispute about that."

"I'm afraid he is."

"Meaning what, exactly?"

"They're not good guys, Paul."

"I know what an oligarch is," Paul said. "What do you want?"

"You're part of the family. You'll be growing closer to Galkin himself. This can be extremely useful to us."

"In what way?"

"You'll be hearing things. We'd like you to report back on anything that might impact our national security, for one thing."

"So, first of all? Whatever it is you're asking me to do, the answer is no. Second, you think Galkin is going to be telling me about his latest conversation with the Kremlin? Alleged, that is. He'll tell me how his cook bakes the best Russian black bread in the world—which happens to be true, by the way. Beyond that . . ." Paul raised his eyebrows, shook his head.

"You'll learn a lot about the kind of financial deals he makes. And the more he gets to know you, the more he'll trust you."

Paul took a long sip of his Scotch and put the tumbler down firmly on the wooden table. "The answer is no, Mr. Addison," he said. "You're asking me to turn against my bride-to-be and the father she adores, my future father-in-law. That's not who I am."

Addison slid a business card across the table. "Keep this in your wallet in case you change your mind."

Paul pushed the card back. He didn't want to chance Tatyana's looking in his wallet for something and wondering why he had a business card for someone in the FBI. "No, thanks."

"Well, you know how to reach me," Addison said. "Call Bernie."

41

By the time Paul got home, Tatyana was already in her pajamas, which were Paul's boxers, and a little white tank top. She was sitting at the kitchen table opening letters and bills with the little jeweled gold pen-knife she always used. Once, when Paul had admired it and asked if it was from Tiffany, she'd told him it used to belong to Czar Nicholas II.

She barely looked up at him, and her face was set in a scowl. Was she angry at him for being home so late? He'd texted her a few times to let her know where he was, so his late arrival time wouldn't have been a surprise.

"Who did you have drinks with?" she asked.

He hesitated. "Bernie."

"Bernie? Why? Are you thinking about going back to work for him?"

"Well, he did ask," Paul replied, which wasn't really a lie.

"Will you always be home this late?" she said. She was deep into a bottle of Whispering Angel and was also vaping.

He thought about pouring himself a couple of fingers of Scotch but decided he'd had enough alcohol for the evening, and he was thirsty. Instead, he poured himself a glass of club soda and took a few refreshing gulps.

"Only if I have a drink after work, which I don't think I'll make a habit of."

"How do I make plans?"

"I'm sorry, *milaya*. In the future, I'll call you or text you, let you know if I'm going to be late."

"What if I want to have dinner with you?" She took a sip of rosé.

"You know this job, sweetie. I work till seven or eight most nights."

"So no dinners?"

He shrugged. "Or late dinners?"

She jutted out her lower lip. "You're no fun." She took a puff from her e-cigarette.

"I'm sorry. It's a long day. Your dad's not an easy boss to work for."

"You never said that about Bernie."

"Bernie wasn't such a hard taskmaster."

She sighed, her shoulders slumped, and tears came to her eyes.

"What's wrong?" Paul said, stroking her back.

"I'm sorry. I'm in a bad mood."

"Because I'm so late?"

"Because of Papa."

"Did you have a fight with him?"

She nodded.

"About the wedding?" He knew that Polina was out of control when it came to the wedding planning. She'd hired a planner, was obsessed with giving Tatyana an over-the-top celebration. Polina wanted a showcase event, something that would show up their oligarch friends. She wanted to talk over every last detail of the ceremony, from the wall of flowers she wanted to the designer of her own dress—should it be the one who'd done Kate Middleton's dress, Sarah Burton? What about David and Elizabeth Emanuel, who'd designed Lady Diana's wedding gown— but weren't they now divorced? Who had designed Kim Kardashian's dress? Paul had pointed out that Kim and Kanye West were divorced, too.

It soon became clear that Polina and Arkady considered this wedding mostly theirs. And it was to be lavish. There were discussions about whom they should hire to perform—Lady Gaga or the Stones, Elton John or Sting?

The planning seemed to be largely Polina's obsession, though. Arkady didn't seem particularly interested.

"Of course about the wedding. What else?" Tatyana said.

"Let me guess," Paul said, trying for levity. "About the flavor of the cake?"

Tatyana took a long, annoyed breath. "Papa wants me to wear his grandmother's ring, which looks ridiculous," she said. "It's clunky and very antique-looking. Not my style at all. But he says it's a family heirloom."

Paul thought, *I'm staying away from that one.*

"And there's more," she went on after draining her wineglass and immediately refilling it. "He said he wants to invite all three of his exes, and Polina hit the roof."

"But you have to at least invite your mother, don't you?" Her mother lived in Moscow, Paul remembered.

She nodded, gulped some more rosé. "Polina hates my mother. Because my mama calls her 'the Snake.'"

"They don't have to sit together."

"Polina's so extra. But today she was *extra* extra. She said if my mama is there, she won't go. I can't deal with this anymore."

Paul thought for a moment, taking in Tatyana's distress. "Listen, *dushen'kaya*. It's going to be okay. I have an idea that'll put a stop to all this."

She looked up at him, a sliver of hope visible on her face, her eyes beseeching him to relieve her of her misery.

"What if we just went to City Hall?" he said.

"What do you mean?"

"We just walk in and sign some papers and swear an oath, maybe, and we're married. What do you think? No wedding party, no ex-wives. We just walk in there, you and me, and do it."

"Are you serious?" To his surprise, she was smiling.

"You know I don't joke around."

"No party?"

"Maybe we can have a party later, but not a *wedding*. No wedding dress, no argument over whether to have a rabbi or a Russian Orthodox priest, no ten-tiered wedding cake. No Lady Gaga."

"Really? You mean it?"

"I do." He laughed, touched her cheek lovingly. *And what a wonderful thing, to see how happy you look already*, he thought.

"Oh, Pasha! A huge weight just came off my shoulders."

THAT NIGHT, PAUL WAS BRUSHING his teeth and getting ready for bed when his phone pinged, an incoming text. He glanced down and saw that the text was from Eugene Frost.

Car will pick you up tomorrow 7 a.m. in front of your building and take you to Teterboro. Cancel any appointments you have tomorrow.

Paul read it over a few times. Teterboro, he knew, was the private airport half an hour away in New Jersey. That meant, probably, that he was meeting Galkin's plane. But for what? He hesitated a moment, finally typing, *Where will I be flying?*

Chicago, came the reply.

For how long? He typed back.

He waited a minute, two minutes, but no reply came.

He wanted to ask Tatyana what she thought about Mr. Frost's order and what it was all about, but she already had her Audrey Hepburn *Breakfast at Tiffany's* sleep mask on, turquoise satin with an image of golden eyelashes on it, and he didn't want to bother her anymore.

42

Having no idea how long he'd be in Chicago, he decided to pack for a couple of days, just in case he needed to stay over. Where he was going in Chicago and whom he was meeting with and why, he had no idea. Mr. Frost was apparently determined to keep all that mysterious.

At exactly seven in the morning, a black Suburban pulled up to the curb in front of Tatyana's apartment building. There was no one in the car but the driver, someone he didn't recognize. Paul handed him his garment bag and climbed inside with his briefcase. The driver didn't speak a word the entire half-hour drive to New Jersey. The Suburban stopped at the airport gate, where a security guard asked for Paul's ID and the driver's as well. He checked a visitors' list, apparently found Paul's name, and waved them through. The Suburban drove around the tarmac to where a plane was parked, a gleaming cobalt-blue-and-white aircraft that was smaller than a commercial jetliner. This must be Galkin's private jet, or one of them.

The driver came around to Paul's side, opened the door, and held it as Paul got out. Then he opened the luggage compartment and removed Paul's garment bag, handing it to a waiting man, who took it without a word.

A young woman with an iPad waved at Paul and beckoned him over to the plane's movable staircase. "Hi, Mr. Brightman," she said, as if she knew him. She was black-haired, attractive, of Asian descent. "Welcome aboard."

Paul followed her up the stairs and into the cabin.

"You're in seat four," she said.

He found his seat up front, white leather and extravagantly cushioned, off by itself against a large window. As he sat, he looked around for Galkin but didn't see anyone farther back. He was the first passenger. Presumably not the only one. He saw a long white leather sofa. A dining table at the back, draped in a white cloth, and set for one, with twinkling crystal glasses and gleaming silverware.

He unsnapped his briefcase, pulled out his laptop and opened it, and found the Wi-Fi. Checked his emails, looking for anything from Eugene Frost. But there was nothing. The cabin attendant, who introduced herself as Robin, approached and asked if he wanted anything to drink—coffee, tea, or juice. Or water, still or sparkling.

She had a hard job. She had to get to the hangar while it was still dark to supervise the catering, order Nespresso pods, do the dishes, and look unruffled as she did it all. It took someone with the politesse of a diplomat.

"Who else is traveling this morning?" Paul asked, looking out the window at the tarmac.

"Mr. Galkin and a few of his aides," said Robin. "They should be here in the next half hour." She glanced at her watch, gave a confident smile. More than thirty minutes later, a helicopter thundered into view. Steadily louder, it landed on the tarmac a few hundred feet away. The doors popped open as the blades slowed, and Arkady Galkin emerged, followed by Berzin, his security chief, who carried a briefcase. Then two other briefcase-carrying minions, both blandly good-looking young males Paul didn't recognize. Galkin's entourage.

Galkin bounded across the asphalt and up the stairs, bursting into the main cabin with Robin the flight attendant right behind. He was dressed in a suit and a ball cap with a logo on the front that Paul had seen before. It was a foot with wings, no words. The logo of one of the most exclusive golf clubs in the world. Winged Foot, in Westchester County. Very subtle, that hat. You had to recognize the logo to know where the cap was from.

Galkin trundled toward the rear of the plane, not even seeming to notice Paul as he swept by. Paul could smell freshly made coffee and jet fuel. On the public address system, Robin announced that they would be leaving momentarily. Paul turned around, saw Galkin seated at the cloth-draped table in the back, drinking coffee. His laptop was on the table in front of him, next to silver and porcelain dishes.

Shortly after they lifted off, breakfast was served. Robin asked Paul again if he wanted any coffee. This time he asked for a decaf espresso. "How long is our flight?," he asked.

"Two hours and thirty minutes," Robin replied.

The minutes passed. For forty minutes, no one came up to him except Robin, occasionally, so he decided to order breakfast: a plain omelet, Canadian bacon, berries. Breakfast came quickly. Paul had lifted his fork and taken a first bite of his omelet when Robin approached diffidently. "Mr. Galkin would like you to come back."

One of the young minions who was seated across from Galkin got up and yielded his seat to Paul.

"Paul, nice to see you. Sit down," Galkin said. "How you are liking new job?" He was in a sociable, expansive mood. He wore a pinstriped gray suit, lavender shirt, and purple tie. On the seat next to him was his briefcase.

"It's good," Paul said. "A smaller organization than Aquinnah, but that's not a bad thing."

"Your office?"

"Very nice." Paul wanted to ask for details regarding this trip to Chicago, but he let Galkin speak first.

"Do you know how Russians hunt for mushrooms?"

The question caught him off guard. "Not really," he said. He knew, from Tatyana, that Russians loved varieties of mushrooms and enjoyed hunting for them; that was all he knew. But what that had to do with anything . . .

"We love to hunt for mushrooms. It is . . . You are one with the nature. If you have fight with someone, you only must to go mushroom hunting together, and after—you are friends again. But you must be very careful. Some mushrooms are what they call 'false twins': they look just like edible mushrooms, but dangerous. Highly toxic. Even experienced mushroom hunters can be fooled. It could be a death cap, and a sliver will kill you." He wagged an index finger. "So you never go to unfamiliar forest alone to collect mushrooms, you understand? If you do, you may die."

Your point? Paul thought. But all he said was "Okay."

"When you are buying stocks for me, you are looking for hidden treasures. But you listen also to advice from those who know."

"Is this about StratforTech?" Paul had ignored Mr. Frost's directive and done nothing about it yet.

"Yes. Listen to me," Arkady said. "I know it seems like sleepy stock, but appearances can be deceiving. We have excellent source that tells us StratforTech will win very big contract from Homeland Security Committee. Next month. This news will make stock shoot up. You must to buy this soon, and no more games."

"Arkady, you and I both know the risk here. This is called inside information, and . . . it's illegal." Paul had to stop himself from saying "in this country." He continued: "If I were to buy this stock, and it went up when the contract was announced, you could pretty much be guaranteed the SEC would investigate. And I'd go to prison. And I don't want to go to prison. And I'm sure you don't want to, either."

Galkin stared at Paul but did not speak.

Paul went on. "If you have a source on the Homeland Security Committee, he's not allowed to divulge information about future contracts, period. If you make an investment decision based entirely on material nonpublic information, that's illegal."

Galkin smiled but said nothing.

Robin approached Galkin with a tray holding a large silver bowl heaped with berries. "Berries, sir?" she asked.

Galkin nodded.

"Would you like heavy cream on your berries, sir? Or clotted cream? Or crème fraîche?"

Galkin grinned joylessly. "I will skip the cream today, Robin." He patted his gut. "Some might say I have Dunlap's disease."

The walls have ears. Paul's stomach clenched.

"One more thing," Galkin said. "I'm going to Moscow on Monday for some business, and you're coming with me. Brush up on your Russian."

It became clear that Paul was being dismissed. He got up and returned to his seat.

THE PLANE LANDED IN CHICAGO, and as soon as it had taxied to a stop, Galkin and his entourage rose from their seats. Galkin glided toward the exit without glancing Paul's way.

As Paul started to stand, Robin came right over. She handed him a ticket. "Uh, you're returning to New York, Mr. Brightman. On the next Delta flight." He looked at the ticket. It was in coach.

43

Paul arrived home in a sour mood. He'd wasted an entire day because of his future father-in-law. An entire fucking day. He paused with his key in the lock, wanting to respect the boundaries between home life and work life on the one hand but, on the other, wishing very much he could just vent to his girlfriend about his asshole boss.

Tatyana lit up as he came through the door. She ran over and hugged him. "I have some news," she said with a big smile. Then, sensing his mood, her smile fell away. "What's wrong?"

He shook his head, scowling. "You don't want to know."

"I do, Pasha. Tell me."

He took a breath. "Okay—truthfully? My day sucked."

"Oh, no. Why? What happened?"

"Well . . . what happened is that your father flew me all the way out to Chicago and back just so he could talk to me in private for five minutes. I feel like he was making a point. Humiliating me, putting me in my place."

"What happened, specifically?"

"He wanted me to buy a stock, but before executing it, I did some research and—"

"He told you to make a buy, and you disregarded his instruction?"

"'Disregarded'? I was doing my *job*, Tatyana. He could have saved me the entire day by just calling me. He could have taken me aside at dinner on Sunday night . . ."

"Well, if you're doing your *job* and your boss tells you to get on a flight out of Teterboro, then you do it, right?"

Paul paused for a few seconds, looked at her. "He told you about this already, didn't he?"

Tatyana flushed. "He might have mentioned . . ."

"He shouldn't be telling you about what goes on at work."

"I mean . . . why not? We're family—why does that bother you?"

"Because he's . . . lobbying you. He's using you to get to me."

"No, he's not. He told me because he was . . . upset."

Paul could see an ugly quarrel lurking nearby. They'd never really had a bad fight, and he didn't want to start one. So he just shook his head, putting up mental guardrails to ward off an argument.

"Pasha," she said more quietly now, "Papa says you make fun of him. Dunlop's disease, something like that?"

So much for the guardrails. "It was a stupid joke, and I said it in the break room. And do you know *how* he knows? He must have the place bugged."

"Or maybe someone told him or Zhenya."

"Zhenya?"

"Eugene Frost. You can't make fun of my father. I mean, *I* can, and I do, but *you* can't. You really can't. You're not just his employee, you're his future son-in-law."

"True," Paul conceded. "But I can be honest with you, can't I? Flying me out to Chicago and back for a five-minute conversation is the act of a . . . a tyrant. A despot. A Mussolini."

"My father is a warrior when he needs to be. He's a self-made man. He's had to be tough. But he'd do anything for those he loves."

"Self-made . . . I guess so."

Tatyana pulled up short. "What does *that* mean?"

Paul saw her pupils dilate, anger color her cheeks. He immediately regretted saying it. "Never mind," he said. "Sorry I said anything."

"When he was your age, he was already a billionaire." She stopped. "I feel like you're trying to estrange me from my own father because your father is such a disappointment to you. I don't mean to lay you out on the couch, Pasha, but that's how I feel. That's what it seems like. Don't make me choose between defending you and defending Papa. Don't pit me against my father."

Paul had seen his parents fight so many times, recognized the rhythm, the jousts, the moves and countermoves, the way an argument could quickly spiral out of control. He didn't want to be that way with Tatyana—they weren't even married yet.

So he shrugged. "Okay, *dushen'kaya*. Maybe so. I'll try to be more careful. And just to be clear, I'm grateful for your father—today notwithstanding!" He forced a smile. "Oh, and did I mention? He wants me to go to Moscow with him. On Monday."

"So soon!" She smiled. "He really must think you're hot shit."

"Who knows what he thinks."

"Will you give me a kiss?" Tatyana said.

Paul hesitated a few seconds. "Of course," he said, and he leaned over and kissed her.

"I don't want to fight with you," she said.

"Neither do I."

"Would you like a glass of wine? I told you I have some good news."

"Sure," he said.

By the time she returned with two glasses—something red for him, a rosé for herself—and handed his to him, he was already beginning to calm down. "An appointment at City Hall suddenly opened up, and I grabbed it."

He was caught off guard. "When?"

"Tomorrow."

"*Tomorrow?* Wow, that's . . ." *Soon!* he almost said. *Sudden!*

"Fate," she said. "Right?"

They agreed not to tell anyone what they were doing, particularly not Arkady or Polina. They didn't want objections or interference. They'd tell them later, after it was done. They needed a witness, so of course he called Rick.

PAUL WASN'T SURE EXACTLY WHAT had happened on Galkin's private plane, how things were left. Had he succeeded in convincing Galkin that they shouldn't buy shares of StratforTech? Did Galkin now get the point that he was flirting with insider trading, which was illegal, and that he'd probably get caught? Had he done this before? If so, how was the firm still in business?

So when he got into work the next day and looked at the morning report, which told the senior people what had happened to the fund overnight, he was shocked to see that the firm was now the owner of five hundred thousand shares of StratforTech. Because he sure as hell hadn't bought them.

The first thing he did was to call his broker at Goldman Sachs, Carla Wachtell.

"So, five hundred thousand shares of StratforTech? What the hell?"

A long pause. Carla said, "What's the problem, Paul?"

"Who authorized that purchase?"

Carla didn't hesitate. "Gene Frost. Something wrong?"

"Did he buy call options on StratforTech, too?"

"Uh, ten million bucks' worth, yeah."

Don't fight it, Paul told himself. *It's not worth it.* There would be legal consequences, but as long as his name wasn't attached to the purchase, he would probably be okay.

Probably.

HE AND TATYANA WOKE UP early the next day and made love. They talked about the ceremony at one p.m. and how they'd get there, what they'd wear.

Paul got to work early and spent a few minutes looking at real estate websites, in search of a bigger apartment. Tatyana was willing to consider Brooklyn but preferred Manhattan and definitely didn't want to live in New Jersey. She wanted to be near other artists.

He was astonished at the price of real estate in the city. Even for someone like him, who worked on Wall Street, nice apartments were prohibitively costly. Even with his salary at Galkin's firm doubled.

It was funny: left unspoken between him and Tatyana was the plain fact that her father had offered to buy them a place, whatever its cost. But Tatyana didn't want a place that advertised her wealth, and Paul wanted a place that he could afford on his own. He wanted them to live within their means—not her father's means.

He called Tatyana. "I found a place I think you'll like," he said. "But we have to look at it quickly."

"Not today!" she said.

"No, not today. Of course not. But soon."

PAUL SNUCK OUT OF THE office—"Taking a long lunch," he said breezily to Margo Whitworth—wearing his best blue Armani suit, a white shirt, and a patterned gold Armani tie that sort of sparkled in the light. He'd stopped at a florist to pick up the bouquet of white peonies he'd ordered, Tatyana's favorite, adorned with a spray of white lily of the valley. Tatyana wore a white halter-neck jumpsuit with a fitted waist and wide, straight legs, along with stiletto heels and diamond earrings. He'd never seen her so dressed up.

He was nervous, of course, but more than that, he felt like he was observing the world from outside his body. He was aware of everything: the funky smell of the taxi, the sunlight bouncing off the glass of the skyscrapers they passed, Tatyana's perfume, the brass letters on the side of the building that announced OFFICE OF THE CITY CLERK, CITY OF NEW YORK.

They waited a little less than half an hour, watching the other brides and grooms, grooms and grooms, and brides and brides. There were Asian and Blacks and Latinos. Some were cuddling, some bickering. You could tell by looking who were the intended and who were the guests. There was a gift shop that sold emergency bow ties. The bathrooms were big and clean and had lots of mirrors. Paul overheard someone saying there were more marriages performed here than in Vegas. Rick arrived and gave Paul a hug, Tatyana a kiss.

When their names were called, they clasped hands and entered the wedding chapel, which was really just a room with lavender walls and a green vinyl bench and fluorescent lighting. Their officiant was a kindly middle-aged judge with a white beard who reminded Paul vaguely of Santa Claus. He wondered if the guy did freelance gigs during the holiday season. They all signed the marriage certificate. Rick congratulated them.

Tatyana glanced at Paul with mock terror, and he did the same, then they kissed, and he put his arm around her waist. He gave Rick a scared look, too, and then smiled to make clear he was kidding. "Thanks for coming," Paul said. He felt, on some deep level he didn't understand, that he was saying goodbye to his friend, that he was leaving Rick behind and entering a new world.

AS THEY WERE COMING OUT of the Office of the City Clerk, he heard a familiar voice speaking loudly in Russian: Arkady and Polina came rushing up to them. Galkin held a huge bouquet of pastel peonies and ranunculus in both his hands. How the two knew they were getting married at City Hall mystified Paul. But Arkady seemed to have his own sources of information. Polina kissed Tatyana on both cheeks, while Arkady handed the flowers to his daughter.

Polina said to Tatyana, eyeing her attire, "Wonderful! I'd never be able to pull off that outfit."

"Why, thank you, *sestrichka*," Tatyana replied. She gave Paul a secret smile.

Polina gave Paul a surprisingly intimate hug, both her arms around his waist, pulling him in tight for a long time. Then she put both hands on his shoulders. "I'm so happy for you," she said. "Tatyana was lucky to catch you."

Then Arkady moved in, offered Paul both hands and drew him in for a hug.

"Paul," he said, "just promise you take care of my little girl."

"You can count on it," Paul said.

Arkady smiled and spoke quietly, out of Tatyana's earshot. "If you ever leave her or cheat on her, I will have you killed. The prenup will be least of your concerns." Then he laughed, and then Paul pretended to laugh, but somehow he didn't find it very funny.

44

That night they went for dinner at their favorite unfancy French bistro, just the two of them. The next day, when Paul had returned from work, they went to look at the apartment he had picked out online. It was a nice, roomy "classic six" in a prewar Park Avenue building.

The apartment was in terrible shape. Its owner had been an elderly widow who'd recently died and seemingly had never done any renovations to it ever. But it had great views, beautiful hardwood floors, and fine details like window seats, the original moldings, built-in bookcases, high beamed ceilings, thick walls, and wide hallways. The kitchen was big but equipped with 1950s-era appliances. It was badly in need of a refresh. But the apartment was located in a doorman building with a handsome limestone façade on a quiet, tree-lined street.

While the Realtor was still there, Paul and Tatyana walked across the apartment to the kitchen and huddled.

"Oh, my God, Paul, it's got such potential, don't you think?"

"We're going to have to sink a lot into a serious renovation," he said. He was pleased by her response, even so. He'd wondered what she would think, given the double-wide town house where she'd grown up.

"Papa can help us with this, you know," she said.

"I'm sure he can. But I want us to do this on our own." Meaning, of course, on *his* own. "I want to earn it."

She gave a sweet smile. Her eyes shone. "I love that. But it's there for the taking."

He shook his head, smiled. "Do you think it's more space than we need?"

They put in an offer that night.

THE NEXT MORNING, WHEN PAUL went to the break room for coffee, he encountered Chad Forrester in quiet conversation with a short guy with spiky black hair. His name, Paul remembered, was Ethan Carswell.

Chad explained, "We're talking about Larsen."

"What about him?" Paul said. Jake Larsen, he'd noticed, hadn't been in the morning meeting. "He get fired?"

Both men immediately looked at each other. Finally, Chad said, "He OD'd."

"You're kidding!" Paul said, incredulous. "Overdosed? On—on what?"

"Speedball. Cocaine and heroin and fentanyl."

"But . . . I mean, I haven't been here long, but he sure didn't seem the type."

Chad and Carswell exchanged a glance.

"What?" Paul asked. "Did I read him wrong? He seemed afraid of his own shadow. Hard to imagine him having such a druggie alter ego."

"You smoke?" Chad said to Paul.

Paul at first shook his head, then, getting it, said, "I'll join you."

OUTSIDE THE BUILDING, ON FIFTH Avenue, a knot of people stood around on the sidewalk smoking. The smoke irritated Paul's eyes.

After exhaling a lungful of smoke, Chad said, "Thing is, Larsen was a Mormon."

Paul nodded slowly. "And Mormons . . ."

"Don't do drugs."

Paul pictured Larsen, a tall, lean guy with floppy brown hair parted in the middle. Their VC guy. He dressed conservatively, in blue blazers over button-down shirts. Very uptight and a bit stiff. Not the personality type you'd expect to be doing speedballs. He remembered Larsen ordering ginger ale at the pizzeria.

"Right," Chad went on. "But I got the sense that he was unhappy here."

"Based on what?"

"On what he'd say to me in the break room or over email or whatever."

"It's a tough gig, working here."

"Sure, but it's tough anywhere in our business."

"No doubt. So what did he say to you?"

Chad took a long draw, blew out a large cloud of smoke. Then he said, "He was complaining about some of the deals he was asked to make . . ." His voice drifted off.

"What—like insider trading or whatever?"

"Something like that," Chad said vaguely.

"You think—you really think—they did it? Like some . . . Russian or something?"

Chad blew out again, a whole lungful. He shook his head. "Hell do I know? Just . . . just don't do what Larsen did. Don't put your unhappiness in writing. Or say it aloud in the office. Again. Understand?"

Paul nodded.

"You know your email is read, right?"

"I guess they have the right to do that, legally."

"They do," Chad agreed. "I'm telling you, there's no such thing as privacy here."

"Even in the bathroom?"

He shrugged. "Unknown."

"Wow."

"You know the rule around here."

"Keep your mouth shut?" Paul said.

"You know it. Larsen broke the rules. Sounds like he talked to outsiders."

Paul felt dizzy. His mouth went dry. "How would anyone know that?"

"I don't know. The phones, maybe? Or maybe someone saw him meeting with someone from the U.S. Attorney's Office. Anyway, he was terrified." Chad's voice grew quiet, hard to hear over the traffic.

What was Chad saying—that Larsen had been *killed*? That his overdose was staged? And by whom—by someone in Galkin's orbit, like the security director, Berzin? That seemed a preposterous allegation. Paul had seen a Tom Cruise movie where his character goes to work for a law firm that seems too good to be true, only to discover that anyone who steps out of line turns up dead. Was that sort of thing happening here—disenchanted employees getting murdered? Instead of just being fired?

Chad pursed his lips in a crooked smile. "Like they say, no one is indispensable."

The sidewalk tilted under Paul's feet. It took him a moment to steady himself. Then he cleared his throat and said, "I should get back inside."

When he returned to his office, he found Mr. Frost sitting behind his desk.

PART SEVEN

TRAIL ANGELS

Present Day

45

Maybe the helicopter overhead had nothing to do with him.

But what if it did? What if Berzin had hired people to search the vast wilderness from above, for a lone man on the run? He'd probably use the pretext that they were searching for a lost hiker.

The helicopter's din, the whapping, roaring noise, remained constant. The helicopter was directly above.

He had to avoid any open areas, where the searchers would definitely spot him. If he remained in the densely wooded parts of the forest, they wouldn't see him. He'd be the proverbial needle in the haystack.

And what if the searchers in the helicopter were using an infrared technology that would allow them to look for heat given off by a living creature? He'd read enough newspaper articles about searches using infrared. With such technology, you could even see someone, from a helicopter above, hiding inside a house.

So he had to hide. Conceal, obscure his heat signature. But how the hell to do that? Somehow he had to get into a shelter of sorts where his body heat wouldn't be detectable. He didn't have time to build one. A cave would be ideal. Or a cleft between boulders like the one he'd recently taken shelter in, but that was probably miles behind him.

He needed to hide *now*.

Then he remembered his space blanket. The emergency Mylar covering, which resembled a giant sheet of very thin aluminum foil. Maybe it would block the infrared signature. He'd read somewhere about a search-and-rescue in the forests of New Hampshire that failed because the lost hiker was covered in a space blanket.

Paul got the Mylar blanket out of the go-bag, where it was crumpled into a loose ball. Impossible to fold. He quickly collected a pile of leaves and twigs and downed branches. He spotted, ten or so feet away, two scrub pines that had grown close together, with branches low to the ground. He tossed the Mylar blanket on top of the lower branches so it acted like a tarp, a canopy. Foil side down, so it wouldn't flash and glint in the sun and attract attention. On top of the blanket, he scattered the twigs and leaves as camouflage. Then he dove under the blanket, lying flat on the damp ground. Between his body and the Mylar was around a foot of air. He figured this would further block his heat signature, prevent heat transfer, and make him less visible from above. Of course, this was all speculation, a theory. He didn't know if it would work in practice. If he'd even remembered it correctly.

From the whumping of the helicopter, he determined that the aircraft was still overhead, hovering.

Had he been detected?

He breathed in and out slowly, to steady his nerves. His heartbeat pounding in his ears.

He waited . . .

Closed his eyes like a kid playing hide-and-seek who imagined that closing your eyes meant the seeker couldn't see you, that you, magically, could never be found.

Gradually, the helicopter racket diminished, and soon it was apparent the chopper had moved on.

But he stayed in position, under the Mylar-and-leaves canopy, and waited. And pondered.

A FEW MONTHS AFTER HE became Grant Anderson, he saw a *New York Times* piece online about the disappearance of the young American husband of an oligarch's daughter. There was speculation that the husband had been killed, but so far, investigations had turned up nothing. After a flurry of interest in the lurid story—did a Russian oligarch have his American son-in-law killed?—there was a gradual fading of interest. As far as he knew, there was never any follow-up.

In the meantime, he became Grant Anderson. A less-than-prosperous but talented boatbuilder, a good and helpful neighbor who volunteered at the town's one church, modest and reclusive but well liked. A good citizen of Derryfield.

In his first year of being Grant, he was beset by worries. He would see someone and think he recognized them; he was constantly afraid the Russians would track him down. But he was disciplined. He lived his Grant life, making friends, working for Mr. Casey and then, after

Mr. Casey's death, continuing his business. Casey, who had no children, had left the business to him.

He never called anyone from his Paul Brightman life. He'd left behind his old friends, even Rick. And now, this made-up Grant Anderson was going to disappear, too, shrink into nothingness.

Years before, while Grant, he had concocted a plan in case he needed to go on the run again. There was a powerful, well-connected senior statesman he knew, Ambassador John R. Gillette. The father of J.R. Gillette, a Reed College classmate of his and Rick's. The kid was troubled, but the father had always liked Paul. Paul felt Gillette would help him, if it ever came to it.

THE HELICOPTER APPEARED TO BE gone. Paul removed the Mylar blanket from under the tree branches, shook off the leaves, and jammed the blanket back into the go-bag.

He resumed walking through the dense woods until he came to a broad mountain stream. The water was flowing quickly, which meant it was safe to drink. He filled his water bottle and took a drink, then filled the bottle up again. Now he had to cross the stream. He looked for rocks to step onto to avoid the water, but there were few. He was forced to wade through the stream, which got his leather boots wet and cold.

On the other side, the terrain went steeply uphill. He consulted his map, wondered if he'd arrived at the southern base of South Hancock Mountain, and wasn't sure. If he'd somehow gone north, to North and South Hancock Mountains, he saw that he was more than halfway to Lincoln. But there were no signs. Maybe there were signs on established trails, but he didn't dare use them.

He skirted the peak of the mountain, avoiding the high land where he might be spotted. Then he found himself walking steeply downhill. He nearly slipped a few times on the loose soil and rocky debris.

A few hours later, he'd reached a valley between the two mountains. The area here was thick with pine trees and hobblebush. Soon, he came to another mountain stream. This one was rocky and surrounded by granite boulders. The rocks and boulders were moss-covered and, he found, slippery as ice. He moved carefully across the stream, hopping from rock to rock. When he had nearly reached the other side, he stepped onto a rock jutting out of the water, and the rock moved. He slipped and fell into the icy-cold water, twisting his left ankle painfully and crying out. Now, his pants soaked with water, he was at risk for hypothermia. He limped ahead slowly for a minute, wincing with the pain.

He would never make it to Lincoln this way.

46

Paul sat on a boulder, resting his ankle, and looked at his map. If he was right and he was somewhere near the Hancock Mountains, the town of Lincoln was a dozen miles or more away. And hobbling twelve miles with this injured ankle was simply out of the question. Yesterday, he had planned to hike through the forest and make his way to Lincoln, avoiding well-trafficked roads where he might be caught. Now he knew he had to get to a trafficked road as soon as possible, then hitchhike to Lincoln. It was a risk, but he had no choice. The nearest road was directly south: the NH 112, the Kancamagus Highway, or "the Kanc," as locals called it. It was a heavily traveled two-lane road. At this time of year, it would be busy with leaf peepers.

The Kanc, he knew, was a dangerous area for his purposes: Berzin would probably expect him to take it. But it was the only viable choice. He could stagger on for another eight to twelve hours toward the Kanc, but twelve miles west to Lincoln would take him several days in his condition, and he wasn't sure he'd make it. He was in great pain, needed some kind of painkiller—Tylenol or Advil. But he didn't have any in his bag. Coulda, shoulda, woulda. He also needed something like a bandana to tie around his ankle, to stabilize it. But he didn't have that, either.

So he'd have to hobble along and endure the pain.

Suddenly, he heard faint voices again. He scrambled to his feet, nearly fell when his ankle gave way, and spotted a dense copse and made for it. In a minute, he was concealed behind a thicket of trees. The voices grew steadily louder. A couple of people speaking in English. He stood there, his ankle throbbing, and waited.

If it was Berzin and his minion, what would he do?

Now two men came into the clearing, maybe a hundred feet away. Both were in their sixties, with long gray beards, long gray hair, and deeply creased faces, the faces of people who'd spent a lot of time outdoors. They wore raggedy jeans and backpacks and were carrying buckets. The two men stood at the bank of the river and filled their buckets. Were they hikers? Were they survivalists? Paul had no idea.

He wanted to ask them for help, for Tylenol and a bandana or something else to wrap his ankle with, but just as he was about to emerge from the woods and ask them, he stopped himself at the last second. He'd be taking a big risk, he realized. What if Berzin came upon these men and asked if they'd seen someone matching his description? He couldn't take that chance. So he remained there, frozen in place, until the men were gone.

Then he pulled out his map, unfolded it carefully so it wouldn't make a rustling sound, and tried to orient himself, though he wasn't sure he was heading south; the sky was too cloudy to make out the sun. Still, he had to move, and he headed in the direction that he thought was south, to the Kanc.

Walking was now painful. His limp slowed him down considerably. He stopped and retied the laces of his left boot very tight, turning the boot itself into a splint of sorts. Taking out one of his burner phones, he switched it on. There was only one bar of signal strength, but it might be enough. He called Sarah on her burner phone, let it ring a long time.

No answer.

Where the hell was she? Had the Russians gotten to her? He switched off the phone, his chest tight.

And he kept going, at a glacial pace. An hour or so later, he came upon a crumbling brick foundation.

He froze. He'd seen that brick ruin before. A realization set in with a kind of cold terror.

He had gone in a large circle. He'd arrived at the exact same ghost town he'd seen yesterday.

He could almost hear his father berating him: *You're doing it wrong.*

47

The rain had stopped, and the sun hung low in the sky, and he knew that way was west. Orienting himself, he proceeded south, mostly downhill. He was weak with hunger and parched and in pain, and when he heard distant voices, he nearly panicked. A woman's whoop. The map told him he was near the Sawyer River Trail; maybe that was where the voices were coming from. He limped closer and saw, through the trees, a wide dirt trail with cyclists whizzing by and two or three women walking in the same direction.

Of course, he didn't want to walk or, rather, shuffle along such a well-used trail. Far too visible. But after consulting his map, he saw that the trail ran south to the Kanc. If he hand-railed the trail—went parallel to it, but at a distance so that he wouldn't be seen—it would lead him all the way to the 112.

Though, at the pace he was going, that would take hours.

He had reached a low, flat valley, where the going was much easier. He shuffled through the forest. It felt like his left ankle was swelling, his injury there exacerbated by the walking. He was only a few miles from the road, though he wasn't sure exactly how many. He was cold, his pants and boots still wet from his splash in the stream. Whenever he took a break, he found himself shivering. When it became too dark to navigate through the dense woods, he briefly considered assembling a makeshift tent and resting overnight. But he felt urgency: he needed to get out of the woods and to Lincoln, no matter what time it was.

It wasn't safe to continue through the woods in the dark, so he took another risk and moved over to the trail. He was cold, still shivering, and he knew that the cold and the stress and the exhaustion were compromising his decision-making process. He was driven by instinct: the need to get out of the woods and get to safety, if that was even possible anymore, the need for a hot shower, the need for sleep.

So he kept going along the now-deserted trail. The moon was covered by a scrim of clouds. He heard the distant hoot of an owl, the howl of a coyote somewhere. And the rustling of leaves. Was it deer? Foraging squirrels? Or just the wind? The shadows seemed to shift and move, as if alive with creatures. Tree branches reached out from the shadows like gnarled fingers.

A little after one in the morning, he came to a sign that read DANGER-OUS CROSSING. He heard water running. He'd come to the Sawyer River, and he soon saw that it was running deep and fast. It must have been swollen from all the rain over the past few days.

Crossing the river, which had to be done, was indeed dangerous, especially in the dim moonlight. Fast-moving water could make him lose his footing, carry him away. But he had no choice: on the other side was the 112, the Kanc. That way was safety. He had to ford this river.

He returned to the woods and soon found a long, sturdy stick from a downed branch. It was tall enough to use as a walking stick, a trekking pole. He stood on the bank, heard the rush of water, and saw how power-ful the river was. He estimated that it was around seventy feet wide at this point. You were supposed to pick the widest point to cross a river: the narrow points are usually faster and deeper. Ordinarily, he'd have tried to rock hop, jump from rock to rock, but with his injured ankle, that would be nearly impossible. So he found a spot that seemed shallowest, then he walked through the water, using his makeshift pole as a third point of contact, a tripod. The fast current grabbed the pole, nearly yanked it out of his hands. He dragged it along the river bottom, facing upstream, sliding his feet. The river was deeper here than he'd expected. The frigid water came up nearly to his hips. He inhaled sharply at the shock. He moved one foot, then the other, then he moved the pole, and in this fashion, he arrived, a few freezing minutes later, at the opposite bank.

He was shivering violently. He heard the occasional vehicle pass by on the Kancamagus Highway—surprising, given the hour. Up above him, he glimpsed the guardrail bordering the road, which was elevated above the river by a couple hundred feet of steep, muddy embankment. His left ankle throbbed.

How the hell was he going to get up to the road with a twisted ankle? But he didn't have time to hesitate; he was bitterly cold and didn't think he could last. So he gritted his teeth and powered ahead, hobbling along as best he could. When the ground started getting steep, he found low shrubs and other vegetation to grab on to, slipping in the mud whenever he didn't have a firmly rooted plant to pull on, the sludge coating his pant legs. He kept on, exhausted, and finally—*finally!*—he was able to grab on to the steel guardrail and haul himself up onto the narrow shoulder of the 112.

Shivering, cold as hell, and entirely covered in mud, he stuck out his thumb.

He heard remote traffic sounds, and a few seconds later, a pair of headlights pulled into view . . . and then passed right by. A minute or so later, another pair of headlights appeared and just as quickly zipped past.

Understandable, he thought: *he* probably wouldn't pick up anyone looking like him, like an escaped killer or a crazy man. He looked like he was running from something.

This thought might ordinarily have made him laugh, if he hadn't been so miserably cold and tired.

He kept his thumb out. A truck zoomed by, a car, and then another car, and another. This went on for some twenty minutes. Meanwhile, his shaking grew more violent. But no one would stop for him, and it was easily twenty miles to Lincoln.

He had heard about people in the North Country called "trail angels," who would stop along the highway to pick up those in need of help. Some of these angels drove the trail during heavy hiking season just to pick up pedestrians and take them to the next point, offer first aid and nourishment. They weren't in it for the money: they didn't expect compensation.

But, apparently, no trail angel was driving the Kanc at two o'clock that morning.

He decided to give up and walk as far as the next overlook, which, on his sodden map, looked to be two or three miles away. But in order to do that, he'd have to get down from the embankment; it was too steep there to try walking alongside the road. And to get down from the embankment, with his injured ankle, would be painful and would no doubt involve a lot of sliding, which he wasn't looking forward to.

Then, suddenly, a truck approached, pulled over to the side of the road, and put on its flashers. Paul hobbled over to the passenger-side door of the GMC pickup as it popped open. Warily, he looked inside the cabin.

The driver was a plump, short, ruddy-cheeked woman in a plaid flannel shirt. The only other occupant of the vehicle was a big white dog in the backseat. The truck's interior was wonderfully warm and smelled of dog.

"Well, are you going to get in or not?" the woman said.

PART EIGHT

PHANTOM

Five Years Earlier

48

Paul's stomach went tight. Now what the hell did Permafrost want? He couldn't shake the paranoid suspicion that Mr. Frost always knew what he was up to.

"Why don't we trade places?" Frost said, getting up and reseating himself in Paul's visitor chair.

"How can I help you?" Paul said pleasantly.

"Are you a smoker?"

What had Frost seen or heard? "No, but every once in a while I need to get out of the office. Get some fresh air."

"In a smoking area?"

Paul shrugged. "How can I help you?" he said again.

Frost had an unnerving way of looking directly into your eyes without blinking, lizard-like, and without looking away, as if he were interrogating you under klieg lights. "The U.S. Navy is planning to build ten new destroyers," he said. "Five defense firms are bidding. The usual suspects. We'd like you to buy call options on BAE Systems and buy put options on the others."

So, a gamble, Paul thought. "How big an investment?"

"Fifty million dollars, all in."

"BAE Systems is a British company," Paul said. "Doesn't seem likely that a British firm would beat an American firm on a U.S. Navy contract."

Frost smiled, one of his rare smiles. "Nevertheless, our prediction is that BAE will prevail, and we're comfortable with the risk."

"What's the logic?"

Frost paused, his smile fading. "The logic is because Mr. Galkin says so." He shrugged and got up. "Oh, and congratulations on your wedding."

After Mr. Frost left, Paul checked his email and then all the usual databases. The coverage all said that the likely winner of the contract would be a General Dynamics subsidiary, Bath Iron Works. The other bidders included Huntington Ingalls, Fincantieri, and Austal USA. If Galkin and Mr. Frost were spinning the roulette wheel, they were probably going to lose.

Unless they knew something they shouldn't.

49

"Where were you?" Tatyana said when he entered the apartment. "I called and called." Her hair was in a long braid. Pushkin was in her lap as she sat on the couch. She was wearing her Athleta yoga pants, and her face was free of makeup. She looked weary.

"I left my phone on my desk at work. Must have spaced out."

"But I called your secretary, and she said you were gone for the day."

"I was working out in the company gym," he said. "Really needed it. Margo left before I got back." He held her eyes. "You're upset. Something's on your mind. Something else."

"I talked to the gallery. I sold only three pictures."

"I thought you said you sold out."

"I did. Do you want to guess who bought all the others?"

"Well, he loves you, that's obvious." *And he owns the gallery*, Paul thought. *There's that, too.* "And it's your first show, don't forget. It takes a while to build word of mouth. And what if you get a review?"

"*Artforum* never reviewed the show."

"They will. Or the next one."

He poured them drinks, realizing that he had fallen into the bad habit of drinking hard liquor every night when he got home. Alcohol relaxed him, but it was beginning to depress him, too. It made him moody, pensive. Tonight, sipping his Four Roses, he found himself thinking about his new bride. The thing that had attracted him to her, at first, was her impetuousness, her spontaneity. He wasn't a spontaneous person, more of a planner, a plodder, and she was an antidote to that. Then, as he got to know her better, he loved the way she rejected her father's gaudy displays of wealth, the way she wanted to live a normal life. She had dismissed that explanation, saying that it wasn't a rejection of her father, but simply a desire to live differently, to establish her own identity.

Whatever the truth—and maybe he'd never know—it was unclear to him where the lines were, what about her upbringing she rejected and what she'd never reject. Did she know what her father was up to? Would she always defend him? Was there a bridge too far?

"Looking forward to Moscow?" she asked as they were undressing for bed.

"Don't know. It'll be interesting. Since I've never been to Russia before."

"I've decided I'm going with you. I want to visit Mama."

"Oh?" A splinter of ice formed in his stomach. He didn't think she'd be accompanying him. "Great. Look forward to meeting her."

When he was sufficiently liquored up, he said to her, "A friend of mine—a colleague at work—died of an overdose."

"Overdose of what?"

"Heroin and cocaine and fentanyl."

"I'm sorry to hear it. That's too bad." She said it offhandedly. "Was he a druggie?"

"He told me he didn't drink. He was a really straitlaced guy. He . . ." His voice trailed off. He couldn't bring himself to repeat aloud to Tatyana what Chad Forrester had speculated.

"Maybe he killed himself," she said. "Too much pressure at work, you know? Maybe he couldn't take it."

"Uh-huh." Paul stared at the ceiling while Tatyana spoke.

"Some people, you can never really know them."

HE AWOKE AT SIX, EYES red and gritty, feeling anxious and depressed, his head aching. Drinking a third cup of coffee was a bad idea; it would only make him more jittery. As he ate a bowl of Rice Chex, he read the *Wall Street Journal* on his phone, and there a headline snagged his eye.

"BAE Systems Wins Billion-Dollar Contract for 10 Destroyers."

50

They had missed several Sunday night dinners in a row, either because Polina was traveling or Arkady was gone on business.

But the next one was scheduled for that Sunday—the night before Paul's flight to Moscow. Normally, he enjoyed these meals. Arkady was relaxed, as he was rarely at the office. There was always vodka, wine, and cognac. Paul loved the food, of course. The family often bickered—it wasn't a Norman Rockwell illustration—but they also laughed a lot. Tatyana seemed to be at ease. Paul liked how happy she seemed when she was with her family.

These dinners were like sitting beside a roaring fire. They warmed him. Coming from the kind of deprived, anxious, cold and dark and gloomy childhood he'd had, he felt with Tatyana's family as if he had entered a warm house after hours in the cold snow and been served a cup of hot cocoa. It melted him inside.

ARKADY WAS WEARING HIS BLUE-AND-WHITE-CHECKED L.L.Bean fleece and jeans. Polina wore a deep-V-neck pink sweater and dark, tight jeans that looked uncomfortable but showed off her butt. Tatyana wore faded jeans and a white button-down.

Arkady greeted them as they entered. The home Arkady, as opposed to the office Arkady, was ebullient and twinkling. "I haven't seen you two together since your wedding. *Pozdravlyayu*! Congratulations!" He hugged first his daughter and then Paul. Speaking with a broad smile, he said, "You two—rob me of putting on greatest wedding in world. But you will not rob me of giving you wedding present." His tone communicated no resentment. He seemed jovial.

Paul noticed Arkady's bald head, smooth and pink like a baby's skin; it looked vulnerable, like a baby's.

"Tatyana tells me you have bought an apartment, finally."

"Yeah, we think this is the one," Paul said. "It'll require a lot of renovation, but it's awfully nice."

"I looked at it online, and all I can say, thanks God my daughter will be moving out of shithole." Galkin lowered his voice, standing close, a hand on each of their shoulders. "Will you please allow me to pay for it?"

"No, Papa," said Tatyana.

Paul shook his head. "Very generous of you, Arkady, but the deal is done. We've had the closing."

"We're about to start renovations," Tatyana said. "Paul has a friend who's a contractor . . ."

"Contractor! This is big responsibility. Is a world I know well." Arkady looked first at Paul, then at Tatyana. "As my present to you, let me handle renovations on apartment. I have people who do excellent work. You're both too busy to supervise renovations. It will make you argue. It is barrier to good marriage. We will talk about your taste, your vision, and I will handle it all. My gift to you both."

Tatyana looked at Paul, who looked back. They both mumbled, hesitated. Tatyana, who would be in charge of the renovations, said, "That would be wonderful, Pápachka. Thank you."

"Yes? And you, Paul? Will you accept my gift?"

"It's too generous, Arkady—but if you insist . . ." Paul said. "Very kind of you."

Arkady turned to face the table, where most of the family was already seated, drinking. "A toast to newlyweds!" he declared.

51

Arkady Galkin reclined in his leather airplane seat. He was wearing a burgundy polka dot dressing gown and embroidered smoking slippers, and he was smoking a cigar, which was stinking up the whole plane. But it was his plane.

It was a long flight to Moscow. Nine hours from Teterboro. The Gulfstream G650 would fly nonstop to Vnukovo Airport.

Tatyana had brought her best camera, a Leica M11. Paul had never seen her so excited, not even before her gallery opening. Now she was in the front of the plane watching a movie, *The Notebook*, which she'd seen dozens of times.

Galkin had invited Paul to the back of the plane to join him for dinner. Over steak and a great red wine (a 1989 Pétrus Pomerol), Galkin talked, and Paul listened. Robin, the flight attendant, poured. Paul could get used to wines like this one.

"You never been to Moscow? What you expect?"

"Gray and cold," Paul said with a wry smile.

"Very American. You listen to propaganda. Watch silly movies, read silly thrillers." Galkin stabbed an index finger in Tatyana's direction as he chewed a large mouthful of steak. "Moscow is world-class city now. World-class. Greatest, most fun city in Europe. Sexiest women, best restaurants, best hotels. Better Italian food there than Rome or Milan."

"So I've heard," Paul said.

"Yes! Streets clean, stores full. Is even naked barbershop. You get hair cut by naked women. Is completely different, Moscow today, than when I was young. When I was boy, I had one pair jeans. My mother constantly—" He mimed sewing.

"Repaired. Darned."

"Yes. I would save my seven kopecks for ice cream. When I was teenage, friend got Rolling Stone record, and we played it and played it till it was too scratched to play music anymore. You know 'Let It Bleed'? Now I hire Mick Jagger to play for me."

"Amazing," Paul said. It really was.

"Chekhov said, 'In Moscow, you sit in huge room in restaurant and you don't know nobody and no one knows you—but you don't feel a stranger.'"

A little drunk, Paul asked, "Why did you want me on this trip? Obviously not for how well I speak Russian."

"Is because you are smart. Also, is useful to have American face in meetings."

Neither Galkin nor Frost, who wasn't on the trip, had filled Paul in on what exactly the business was in Moscow. It remained a mystery. Maybe his Russian-speaking colleagues knew more. And what meetings was Galkin having? Paul wondered. Fortified by the wine, he asked, "Who are we meeting with?"

"*You* are meeting with venture capital funds. I have my own meetings."

"What sort of meetings do you have lined up?"

Galkin gave him a hard look. "Is personal." He took a sip of wine and signaled for more.

"Got it," Paul said, forcing a chuckle.

"Don't drink tap water in Moscow," Galkin said sternly, pointing directly at him. "Only bottle."

PAUL WAS A BIT WOOZY from the wine, and he had a headache. He'd been having headaches more and more often, and he knew it wasn't from the stress at work. Work stress he was used to, after years at Aquinnah. No, it was something else, a tension headache that had started when he'd made a decision that was irrevocable.

52

Paul had left work early the day he learned about Jake Larsen's death.

He walked several blocks until he found a Duane Reade, where he bought a prepaid cell phone. He went to a nearby Starbucks, set the phone up, and called Bernie Kovan's cell.

"Brightman!" Bernie said when Paul had identified himself. "You get a new phone number? You want to come home?"

"Your friend Mark Addison—I didn't save his business card. I'd like to talk with him. Can you reach out?"

"What's going on, Paul? You okay?"

"I'm fine, Bernie—nothing to worry about. But I need to talk to your friend. Here's a number to use—tell him not to call my cell."

SPECIAL AGENT MARK ADDISON HAD given Paul a long set of instructions. Paul left work the next day at a little after six o'clock. *Bring a change of clothes in a gym bag,* Addison had said. *Leave your phone and your Apple Watch, if you have one. Walk to Grand Central. It'll be rush hour: easier to lose a tail. Walk down to the dining concourse level and find a public restroom. Change into different clothes—jeans, a baseball cap.*

How will I know if I'm being followed? Paul had wanted to know.

If they're any good, you won't.

Once he'd changed, he headed back to the subway. He took the uptown 2 toward the Bronx to 125th Street and got off.

It took over an hour to reach Doris's Harlem Restaurant ("Queen of the Soul Food") on Malcolm X Boulevard. The fried chicken smelled incredible, and Paul was hungry.

Addison was sitting at a two-top in the back. Paul had forgotten what he looked like, but then he saw the big ears. The FBI man was nibbling on a large square of corn bread. He put it down when he saw Paul.

"How do I know you're really FBI?" Paul asked as he sat down.

"Fair question," Addison said. He produced a black leather flip case that held an FBI badge, gold with an eagle on top, and a photo ID card.

"You can probably get that made on Etsy."

"Or you can call the New York field office and ask for me, if you want. Or you can ask Bernie—he'll vouch for me."

"Okay."

"You're suspicious. That's good. I respect that."

"So why aren't we meeting at your office, anyway? Because it's watched?"

"Partly. And because we—my section—are working in isolation from the rest of the office."

"Isolation?"

"OpSec. Operations security. Some of our special agents are undercover."

"What's your section?"

"We deal with Russian oligarchs in the U.S."

Paul nodded slowly, his eyes widening.

"So what changed your mind?" Addison asked. "Last time we met, you sent me packing."

Paul told him about Jake Larsen's overdose.

"And you don't think Larsen did drugs?"

"I didn't know him well. . . . but something doesn't feel right. He didn't even drink alcohol."

Addison looked somehow satisfied—and also like he knew a lot more than he was willing to say.

"Is it possible," Paul asked, "that Galkin has people on call who, you know—what do they call it, 'wet work'? I mean who actually murder people? Like this guy Berzin—Andrei Berzin?"

"Galkin's security chief."

"He's ex-KGB," Paul said.

"And more recent than that, ex-FSB. Left the service not long ago. Are you asking, would a Russian oligarch arrange the death of someone he wanted out of the way?"

Paul looked at him.

Addison answered his own question. "Of course he would. Haven't you been reading the news? It's a whole new world."

Paul had read, like everybody else, about Russian defectors who'd been assassinated in Britain. Served tea infused with deadly radioactive poisons. "What does that mean, exactly?"

"Since the Cold War ended, the Russian intelligence services—we're talking the last decade, mostly—have been more aggressive than ever in targeting enemies abroad. I mean, it usually happens in parts of the world Americans don't pay attention to. Chechen émigrés in Istanbul, places like that. But they also target Russian émigrés who are outspoken Kremlin critics. People they label traitors. Most of the time, they're careful about covering their tracks."

"Making it look like an accident."

"Right. Or a suicide."

"Hence the overdose," Paul said.

Addison shrugged. "And you're here because . . ."

"I want protection."

"Makes sense."

"So what are you going after Arkady Galkin for?"

"Money laundering for the Kremlin. Stock fraud. Ever hear of the Racketeer Influenced and Corrupt Organizations Act?"

"You mean RICO? You guys use that against the Mafia."

"Exactly. And when we take Arkady Galkin down, the whole family goes down with him. Employees, too. Including you and your wife. Congratulations, by the way."

"But the work I do there is a hundred percent legit. His outfit is a real investment firm. I know, because I do real investment work."

"Based on what you know. But whose money is he playing with? Who are your investors?"

Paul thought for a moment. Hesitated. Decided this was the moment. "I know about several instances of insider trading, and I'm willing to give you that information as long as I'm protected. I want immunity."

"I think that can be arranged."

"I also want absolute confidentiality. I do not want to testify against my father-in-law. I do not want it known that I was your source. I do not want Galkin finding out about my role."

"Understood. Can do. Unless the case goes to trial. But these cases rarely—almost never—go to trial."

"And I want Tatyana protected."

Addison shook his head. "That I can't guarantee. She's part of the family, lives on money that was illegally obtained. Illegal proceeds."

Paul folded his arms. "It's nonnegotiable. She knows not a god-damned thing about her father's business. She's a fucking photographer. She's an artist."

"She's going to lose all her money."

This didn't seem like a hill to die on. "But I want you guys to sign a nonprosecution agreement on her."

After a long pause, Addison nodded. "All right, I'll make it happen."

What would happen to his marriage once Tatyana learned he was cooperating with the U.S. government to bring down her father? How could the marriage even survive?

Addison brought him back to the present moment.

"What kind of briefcase does Galkin carry?"

Paul tilted his head, smiled. "A Berluti. I googled it—it costs like six thousand bucks. Why?"

"I'll explain later."

Paul took a sip of his Coke. "One more thing. There's been a big new development."

"Tell me."

"I'm going to Moscow next week."

Addison's brows shot up. "Whoa. With Galkin?"

Paul nodded gravely.

"Business or pleasure?"

"Does anyone go to Moscow for pleasure?"

"So it's a business trip."

"Honestly, I don't know much about it. He said, 'You're coming,' and I said, 'Yes, sir.'"

"But he's bringing you."

"Right."

"Interesting. We might have a job for you there."

"And if I refuse?"

"Look, Paul, you're a free citizen. You're free to do whatever you want. You want to hang out in Moscow alone with Galkin and Berzin without protection, go ahead. Be my guest."

"What's the job?"

53

It was a small crew in Moscow, the oligarch and his daughter, Paul, and a couple of fluent Russian-speaking investment officers from the firm, Ivan Matlovsky and Matt Orlov.

The five were driven in two armored Bentleys: Paul, Tatyana, and her father in one. The weather was gray and drizzling, and the first stretch beyond the airport facilities was ugly. Mostly warehouses and commercial buildings, gray and unsightly. When they reached the outskirts of Moscow, Paul saw high-rise apartment complexes, enormous housing blocks built in Soviet times. As they entered Moscow proper, the buildings became commercial and surprisingly international in style. They drove along Kutuzovsky Prospekt, one of Moscow's main drags, past Gucci, Louis Vuitton, Prada, Versace, Dior. A Rolls-Royce showroom. It was like Rodeo Drive in L.A., except cold. Moscow in May could be cool and rainy. Paul had read that Kutuzovsky Prospekt, named after a famous Russian general who defended the city against Napoleon, was now the Park Avenue of Moscow. But a lot flashier, he decided. The buildings were lit up purple and blue. There were huge electronic billboards—ads for the Armani Exchange, Chanel, Omega watches, and something called Megafon, which he later learned was a major Russian mobile phone network operator. Neon and LED lights everywhere. The city sparkled in the night. It wasn't at all what he'd expected.

He thought anxiously about his assignment. Special Agent Addison hadn't prepared him well for Moscow; he'd made the city sound gloomier and more Soviet than it actually appeared to be. So Paul wondered if Addison was up on what surveillance was like in Russia these days. Paul would be in meetings most of the three days they were scheduled to be there. And he didn't even know how paranoid to be, a thought that made him paranoid. Would he be followed around town, the way foreigners were in the movies?

They checked into what he was told (and soon believed) was the finest hotel in Moscow, the imposing, grandiose building that was once the Hotel Moskva, designed by the same architect who designed Lenin's Mausoleum. It was 2 a.m. Moscow time. Even though they'd flown private, in luxury, with lie-flat seats, they were all exhausted. Tatyana and Paul checked into their room, a gorgeously appointed suite. Surely, he got the upgrade only because Tatyana was with him.

"How are you feeling about being back?" he asked her from the bathroom as he was brushing his teeth. But she was already snoring softly.

He noticed he had an incoming message on the Signal app. It was from Addison. The FBI agent had assured him that Signal was safe to use, that it was secure, as opposed to WhatsApp or the Russian messaging app Telegram. WhatsApp had a history of exploits, and Telegram wasn't encrypted. The Russians, Addison had said, hadn't broken Signal. Paul hoped he was right.

Meet friend Tues 1pm Moscow time @ GUM Burberry boutique. You should be out of your meetings by then.

Meet who? Paul texted back.

Colleague of mine. Leave your phone in hotel.

IN THE MORNING, AS TATYANA slept, Paul took a shower and shaved and went downstairs to the Bystro restaurant on the second floor to have breakfast with the other two AGF guys. He was bleary and half-asleep, whereas Matlovsky and Orlov looked wide awake. He got the explanation a few minutes later, after the waiter had poured them all coffee, when Orlov offered him some Provigil, saying that airline pilots took it all the time. It made you alert and wakeful and improved your cognitive performance. Paul pocketed a pill, but he wasn't exactly in the mood for experimenting with a drug he'd never tried before.

Matlovsky had black hair, short on the sides and longer in the middle, and a large, sharp nose. Orlov had long blond hair, fair skin, gray eyes, and high cheekbones and looked very Slavic. They were both American-born ethnic Russians who spoke Russian fluently because they'd grown up speaking it with their parents.

Matlovsky and Orlov decided on the Russian breakfast buffet, returning with their plates loaded with cold cuts and cheese and sausages and yogurts. Paul ordered an American breakfast of scrambled eggs, bacon, and toast. He wasn't ready to go full Moscow yet.

"What's the purpose of this first meeting?" he asked them. "I have briefing books and a PowerPoint deck, but Frost never filled me in."

"We're mostly just entertaining pitches," said Orlov.

"A thought shower," Matlovsky said.

"Where's the boss?" Paul asked.

"Which boss?" asked Orlov.

"Galkin."

"We don't ask," said Matlovsky. A waiter came by and filled their coffee cups. Paul knew only that Arkady was staying in the Presidential Suite alone, without Polina, who for some reason usually didn't want to go to Moscow. Galkin went several times a year, the guys had told him earlier.

Maybe his father-in-law was still asleep, Paul thought. It was clear that he kept his own schedule. Paul and the two Russian American guys were on their own.

They met in one of the hotel's conference rooms with five people from Propulsion, a Moscow-based firm that was pitching ideas all over the place. At one point, the lights went out so they could watch a PowerPoint presentation, and Paul came close to drowsing, but instead he poured himself a fourth cup of coffee. The Russians—two women, two men—spoke English fluently with British accents. They also used the jargon of the corporate world: "boil the ocean" and "robust" and "best practices."

The meeting with Propulsion broke for lunch. Paul was slowly coming to the realization that their meetings were pointless, just for show. Nothing more than busywork for him while the real show took place. And the real show must be whoever Galkin was meeting with. Paul and Matlovsky and Orlov were there only to provide a pretext for Arkady's Moscow trip.

Paul went out to the hotel lobby. It was spacious and stunning: high ceilings, ornate chandeliers, polished marble floors, and plush carpets in beige and cream. He was waiting for Tatyana; they would be meeting up with her mother. Soon he noticed an elegant, slim-hipped woman in her late fifties standing off to the left of the front desk, wearing what he knew from Tatyana's closet was a St. John suit in a powdery olive hue. She could have been a retired model. She had silver hair and very red lipstick.

Just then, Tatyana emerged from the bank of elevators and, seeing the silver-haired woman, half-ran toward her. "Mámochka!" she called out. There were tears in her eyes.

The two embraced tightly, for a long time. This was Galina Borisovna Belkina, Arkady's first wife and the mother of his two children. Speaking in machine-gun Russian, Tatyana introduced Paul. He extended a hand, but Galina leaned in and kissed him on both cheeks.

"Wonderful to meet you," she said in Russian. "*Moi zyat*. My son-in-law." She spoke with the deep rasp of a longtime smoker. "Will you come with us or . . . ?"

"I can't join you for lunch, I'm sorry," said Paul. "Business meetings." More rapid-fire Russian.

"She wants to invite you to dinner at her dacha tonight," Tatyana said.

"I'd love it," Paul said.

"Have you ever been to Moscow before?"

Paul said he hadn't.

"You should be a tourist for a while. Will you have a chance? Hire a guide from the hotel."

At that moment, Arkady Galkin emerged from the elevator bank. He was wearing a blue suit, a silver tie, and very shiny black shoes, more dressed up than Paul had ever seen him. He smelled of cologne and cigars. Galkin approached Galina, kissed her chastely on her cheeks three times. Tatyana was holding onto her mother's hands as if afraid she would leave.

Galkin and his ex-wife spoke for a few minutes, civilly. At one point, Paul understood him to say that he was visiting a friend's dacha on the Rublyovka. Paul knew that was a tony area west of Moscow where the rich had dachas, or country houses.

Galkin turned to Paul and said, "So you want to see Moscow." Sardonically he added, "I suppose you will see Lenin Mausoleum."

"Maybe."

"No Muscovite goes there. Only for tourists."

"Just like I've never been to the Statue of Liberty. Is the great man's body really there?"

"Looks like wax, but really is his . . . body. At least head. How you get around?"

"What do you advise?"

"Take company car. Driver is also security guard."

54

After his business meetings were concluded, Paul returned to his hotel suite to find Tatyana napping. She hadn't closed the drapes, and the amber late afternoon light was pouring in, striped across the bed. In the sitting room, he stood at the window and took in its view of Manezhnaya Square. Too agitated to sleep, he watched some Russian TV, the volume low so it wouldn't wake Tatyana. He switched from some kind of sketch comedy channel to coverage of ice hockey to a nature documentary, eventually settling on a news program on Rossiya 24. It was, of course, entirely in Russian, and he understood only a phrase here and there. After a few minutes of mute incomprehension, he turned it off.

Tatyana came into the sitting room, stretching, and leaned over to kiss him. She was wearing an oversize T-shirt that hung down to her knees. "Mama wants us to come early so we can take a walk in the woods around her dacha."

"Okay. How was your time with her?"

"We went to Petrovsky Passage and Tverskaya Street," she said, "mostly looking at jewelry. We had coffee, then we went to the Old Arbat and looked at antiques. And we talked, Pasha, we talked. I miss her so much."

"Do you miss Moscow?"

"It's sentimental for me, you know. It's my childhood."

"But you were so young when you left."

"I know, I know. But it's in my . . . *maya dusha*. You know what I mean?"

It meant "my soul." He understood. She was an American, had lived most of her life outside Russia. But she was at heart a Russian.

"Did you have a chance to take any pictures?" he asked.

She beckoned him over to her laptop and showed him some photographs she'd taken. An old lady in a black coat and gray knit cap squatting before an array of junk spread out on the ground, probably her life's possessions. A lineup of street vendors in front of a train station. A young man standing in the middle of a dump, garbage as far as the eye could see, birds flying just overhead.

"Remarkable," he said.

She smiled shyly. "You didn't see any of these people, did you? In the center of the city, they hide the homeless and the poor. You have to know where to look." Glancing at her watch, she said, "I should get dressed."

Half an hour later, they were walking across the opulent lobby and saw her father sitting in one of the plush armchairs, looking impatient. Tatyana hurried over to him and put a hand on his shoulder; he got up, and they hugged. Paul hung back so the two could talk.

A man in a cheap blue suit, clearly security or a driver, approached Galkin and said, in Russian, "Very sorry, sir, very sorry."

"Let's go," Galkin replied sourly. The driver appeared to be late, which Galkin detested.

"Right away, sir," the driver said.

"Come on," Galkin said brusquely to him. He hugged his daughter again and then walked with the driver out the front doors. Where Galkin was going, Paul had no idea. Paul had been invited to dinner with his colleagues but had had to pass, for family reasons, he said.

In the car—this one a new Mercedes S-Class that smelled of rich leather—he and Tatyana talked quietly. "Where's your father going tonight?" Paul asked.

Tatyana shrugged. "He never tells me. Business meetings."

The driver took Kutuzovsky Prospekt all the way to its end, marking the beginning of a residential area, the Rublyovka. This was no ordinary residential area. It was lined with immense mansions, and some, probably even more immense, hidden behind trees and gates. This was where the Russian elite—oligarchs, generals, celebrities, politicians—either lived full time or kept their weekend dachas.

Galina Belkina's dacha was at the end of a long, tree-lined dirt road. It was a low, rambling wooden house, its cedar shingles weathered to gray. It looked a hundred years old at least. Galina emerged from the green-painted front door just as the Mercedes limo pulled up, her arms outstretched theatrically. She was wearing a beige quilted jacket with a

Burberry lining. "Come, let's walk," she said in English. "Are you ready for a . . . *pro-gulka po prirode*? 'A walk in nature'? We will get fresh air."

Tatyana was wearing flats, which she knew wouldn't do for a walk in the woods, so she slipped into an old pair of green rubber wellies that had been left on the porch. Paul, who was wearing street shoes, put on a pair of brick-red wellies from the jumble that was probably there for guests.

Galina had several acres of land on the edge of which the forest began. They entered the forest, Galina leading the way through a dense copse of trees, birch and pine and spruce. It reminded Paul of the forests in Bellingham, Washington, where his father would take him on nature walks. She seemed to know the woods well, leading them along paths and well-maintained trails that wound around the trees. Much of the way was shaded by the thick canopy. Galina and Tatyana talked for a minute or two in Russian, then Galina said to Paul, "You see a little bit of Moscow today?"

"Not yet. I think tomorrow we'll have a little time. I want to see St. Basil's Cathedral."

"Inside, it's nothing. But the domes—do you know why they're so brightly colored?"

He shook his head.

"It was built during Ivan the Terrible, when churches were painted in bright colors and intricate patterns. You know, St. Basil's was modeled after the Book of Revelation—it's what it says the Kingdom of Heaven will look like. They say that Ivan was so pleased with the cathedral that he blinded its architect."

"Why?"

"So that its design would never be replicated."

"Some payday," Paul said.

"Tanya tells me you now work for Arkady Viktorovich?"

Paul nodded.

"You are an investments manager?"

"Something like that."

"Well, I don't know what I'm talking about. I just know he has a lot of money. He takes care of me, but only because he has to." She gave a short, scornful bark of a laugh. "He's not exactly generous."

"The rich stay rich by not giving it away," Paul said.

She laughed again, more openly, and it sounded like Tatyana's laugh.

AS THE SUN WENT DOWN, they circled back to Galina's dacha. Inside, the house was open and spacious. Exposed beams on a pitched ceiling. There were old-looking caramel-colored leather couches with rolled arms, Persian throw rugs, and icons hung on the maroon-painted walls. Paul smelled something delicious being cooked. A young man in a white shirt and dark jeans, apparently a member of Galina's staff, offered them flutes of champagne from a tray.

Mother and daughter were in the middle of a conversation about a childhood friend of Tatyana's who had gotten into trouble. That was as much as Paul could discern; they were speaking only in Russian. Galina asked for more champagne, and so did Tatyana. Paul didn't want to get drunk, not in front of his mother-in-law—plus, he had a business meeting in the morning. He asked for mineral water.

Dinner was leg of lamb with whipped potatoes and green beans, simple but savory, all served by the butler, who seemed also to be the cook.

"We are being very rude to your Pasha," Galina said. She had just told Tatyana a story about a woman with whom Arkady had been conducting an affair when Tatyana was a toddler. Galina spoke in Russian, but Paul was beginning to understand spoken Russian more and more.

He said, in English, "I assume this was after he'd gotten rich."

"In fact, yes," said Galina with a grin.

"Arkady says that women are attracted to rich men like flies to shit," Paul said.

Both women laughed. "He's very direct, your husband," Galina said.

They started on the lamb and were silent for a moment as they ate.

"How'd you meet Arkady in the first place?" Paul asked.

"I went to a party with a lot of people from the Bauman Institute, and we were immediately attracted to each other. In those days, he was kind of cute." Galina took a long sip of red wine. "Forgive me for saying this, but the lady engineers he went to school with were not exactly *Playboy* centerfolds."

"Not his type, huh?" Paul said.

"What about that professor?" Tatyana asked. "Didn't they have an affair?"

Galina's eyes lit up. "Ah, yes." Turning to Paul, she said, "One of his teachers took a shine to him. Ludmilla something. A younger faculty member."

"One of his teachers?" Paul asked.

"I remember she had very thick glasses. Coke-bottle glasses, you would say. But very *connected*." A long, significant pause. "She made him rich, you know." This was directed at her daughter. "She was connected."

"How'd she make him rich?" Paul asked.

"She knew the right people in the Kremlin. Ludmilla was kind of a recruiter."

"Recruiting for what?"

Galina shrugged, uninterested in explaining further. "The Kremlin was looking for promising young Russians to take the economy private. All the men who became oligarchs—and they were all men—were well connected to the power structure. You had to know the right people. This is how it is in Russia—who you know."

Not so different in America, Paul thought.

"Didn't you say Ludmilla tried to convince him not to marry you?" said Tatyana.

"Ah, yes," Galina replied. "My biggest enemies were not his girl-friends but the women, his platonic friends he made at Bauman. They thought I was a . . . I believe the term is *bimbo*, right? Worst of all was Ludmilla. Maybe they were threatened by me."

Paul was about to ask what Ludmilla's last name was when Tatyana said, "Polina had her eyes on Papa for years"—and the opportunity passed.

In the car on the way back to the hotel, Paul saw another chance and asked Tatyana for Ludmilla's surname. Tatyana was drunk, pleasantly so. Too drunk to ask him why he wanted to know.

"I don't remember," she said after a moment. "Ludmilla Sergeyevna something." She remembered only Ludmilla's patronymic, but maybe that was good enough.

Tatyana crawled into bed as soon as they arrived in their room. Paul brought her a couple of aspirin and a glass of water to ward off a hangover in the morning.

He had begun getting undressed himself when his phone rang. He didn't recognize the number, which began with country code 44, which he knew was the United Kingdom.

"Paul Brightman?"

"Yes?"

"Dick Foley, I'm a friend of Rick Jacobson's. Sorry to be calling so late."

A Brit, by the accent, Paul thought. "That's okay, I'm up. What can I do for you?"

"Can I buy you a drink?"

"I'm out of the country at the moment."

"You're in Moscow. I am, too. We're at the same hotel."

"How do you know what hotel I'm at?" Paul had barely seen Rick in months. Had he told him he was going to Moscow? He was sure he hadn't.

"Long story," the man said.

"I'd like to hear it."

"I'm working in Moscow, and I saw Arkady Galkin here, and I know from Rick that you work for him. He gave me your number."

"He did?" Was this someone from the FBI sent by Addison? Paul wondered. "Okay, well, I've got a full schedule of business meetings while I'm here." *Pointless ones*, he didn't add. "When were you thinking?"

"How's now?"

55

The man at the hotel bar had gray-blond hair and was dressed in a dark-gray suit, no tie. He had nearly invisible eyebrows and deep-set gray eyes. He looked to be around fifty. "Dick Foley," the man said as they shook hands.

"Paul Brightman. How do you know Rick?"

"We've met in charity circles in London. My company funds some of his efforts. Anyway, I saw Galkin here, and I remember Rick saying you'd started working for him, and I thought I'd give you a call."

"Nice to meet you."

"May I take you to a bar I think you'll like? It's a speakeasy called Schrödinger's Cat. I have a car."

Paul hesitated a long time. Then he said, "It's late. I'll have one drink, here, in the hotel bar."

The bar was dimly lit, with black tables and jazz playing low. Paul and Foley took stools at the bar. The Englishman ordered Zubrowka, and Paul ordered the same. Foley explained that it was a Polish vodka flavored with bison grass, which gave it a pale green color and a distinctive zing. They each had it straight. It had a slightly medicinal aftertaste, but Paul liked it.

"You know my boss?" Paul asked.

"He's a clever man, your father-in-law. A shrewd negotiator. You shake hands with him, you count your fingers afterward, right?" A nervous titter. Foley was watching Paul closely, as if to gauge his reaction. He added, "You can't help but admire him for his skill."

Paul was intrigued but didn't want to seem too interested. He didn't smile or laugh. He didn't want to show this stranger any kind of disloyalty to Galkin. "What kind of business are you in?"

"I'm a commodities trader. I work in the City."

Paul looked around, hoping not to be spotted by either Galkin or Berzin.

Foley drained his glass, signaled the waitress for another. "Who are you meeting with in Moscow?"

"Don't think I want to tell you that. You might be a competitor."

"I can be very useful to you."

"Oh, yeah?"

"Sure. You're trying to impress the big man. But you're in a little over your head, aren't you? You don't know the lay of the land. And I can help."

"I didn't ask for your help."

"Let me tell you a few things that might be very useful to you, something you can't get on your Bloomberg terminal. You're looking to buy a stake in a Russian paper company called Hyperion—'*Giperion*,' as the Russians call it."

Paul was surprised the man knew that one of the companies AGF was looking at was a huge pulp and paper mill in Siberia. "What about it?"

"Well, for years they've been pumping toxic waste into Lake Baikal. Which you may know is the largest freshwater lake in the world. And they were just shut down by a regional Siberian court. You don't want to own the biggest polluter in Russia. Not to mention, any equity stake you take in this company is going to come with a bloodbath of red ink. That company is what Russians call a bear trap. Don't take my word for it. Do the research yourself."

"So why are you telling me all this?"

"I'm establishing my bona fides."

"Meaning you want something from me."

"Of course I do. I can help you, and I suspect you can help me. I want to know who he's meeting with in Moscow. I don't mean you, the junior lackeys. I mean the great man himself."

"That I can't tell you, because I don't know."

"But you're a smart young man and, in this instance, well connected. You can find out."

"I don't think I can help you. I know what I know, and I know what I don't know." Paul put his drink down onto the wooden bar top with a thump. He took out a handful of rubles, but Foley waved them away.

Paul got down from the stool and extended a hand. The men shook, and Foley said with a smile, wriggling his fingers, "All my fingers—all there!"

56

The business meeting the next morning was as pointless as the one the day before had been. Paul and the two other AGF men had gone to the modernist headquarters of Lukoil, a Russian energy giant, to explore various investment opportunities. They discussed a couple of deals, including selling Lukoil's refinery in Sicily. But it was all hot air, another time waster.

When the meeting broke up, and they were leaving, Orlov and Matlovsky invited Paul to join them for lunch at the White Rabbit, a Michelin-starred restaurant with a panoramic view of the city. But Paul had other plans. He told them he was going to meet up with his wife. He returned to the hotel to check in with Tatyana, but she was already gone. She'd left a note saying she was meeting her mother for lunch at Café Pushkin.

Paul came out the front entrance to the hotel, where he saw a cluster of black luxury vehicles—a Bentley, a Range Rover, a Mercedes S-Class. The Bentley rolled down its driver's-side window and a voice called out, "Meester Bright-man!"

His driver: a rotund young man with greasy black hair.

"Thanks, but I'm going for a walk," Paul told the man. "I'll be back in about an hour. *Spasibo.*" Thank you.

He wished he had his iPhone with him to help him navigate, but he'd left it in his room, as Addison had instructed. He'd brought with him a small map of central Moscow he'd gotten at the front desk. The hotel was near Revolution Square and GUM, the famous Russian department store where he'd been directed to go.

So was he being followed?

He'd have to assume so, even though he didn't see anyone walking behind him.

Addison had told him that too many foreigners came to Moscow these days for the FSB to follow them all. There weren't enough FSB agents. Plus, there were surveillance cameras everywhere, in this new Moscow.

GUM—the initials in Russian mean "main universal store"—was an enormous, handsome structure built in the nineteenth century in the Russian Revival style, with an arched entrance, white and pale yellow. It was directly across from Red Square. Inside was a shopping arcade consisting of three levels of walkways and a glass roof and bustling with people speaking all kinds of languages—French, Italian, Japanese, Russian, and English.

It was elegant, nicer than a lot of high-end shopping malls Paul had seen elsewhere. It was also crowded. He saw Prada and Louis Vuitton and all the brands you'd expect to see. Famous-in-Moscow restaurants like Canteen No. 57 and Beluga Caviar Bar. In the crowd in front of the Burberry boutique, he was jostled by someone, a young woman, who apologized in Russian. When he entered the boutique, a phone began ringing. He was startled to realize the ringing was coming from his own coat pocket.

He reached inside his pocket and found an iPhone identical to his own and a little white AirPods case.

The woman he'd bumped into.

He answered the phone.

"You have a tail," a man's voice said. He had an American accent.

"What am I supposed to do about it?"

"Did you tell someone you were going to GUM?"

"No."

"Take the nearest exit to the street. It'll be on your right. Don't hang up."

He put in the AirPods.

57

Who was following him? Everyone, it seemed, was watching him. Everyone could be. That car idling by the curb whose middle-aged driver was staring at him? The teenage girls walking next to him on the sidewalk, glancing over and giggling? Well, maybe not them. But the lone older man in a T-shirt with a backpack and ear buds in, a few paces behind? Or the young guy holding his phone in front of him and talking into it? Muscovites didn't look the way he'd expected. He didn't see many old grandmothers, *babushki*, with scarves over their heads. It was a chilly morning, but he didn't see many fur hats, either. Maybe they were out of season. A lot of smokers, though, more than on the streets of New York.

The man on the other end of the phone began to speak again. "I want you to stop in front of the souvenir shop on your left and look down at your phone."

Paul did as he was told, and as he stood with his back against the plate glass, he saw a couple of burly men pass by and glance at him. Were *they* the tail? They kept going without glancing again. So maybe not.

He noticed surveillance cameras on the street, mounted to the sides of buildings and to lampposts. Addison had told him there were more than a quarter million CCTV cameras in Moscow powered by facial recognition software. Not as many as in London, not yet. Nor as in China. But Moscow was racing to catch up. Surveillance cameras were used to identify protesters and journalists.

"Now what?" Paul said into the phone.

"Go to Yandex and order a cab."

"Yandex?"

"The app's been preloaded onto your phone under a false name and a different credit card. It's a cab-hailing service. Order a cab to meet you in front of the Hotel Metropol in twenty minutes. Your name is Robert Langfitt."

"Where am I going?"

"To meet me. We want to make sure you're not followed, obviously. Just follow my instructions, and everything will be fine."

"Okay." Paul checked his new phone and found the app, called Yandex Go, and opened it. The language was already set to English. He fumbled around for a few moments until he figured out how to call for a cab and then put in the desired location. "Done," he said.

"Okay. Now, when you get to the end of this block, I want you to take a sharp left and then enter the building on the corner. It's a small boutique hotel. See it?"

He spotted a graceful art nouveau building on the corner and entered it. Inside was a bright, surprisingly modern lobby furnished in bold purples and pinks. The air was delicately perfumed. Loud electronic dance music was playing. He glanced back, didn't see anyone who looked like they'd followed him inside.

"Head to the front desk and give them the ticket."

"Ticket?"

"It's in your pocket. A claim check."

He reached into the same jacket pocket where he'd found the iPhone, and sure enough, there was a paper stub with numbers printed on it in red. At the front desk was a stylish young woman with short brown hair and a lot of makeup on, teased eyebrows and full red lips. She smiled at him, must have instantly assessed him as a foreigner, and said in English, "May I help you?"

"Good morning," he said, handing her the stub.

"One moment, please."

She disappeared into the back and returned a minute later with a black nylon carry-on case. She wheeled it around the end of the counter. "Thank you for staying with us, Mr. Langfitt."

"Thanks," he said. How, he wondered, did she know his cover name? In his ear, the voice said, "There's a men's room behind the front desk. Take the suitcase with you and change into the clothes we've provided. Hang up now, but call me back when you've changed."

"Okay."

Change clothes? This was crazy. He was an American businessman in Moscow, accompanying a Russian oligarch. But maybe it was inevitable that the Russian authorities wanted to keep close tabs on him. Or maybe it was Galkin's people. If he was indeed being followed, as this disembodied voice claimed, it wouldn't be that surprising.

Yet, if he was seen meeting with a known FBI agent, he was screwed. Addison had told Paul that the FBI had special agents stationed in Moscow, in the American embassy, as legal attachés. That the FSB would recognize all FBI special agents working in Moscow. So this particular agent was right to be careful.

They could arrest him on any pretext.

He had to lose the tail.

Paul locked the bathroom door and placed the case on the counter next to the sink. Unzipping it, he found a silver-gray Adidas track suit jacket; on the front, the image of a soccer ball, the logo of some Russian football team. There was also a pair of worn blue jeans, a green-striped T-shirt, a pair of battered Nike Air Max 95s, and a black Russian flat cap. In a glasses case, a pair of glasses with thick black frames. He put them on and saw that the lenses were clear.

In a few moments, he'd changed into his Russian costume and folded his suit jacket and pants and Oxford shirt into the case. He regarded himself in the mirror and almost laughed at how different he looked. He could now pass for a Russian.

Paul hit the Call button on the phone. "What now?"

"I want you to exit the hotel through the service entrance in the back, next to the kitchen. That will lead you to an alley. You'll be taking a left out of the alley and back onto the street. Two blocks away, you'll find the Metropol and your cab."

He left the restroom, carrying the case, and saw no one there. He found the service entrance, pushed the door open, and exited next to a foul-smelling dumpster. A couple of kitchen workers were standing next to it smoking. They nodded at him. One of them said something to him in Russian, but he ignored it, nodding back and smiling, and kept going down the alley.

The voice in his ear said, "You'll be passing the Lubyanka, where there's a prison you don't want to see the inside of."

"Uh, yeah."

"Used to be KGB headquarters. No longer. Still not a nice place to visit."

It was a large yellow-brick building with hammer-and-sickle symbols on its lower façade. He'd seen this place before, in spy movies, and the sight of it made him reflexively nervous.

A few blocks away was an enormous and beautiful hotel the size of a city block, the Metropol. He found the main entrance, beneath a canopy with the hotel's name emblazoned in English. In front of it idled buses and luxury vehicles and several yellow cabs. He found the cab with the right number and got into the backseat. The driver, who'd been standing outside the cab smoking, dropped his cigarette to the pavement and ground it out with what appeared to be disappointment.

"Meester Langfeet?" he said as Paul got in.

"Yes."

"Tretyakov Gallery?"

"Right."

"Is close."

Paul nodded.

"Short ride." The driver sounded annoyed.

Paul shrugged, said nothing.

The voice in his ear spoke. "You're in the cab?"

"I am." The driver looked like a Muscovite but had a British or American name and spoke English. It didn't make sense to him, but he didn't raise the point with the FBI man on the phone. This wasn't the time.

"Okay," the voice said, "I'll meet you in front of the *Princess Tarakanova*."

"Who?"

"You'll find it easily. Second floor, Hall Sixteen. *Princess Tarakanova*. Every Russian knows her. I'm signing off now."

58

The cab took him to 10 Lavrushinsky Lane, and he entered the ornate nineteenth-century building. He paid five hundred rubles for a ticket, checked his carry-on case at the museum's cloakroom, and joined a crowd of tourists. On the second floor, he found *Princess Tarakanova.*

The painting was extraordinary, arresting. A large crowd had gathered in front of it. The canvas was large, eight feet by over six feet, and dramatic, painted in the Russian realist manner. A beautiful young woman stands on a bed trying to escape a rising tide of water flooding her gloomy prison cell. She leans back against a crumbling wall, helpless, her face wracked with despair.

Paul looked around for the FBI agent, heard Japanese and French being spoken. A guy standing next to him said, "Pretty great, huh?"

Paul turned. It was a craggy-faced American tourist, a bulky white-haired man wearing a Chicago Cubs cap and holding a guidebook to Moscow.

"Great use of light and shadow." Paul said.

"Notice the rats scrambling onto the bed?"

"Oh, yes."

"This chick," the man said, pointing at the young woman standing on the bed, "was going around the salons of Rome during the reign of Catherine the Great claiming she was the *real* heir to the Russian throne. She said she was the daughter of Empress Elizabeth. Turned out to be a real threat to Catherine—who'd seized power in a coup. So Catherine laid a clever trap. She sent her former lover, Count Alexei Orlov, to Italy to seduce the woman. He pretended to fall in love with her and then invited her to get married on board his ship in the waters off Tuscany. Soon as she boarded the ship, she was clapped in shackles, kidnapped, and hauled back to Mother Russia. Imprisoned for life. Died in prison."

Paul smiled at the chatty older man. "So was she really the daughter of the empress?"

"No one knows. She was just one in a long line of pretenders to the

Russian throne. Russia had lots of them. More than in most countries. And this was Catherine's way of saying to all of Russia, 'Don't fuck with me, fellas.' Now, that's how you stay in power in this country. I'm Andrew, by the way." He shook Paul's hand firmly and turned to leave.

Paul felt something in his hand, something small and rigid, like a hotel key card, and when he glanced around to look for the tourist, the man had already disappeared into the crowd.

BY INSTINCT, PAUL DIDN'T LOOK at the little card until he'd left the hall.

On it was printed, in Russian, "11 Lavrushinsky Lane." Underneath that, in black Sharpie marker, was scrawled "9C." The Tretyakov Gallery was also located on Lavrushinsky Lane, so the hotel the card was from had to be nearby.

He retrieved the carry-on case from the cloakroom on the first floor and exited the building. As he did so, he hit the phone number he had called back fifteen minutes before. "What's going on?" he said when the man answered. "I thought we were meeting in front of the painting."

"Last-minute change of plans. Didn't want to take the chance."

"Was I followed?"

"Apparently not. You weren't. Well done. Me, I can't be certain. I'm in the apartment building right across the street."

Paul spotted the modern apartment complex and crossed the street. Passing a well-tended flower garden, he found the entrance. A small, empty lobby furnished with a few easy chairs. There was a bank of mailboxes and an internal door with a card reader affixed to its side, which the key card buzzed open.

Down a gray-carpeted hall on the right was an elevator. He entered it and hit 9. Nothing happened, so he waved the key card in front of the card reader under the number panel, and the elevator doors closed.

Apartment 9C was down the hall on the left. He tried the key card there, but got no response. He hit a doorbell, and the door came right open.

Standing there was "Andrew," the tourist from the gallery, the bulky white-haired man, only now he wasn't wearing a Cubs cap. Paul entered quickly, and the door shut behind him.

He'd entered a spacious and utterly empty apartment: an expanse of polished wooden floors in a herringbone pattern, white walls, no furniture. "I'd offer you a seat, but as you can see, I don't have any. My name is Aaron. I'm a friend of Mark Addison's." The man had an acne-scarred face, chapped lips, and thinning white hair.

"What happened to 'Andrew'?"

Aaron shook his head. "Sorry about all the precautions. It's for your own good."

"Mark said the KGB doesn't follow foreigners around so much anymore."

"It's the FSB now, and it's different for American embassy employees. For us, life hasn't changed that much. Listen, I'll make this quick." From the floor, he pulled a burnished leather briefcase—identical, Paul realized, to the one Arkady Galkin carried. "This way."

Paul followed him into the spacious empty kitchen, where they stopped before a large island topped with black granite. There the man set down the briefcase. He unzipped it and pulled out a small, squarish white tile.

"That an Apple AirTag?" Paul asked.

"Modified. It doesn't reach out to other Apple devices like the AirTag does. It's a non-emissive passive transponder. Here's all you do."

He slipped the tile into the briefcase and immediately pulled his empty hand out. "You put it into the inside-facing side of a pocket. It'll adhere to the leather. Try it."

"How am I supposed to do this?"

"All you need is twenty seconds alone."

"With Galkin's briefcase?"

"Right."

"And when's that supposed to happen?"

"You're a member of the family now. You'll have opportunities."

"Easy for you to say. Am I supposed to keep this phone?"

The FBI man nodded. "It's clean. No bugs."

"If the . . . FSB can tap my iPhone, they can tap this one."

"But they don't know you have it, see. It's called security through obscurity. Nothing is uncrackable anymore. Security is a dated concept. I mean, the only uncrackable safe is one that no one can find to crack."

Paul nodded dubiously. He had to make sure to keep the two phones separate. Maybe one in his pocket, one in his suitcase. He didn't want Tatyana discovering that he had two identical iPhones. "By the way, I had dinner with Tatyana's mother last night."

"I know," Aaron said. "How'd that go?"

Paul nodded. "Galina Borisovna said something interesting about her ex."

"Oh, yeah?" The man seemed to perk up.

"She said when he was a student at the Bauman Institute, he had an affair with one of his professors, who made him rich."

"What does that mean, 'made him rich'?"

"She was apparently a recruiter for the Kremlin."

"You catch her name?"

"Ludmilla something."

"Last name?"

Paul shook his head. He knew more but didn't want to say. Knowledge was power. "Tatyana's mother said Ludmilla even tried to talk Arkady out of marrying her."

"Jesus, that's the woman who recruited him for Mother Russia. Need her full name."

"Sorry . . ."

"Would your wife know?"

"She doesn't remember. Anyway, that was before she was born."

"Find the name, if you can. Help us, and we help you. You know how this works. You want the Bureau's protection, you gotta play ball."

"Actually, I thought I was helping you by planting this fucking tracker," Paul snapped. "Isn't that *playing ball*?"

The man smiled. His smile seemed to crack the lunar surface of his face. "That's playing ball, all right. But you'd better practice. Right now." He handed Paul the briefcase. "You don't want to strike out."

59

On his way back to the hotel, Paul stopped at a Russian fast-food chain called Teremok and got a chicken Caesar blini. As he ate, he wondered how the hell he was going to get access to Galkin's briefcase—alone. And what would happen if he got caught trying to insert the tracker? He looked around the restaurant, sensed that he was surrounded by Russians, not tourists. He didn't know if he was being followed anymore and didn't feel qualified to know for sure. He'd changed back into his own clothes at the FBI man's apartment and looked like an American again.

At the hotel, he found their suite empty except for a maid cleaning the bathroom. Tatyana was gone, maybe still at lunch with her mother. He would have to explain to her where he'd gone, have to make up a story about how he wandered around Moscow as a tourist. He switched off the iPhone that the FBI had given him, then hid it in a pocket of his suitcase. He pulled out his own iPhone, saw that he had a few messages. One was from Arkady, inviting him to a "business dinner" at a nearby restaurant called Aragvi.

He called Tatyana.

"How's your day going, sweetie?" he said when she answered.

"Good. We're in Van Cleef and Arpels. Mama wanted to show me something. Are you in boring meetings all the time?"

"Not at all. My meetings finished early. I've just been wandering around the city, being a tourist." Trying to be casual, he asked: "Where's your dad?"

"He's not with you?"

"I have no idea where he is. Any idea what his plans are?"

"Pasha, when we go to Moscow, we go our own separate ways. Why are you asking me?"

"Curiosity, that's all."

"Are you free for dinner? We're going to La Marée—I wanted fish. Can you join us?"

"I've been asked to join your father for dinner at a place called Aragvi. Kind of a command performance."

"I understand," she said.

Next, he called Rick Jacobson's mobile number, using the hotel's Wi-Fi. Late afternoon in Moscow meant it was around eight thirty in the morning in New York. His friend would either be at work or on his way there.

"Tell me about Dick Foley," Paul said when Rick answered.

"Who?"

"The Englishman. Commodities trader in London who does business in Moscow."

"Commodities trader? I don't know any commodities trader."

"He's a funder of your foundation . . ." Paul's voice trailed off. "Dick Foley?"

"Believe me, if he were a funder, I would know his name. I don't know any Richard Foley or Dick Foley or anything like that. Can't help you. Sorry."

60

The thought occurred to Paul that his meetup with "Dick Foley" could have just been a test set up by Galkin to check his son-in-law's loyalty. Would his father-in-law have resorted to arranging a ruse like that? If not Galkin, then maybe Berzin? Or was it the FSB? It couldn't have been Addison . . . could it? The FBI man's agenda was murky; Paul still didn't know what he'd wanted, besides planting a tracker.

But he didn't have time to obsess any longer over the strange meeting with "Dick Foley," because he had to figure out how to plant the tracker in Arkady's briefcase, and the more he thought about it, the less likely it seemed he'd succeed. They were in Moscow for two more days. There was a deadline.

Galkin was rarely without his briefcase. Like it was part of him. Except at home, when he left it in his study there. Here, in Moscow, the trick was to get Galkin into some private setting and then wait until he temporarily left the room, went to the bathroom. Maybe in his hotel suite.

He knew Galkin would be at dinner at seven, in a few hours, but he didn't know where he was right now. Maybe back at the hotel. Paul had his father-in-law's mobile phone number but knew he wasn't really permitted to call him. Certainly not now, when the man might be napping. He called the front desk and asked to be connected to Galkin's suite.

The phone rang and rang. The hotel operator got on the line and said, "I'm sorry, I believe Mr. Galkin is not there."

So he wasn't back yet. He would see him in a few hours. Maybe there'd be an opportunity at dinner.

THE ARAGVI WAS A FIVE-MINUTE walk from the hotel. It was an old Moscow restaurant that specialized in Georgian cuisine. Inside the entrance, the maître d', a middle-aged man as wiry as a greyhound, greeted him in Russian. Paul asked for Mr. Galkin's table and was escorted to a private room at the center of which was a large oval table. Around it sat

Paul's colleagues and a few people he didn't recognize, and at the head of the table was Arkady, who called out, "Mr. Brightman is good enough to join us."

"Apologies," Paul said, nodding. He'd fallen asleep in his suite, still dressed in his business clothes, and gotten up late.

Arkady began the introductions. The others at the table were Russian lawyers and consultants whom Galkin had done business with in the past, along with Orlov and Matlovsky and Berzin and one of Berzin's security guards. Paul's glass was filled with a Georgian white wine called Tsinandali, his plate heaped with khachapuri, Georgian cheese bread; khinkali, Georgian dumplings; and shashlik, a type of shish kebob. The wine had a pleasant floral taste.

Berzin was regaling the party with stories of the restaurant's heyday, when Aragvi was the favorite haunt of the KGB. Kim Philby used to love coming here, Berzin said. "The rumor was that all the tables were equipped with microphones." He had a reedy, quiet voice. "You had to be very careful what you said here."

Galkin was relaxed, more relaxed than Paul had ever seen him before, even at home. He was telling stories, trading quips, laughing uproariously. He was in his motherland and seemed somehow different, more at home. He was holding forth. Was he making jokes at the expense of the other oligarchs who were loyal to the Kremlin? It seemed so. "Russians under czar, under Soviets, under capitalism—always same. Always there is court in Moscow filled with obedient . . . puppets." Looking hard at Paul, Galkin said, a crooked index finger pointed at him, "A puppet thinks he is free if he loves his strings."

The dinner broke up after midnight. Paul and the others from Galkin's party separated in the lobby of the hotel. Galkin didn't have his briefcase with him. It was probably back at the hotel. There hadn't been a possible moment at the restaurant, anyway. For the first time, Galkin looked tired and older than his seventy-some years, yet still happy. Paul kept thinking about what his father-in-law had said, that a puppet thinks he's free if he loves his strings. Did that mean *he*, Paul, was a puppet? Or the opposite: that Galkin felt himself to be one?

The two men waited side by side at the elevator bank.

"You see some of Moscow?" Galkin said.

"I did, yes. A little bit."

"Tatyana take you around?"

"To be honest, I've barely seen her! She's been with her mother most of the time. When she wasn't taking pictures. But, listen—I need to talk to you for a few minutes."

"When, now?"

An elevator dinged, its doors opened, and they got into the car. "It won't take long," Paul said.

61

The Presidential Suite was on the tenth floor. It was spacious, of course, and modern in décor, with sweeping views of the Kremlin at night and St. Basil's Cathedral; the white drapes were now open on the city vistas. Galkin led him to a sitting room with a couple of facing white couches, a glass-topped coffee table between them, topped with a spray of irises and a large platter of exotic fruits.

Slumped on the floor next to the coffee table was Galkin's briefcase.

Each man sat on a couch facing the other. Galkin leaned back, crossed his legs, and dangled one of them. He looked a little drunk.

Paul hadn't seen his father-in-law use the restroom at Aragvi. So soon he would have to. There'd been a fair amount of drinking at the table, and the man was afflicted with the same ailment that plagued a lot of men his age: he often had to pee, Paul had noticed. All Paul would have to do was wait him out. Talk until Galkin had to get up to use the bathroom. Then make his move.

"You are not liking Moscow, you are liking Moscow, what?" Galkin began.

"Beautiful city."

Galkin nodded. "Where you go today?"

Paul shrugged. "Red Square, St. Basil's, the usual places."

"You like GUM?"

Had his father-in-law had him followed?

"Great shopping mall." Paul tried to feign enthusiasm.

"No museums?"

Paul paused. His stomach went hollow. How much did Galkin know about where he'd gone in Moscow? "Briefly went to the Tretyakov Gallery."

"Briefly?"

"I get museum-ed out pretty quickly. I'm not proud of that."

"And my Tatyana is enjoying herself?"

"Think so. We've barely—"

"Yes, yes, you've barely seen each other, I know. She spends lot of time with her mother?"

"She does."

"Tatyana also loves Moscow. You have dinner with Galina Borisovna?"

"Very elegant lady."

"Not when she's yelling," Arkady replied. He smiled sheepishly. "I sorry, I must be drunk. She's good mother. Beauty, once upon a time." He looked down, folded his hands. "You have to say to me something?"

"Yes, I was doing—"

"You will excuse me. I have to go to gulag." Galkin got up from the couch, almost stumbling at first.

"The gulag?"

His father-in-law smiled as he walked toward the door. "What we say when we use toilet." He chuckled.

Galkin made a motion for Paul to get up as well. "You know, Paul, I am tired and not at most sharp," he said, waving him out. "Goodnight."

Shit. "To be continued in the morning?" Paul said, trying not to sound desperate.

"Everything will wait."

"When can we talk in the morning?"

"I have breakfast with Berzin at nine."

"Before that, then?" And hope Berzin didn't come early.

"You come at eight."

Paul had meetings starting at nine. "Eight is perfect," he said. It was worth a try.

HE GOT UP AT SEVEN the next day, had a leisurely coffee in their suite, and got dressed.

Galkin answered the door to his suite. He was wearing an expensively tailored–looking suit and a tasteful maroon tie. He looked a little grumpy, maybe hungover.

They went to the same sitting room. Coffee was set out on the glass coffee table, next to Galkin's briefcase, in the same place where Paul had seen it the night before.

"So Polina doesn't come back to Moscow very often." Paul poured them both cups of coffee.

"Bad blood, I think," Galkin said and didn't explain further. He changed the subject. "Your meetings go well, yes?"

"Yes. And yours?"

Galkin ignored that question as if it were impertinent. "Marriage is good?" he asked abruptly. "You don't look at other women, I hope. Or maybe you do—but look, but don't touch."

"Marriage is good." There was a pause during which both men took sips of their coffee. "So I've been doing a little research into Hyperion," Paul said.

"Giperion?"

"I had a bad feeling about something, so I did a little digging." He told Galkin how the company had just been shut down by a Siberian court for polluting Lake Baikal. Paul hadn't seen anything online about this, so he was taking the chance that "Dick Foley" had been telling the truth.

Arkady narrowed his eyes, nodded shrewdly. If he'd had eyestalks, they'd have been waving.

"We don't want to own the biggest polluter in Russia," Paul explained.

"No," Galkin said quickly. "Is bear trap."

Paul outlined for him what Galkin himself had surely already figured out: that by buying a share in that company, they'd be taking on enormous debt. Then Galkin said, standing up, "Is time to take leak."

Paul watched him lumber out of the room. He heard the bathroom door close. *Finally,* Paul thought. *Now I'd better hope the pee takes him a while.*

His heart galumphing, he leaned to his left and picked up the briefcase. It gave off a nice musky, animal smell.

It wasn't locked.

His ears remained alert for Galkin's return.

He turned the brass clasp lock and opened the flap. The bag was stuffed with papers. He saw the inside pocket he'd been instructed to look for. Pulled the tracker out of his right pocket, quickly peeled off the paper on the adhesive, and holding the tracker carefully, stuck his hand into the intended briefcase pocket.

And he listened . . . because if Galkin returned right now and saw him with his hand inside the briefcase, there would be no way out. No way to explain what he was doing. Nothing he could think of quickly, anyway.

Swiftly now, he slipped the tracker into the bottom pocket, sticky side out so it would adhere to the inside of the pocket. He patted the tracker into place.

He closed the flap of the briefcase, turned the clasp, and looked up.

Arkady was standing there watching him.

It had been an unexpectedly quick pee.

Paul's heart rocketed. He held up the briefcase, his face flushed. "What is this, hand-rubbed calfskin?" he croaked with an admiring smile.

Galkin, smiled, seemingly flattered, and looked as if he were about to say something when the doorbell rang. It was nine o'clock exactly. The Russian turned to let Berzin in.

"Good morning," Berzin said.

Paul stood up as Berzin entered the suite. The chief of security eyed him suspiciously. He, too, was wearing a suit. Paul wondered where the two men were going, and if they were going together.

62

Tatyana was just waking up when Paul returned to their suite, her sleep mask pushed up into her nest of tangled hair. "Where were you?" she asked.

"Meeting with your dad," he said. Fifteen minutes after planting it, he was still anxious about the tracker. If it were discovered, he'd be the obvious culprit. Galkin had seen him with the briefcase, but did he suspect anything? And maybe Berzin would search his boss's briefcase. Paul didn't want to think about that possibility.

"When do you get finished with meetings today? Lunchtime again?"

"Probably," he said.

"Mama wants to see you again. Lunch or dinner today. Tomorrow we're leaving."

Paul, however, had something to do this afternoon. He couldn't use the line again about just being a tourist. That wasn't a good enough excuse to get out of lunch or dinner. So he said, "I have to leave the afternoon open for a business lunch and all that. Let me join you two for dinner."

While she was in the shower, he took out the second iPhone from his suitcase, switched it on and opened Signal. *It's done*, he messaged Aaron.

Congratulations, came the reply a minute later. *Better late than never*.

AFTER ANOTHER SERIES OF POINTLESS-SEEMING morning meetings with more potential clients, there was indeed a business lunch at a two-Michelin-starred restaurant called Twins Garden, run by twin brothers. Farm-to-table modern cuisine, dishes that resembled Magritte paintings, and an exhaustive wine list. After lunch, his two colleagues asked Paul to join them on a tour of the Kremlin Armoury, the Imperial Treasury, and the Diamond Fund, which housed the crown jewels, the ivory throne of Ivan the Terrible, and the Kremlin's collection of ten Fabergé eggs.

But he turned them down, claiming he was going to join his wife. A plausible excuse.

In truth, he wanted to find the woman who had made Arkady Galkin rich.

THE CLOSEST METRO STOP WAS Mayakovskaya, named for the famous Russian futurist poet Vladimir Mayakovsky. The entrance was half a block away, just past a KFC. An escalator took him deep underground. He'd read about how deeply into the ground the Moscow Metro system was dug: deep enough for its stations to serve as bomb shelters for the citizens during wartime. But he wasn't prepared for how stunning it was. Chandeliers and marble columns, vaulted ceilings with vibrant mosaics depicting scenes of Soviet life and glorifying the past achievements of the Soviet Union. Soft lighting created a warm glow.

A few other people entered the station when he did, but they didn't seem to be following him, at least as far as he could tell. At a ticket machine, he saw that a single trip cost 57 rubles. He bought a day ticket for 265 rubles, about 3 dollars. The signs were in both Russian and English, fortunately. After a moment's confusion, he saw that he needed to take the brown line, Koltsevaya. After several changes, he exited at the Baumanskaya station. This one was far plainer, though it did have a mural of Vladimir Ilyich Lenin looking heroic.

Paul took the steep escalator up to the street and saw before him a huge, beige wedding cake of a building built in the Stalinist Empire style: the Bauman Moscow State Technical University, from which Arkady Galkin had graduated over fifty years before. The entrance to the building was red stone with heavy columns bedecked with statues of both ancient gods and renowned Soviet scientists. Paul entered and, after a while, found on the first floor the library. In his crude Russian, he said to the first librarian he encountered, a small man with a thick thatch of prematurely gray hair, "I am looking for a yearbook for 1969."

The man replied quickly in Russian with a scowl, seeming to correct him. Then he switched to English. "Are you student? Tourist?"

"My father graduated from Bauman in 1969."

"Oh, very impressive," the librarian said, smiling. "What did he study?"

"Chemical engineering. I was hoping to see his yearbook entry."

"Come with me."

The man led Paul up a set of stairs and through the stacks to the yearbook section. In short order, the librarian located and pulled off a high shelf a book entitled *Scientific and Technical Bulletin of Bauman Moscow State Technical University 1969.* Which was presumably a yearbook. Paul thanked him, took the book over to a table, and began to look through it. The librarian had told him to come find him if he had any questions.

Paul skimmed through the book. How many of the Class of 1969 would still be alive after fifty-six years? he wondered. That would make them seventy-six, seventy-seven years old. Most of them were men, and the average lifespan for a Russian man—Paul had looked this up—was sixty-eight. But the classes were small, he saw. Around two hundred students.

Once he figured out how the book was laid out, he located Arkady Galkin. A small, square black-and-white photo showed a young man with a head of curly hair and an unsmiling face. No question it was Galkin.

Then he went through the faculty pages, looking for Ludmilla Sergeyevna, the surname Tatyana had mentioned, or Ludmilla S. Something.

There were five Ludmillas on the faculty. Paul jotted down their full names on a piece of scrap paper, the five Ludmillas. One was high in the administration, a majestic-looking blonde named Ludmilla Aleksandrovna Khramova. Too beautiful and too senior to be the right one. And besides, Tatyana had given the patronymic "Sergeyevna."

Then there was was Ludmilla Artemevna Sidorova. And Ludmilla Maximovna Mikhailova.

And then Ludmilla Sergeyevna Zaitseva. A picture of a dark-haired young woman with very thick black-framed glasses.

That was his Ludmilla. The right name, the right look.

On one of the computer terminals in the Reference Room, he opened a Russian search engine and entered her name. It popped up with a Moscow address: 322 Kedrova Street in the Chertanovo District. He entered her address and phone number into the iPhone the FBI had given him.

If he was able to find out who she was and what her role was in Arkady Galkin's rise, he would then own information the FBI didn't.

And information was power.

63

On the street outside the institute, where there was decent mobile phone reception, Paul called the number for Ludmilla Zaitseva using the FBI's iPhone. If she wasn't there, he wouldn't bother with the long journey to her apartment. But if she answered . . .

A brusque *"Allo?"*

"Ludmilla Sergeyevna?"

"Da? Kto eto?"

He switched to English, hoping she spoke it, too. "I am a friend of Arkady Galkin's," he said.

A long pause. "Yes?"

"I need to talk with you."

Another long pause. Paul thought she'd hung up. Then: "Who is this?"

"My name is Robert Langfitt."

"Yes?"

"Will you be there in an hour? Something I'd like to speak with you about."

Before she could demur, he hit End.

It was a long Metro ride to the Chertanovo District, on the outskirts of the city. The Metro station there was plain and unadorned, probably built recently. When he emerged from it, he saw that he was in a very bad part of town. No tourists here. An apparently homeless man slept on a park bench. Garbage was strewn across the ground. The asphalt was full of potholes. Paul passed a monument honoring the Soviet space program and quickly found Ludmilla Zaitseva's address, a decrepit-looking high-rise. The main doors to the building were unlocked, and the entryway was littered with vodka bottles and discarded hypodermic needles. In the lobby, he found a row of intercom buttons labeled with surnames; he pressed the one that read, "Zaitseva, 6F."

He waited for the inner door to be buzzed open. And waited. He rang again. Still no answer. Maybe she was out. Maybe she was at work, if she still worked.

A woman entered the lobby from outside and keyed open the inner door. Paul followed her inside.

The elevator bore a sign in Russian that said it was under repair. Apartment 6F was probably on the sixth floor. Paul climbed six flights, passing more scattered hypodermic needles, a spill of food garbage on the third floor—orange peels, melon rinds, chicken bones, coffee grounds—and a discarded and evidently used condom. By the time he got to the sixth floor, he was a little winded. *You need to exercise more,* he chided himself.

He knocked on the door to 6F. There was no bell to ring.

Nothing. He waited a minute, knocked again.

From deep inside, he heard a woman's voice, high-pitched and harsh and scolding. The voice moved closer to the door. "*Shto, shto, shto?*" it said. "What, what, what? Who is it? What do you want?"

The voice continued babbling stridently as the door opened a few inches, and Paul found himself looking at a short, broad-faced, portly woman whose eyes looked peculiar, cloudy and opaque.

"Ludmilla Sergeyevna? I called you."

"Yes, yes. Mr. . . . . Langford."

"Langfitt." Then he made a decision and said, "I got your name from Galina Borisovna." He added her surname for good measure: "Belkina." Galina had indicated that the two women had detested each other, but some personal connection would still be better than none.

The apartment smelled of fried onions, which wasn't unpleasant. But also of something putrid. He looked around. The place was squalid, the dwelling of a pathological pack rat. Piles of magazines and newspapers everywhere, drifts of dust, food-encrusted dishes.

"Oh," the woman chastised him, referring to Galina: "*Kakaya skuchnaya lichnost.*" "What a bore." Then, still in Russian, "What an idiot. She gives you my address? This Galina, she gives you my address?"

"Just your name," Paul said, not wanting to detail how he'd located her. "I'll tell you why I'm here," he said in English. "I just started working for Arkady Galkin, and I have some concerns."

She looked in his general direction, her eyes unfocused. She seemed to be blind. Maybe she didn't understand English. So he repeated the words in simple and, he hoped, correct Russian. Then: "May I come in?" in both English and Russian.

With a deeper scowl, she pulled the door open just enough for him to enter. "You are American?" she said.

"Yes."

"You work for the great man?" Her sarcasm was sharp and obvious.

"Yes." He entered the apartment.

The woman backed into a chair, and Paul sat on the piano bench facing it. The lights were all off in this malodorous apartment, and the room was dark.

"Why? You can't get other jobs in America?"

Paul realized he'd misunderstood Galina's words about this woman. Ludmilla Sergeyevna may have urged Arkady not to marry his first wife, but she was no friend of Arkady's. She also spoke excellent English.

He gave an uncomfortable smile.

"I know this man well," she said. "You see, Arkady was a small, unimpressive man. Not very good looking, but very ambitious. And very very smart. None of the women in his class were interested in him. You think he is now rich and powerful oligarch married to what you call bimbo? Back then, bimbos didn't even look at him . . . until he started to become rich, and then they flocked like, like . . ." She said it in Russian: "Like moths to the light. I warned him that the gold diggers will come. But men are ruled by their . . . *sexual organ*, even smart, ambitious ones like Arkady Galkin. Maybe *especially* that type of man. So he marries this shrew."

"Galina."

"Yes, of course." Her eyes looked just past his.

She was definitely blind, Paul decided. She was also quite elderly looking, like a woman in her nineties. *Russia must age people*, he thought. *Maybe it's the poverty.* He changed tack: "You were one of his professors."

"I taught economics at the institute and also was on Kremlin advisory committee. This when Russia was changing from communism to capitalism. Back then, I just had bad vision. I didn't know I had retinitis pigmentosa and was steadily going blind."

"And he was your student."

"I discovered him. I was a talent scout. I mentioned him at my weekly committee meeting in the Kremlin. They investigated him, liked his story. . . . He was agreeable. Back then, you know, we were all on one side. We all knew that someone young and energetic and ambitious could be immensely valuable."

"Valuable how?"

"We needed some of our biggest state-owned companies to go private, and so we needed smart capitalist types. Galkin was a student by day, a black market hustler by night. He'd sell jeans and then cars. Made a lot of money. That attracted our attention. He was a brilliant young man."

"I don't understand. You made him rich?"

"I did what I thought was best for everyone."

"How? What did you do for him?"

"No, no. We *let him* make his fortune. Let him take over distressed assets. Cut through the miles of red tape. Gave him the chance to get rich. He was smart enough to amass his own fortune. As long as the Russian bureaucracy stayed out of his way."

"So now . . ." Paul faltered. "Not sure I get this. Is he independent? Or is he controlled by the Kremlin?"

"All these oligarchs, they're marionettes. Marionettes with their own bank accounts."

"And the Kremlin's pulling the strings." Paul thought of what Galkin had said at dinner at the Aragvi: *A puppet thinks he is free if he loves his strings.*

"As for who pulling strings," Ludmilla continued, "that's where things get complicated."

Paul paused. "Does that mean you're still connected to the Kremlin?"

She shrugged. "Look at me. You think I am still part of government now?"

He nodded that he got it, didn't reply.

"We were all squeezed out years ago. And I? I am thrown away like so much garbage. Look how I live."

"But *who* threw you away?"

She shrugged again.

Paul shook his head. "Galkin must know you're in desperate straits, but he doesn't support you?"

Her eyes flashed. "He wants nothing to do with me."

"Why not?"

Another shrug. "Maybe he wants everybody to think he became a rich man because of his genius. He doesn't want anybody to know he got help."

"Or that he's two-faced."

"*Two*-faced? Count again!"

"Huh?"

"For a thousand years Russia has had an imperial court in one form or another. And everyone interested in power in this court develops at least *three* faces." She held up one finger after another as she said, "The face you turn to the empress. The face you show your peers. And the face that confronts you in the mirror."

"Ah," he nodded.

Wagging a crooked forefinger, Ludmilla said quietly, "The moment you think you have it all figured out is when you learn how dead wrong you are."

Paul nodded, and said, "Russia is a riddle wrapped in a mystery, or whatever the Churchill quote is." One of his Russian teachers at Reed liked to quote that.

She shook her head. "No riddle. You Americans, you believe in brute force. We believe in innuendo and disinformation and a slick of poison on the doorknob. And now you have a new prime minister in England named Boris!"

Her phone rang. It was an old-fashioned black rotary dial phone like you'd see in the United States in the last century. She reached for it and after just a second or two of fumbling was able to grasp the receiver in her hand.

"*Allo!*" She listened. Spoke in rapid Russian, then hung up.

"You were followed here?" she said with alarm.

Paul's stomach dropped. "I don't know. I can't be certain, but I didn't think so. Why do you—?"

"The FSB is coming. Not regular police. I have friend in FSB."

"What do you mean they're coming? For what? Meeting you isn't breaking any law."

"You are in Russia, my friend. Knowing the law won't help you. It's no defense. If they wish to arrest you, they will. They will make up a pretext."

"Why FSB?"

"I have spoken critically of government, so they put watch on me. They listen to my telephone. Is easy to do now. Is automated. Someone calls me, a light goes on, maybe a bell rings somewhere. I don't know how. They want to know who I am meeting with. American, they know this. Now, *go. Now.*"

"How close are they?

"Please! *Move!*"

64

He clambered down the inner stairwell of Ludmilla's building, down floor after floor, his footsteps echoing in the space. On the ground floor, he looked around quickly for a rear exit, but didn't find one. There was no one in front of the building, so he chanced it and ran out that way.

He tried to call to mind the map of the Chertanovo District as he ran back the way he came. He saw the statue of the cosmonauts in the small park, saw the Metro entrance, and decided not to go that way. *Don't go the way you came*, he directed himself. *If the FSB is coming for you, don't make it easy for them.*

They've probably come to question me, he thought. To find out who was meeting with Ludmilla Zaitseva. But why? Being publicly critical of the Kremlin would get you arrested in Russia these days, Paul knew. That was a fact. So meeting with someone like her—was that enough to get him arrested?

He didn't want to find out. But if he were detained, couldn't he simply call Arkady Galkin? Galkin had to be connected to the top. He could surely make one call and have the whole thing go away.

Still, Paul didn't want to be taken into custody and questioned. He had to elude the FSB, in a city where he was a novice, in a country where they had their own rules. Heart thudding, he walked past the Metro entrance and crossed busy Chertanov Street. He knew he looked like an American, and there weren't a lot of them around this remote part of town.

Down Kedrova Street, then a right onto Trade Union Street, crossing the street and striding down the median separating opposing lanes of traffic. He glanced at his watch.

There wasn't time to call an Uber, so he went to the side of the road and waved his arm. A compact SUV, a black Chevy Niva, pulled over, its tires squealing. A gypsy cab. A rip-off, he knew, but he didn't have time to do anything else.

Heaving a sigh, Paul sank down in the car's backseat.

The driver, who wore a flat, gray woolen cap, said, "*Kuda?*" "Where are you going?"

65

No one from the FSB was waiting for him back at the hotel, as far as he could determine. Somehow he felt safer amid the luxurious trappings of the finest hotel in Moscow, as if the locals wouldn't dare intervene here. Then again, the FSB didn't know his name. They knew only the name "Robert Langfitt." That was all the old lady knew, too.

Unless his face had been caught by a CCTV camera. Paul hadn't noticed any in or on Ludmilla's apartment building. But if he'd been identified . . . he didn't want to think about that. Because then Galkin would know he'd been going around Moscow looking into his past, that he'd met with the woman who'd recruited Galkin to work for the Kremlin. And maybe then he wouldn't be so forgiving.

Paul had courted danger. The question was, would he face the consequences?

He went directly to their suite, didn't find Tatyana there. On his iPhone was a text from her telling him to meet her at eight at a restaurant on Novinskiy Boulevard called Selfie.

On the other iPhone was a Signal message from Addison that simply read, *Congrats!*

For what? Paul wondered.

Another Signal message, this one from Aaron, saying, *Success, thank you.*

The tracker he'd put inside Galkin's briefcase. For a moment, he'd actually forgotten he'd done it.

A few hours later, he left for dinner, taking Galkin's Bentley to the restaurant. Lowercase English letters on the outside of a modern building spelled out "selfie." Inside, the décor was very hip, with a sleek open kitchen. He found Tatyana and her mother at a desirable-looking table, rapt in conversation.

THEY STAYED AT THE RESTAURANT until past midnight. After many vodka toasts, mother and daughter were fairly blitzed. They said a protracted goodbye—Tatyana and Paul were leaving Moscow in the morning—and Paul finally managed to trundle Tatyana into the waiting Bentley and back to the hotel.

He took her arm as she walked unsteadily into the empty lobby.

Then he saw that the lobby wasn't quite empty. Two men in ill-fitting suits and one in a green uniform were standing before the reception desk, questioning the night clerk.

Maybe this was routine . . . but maybe it wasn't.

Were they FSB, and were they looking for an American businessman named Langfitt? They wouldn't find him here. But what if they had a photo of "Langfitt's" face, from a camera Paul hadn't spotted? When he walked by, they'd see him, they'd detain him . . .

He switched places with Tatyana so she would be on the side nearer the reception desk and he wouldn't be as visible, and together they passed by reception and reached the elevators, Tatyana tottering, her heels clearly uncomfortable after a long day.

Before they could push a button, though, Paul heard a loud male voice calling out in Russian. It was Arkady, approaching the elevator, and he seemed a little unsteady himself. Like father, like daughter. Gripping his briefcase in one hand, Galkin gave his daughter a half hug with the other and said something in Russian about *doch'*, which Paul knew meant "daughter." He reeked of cigars and booze. Then Galkin turned to Paul. "How was your last day in Moscow?"

"Very nice, thanks."

"Your meetings go well?"

"Quite well, thanks."

"What you do after meetings? While my daughter and my ex-wife are spending my money?"

Why was he asking? "Mostly walked around aimlessly."

"Yes?"

"Beautiful city."

A long pause, and Galkin's eyebrows furrowed, his eyes glittering. "Why you go to Bauman?"

Paul's stomach sank. *He must have had me followed*, he realized.

Laughing, Tatyana said in disbelief, "You went to the Bauman Institute?"

"I did," Paul said to her. "I knew your father went to school there, and I knew it was important to him, so I read about it. Saw an interesting mention of its architecture." Turning to Galkin, he said, "Partly nineteenth century, partly Soviet, but it's harmonious. It works." Paul the architecture critic. How much did Galkin know about what his son-in-law had researched at his alma mater?

Had he been followed to Ludmilla's apartment, too? He would have no way to explain that.

Galkin gave Paul a hard look. "Architecture of Bauman not interesting" was all he said.

66

The days after Paul's return from Moscow were filled with anxiety. He found himself waiting for the hammer to come down, for Moscow to catch up with him. Had Ludmilla given the police his phony name, pointed out his connection to Galkin? Would Galkin learn that Paul had been going around Moscow looking into his past?

He found it hard to concentrate on work. Tatyana seemed energized after seeing her mother; she seemed to float. Paul, for his part, was glum and fretful. She asked why he seemed so ill at ease. He told her there was a lot of pressure at work.

The third time he met with Special Agent Mark Addison was in a Starbucks at the corner of Astor Place and Lafayette Street—the foulest Starbucks Paul had ever been in. Several vagrants were sleeping at tables; a disordered man shouted at a mirror near the bathrooms; not even the smell of coffee could mask the low-lying ambience of urine and body odor.

When they were settled at a table, each man with a coffee, Paul recounted for Addison the tension-filled days in Moscow, what he was able to accomplish, and then said acerbically, "Was it worth it?"

"Was *what* worth it?"

"Putting the tracker in Galkin's briefcase. I nearly got caught."

"But you *didn't* get caught, did you?"

"Hard to know for sure. I don't know exactly what Galkin saw, what he thought."

"Well, you didn't. Because it worked."

"How so?"

"We were able to track Galkin to a meeting in Novo-Ogaryovo, on the outskirts of Moscow."

Paul shrugged. He didn't know what the place was or its significance.

"Do you know what Novo-Ogaryovo is?" Addison said. "That's the Russian president's dacha. Heard of him? That's his official residence. We would not have known this if not for you. So what you did was extremely important, Paul. We can confirm now, thanks to you, that Galkin is working with the Kremlin. That's huge."

Working with the Kremlin, Paul thought. Jesus. What had he gotten into? "And what happens when Galkin finds the tracker? Because eventually he will. Or Berzin? Or someone working for Berzin, doing a security sweep?"

Addison appeared unworried. "Galkin has enemies. Plenty of enemies. Someone did it. Not you. Probably someone in Moscow, they'll suspect."

"He saw me holding the briefcase."

"You're hardly at the top of the list of suspects."

"I don't find that very reassuring."

Addison tilted his head to one side. "My colleague Aaron tells me you got the name of the talent spotter who originally connected Galkin to the Kremlin. You have a name—Ludmilla?"

Paul just nodded.

"No last name?"

Paul hesitated. "I may be able to get that for you."

Addison looked puzzled.

Paul changed the subject. "One more thing. I had a strange encounter in Moscow. With a guy who claimed to be a friend of a friend of mine. Turns out he wasn't." He told Addison about his drink at the hotel bar with "Dick Foley." Then he took out his iPhone and showed Addison a photo he'd covertly snapped of "Foley" at the bar.

The FBI man peered at Paul's phone, squinted at the high-res photo. "Oh, jeez," he said after a moment, his voice taut. "That's Igor."

Oh, shit. "Igor . . . ?"

"Igor Krupin. SVR. Known to us. Very smooth."

"SVR is . . . ?"

"Russian foreign intelligence. Used to be KGB, back in the day."

"This guy spoke perfect English, with a British accent."

"Krupin's fluent in like six languages. What was his pitch?"

"He wanted to know what I thought about Arkady Galkin. Also, what kind of business Galkin was doing in Moscow."

"How much did you tell him?"

"Very little. So what the hell did the SVR want with me?"

"Maybe they wanted to find out if you have some sort of agenda. How loyal you are to Galkin. What did you say about your boss?"

"I don't remember. Something vague. Nothing critical, that's for sure."

Addison pulled out a small black nylon sack. "My bag of toys," he said. The bag contained only one toy, though. "This," Addison said, after glancing around the coffee shop, "is called a KeyGrabber." It was a black cube half an inch long, clearly a piece of computer electronics. "It's all you need. That and a little luck."

IT TOOK ADDISON ABOUT FIFTEEN minutes to give Paul instructions on using the KeyGrabber, but only because he repeated himself three times. Then he handed him a digital RFID key card. It was blank. "When you enter the AGF office to do your work for us, you obviously don't want to use your own key card showing your name and entry and exit time."

"Whose is this?" Paul said, turning the RFID card in his hand.

"A member of the custodial staff who's cleared to be in the office late at night and early in the morning."

"And what am I looking for?" Paul asked.

"Formation documents. The documents used to set up the firm. Information that's buried in the old files. Where the money came from that set Galkin up in business. Who the original investors were."

"But how could you not have information on AGF's investors? You're the FBI, man! You know everything."

"Very funny," Addison said, not amused. "There's plenty we don't know. That's why we need you. Galkin is running a private limited partnership, an LLC. So the underlying documents are not on file with state or federal authorities. To us, it's a black box."

Paul slipped the KeyGrabber and the RFID card into the small black canvas bag and then put the bag into his briefcase. The next day, he brought it into work. The FBI project, he figured, would take no more than three days. He would be careful and methodical. He didn't like having to count on luck.

He waited until things at work were slow, when people were unlikely to drop into his office and Margo was on break. Then he disconnected his keyboard from the USB port at the back and plugged the little black device, the KeyGrabber, into the port and reconnected the keyboard's black cable into it. The KeyGrabber would copy every single keystroke made on his computer. "Keyloggers have been around for years," Addison had told him, "and most IT professionals recognize them easily. This one, though, is nearly invisible. Undetectable. No one's going to notice it."

The IT department in Galkin's firm consisted of one employee, Volodymyr, who was Ukrainian. Volodymyr was in his twenties and said to be a whiz. He was small and scrawny and somehow always had a few days of stubble on his jaw. On Slack, Paul messaged Volodymyr—he went by the nickname "Vova"—and told him he was having trouble with his computer.

Not more than four minutes later, Vova knocked on Paul's open door. Clearly he was having a slow day. "How can I help you, sir?" he said. His American English accent was nearly perfect. His "sir" seemed to be ironic.

"This is weird," Paul said, "but I'm having speed issues with my web browser. It sort of randomly won't load our website. Or it's really slow to load. Like that."

"Can you show me?"

"Will you excuse me, Vova? I've got to use the restroom. Why don't you reboot it and try it yourself?"

"Sure," Vova said as Paul left his office. He wanted Vova to reboot his computer and then enter his own password.

Paul returned some five minutes later.

"Sorry to tell you, I wasn't able to reproduce the issue," said Vova. "You said the company website won't load?"

"Right."

"Loaded just fine, sir."

"Hmm, weird. I'll try and get a video of it happening next time. Thanks for trying. And sorry to bother you."

"No worries," said Vova.

The next step was a little complicated, because Paul didn't really have any privacy at home, in Tatyana's small apartment, and their new place was still being renovated. She would ask what he was doing. More

THE OLIGARCH'S DAUGHTER 255

accurately, she would want him to stop work for the day, have a drink.

accurately, she would want him to stop work for the day, have a drink. So after work, he stopped at a Blue Bottle, ordered a decaf latte, and grabbed a table. He inserted the KeyGrabber, which he'd unplugged from his computer, into a USB drive on his personal laptop.

The KeyGrabber had recorded every keystroke Vova had made, including his login credentials and password. As the firm's IT specialist, Vova probably had permission to go anywhere in the company's system.

Now Paul had it, too.

He had everything he needed to penetrate the firm's network.

Everything except the courage.

Addison had outlined for him how he should do it. Because there were problems. Challenges to meet. Addison suggested that Paul do it at night, after hours, after everyone had gone home. He should badge in using the RFID key card the FBI had supplied, using the janitor's credentials. Of course, some employees worked late, till ten or eleven at night. Which meant he might have to stay as late as midnight or later— and concoct some story for Tatyana as to why he would be coming home so late. She might suspect him of seeing someone, having an affair. And if she suspected that, she might tell her father, in casual conversation— they talked a lot. So his alibi would have to be convincing.

But that was the least of his problems.

There was also the issue of the firm's security cameras. There were CCTV cameras at the entrance and the fire exits. If anyone bothered to look, Paul would be seen leaving the office at, whatever, one or two in the morning. That would raise questions.

From his burner phone, he texted Addison and asked for another meeting.

THREE DAYS LATER, HE TOLD Tatyana he had to work late that night. "I've been putting it off for weeks," he said, "but I have to make a presentation at the morning meeting tomorrow."

That was almost true. He did have a presentation to make, but he'd already finished work on it.

"How late will you be?"

"Midnight or after, I bet."

"You're kidding!" she said with a pout. "I'll be asleep!"

"I know, *dushen'kaya*. I'll be quiet."

"Does my father know how hard you work?"

IN THE MORNING MEETING, PAUL took notice of what his colleagues were wearing. Mostly button-down shirts and quilted navy vests and khakis, with various types of sneakers, leather or not.

He left work around five thirty, earlier than usual, telling Margo he had some errands to run. He made it to the Orvis store on Fifth Avenue just in time. The Adidas flagship store, a few blocks away on Fifth, was open later. At J.Crew, after buying a pair of chinos, he changed clothes in the dressing room.

To kill time, he browsed at the Barnes and Noble and then stopped at a pizza place for a slice, but he didn't have an appetite. He was too tense. The time dragged by. He picked up a Yankees cap at a tourist shop on Sixth Avenue, then walked around aimlessly, hoping he wouldn't run into anyone he knew. This was Manhattan, where you could go for weeks without bumping into anyone, but then run into an old friend from high school when you least wanted to.

Finally, at a few minutes before nine, he returned to the office. His colleagues worked late, many of them, but usually by eight, eight thirty, the office was nearly deserted.

Wearing his brand-new quilted Orvis vest and his brand-new Stan Smiths and his brand-new Yankees cap, he entered, looking down at his feet, his face turned away from the security camera. His outfit could have belonged to anyone in the firm. He was wearing a Covid face mask, too, so there was very little face to identify. He waved the RFID card Addison had given him at the reader.

As far as the system knew, a custodian had just badged in. But if anyone bothered to look at the video feed, they wouldn't see a face.

67

The office was empty. The lights were on; they always stayed on.

But Ivan Matlovsky was still at work, at a hot desk, used by different people, on the corridor outside Paul's office.

Paul didn't want any witnesses, so he went into his office and, every once in a while, glanced through the glass wall to see if Matlovsky was still there. Paul couldn't log onto his own computer. As far as the office security system knew, he wasn't there.

At eleven thirty, Matlovsky finally left. Paul remained in his office a few minutes longer, just to make sure Matlovsky hadn't simply gone to the men's room. After fifteen minutes, no Matlovsky.

Paul went to the break room to brew himself a cup of coffee. Carrying the cappuccino, blowing on it to cool it off some, he wandered around the floor. On the far side, he found Jake Larsen's tiny office, thinking he might use Larsen's work station, but of course the computer had been removed.

Nearby was Steve Gartner's desk. No one was in sight. This looked perfect. He looked at his iPhone. Ten minutes after midnight.

He walked over to Gartner's desk and sat down. Looked around, listened. He saw no one, heard nothing. He was as sure as he could be that the office was empty.

He took out the slip of paper on which he'd written Volodymyr's login and password. The login was simply his Gmail address. The password was a long, unmemorizable string of numbers and letters, which somehow the IT guy had memorized.

The first few attempts, he mistyped some characters and got an error message. He typed the password in again more carefully this time. He was in.

He'd been in the online files a few times before, mostly to get old research on companies he was considering investing in. But now, with Vova's universal admin permissions, he saw the whole filing system, color coded, areas of the system he had no access to as Paul Brightman.

The top-level folders had labels like "Legal," "Finance," "Operations," "Human Resources," and "Investments." Within each folder, he saw, were subfolders—Financial Statements, Tax Documents, Expense Reports, and so on. He poked around for ten or fifteen minutes, looking for the files he wanted.

They were in the Legal folder. Within that, along with Litigation, Regulatory Compliance, and Contracts, was the subfolder he was interested in: Formation Documents.

These were the documents used to set up the firm. That was where he'd find what Addison wanted.

The Formation Documents folder had special-access privileges. Only Galkin, Frost, the CFO, and the general counsel could look at these.

And Vova.

Within this folder was a subfolder: Subscription Agreements. Paul knew this was where AGF kept files on the investors who'd put money in the fund.

This was where the gold ore was.

He glanced at the time on the computer screen.

1:05.

There were originally five investors, he saw at once.

Five very rich people, that meant, had put money into Galkin's firm. Maybe they were oligarchs.

Of course, just because he had the folders on the five possible oligarchs didn't mean he had their names. They would use shell companies. That was what oligarchs did. Not just oligarchs, but plenty of rich investors cloaked their identities in shell companies.

But Paul would get what he could. He would look—

Just then, he became aware of a clatter and mumbled voices and looked around with alarm.

It was a custodian with a vacuum cleaner strapped to his back, a middle-aged, slump-shouldered man with dusky skin.

"Hello," Paul said.

"*Boa noite, senhor,*" the cleaner said.

He was the only cleaner in the office now, he was quite sure, but the custodian had likely seen employees working late before. It would not be good if someone saw that Paul was working at someone else's computer. But the cleaner probably had no idea whose desk was whose.

This would not be one of his problems, he assured himself.

He went back to Gartner's computer screen.

SEVENTEEN YEARS AGO, FIVE INVESTORS had put money into Galkin's fund.

Five investors.

Paul looked in each folder, one by one. Looking for the names of the investors.

Instead, he found the names of shell companies and the banks they'd used.

Ocean Palm Holdings Ltd., Pacific Private Bank of Vanuatu
Windward Northern LLC, Partners Bank of St. Lucia
Duchy Investments Ltd., DBS Bank, Guernsey

All sketchy-sounding banks in sketchy jurisdictions. In other words, he knew nothing about where the money came from.

He opened his laptop, opened a new Word document, and typed in the names of the shell companies and their sketchy banks.

He totaled up the money each mysterious shell company had deposited into Arkady Galkin Finance LLC. It added up to $2.3 billion.

Then he had a brainstorm.

Within the Legal folder, he found another folder titled KYC, for "Know Your Client." Or maybe it was "Know Your Customer." A mandatory process ordered by the U.S. government shortly after the attacks of 9/11, KYC forced banks and financial institutions to verify that a client was really who he said he was. As Addison had pointed out, the government didn't get to see the KYC documents. Not with a private equity firm. They were kept private.

Yes. There they were. For each depositor, there was a KYC document. A "Customer Information Form."

He opened the first one, for Duchy Investments Ltd., and there was the information:

Full Name: Natasha I. Obolensky
Date of Birth: September 6, 1977
Nationality: Irish

On and on it went. All of Natasha Obolensky's personal information, a copy of her Irish passport, etc. Natasha's signature. Whoever she was. And then one curious line:

Beneficial Ownership: Phantom.

So here was one of the investors: an Irish citizen with a Russian name. Bizarre. The whole thing sounded fake. A woman named Natasha Obolensky who had wired in $460 million.

Then he looked at the next KYC document, for Kent Ridge Ventures Ltd., sent in from Hermes Bank of Singapore.

Full Name: Natasha Obolensky
Date of Birth: September 6, 1977
Nationality: Irish

Four hundred seventy-five million dollars.

Beneficial Owner: Phantom.

Seventeen years ago, Natasha Obolensky had deposited $2.3 billion in five separate tranches over the course of five days.

Who the hell was Natasha Obolensky and where did she get $2.3 billion? And who or what was Phantom?

PAUL COPIED THE FIVE KYC documents to a thumb drive. He blinked a few times. His eyes were dry and irritated. He pocketed the thumb drive, then signed Vova out from Steve Gartner's computer, slipped his laptop into its carrying case, and got up.

It was 2:26 in the morning.

The nearest security camera, he was fairly sure, was at the entrance/

exit. He donned his face mask and his Yankees cap. When he got to the exit door, he badged out using the prox card the FBI had given him, while looking down at the floor.

As far as the office security system was concerned, Paul Brightman had left the building at 5:30 p.m. At a few minutes after 8 p.m., someone on the custodial staff had badged in, leaving at 2:30 a.m.

When he left the office, he pulled down his mask so he could breathe normally. On his way out of the building's lobby, he saw someone entering from the street.

It was Volodymyr, his hair sticking up wildly, looking like he'd just gotten out of bed.

Paul pulled his mask up. Had Vova seen him or not?

He couldn't be sure.

PAUL GOT HOME AT THREE in the morning.

Tatyana gave a sort of grunt-moan when he climbed into bed, then rolled over to give him room.

He had maybe four hours before he had to get ready for work, but he was unable to sleep. He flip-flopped in the bed, his mind playing and replaying the image of Vova entering the building.

Did he see me?

Vova had obviously been awakened by some kind of software alert. How much did that alert tell him?

HIS PHONE ALARM GOT HIM up at seven. His eyelids felt like they were glued together. His head pounded. He rose from bed carefully, trying not to jar his thudding head.

He made coffee, which unfortunately involved grinding the beans—this was his own fault; he liked his coffee fresh—which woke Tatyana. She appeared beside him, kissed his cheek. "Did you get your presentation done?" she asked sweetly.

"I did. Sorry to wake you." He held the glass carafe under the tap and filled it halfway, then slid it into the complicated coffeemaker.

"That's okay. I want to catch some morning light. I talked to my papa last night."

"Yeah?" He felt a jolt.

"Our apartment should be ready in a week or so. He says his crew is working full speed."

"That's great. It's . . . Does he know we don't want the décor to look like his town house? I mean, we agree, don't we?"

She laughed, a sound high and lilting. "We've talked about it a million times. He knows we have a different aesthetic."

He looked around at her apartment. "Do we have one? An aesthetic, I mean."

"I like things simple and basic, and I think you do, too."

"No gold fixtures."

"Ha ha ha, very funny."

"Have you seen it yet?"

"No," she said, vaguely exasperated. "I asked, but he won't let me. He wants it to be a surprise."

PAUL ARRIVED AT THE OFFICE shortly before eight. He'd showered and tried to make himself look presentable, but the lack of sleep showed on his face, especially under his eyes. Margo wasn't there yet; she normally came in at eight thirty.

The morning meeting took place in a glass-walled conference room with a long, coffin-shaped conference table made of dark hardwood. All the firm's principals were in attendance, the twelve most important people in the company. When Paul got there, people were talking about the New York Giants game that weekend and some high-profile, over-the-top wedding in the Hamptons that a few of them were invited to. As soon as Eugene Frost arrived in the room and sat down at the head of the table, all conversation stopped. Mr. Frost was a buzzkill and ran a tight ship. Not like the morning meetings at Aquinnah, which were looser and leavened with schmoozing and joking.

Almost everybody was drinking coffee, and no one touched the breakfast pastries arrayed on the sideboard. Either they'd already had breakfast or they were watching their glycemic profile. Dunlap's disease and all that.

Mr. Frost began the meeting right on time by clearing his throat.

"I have an important announcement," he said somberly. "Our network was accessed last night in the 'wee hours.'" He said "wee hours" with audible quotation marks. "We are currently conducting an investigation. We know a few things right now. We know that the attack was not done remotely. It was done locally. From within our offices."

People were glancing around, murmuring. "Wow. Was anything taken?" someone said.

Paul tried not to show his terror.

"Can you tell who signed on?" asked Ivan Matlovsky.

"We know which computer was used. Our investigation is proceeding quickly, and we will find the intruder. If any of you knows anything, please consider it your urgent responsibility to notify me at once." He paused. "And now to work."

Then each principal gave an update on his area. There was some high-level stuff on the market in general. The meeting was over in an hour and a half.

As it came to a close, Mr. Frost turned to Paul. "May I speak to you a moment?"

Paul's stomach went taut. "Of course." He drew closer to Mr. Frost, smiled expectantly, concealing his panic.

"An interesting deal possibility has come in. From a friend of mine I saw at a Hamptons party yesterday. I'll forward you the PowerPoint deck on them. I'd like you to take a look at it. It's an online gambling company called FanStars."

"Sure," Paul said. Mr. Frost peeled away, walking quickly down the corridor.

WHEN PAUL RETURNED TO HIS office, his colleague Ethan Carswell knocked on his door, entered, and then closed the door behind him. He'd been at the meeting moments earlier.

"I overheard Frost mention FanStars," he said.

"Yeah, he wants me to look into it. You know anything about them?"

Ethan glanced sideways, then at Paul. "I do. Because actually *we* looked into FanStars, some years back."

"And?"

"We, you know . . . we passed on it."

"When was this?" asked Paul.

"I don't know, five or six years ago."

"Before online gambling was legal."

"In the U.S. anyway. Good ol' puritan America. We did an exhaustive study of the gambling space. Looked really hard at a couple of deals."

"But you passed on them?"

"Yeah."

"Any particular reason why?"

He shrugged. "Legal exposure, probably. But I wasn't point on the deal."

"Thanks."

Paul shook his head. Maybe it wasn't so weird that Frost wanted to go back to this online gambling site after so many changes in the marketplace.

But Paul was obviously far more concerned about Frost's announcement at the meeting, how they were investigating the network break-in. If they discovered it was him, he was fucked.

He took out his burner phone and texted Addison.

68

Paul was living in a state of anxiety, afraid that at any moment Mr. Frost or Berzin was going to take him aside and interrogate him. So he decided he was going to do some serious due diligence on FanStars. Maybe he'd turn up something like he did on Cavalier, when he was at Aquinnah. Busy work like that would take his mind off the constant nervousness.

The first thing he did was read the twenty-eight-page PowerPoint deck on the company that Frost had shared with him, taking notes in a new document. The research was mostly fluff. It talked about the technology FanStars used, who its potential customers were, why AGF was going after this particular firm. That sort of thing. Then he turned to Bloomberg to see who the investors in FanStars were. It was a private company, so there wasn't much information available. He combed through the other databases on his desktop—FactSet, Capital IQ, TechCrunch— gathering whatever miscellaneous information he could. Paul had researched hundreds if not thousands of companies and had a pretty good idea what he was looking for: the people who ran the firm. It's always the people at a company who cause the problems. As the saying goes, you're betting on the jockeys, not the horses. So he collected the names on the management team and then started digging into them— looking at their LinkedIn profiles, what sports they'd played in college, if any. He looked at Dun and Bradstreet to see whether these people were creditworthy or not, whether they paid their taxes, what the approximate size of FanStars was.

FanStars was legally based in Cyprus. This didn't surprise him. Gambling companies liked to be based in countries like Malta or Cyprus, where there weren't too many rules and where nobody asked questions.

Everything seemed to check out okay—no big surprises, no reason to stay away from making a deal with FanStars—until he logged into one of the websites where employees (and ex-employees) anonymously reviewed their own companies. He looked at FanStars's employee reviews. Most of the reviews said benign, bland things like "Great company" or "Good company to work for and flexible benefits" or "Great working environment." Then, one caught his attention, an anonymous post from seven years ago:

"OK company but . . . my girlfriend temped there, and they offered her a full-time job, but she heard rumors. Too many stories about too much weirdness going around."

Rumors . . . weirdness going around . . .

That could mean anything. Or nothing.

He decided to dig some more. He wanted to be thorough with his due diligence. Do another Cavalier. See what he could find. That meant he needed to look at whatever was in the files from five or six years ago, when AGF last looked at the company. See why they ultimately decided against doing a deal with FanStars.

Paul emerged from his office and said to his admin, Margo, "I need to find some files from five or six or seven years ago. Where should I look?"

"Five years ago or more? That stuff's stored offsite," she said. "The SEC makes us keep them going back seven years."

"What's offsite?"

"Upstate."

"How far upstate?"

"I think it's in Ulster County. It's a place—hold on." She tapped some keys. "It's called Hudson DataVault. Underground storage, in some kind of old decommissioned mine."

"Got it. Thanks."

ALL MORNING, HE EXPECTED TO be called in for questioning about the network "attack," but no message came in, by phone or Slack or any other way. At lunchtime, he said to Margo, "I should be back in an hour. Meeting a friend for lunch."

He walked to Fifty-Ninth Street and took the downtown C Train to the Chambers Street station. The coffee shop was a few blocks away, on Reade Street in Tribeca.

Addison was sitting at a two-top at the back of the shop. "You look like shit. Coffee?"

Paul shook his head. "Too nervous." He looked around, slipped the flash drive out of his pocket, and handed it to Addison.

"Great work," Addison said.

"I may have been caught."

"*May* have been?"

Paul explained.

Addison nodded calmly. "The intrusion detection system was probably triggered by an unusual combination of suspicious actions. Like logging into the system at a weird hour, plus accessing sensitive files and exfiltrating the data."

"Exfiltrating . . . ?"

"Saving it to a flash drive might do it."

"Hold on," Paul cut in furiously. "If saving to a flash drive would trigger the intrusion detection system, why the hell did you tell me to *do exactly that?*"

"I didn't have good information," Addison said, and apologized.

"Great. So now they know it's me."

"If they knew it was you, you wouldn't be here. Okay? No, they don't necessarily have any idea it was you. The alarm would tell them which machine the activity occurred on."

"That's all?"

"Further investigation will make it clear which account was logged into the system at that time. When the IT guy realizes that it's his own account, he's going to go into full panic mode."

"Which will lead to me."

"It'll lead to whoever badged in."

"Not me." *Some custodial worker,* Paul thought. Whose name he didn't know. But what would happen to *that* guy?

"You're not going to be identified on the CCTV. Did you disguise yourself?"

Paul nodded.

"Nothing links back to you unless the camera caught your face."

"Which I'm sure it didn't."

"So no need to worry. Don't borrow trouble, Paul." Addison changed the subject. "What did you find in the Formation Documents?"

Paul explained about the billions of dollars wired in by one improbably wealthy Irish citizen, Natasha Obolensky.

Addison nodded. "We know the name."

"You do?"

"She was a front for Moscow."

"Jesus. So Arkady Galkin is a money manager for the Kremlin," Paul said, as much to himself as to Addison.

"Exactly."

"So what is Phantom?"

Addison startled. "Where did you come across that name?"

"It's in the KYC forms—the 'Know Your Customer' documents. Beneficial owner in every case was something or someone called Phantom."

"That was in there?"

Paul nodded. "What is it?"

"That's what I need you to find out. Anything you can. Anything in Galkin's files."

Paul shook his head. "I think I'm done here."

"Almost. Not quite."

"Don't I have a choice? Are you going to push me so hard that they finally catch me?"

"You need to take another deep dive into Galkin's files. You know, do your due diligence. Find out what you can about Phantom."

"Shit."

Addison tented his fingers and leaned back slyly. "So I hear you have a name. 'Ludmilla.' A fine old-fashioned name."

Paul just nodded, waited. Addison was studying his face.

"There were five Ludmillas on the faculty of the Bauman Institute when Galkin was a student there," Addison said.

Now Paul smiled. Some junior FBI research associate had done grunt work.

"What will it take for you to give us her complete name, or as much of it as you have? I think we've been pretty transparent with you and very reasonable."

"And I think you know what I want."

Flatly, Addison said, "You want your wife shielded from our efforts."

Paul nodded again.

"She's quite central to our case, that's the problem, Paul."

"That's *your* problem. You already agreed to it. I want it in writing."

A long moment passed. Paul listened to traffic noise from the street. Finally, Addison said, "Would a handshake do? We're both men of honor."

Paul looked at him hard. "What if something happens to you?"

"I'm a survivor of a lot of knife fights, Paul."

69

Up till now, he had almost bought into the myth of Arkady Galkin, the self-made man who'd built his fortune over the years steadily, maybe ruthlessly, but on his own.

Until Moscow. And what Ludmilla, the nearly blind woman, had told him. And what he'd found in the files.

Was that why Jake Larsen had been killed, for asking too many questions about a Russian operation? It was no secret that the Russian intelligence services resorted to deadly means to deal with their enemies.

And was he next?

Would what had happened in Moscow catch up with him?

He rented a Chevy Malibu at Hertz. As he got on 495 West at Tenth Avenue and then, a few minutes later, I-87 North, he found himself thinking obsessively about his father-in-law and the danger he had stepped into, about Frost and Berzin. And Mark Addison and the FBI. And Tatyana. Addison had promised that the FBI would provide protection for Paul, but he hadn't been specific enough to settle Paul's qualms.

Would it be enough? And would they protect his wife, too?

The view as he drove got increasingly picturesque. It was jarring, the beautiful scenery juxtaposed against the paranoia he was feeling, the sour plumes of acid it jetted into his stomach. By the time he reached Ulster County, he was driving across farmland, beside pastures and herds of cows and grain silos and stacks of hay. It made him think about his childhood, the time he spent with his father in the woods outside Bellingham. In some ways, his New York City life had been an unsettling change for him. He'd grown up identifying trees and hiking through forests, spending much of his time outdoors. But he'd given all that up to move to Manhattan and get a job on Wall Street. It had been a trade-off, and he wondered if he was really happy as an urban guy. Tatyana, certainly, wouldn't want to leave the city. He was reminded of a TV show, *Schitt's Creek*, where a once-wealthy family moves to a small rural town. Hilarity ensues.

He didn't see any signs for Hudson DataVault, so he placed his trust in his GPS to guide him to the facility. The route there was a series of perfectly straight farm roads. Then the landscape became hilly and more densely forested, and the roads were winding. Finally, a newly paved access road took him to a small, low-slung, white-painted cinderblock office building built into the side of a mountain. Next to it was a tunnel, down which a couple of large white Hudson DataVault trucks were then driving, probably dropping off boxes of files. Or other things besides files. He had read that the storage facility, which was located in an abandoned limestone mine, held a whole range of things: racks of computer storage devices; studio master recordings from music companies; original negatives of thousands of movies, new and old, stored by movie studios, some of them extremely valuable; videotapes of years of Major League baseball games; priceless paintings that belonged to rich people—all kept in giant underground vaults.

And according to his research, the facility held *miles* of file boxes on steel shelves, mountains of paper documents deposited there by financial institutions and thousands of other corporations. So much for the myth of the paperless office. You needed someplace to store all your old stuff, the photocopies, minutes, tax returns, personnel files, invoices, and correspondence—all the documents you're required by law to keep, for compliance reasons. (*Compliance* was the big buzzword in the corporate world these days.)

Somewhere in the seven underground levels were boxes containing the old files from Arkady Galkin's firm. And included among them would be a few files—not a whole box, surely—about the gaming company FanStars.

70

He parked the rental in one of the few designated visitor spaces and walked up to the front door. A moment later, he was buzzed into a small office. Behind a counter sat a receptionist: a short-haired blonde in her twenties. "How can I help you, sir?" She had a husky voice. A sign on the counter identified her as Amy Scardino.

"Good morning, Amy. Paul Brightman up from New York City. I'm ready to look at the boxes ordered by my firm, AGF LLC."

"I'm sorry, who are you again?"

"Paul Brightman. AGF LLC. We placed an order for a retrieval."

"I don't think we received any retrieval request. We weren't expecting anyone this morning."

"I'm sorry," Paul said in a voice that made clear he wasn't at all sorry, "but we dealt with a 'Tim.'" He had gotten the name "Tim O'Brien" from the Hudson DataVault website, under "Our Team." Tim was a "customer experience specialist." He was who someone from Galkin's firm would have emailed to request that a certain box of files be retrieved from the vault.

"Tim O'Brien?"

"That sounds right. My admin made the appointment, but I believe that's the name she mentioned."

"One moment." She clicked a button on her phone and said, "Tim, we have someone here from—who are you with again, sir?" She had long blue-painted fingernails.

"AGF."

"AGF. He says they ordered a retrieval of some files?" A pause. Looking at Paul: "Sir, he never received any such email." Paul noticed she said "he" and not "we." That was good.

"That's troubling," Paul said, allowing a twinge of irritation to color his voice. "I just drove two hours up from the city . . ."

"I know, I'm sorry, sir."

"Well, can we please retrieve the files now? I know it'll take some time, and I'm willing to wait." He paused a beat, lowered his voice. "I don't mean to sound like a prick, Amy, but I'm not driving two hours back without setting eyes on those files."

He had watched any number of promotional videos on YouTube for Hudson DataVault: a virtual tour of the old limestone mine that had been converted into high-tech storage space, interviews with a customer experience specialist and the CEO. So he knew what Tim wanted: the number of the file carton, that was all. Every carton had an RFID label. Each label had an RFID serial number. Paul didn't understand exactly how it worked, but he figured he didn't have to know. What he did have was a file box number, which he'd gotten in a search, back at the office, of AGF's offsite records database.

He read the file number from the notecard on which he'd jotted it down.

"It can take upward of an hour to get your files," Amy said, and he knew he was in.

71

Amy led him to a room down a hall, not far from the front office, where he sat for a while, checking his email. The room was bare and institutional: gray carpet, conference table, nothing on the white walls. They used this space for clients to wait when they came to look at their employers' old files, or for meetings when clients were undergoing IRS audits. The air here was slightly cooler than in the reception area. Paul heard the roar of dehumidifiers. There must have been a whole lot of dehumidifiers in the seven floors underground, which had to be an awfully humid place.

Nothing in his email inbox was urgent. Nothing from Vova in IT; nothing from Mr. Frost. He had not been discovered, yet.

He answered a few emails, forwarded a few, checked on his portfolio, checked the time. Half an hour later, the door opened and a guy in a Hudson DataVault uniform wheeled in two brown cardboard boxes on a hand truck. He lifted them onto the table in front of Paul. At one end of each carton was an RFID label, a long sticker with what appeared to be a barcode on it. Underneath the sticker, Paul knew, was a metallic strip that contained a computer chip and the antenna for receiving and transmitting signals.

"That was fast," Paul said. He'd been expecting to wait over an hour.

"Slow day," the guy said. He scanned the RFID label on the box with a hand scanner, then removed the security band. The box had Hudson DataVault's logo on it and a three-inch-tall lid.

When the delivery guy had left the room, Paul opened the first storage carton. In a large, loopy hand on each end of the box was scrawled "FAN-FANZ." The files were organized alphabetically, with plastic tabs sticking up for each one. Each file was barcoded, Paul saw. He pulled out the six folders labeled "FanStars." They contained research and reports and printed-out emails on this company in which AGF had once seriously considering investing. Obviously, somebody had done the work. His predecessor, probably.

Most of the files were six-year-old documents of the sort of financial research he'd just done himself on FanStars. Nothing surprising there. Boring stuff—familiar, if now out of date. He leafed through them to make sure he hadn't missed anything important, and he saw that he hadn't. It was the folder of email printouts that was worth spending time on, and he did, reading over each email.

And then he knew he had discovered a ticking time bomb.

There at the bottom of one page—so small and seemingly innocuous that he'd nearly missed it—was a signature that made the hair on the back of his neck stand up.

The person who had originally brought the FanStars deal to Arkady Galkin, and who'd get 10 percent if the deal happened, was someone named Maxim Kagan. That name was disturbingly familiar to Paul. He pulled it up on his phone to confirm his suspicions.

Maxim Kagan was a Russian citizen wanted by the FBI. Not back then, not at the time AGF was working on the FanStars deal, but now. He was what was known as an SDN, a specially designated national. Which meant he was on a long list put out by a little-known office in the Treasury Department. Do business with an SDN, and you could be fined millions of dollars and put in prison for up to thirty years.

Paul wondered if his father-in-law knew Kagan's background. Galkin might not mind being fined a couple million dollars, but he would definitely mind being in prison for thirty years. If Maxim V. Kagan was behind the FanStars deal now, and AGF invested, Paul's bosses would be in serious legal peril and would soon be visited by the guys in windbreakers.

He removed from the file folders every email print-out from and to Maxim Kagan, laid the pages out on the table, and carefully photographed each page with his phone camera.

Then, his heart rate quickening, he picked up the second file box, the one labeled, in big blue Sharpie, "PHAM-PHAT." He opened the box and quickly flipped through the plastic file tabs.

There was no "Phantom."

Of course not. That would have been too easy.

He went through the file tabs again, more slowly, to make sure he hadn't missed anything, and he hadn't. No such file.

Oh, well. At least he had a trophy to bring home: Maxim Kagan.

And then he had a thought. In the Russian transliteration, Phantom was spelled "Fantom." Beginning with the letter *F*. He opened the first box again. Went through the file tabs again, in alphabetical order: FAI . . . FAL . . . FAM . . .

A tab nearly hidden by the ones around it. Maybe he'd missed it the first time. A slender folder.

Фантом.

He pulled open the folder and found no paper files in it. Just a small silver thumb drive Scotch-taped to the inside of the folder.

It was labeled, with a black marker, **Фантом.**

He thought a moment and then slipped the thumb drive into his pocket.

PART NINE

WOODSMEN

Present Day

72

"Mind putting down that tarp before you sit?" the woman said when she saw him, mud-spattered, in the light of her truck's cab.

Paul took the folded tarp from the floor of the cab and, unfolding it, placed it carefully over the seat and the floor. Then he set down his go-bag, already crusty with dried mud. He hopped up inside and pulled the door shut.

"Thank you," he said.

"No offense, but I just took Audrey to the car wash."

"Audrey?"

"Sorry. My truck's named Audrey. Hey, we all got our quirks, and that's mine. *One* of mine. Where you headed?"

"Lincoln."

"I'm on my way home to Woodstock, but I have to go through Lincoln, of course. Where you want me to drop you off?"

"Any motel that'll take me."

She gave a low, hearty laugh. "Might take a while to find one. You been in the woods a long time?"

"Few days."

The white dog in the backseat poked its snout between the two front seats, and Paul patted its thick coat. It felt coarse and dry. The animal appeared to be smiling.

"That's a long time if you're lost. You a solo hiker? Or did you get separated from your party?"

"Solo. But my compass is broken. Are you a trail angel?"

She smiled as she pulled the truck back onto the road. "You can call me that, yeah. Finished the late shift at Memorial Hospital in Conway. I'm a nurse. Speaking of which, your foot okay? You seem to be limping."

"Twisted my ankle."

"Gotta ice it and compress it."

"I'll get some ice in town," Paul said.

"Hold on. I've got some instant cold packs." She pulled back off the road and onto the narrow shoulder, put her blinkers back on. Opening the console between her seat and his, she took out a rolled elastic bandage and a cold pack and handed both to him. "You know how to use these, right? Squeeze the inner pouch thingy."

"Thank you. And thanks for picking me up."

"Part of my job description. As a trail angel. I'm Angela, by the way."

Angela, he thought. *Like angel.*

"Nice to meet you, Angela. I'm Giles."

She switched off the truck's blinkers and pulled back onto the road.

Paul removed his left boot, twisted the ice pack, and put it on his ankle, securing it with the elastic bandage. The blisters on his toes hurt, too, but he knew there was little he could do about them.

"I'd offer you a bed, Giles, but we don't have a spare one. My wife and I just have the one bedroom. Seven hundred square feet. Room enough for us and Tucker."

Tucker, he assumed, was the dog. "Your dog always smile?"

"Looks that way, doesn't it? He's a Samoyed. Genetically very close to wolves. They all have upturned mouths. Those upturned corners keep icicles from forming on their face in really cold weather."

"Huh." He settled back into his seat, luxuriating in the warmth, and the next thing he knew, Angela was poking at him. "Wake up, Giles. You okay with a Days Inn?"

Paul opened his eyes, saw that they were parked in front of the Days Inn on U.S. Route 3. "Absolutely," he said. "Thank you again."

"Oh, I'm not leaving until you get checked in. Make sure they'll take you."

He put his boot back on, tied it tight, wrapped his ankle with the elastic bandage. Then he got out, grabbed his bag.

Inside the motel, there was no one at the front desk. It was around three in the morning. He hit the call bell, and a minute later, a woman emerged from the back, blinking and yawning. "Can I help you?"

"I need a room for the night."

She looked at him for a long time. She had long brown hair parted in the center and thick glasses. "That'll be three forty-five."

"My credit cards are no good. But I can put down a few hundred in cash as a security deposit if you want."

She shook her head. "Hotel policy. We can't take cash. I'm sorry."

ANGELA WAS WAITING IN HER Denali. "They wouldn't take you?" she said with a laugh.

"Nope." He didn't explain that he had to pay cash, that he had no credit cards.

"There's a motel north a couple miles. The Flume."

"Let's try the Flume," he said.

The Flume Motel was a row of clapboard buildings on Route 3 next to Franconia Notch State Park and Flume Gorge, a major tourist attraction, a natural cavern carved into the granite. The motel advertised free Wi-Fi. The reception area looked clean and well kept, and they took cash. No credit card required.

Paul rolled up a fifty-dollar bill and held it out to Angela.

"Thank you," he said. "Angela, I can't tell you—"

But she refused it. "No big thing, friend. Glad I could be of some assistance."

As soon as he was in his room, he peeled off his sodden boots and took a long, hot shower. Then he got into bed and, within a few moments, sank into a deep sleep.

73

He was awakened by the playful screams of children in the parking lot outside his room. He grabbed his watch from the nightstand. It was nearly noon. He'd slept for nine hours and felt drugged. He could easily fall back asleep for the rest of the day, but he needed to keep moving.

He found the burner phone he'd last used and hit the Redial button to call Sarah.

After five rings, the phone was answered. Sarah said, "Grant? Where are you? Are you okay?"

"Yeah, I'm fine. Sorry to wake you. Are you at Tilda's?"

"Yes. Where are you?"

He didn't want to say anything over the phone.

"I'm in a motel room. Listen, Sarah, you need to get rid of your iPhone, okay?"

"Grant, what the fuck is going on? You got Alec Wood *killed*." Her voice was strained.

"What—what do you know?"

She must be going crazy, Paul thought, *and it's all my fault.*

"There was a front-page article in the *Derryfield Courier* this morning. It said that Alec was killed in front of your house, Paul! It said you're a person of interest."

He tried to calm her as best he could over the phone, tried to assuage her panic, but she was distraught.

"Sarah—Sarah, *listen!* I'm sorry to raise my voice, honey, but I don't have a lot of time, and I need you to pay attention here, okay?"

She seemed to catch her breath after a moment, saying, "Okay, okay, okay," and then he spoke again.

"I have to hang up now—but please know that I'm doing okay, I'm safe, and I've got a plan. We're going to get through this, both of us. But these are bad guys, Sarah, I'm telling you. So I need you to be really careful. Don't talk to anyone with a Russian accent. And don't tell anyone I called. It's important."

74

Paul looked at himself in the bathroom mirror. Though he'd taken a shower the night before, his skin was still encrusted with mud. He took another long shower and then tried to scrape some of the filth off his clothes.

Wearing his old, foul-smelling jeans and shirt, he set out for downtown Lincoln, a few miles away. He went slowly. Both his feet were tender, his ankle throbbed, and the blisters on his toes were pretty bad. He spent a few minutes trying to hitch a ride but had no luck. No trail angels here.

He'd been to Lincoln a couple of times over the past five years. It was a small town with roughly the same population as Derryfield, but was much more spread out, considerably more touristy. It was the home to the Loon Mountain ski resort. Decades before, the town ran sawmills on the Pemigewasset River, a center for logging that featured a bustling paper mill, but all that was gone. Now it was largely a tourist attraction and a ski destination.

The first thing he needed, of course, was new clothes. His jeans, his shirt and jacket, his socks—all were encrusted with mud. In Lincoln, you could buy all the ski attire you wanted—which he didn't need. On a previous visit, he and Sarah stopped at a thrift shop on Main Street, where Sarah had found a set of vintage Yellow Ware cups and saucers she was excited about. He remembered seeing racks of secondhand clothes there, too.

At the thrift shop, the woman behind the counter looked him over, head to toe. "Ooh, now, what happened to you, dear?"

"You don't want to know."

"Oh, my. Well, if there's anything I can do to help, let me know." She had light brown hair done up in a sort of bubble, oversize glasses with thick lenses, and a kindly face.

"I need some clothes that'll fit me. Some jeans, a shirt, a jacket, some shoes or boots."

She looked hesitant, probably wondering if he had any money to pay for them. "Well, I know we don't have any jackets, unless you mean suit jackets, and those we have in abundance. No one seems to wear suits anymore. No shoes or boots, either—those just don't sell. Except for ski boots; those we do have. Those move. I don't think we have any jeans, but let me . . . Hmm . . . would a pair of khakis do you, dear?"

The chinos were a little big, but they fit him okay. He added an old Paul Stuart striped dress shirt with a frayed collar. He changed in the shop's restroom and threw his old clothes in the trash.

"There now, you look much more presentable," the woman declared when he emerged from the restroom.

At a ski shop down the street, he bought a warm Patagonia ski parka and a navy beanie, a new pair of work boots, a pair of binoculars, and a Peak backpack. He knew it was important to change his appearance frequently. He emptied the contents of his go-bag into the new backpack and tossed out the bag. On Main Street, he passed a Rite Aid pharmacy, where he bought some Motrin, elastic bandages for his ankle, gauze bandages and petroleum jelly for the blisters on his feet, another couple of disposable phones, and a candy bar.

At White Mountain Bagel Company, he had a delicious roast beef sandwich and a lot of black coffee. He pocketed the apple he didn't have room for. Someone had left behind on a table a copy of the *Conway Daily Sun*. On the front page was an article about the murder of a local police officer, Alec Wood, in Derryfield. No known suspects yet, it said. Even less information than Sarah had found in the Derryfield paper.

When he'd had enough coffee—maybe too much—he went in search of a bank. Not just any bank, but one he had visited five years earlier, where he'd opened a safe-deposit box. He remembered it was on Papermill Drive, right off Main Street. In his pocket was the small envelope he'd long ago stashed in his go-bag, which contained the key.

As he shuffled along, he looked around at the other pedestrians on the street. They could have been shoppers or town residents going out for lunch. He didn't see anyone suspicious, and he wondered idly if it was possible that he'd actually lost his pursuers. He walked past a Life Is Good store and chuckled dryly at the irony. Life was decidedly not good these days.

It was a good thing, though, that there were people on the streets, so he could better blend in. But because of his ankle, he was unable to change his gait, which was a problem. He limped, and there was nothing he could do about that. If the Russians knew he'd injured his ankle, they'd be able to spot him right away.

At the bank, a pleasant man in his thirties with black-framed glasses showed Paul to the rank of safe-deposit boxes at the back of the lobby.

Paul unlocked his box. Exactly one item was in it: a silver USB drive.

LOU WESTING'S OFFICE WAS ON Main Street, a few doors down from the Life Is Good store, its entrance marked with a painted wooden plaque, in green and gold, that read, WESTING LAW. In the same wooden building, on the first floor, was a restaurant called Pies-n-Thighs. Standing in the entrance to a closed "adventure golf" shop, Paul regarded Westing's building through his binoculars. It was across the street and down about a hundred feet. It was still lunchtime, and a steady stream of customers entered and exited the restaurant.

He called Lou on one of his new disposable phones. While waiting for the call to be answered, he held the binoculars to his eyes with his right hand. Lou answered.

"Lou, it's Grant Anderson."

"Grant. Where are you, bud?"

"I just got into town. Staying at the Days Inn on Route Three. You hungry?"

"Sure."

"Want to meet at that place right downstairs from you, the Pies-n-Thighs? I passed by it this morning, and something smells awfully good in there."

"That would be great. Good choice. Give me, oh, ten, fifteen minutes. I gotta finish up a memo. Then I'll meet you there."

"Perfect."

Paul tried to look into the second-floor windows of Westing's law firm, but the sun was reflecting off the glass, and he couldn't see much.

A few minutes later, he saw something that set his heart clattering in his chest. Three men and two women wearing dark-blue windbreakers with FBI printed in yellow letters on the back came around the corner of the building from behind him.

Were they here to apprehend him?

He considered his options. He could run—no, better to walk, casually, down Main Street, like a local who was supposed to be there, and then turn into the ski area behind the street. But several members of the five-person FBI team seemed to be watching the street, perhaps waiting for him to come from the Days Inn.

A minute later, Paul watched Lou emerge from the law firm's ground-level door and walk toward the restaurant's entrance. He still had the heavy dark brow and double chin Paul remembered, except now he wore a look of determination. He strutted like a rooster.

Paul watched as Lou walked up to what looked like the FBI team leader and said something to her. The woman and the other two FBI agents stationed outside the Pies-n-Thighs door then walked around the back of that building, no longer visible to anyone walking by. Lou entered the restaurant.

Paul waited. His burner phone rang.

Lou's mobile phone number. "Grant," Lou said, "I'm at Pies-n-Thighs. Are you coming?"

"I am. Just a little late, sorry. Something came up."

"Okay. No problem. Listen, I'm glad you called." Lou's voice sounded odd—stilted, almost.

"I need your help," Paul said.

"I know you do," Lou said. "Look, I know you've been having a hard time, but I want you to know you're not alone." He sounded like a hostage reading from a statement prepared by his captors. "I'm here to help any way I can." *Had Lou Westing been in touch with the FBI?*

"On my way," Paul said and ended the call. It was time to move, maybe long past time.

He saw one of the FBI agents come from behind the building that housed the restaurant and cross the street, a hundred feet from where he was standing. Paul's instinct was to run, but he knew that would only attract attention. His mouth had gone dry. He stuffed the binoculars into his backpack, stepped out onto the sidewalk, and began walking down Main Street, calmly, away from the guy in the windbreaker. He tried to act casually but knew they were watching the street.

A few doors down, he came upon the thrift shop where he'd purchased his replacement clothes and entered it.

"He's back," the woman at the desk said, smiling. "Everything fit okay?"

"Everything's great," he said. "I know this will sound weird, but do you happen to have another exit? There's a woman I'm trying to avoid."

The woman behind the desk peered at him for a minute, then laughed. "Oh, yeah? You could take the service entrance, dear. Sure." And she pointed toward the rear of the shop.

75

He tried not to limp too obviously as he slipped out the rear exit of the thrift shop. There was a hardened-dirt parking lot there and, immediately behind it, a thickly wooded area. That way, he knew, lay the Pemi Wilderness.

For perhaps a tenth of a second, Paul considered whether he should surrender. His instinct had always been to obey law enforcement. Most people would. Also, the FBI agents would expect him to try to evade them in town, on foot, and by vehicle. What they would not expect him to do was go back into the woods.

So that was precisely what he would do.

Paul wished he'd bought more articles of clothing than he had, but he hadn't planned on this. He had a warm parka and a good new backpack and not much else. In his pockets he had an apple and a KIND bar (Double Dark Chocolate), the latter because it looked healthier than a Snickers, though he wasn't sure.

But he had been taught a long time ago how to survive in the woods.

So he plunged into the forest. He went as fast as he could, but this wood was dense with vegetation. When he was far enough in that he knew he couldn't be seen from the parking lot, he immediately set about building a debris shelter. This was challenging because if he gathered too much debris from where he was settling down, it would leave a telltale clearing. So he had to collect the branches and twigs from a few hundred feet away, which took considerable time. Slowly, he built a frame, stretched his tarp over it, and camouflaged it with branches and leaves. He stepped back, took an assessing look, was satisfied. Because the sun had begun to set, he got into the shelter and lay down, wearing his parka, and tried to rest.

Maybe they'd given up looking for him.

Yeah, right.

Finally, his thoughts stopped spinning enough for him to fall asleep.

It was the crackle of a two-way radio that jolted him awake. In the crackle, he distinctly heard his last name.

He'd been asleep for two hours. The light had gone. He remembered suddenly where he was.

Now he heard the tread of multiple pairs of feet on the forest floor, the snap of branches. His heartbeat thundered.

He froze. He couldn't judge how close they were. He had no idea whether they'd made out his hiding place. So he decided to wait in place, breathing silently. If they'd found him, they'd found him, and there wasn't a lot he could do about it.

He waited in fear for twenty minutes. Were they Russians? Feds? The transmission from the portable radios had faded. So had the audible tramping of feet. Whoever it was seemed to have passed by.

Then he heard a male voice in the darkness. "Let's go." The voice was close to where he was hiding, within mere feet.

Paul held his breath, hoped against hope that the order wasn't directed at him.

"I mean it, let's go *now*." Even closer.

Another male voice, just as close: "They're on to you. Get up and go.

Wait. Were they speaking to *him*?

"We can help you," the voice said, "but only if you move your fucking ass."

They *were* speaking to him. Paul was perplexed. Maybe it wasn't the FBI. Anyway, what choice did he have? He made a decision and spoke:

"Who the hell are you?" he croaked.

In the next instant, he felt himself grabbed on both sides. Four sets of arms reached into the shelter beneath the tarp. Someone had his left arm, someone else had his right, and as they pulled at him, he stumbled to his feet, his entire body vibrating with fear.

"Hey!" he protested. "What the hell?"

"We're trying to help you, man," one of the men grunted. "Keep your fucking voice down."

Someone else said, "Grab his backpack."

Both men had full beards, one man's black and white, the other's entirely gray. Paul had a vague feeling he'd seen them before.

Now, suddenly, they were trundling him through the dark woods. He limped, trying to keep up with their pace. They torqued him in one direction, pulled him into a stand of trees, then yanked him in another direction through another bunch of trees, then uphill.

"Who the hell are you?" Paul said again.

One of the men hissed at him to shut up.

The other muttered, "They're after you."

"Fucking feds are coming," the first man said. "They're fanning out across the terrain. They know you're in the Pemi."

In a couple of minutes, they came to what looked like a tiny, narrow log cabin in a dense, dark copse. The first man fiddled with the lock on the cabin door, and the door, built of split logs, swung open.

"Get in there," the second man said. "The feds don't have keys. Move it."

Paul wanted to ask these men again who they were, why they were helping him. Were they themselves fugitives, too?

Instinctively, he trusted these guys. He didn't understand their motive, but his gut feeling was to go along with what they were telling him to do.

It was either that or give in to being arrested by the FBI.

"Move it!" the second man said again.

Paul stepped into a darkness that smelled of pine tar and heard the *click-click* of a door being locked behind him.

76

Knowing he was locked in didn't calm his nerves. He didn't feel at all protected.

For several minutes, he stood there in the pitch black, breathing carefully so as not to make a noise. His heart beat so loudly he swore it would have been audible to others, if there'd been any others in there with him.

At first he couldn't tell the difference between when his eyes were closed and when they were not. But in a minute or so, his eyes adjusted to the gloom and he saw tools and rakes and bottles. He appeared to be inside a sort of maintenance shack where the National Forest Service kept supplies to maintain the trails. Such shacks are built to blend into the environment. They're never disclosed on maps used by the hiking public. Tiny cracks of dim light filtered in where one log in the shack's walls didn't completely meet the other. The shack was well constructed; he was impressed.

He wondered again who the hell his rescuers were, what they were doing there, and why. He knew the FBI thought he had killed his own friend, Alec Wood. And who knew what else they suspected him of doing.

He'd impersonated another person, yes. That was true. For five years, he'd been living under the name and Social Security number of Grant Anderson. Criminal impersonation in the first degree was a felony in New York and a lot of other places around the United States. He knew this. He had looked it up several times. It wasn't as serious as pretending to be a law enforcement officer or a U.S. government employee, but in some states it would net you at least three years in prison. In New Hampshire, he was pretty sure, it was a misdemeanor. So: no big deal.

Did it really justify an aggressive pursuit and arrest? He didn't think so.

He knew there was more, much more. He was the man who knew too much.

In roughly five minutes—he didn't know for sure; the hands of his Timex didn't glow in the dark like his old Omega's had—he heard voices in the woods.

"Watch where you're walking—look out for a tripwire. Guy could have set up booby traps for us."

"Spread out as far as you can but stay within sight of each other."

". . . order up a FLIR."

It was the FBI team he had earlier evaded. They were clearly searching the forest for him.

He thought: if they managed to find him in this shack, wouldn't it be better to be held in a U.S. prison facility than to surrender to Galkin's goons—who would almost certainly kill him . . . and probably inflict plenty of other horrors on him beforehand?

The voices had come nearer, and then the doorknob of the shack was turned, back and forth, back and forth. Paul's chest grew tight. He held his breath. He heard something about "locked" and then something about "keys," and then he heard, perfectly clearly, someone right outside the shack's doors say, "Nah, *you* can't get in, *he* couldn't get in. Let's move on."

Paul breathed in silently, out silently, and waited.

He heard footsteps crackling on the forest floor, the crunching of dead leaves and twigs. Heard the FBI agents exchanging words he couldn't make out.

Ten minutes slowly went by. He could just barely see his Timex.

Then, a gentler rustling outside. The doorknob turned again, and this time the door was pulled open. Soft dappled light filled the shack's interior. He felt a jolt of adrenaline.

"Shit, you got a whole SWAT team after you," said one of the bearded men who'd dragged him here. "What'd you do?"

"Long story," Paul said. "Who are you guys?"

"The Deacon wants to see you," said the other one, ignoring his question.

"The who? And for what?"

"Are you going to follow us, or do we have to drag you again?"

"Sorry, but my goddamned ankle's hurt."

He rose to his feet and followed them, limping. "Want to know, who the hell are you?"

They traipsed ahead, not answering, walking skillfully through the forest, their gaits expert, the sounds they made minimal. Paul followed, painfully. Every once in a while, they had to stop for him, waiting impatiently.

The two men didn't speak further. They seemed to weave their way among the trees as if they knew them all. Now and then, they'd come to a stopping point, and the one with the black-and-white beard would look for something, seem to find it, then continue on.

This went on for more than half an hour. The party went uphill for quite a distance, then downhill, then through a particularly dense section of forest until they came to a clearing with a drift of dead leaves around the stump of a scrub oak tree. Standing beside the pile of leaves was a third bearded man, only, his beard was even longer and fuller, a full grizzled Jeremiah Johnson. This had to be the Deacon.

"Why are the feebees after you?" he asked. "It's not homicide, is it? Or kidnapping?"

Paul ignored the question. "Tell me: Who are you guys? You've saved my ass. I don't get it."

"Tell me what you're running for. Or from."

"Long story."

"If you think we're going to protect you without knowing what you did, you're hallucinating."

"Protect me?"

"Hal and Leon locked you in a maintenance shack; that wasn't protecting you?"

"But who *are* you guys? Why are you doing this?"

"You first tell me why you're running from the feds."

Paul exhaled, a long sigh. "I don't exactly know, okay? I've been living under someone else's identity, for one thing."

"And the feds caught up with you."

"Right."

"What'd you do?"

"What'd I do?"

"Why you in hiding?"

Paul heaved another sigh. "I'm on the run from a goddamned Russian oligarch."

The Deacon chuckled dryly. "You rip off some Russian billionaire?"

"Well, I took something that I think belonged to him, yeah."

"You don't know for sure?"

Paul shook his head.

"The feebees coming after you for ripping off a Russki?"

Paul thought for a minute. "Maybe for using someone else's Social Security number."

"So you're trying to keep yourself safe, but all the federal government cares about is that you broke one of their ridiculous rules."

"About right."

"What is government but a protection racket? Organized crime. No different from the mobster in the neighborhood who's extorting money from you by saying your candy store needs protection. You don't pay up, you have an unfortunate fire, burns down the place. Same with the government: You give up your rights to the government in exchange for protection. They make war to protect you, they say, and they tax you to pay for it."

"Right," Paul said, recognizing the rhetoric.

"There's no 'consent of the governed,'" the Deacon continued. "It's submission of the frightened."

"War made the state, and the state made war," Paul said, suddenly remembering something his father used to say.

"Exactly. Violence is legit if the government does it, whether it's the electric chair or the war in Iraq. What most people call organized crime is just less successful and smaller in scale than governments."

"The government has a monopoly on legitimate violence," Paul said, repeating yet another of his father's mantras. He knew all the rhetoric, from his father, and wanted to make nice.

"You got it."

"You guys live in the woods?" he asked, pointing at the two men who had brought him there. These men didn't look like hikers or campers.

The two men said nothing. They looked at him warily.

The man they called the Deacon said, "You can hide in here." He pointed to the drift of dead leaves. Paul furrowed his brow.

The Deacon pointed again at the pile, and Paul could see that it was actually a well-constructed shelter built from forest debris. He glimpsed a hole where a human could crawl in.

"It's a debris shelter," the Deacon said. "You'll want to get in there for a few hours. We can talk later if you want." He held out his hand. "Stephen Lucas."

Paul hesitated a moment, then said, "Paul Brightman."

The Deacon smiled. "I thought so," he said.

PART TEN

A CUP OF TEA

Five Years Earlier

77

Paul returned to the office in the early afternoon. The place was hushed, everyone apparently at their desks.

The Phantom flash drive was burning a hole in his pocket. He felt some of that same paranoia he'd experienced in the office at two in the morning, downloading documents to another flash drive, the tightness in his gut, the prickling of the skin at the back of his neck.

"Your errands get done okay?" Margo asked.

Paul nodded, smiled.

"Mr. Frost wants to talk to you. He wants you to go to his office right away."

"Okay." That couldn't be good. Paul returned to his desk to find the red light on his phone console flashing.

A voicemail from Mr. Frost.

"Mr. Brightman, please come see me immediately when you return to the office." A hushed voice, that barely perceptible Russian accent. A hint of menace.

Interesting that he didn't send me an email or call my cell, Paul thought. *He has my number.* If it was as important as Frost made it sound, he could have reached him right away. Instead, he'd waited for Paul to be back at his desk.

PAUL WALKED TO EUGENE FROST'S office, right next to Galkin's.

No cordiality, no small talk. "Why were you at our remote storage site upstate?"

Hudson DataVault must have called him. Probably not the receptionist, Amy, but maybe the guy from the Pennsylvania office, outside Pittsburgh. A belts-and-suspenders kind of guy. He'd have double-checked authorization to cover his own ass.

"Doing due diligence on FanStars."

"The gaming site I recommended."

"Right. I don't know if you know this, but Maxim Kagan is officially an SDN, a specially designated national. Which means that we can't do business with him. We're talking prison sentences if we do."

"Mister Kagan originally brought in this deal, it's true, but he is no longer affiliated with FanStars in any way."

"I didn't know that. Anyway, that's why I went upstate."

"You should have cleared this expedition with me in advance."

"Understood."

"I appreciate your wanting to be proactive, but you also need to follow procedures."

"Okay."

But Mr. Frost wasn't done. "Why did you not inform us you were going?"

"Frankly, I wasn't sure I'd find anything useful."

"Yet you wanted to dig around in old files and waste more than half a workday."

Paul shrugged. What could he say anyway?

Frost changed the subject: "You are a friend of Chadwick Forrester, is that correct?"

"Yes."

"Has he ever talked with you about his dissatisfaction with our firm?"

"Never." Why, Paul wondered, was he asking? What did they have on Chad?

Frost nodded, his eyes drifting off. He was silent for a few seconds. Finally, he spoke. "Your work on BAE Systems was extremely profitable. You turned fifty million dollars into two hundred and twenty-three million dollars. That's a very big hit for the firm. I congratulate you."

"Thank you."

"You are a valuable employee. Not just because you are Mr. Galkin's son-in-law. But you can't go off on your own whim, looking into things that excite your curiosity. You have to run such projects by me first. Is that clear?"

"Crystal."

"I understand you speak Russian."

"Barely. I took two years of it in college."

"You probably know a fair amount of Russian slang."

"Some."

"It's not an easy language for Americans to learn. But there's a very useful Russian slang word you should know."

"What's that?"

"*Pochemuchka*."

Paul repeated it, stumbling over it, a tricky little Russian word. *Pochemuchka*. "And what does it mean?"

"It means someone who asks too many questions. An overly curious person. A busybody. It comes from the title of a Soviet-era children's book whose hero, Alyosha Pochemuchka, is never satisfied with the answers he gets. When you say it of a child, it's a term of endearment. But not with adults. It's not an endearment."

"Got it," Paul said, and he turned to go. Then, thinking of something, he turned back around. "So what happens to Alyosha Pochemuchka? In the book, I mean."

There was a long pause. Paul could tell that Eugene Frost was debating how to reply. Finally, he spoke, slowly, deliberately. "This was a Soviet-era children's book. One hundred percent Soviet propaganda. What do you *think* happened to the boy who asked too many questions in the old Soviet Union?"

"Understood," Paul said simply as he turned and left the office.

78

In the late afternoon, he texted Special Agent Mark Addison and told him he'd found something of great importance. Addison had assured Paul that it was safe to text him on the office Wi-Fi as long as he used Signal.

Addison replied at once. *Can you meet at 9 tonite?*

Paul thought for a moment. He couldn't stay late at work again. He decided to go home at the regular time, have a quick dinner with Tatyana, tell her he had to go back to the office for an hour or so. He'd meet Addison at nine, hand him the flash drive, and go back home.

When he got home, Tatyana was cuddling Pushkin as she looked at photos on her computer. "Oh, I'm glad you're home," she said. "I have a surprise for you."

"Uh-oh," he said, leaning over to kiss her. He was wary: a surprise? Since Moscow, he'd been feeling strangely awkward around her, like some kind of impostor. A traitor, to be more precise. He was betraying her father; there was no way around it.

"Let's get some takeout, and then we can head over to Park Avenue and meet my father and Polina."

"Park—our new apartment? Is that the surprise?"

"I guess I'm not so good at keeping secrets."

"So it's finished?"

"We're going to meet them at eight thirty or nine."

Which was when he had to meet Addison. "That was when Rick and I are supposed to have a beer," Paul said. "Can we do it tomorrow instead?"

"We can't blow off my parents."

"I'm not blowing them off. I just want to reschedule."

"Out of the question," she said firmly. "Papa's going to London on business tomorrow. We can't reschedule."

"Okay," Paul said, defeated. "We'll meet them tonight." He would have to text Addison and postpone.

THEY TOOK A LYFT TO Park Avenue and pulled up beside their new building, its façade a graceful limestone. They greeted the doorman and took
the elevator to the ninth floor. Paul felt a weird skirmish of emotions:
he was excited to see the place, but a little apprehensive that, after his
in-laws' renovations, it would be dripping with gold.

The elevator doors opened, and they saw not their old apartment door
but large, ornate brass-filigreed double doors. These were flung open,
and Arkady and Polina bustled out, both of them crying, "Welcome!"
Arkady was wearing his blue-and-white bird's-eye L.L.Bean sweater, and
his wife was in a tight-fitting black dress. They hugged Tatyana, then
Polina hugged Paul, and Arkady shook his hand firmly.

"Welcome to your new apartment!" Galkin said.

"What—what the hell did you do?" Paul yelped. The words escaped
before he could bottle them up. "The door . . ."

"Is salvage from sacred mosque in Morocco. Apartment is nice, yes?
Is very simple and spare. The way you both like it, yes?"

But everything looked different. For one, the apartment seemed
much larger.

"I don't understand," Paul said. "What—what happened to the
apartment next door?"

"I buy out neighbor," Galkin said gleefully. "Pay them to move very
fast. Everyone has price." He'd hired the celebrity Japanese architect
Tadao Ando to combine the two apartments into one gracious, high-end
home in the minimalist style. Now the apartment went on forever. It was
a blend of old New York architecture and modern interior design. The
walls were white and gray and beige and pale yellow. The carpets were
an indeterminate shade between gray and beige. The sofas were long and
gray and comfortable looking. Everything was done in a neutral palette.
It was tasteful and simple but not boring. There was no gold plating, no
ticky-tacky.

Tatyana's eyes were wide, her mouth agape, then smiling. She seemed
stunned and delighted. She, who rented an apartment in the East Village
with a problematic toilet, was now thrilled with this beige Versailles of the
Upper East Side, this modernist Taj Mahal.

Paul was silent as he looked around. The apartment was now two classic sixes combined, immense. Inside, he seethed. He had gone to the mat to buy this apartment, had maxed out his finances, had spent everything he had—and now his father-in-law was making him look like a pissant.

One of the many rooms was set up as Tatyana's photography studio. Another, Polina told them, could be used as a gallery to show her photographs. "Pápachka," she said, visibly moved. She spoke to him quickly in Russian and then said, "Thank you."

"I am impressed," Paul said tightly. "Thank you."

"If you don't like," Arkady said, "you can redo how you want."

"But it's perfect," Tatyana said.

PUSHKIN WAS YAPPING WHEN THEY arrived home back at their old place. Tatyana took him out for a walk while Paul poured himself a large glass of bourbon. He took a big gulp.

Tatyana returned with the dog. He and she collapsed on the couch. Pushkin scrambled into her lap. After what they'd just seen, this place really did seem like a shithole, as her father had said. Paul poured her a glass of rosé.

"I know what you're thinking," Tatyana said. "Nobody could do a reno so fast—board approvals, certificates from the city planning office? Impossible, right? But Papa has his ways."

"Meaning substantial payoffs."

Tatyana shrugged. "Papa has his ways."

A long silence passed between them.

"Well, what'd you think?" he said.

"What did *you* think?"

"You seemed ecstatic."

"It was so generous of my father. I don't just mean the money. I mean the time and attention he must have put into the renovation."

"He didn't ask me about enlarging the place. Did he ask you?"

"He wanted it to be a surprise, Pasha."

"Explain something to me. You've lived here for five years." He waved his hands around, speaking softly but with a burning intensity. "You don't want to show off your wealth. Yet now you're happy to live in the . . . the Winter Palace. I don't understand the contradiction."

She looked distraught. "Why are you so, I don't know, so angry about this gift?"

"Your father turned the nice apartment you and I bought together, which was in need of a lot of work, into a place twice the size."

"Yes, but there's a photography studio and a gallery. And if we have kids—" They hadn't talked much about kids, though Tatyana always smiled and cooed at babies they passed on the street.

"I get it," Paul said. "Your father is acknowledging your art. You feel *seen*."

"Exactly! And there's no gold anywhere. It's incredibly beautiful. How can we say no?"

"It's a beautiful apartment, yes, but it's not *our* apartment." Paul was reminded of the old saying "Happy wife, happy life." The enormous, sprawling, yet tasteful apartment seemed to make Tatyana happy. Or maybe it was the thought behind it that made her happy. He wasn't sure.

She nodded. She had half her wine left, and he'd finished the rocks glass of bourbon. "I get it," she said.

"You always shun that kind of opulence. I don't think you really want to live in a place like that. *I* don't want to."

"It'll hurt his feelings," she said. "He'll be crushed."

"Your father?" He couldn't imagine Arkady Galkin having bruised feelings. He wasn't that sensitive. Paul shook his head. "Will you explain something to me about him?"

"I can try."

Paul's friends on Wall Street who'd grown up poor and then gotten rich always had the biggest, showiest houses in the Hamptons, the most impressive apartments or town houses. Great novels had been written about the struggle between old and new money. But for Galkin, it was more complicated than that. "Your father has one of the biggest town houses in New York City, a giant yacht . . . yet he's always wearing the same clothes, and they're not very expensive. He buys them from catalogues."

Tatyana laughed, her laugh high and lilting, always lovely. "Oh, my *pápachka*. You know, in Soviet times, before I was born, he was poor. He lived in a communal apartment with his mother and his grandparents and his sisters. And now that he's rich, he wants to enjoy it. But he still loves a bargain. He doesn't care about what clothes he wears, or shoes, or watches."

"Huh."

"But he always wants his opponents, his adversaries, the people he's negotiating with . . . he wants them to see how successful he is. So he shows off. I know people in Russia, who are even richer than we are, who live much more modestly."

"Okay."

"So what are we going to tell him?" Tatyana asked.

A long, awkward silence passed between them.

How can I accept this gift from Arkady? Paul asked himself. He wanted to refuse, to insist that they sell what Arkady had created for them, get their money back and buy another place, their *own* place. But he was immediately suffused by a flush of guilt for having betrayed Tatyana and her father. No matter the reason, how would she ever forgive him?

"How can we tell him no?" Paul finally replied.

Tatyana beamed and clasped his hands and kissed him. Tears were in her eyes. "So now I can tell you: he invited us to join him on his yacht this weekend," she said.

"His *yacht*? Why? What's the occasion?"

"I don't know. He does that sometimes. Invites you at the last minute."

"Do we have to go?"

"You don't want to? I love his yacht."

I love his yacht. Who is this woman? Paul wondered. This woman who lived in the apartment of a struggling artist, who disdained displays of wealth, but who also now exulted in a ridiculously big Park Avenue apartment and her father's yacht.

Which Tatyana was the real Tatyana?

"Then we'll go," he said.

79

The silver thumb drive labeled "Фантом" was still in his pocket. Tatyana had gone to bed. He waited until he was fairly sure she'd fallen asleep. Then he inserted the device into his laptop. A little icon popped up on the desktop. He clicked on it, and a window opened, filled with what looked like junk.

```
Zmo_7_^UqV/Vj[:_9Mp_;K\K!+ő_'W9@%y_g{s~|w'$I<~IO?__
va+~ D_@2_q__b__rbh_ o@ 8_q"B!Gw?N.Ʉ}_ V;V_U_ *5[?]_Y_
IѰT__.`4_p&)Ëi G.:
```

He stared at the characters for a while, trying to discern a pattern, but he didn't see one. Maybe the thing was just unreadable. Too many years sitting in storage, the flash drive had decayed. He was about to eject it when he had an idea.

Perhaps he was being overly cautious, or just paranoid, but he wanted to save a copy of whatever was on this device before he handed it over to Special Agent Addison. Even if it was garbage. He went to the music-sharing website SoundCloud and logged in. There he found his old collection of mixtapes and music tracks from his college singing group and his garage band. The band wasn't very good, he now realized, but playing together had been fun, and they always got an audience. A small audience. Mostly, they played for themselves.

He uploaded the thumb drive's contents, renamed the file "Stairwaytoheaven.mp4," and then burned the file onto a new thumb drive. Then he went into the bathroom to find a place to hide it. In the kitchen junk drawer, he found a screwdriver. Back in the bathroom, he unscrewed the backplate to one of the wall sconces, put the USB drive in there, and screwed the plate back on.

Then he texted Addison on Signal.

80

At work the next day, Chad stopped by Paul's office around noon and asked if he wanted to pop out to grab a sandwich. This was so unusual a request—given the spread laid out for them every day, there was no reason to go out for lunch—that Paul immediately understood that Chad wanted to talk. He got up and walked out of the office with him, neither of them speaking. It wasn't until they exited the lobby that Chad spoke.

"Dude, I'm scared shitless. They've been asking around about me. Like, am I a troublemaker."

The two fell into silence. The sandwich take-out place, called Baguette, was halfway down the block. They joined a long line that looked like ten minutes of waiting. Chad said hello to a guy who was leaving with his sandwich; he was a pudgy, pasty-faced guy with black curly hair and steel-framed glasses and a nervous tic in his left eye. Paul vaguely recognized him as a new associate but couldn't place the name. He looked around the line, behind them and in front of them. Both sets of people were couples he didn't recognize engaged in conversation.

Chad looked uncomfortable talking about work with other people so near. The two of them discussed football until they got their sandwiches. Chad found an empty table—the take-out place had four or five small, round high-tops for customers.

"Have you seen the security guys Galkin uses?" Chad finally said.

"Oh, yeah."

"Those thick-necked bodybuilding guys who love their weapons?"

"I have."

"They're ex-KGB or -FSB or -GRU. And I hear the Russian security services recruit sadists. I've heard they kill people with flamethrowers."

"Great." Was Chad trying to scare the shit out of him? Unfortunately, it was working. "You think one of those guys killed Larsen?"

"Wouldn't surprise me at all," Chad said.

Paul remembered Mr. Frost asking about Chad and his "dissatisfaction" with the firm, but decided not to tell Chad. He didn't know whom to trust.

Paul turned to look out through the plate glass onto the street. Walking past was Andrei Berzin, Galkin's security director. Berzin turned, peered in. He made eye contact with Paul.

Adrenaline coursed through him. Had Berzin seen him talking with Chad? Maybe so.

Maybe not.

"THIS IS A GOLDEN OPPORTUNITY," said Special Agent Mark Addison. He was wearing another one of his nondescript gray suits with a nondescript blue tie. The normally phlegmatic Addison was more excited than Paul had ever seen him. The two were sitting in a coffee shop a few blocks from Grand Central, a short walk from Paul's office. It was a crunchy sort of place—brick walls, battered leather sofas, Latin music on the playlist.

"Opportunity for what?" Paul asked.

Addison lowered his voice. "Galkin sails with family and close friends and certain business associates, and we want to know who. Names, nationality, passport numbers, port of embarkation, all that."

"How the hell am I supposed to get passport numbers?"

"They'll be on the ship's manifest. Maybe IMO Form 98. Or the IMO FAL Form. And take note of names when you meet people."

Paul exhaled. "How am I supposed to get the ship's manifest?"

"It's always on file in the captain's office, and it's often posted around. You'll find a way."

"Is there security on the boat?"

"Nothing like at his office. Because his passengers are his friends, and he trusts them."

"I don't think Arkady trusts anyone."

"He's starting to trust you."

"I think he did, for a while. But then I went to his institute in Moscow, and I took a trip upstate to the offsite files, and . . . his people suspect me, and I can tell he's wary of me. I feel like something's changed."

Addison didn't say anything.

"So what is Phantom, do you think?" Paul said. He'd handed Addison the little silver object when he arrived, and the agent now palmed it like a magician doing legerdemain.

"We'll see when we examine the flash drive. But our working theory is that 'Phantom' is the code name for the entity that sent all that money to Galkin. This little doodad might well contain all the financial records. It's like gene sequencing—it will likely reveal the actual origin of the funds."

"If there's anything on it," Paul said. He wondered if it was okay for him to admit that he'd inserted the drive and looked at it, that it was all garbage text, or so it seemed. Or that he had made a copy. He decided against it.

He changed tack. "Let me ask you something . . ." he began.

He'd once heard from his uncle Thomas that hundreds of seafarers went missing every year and were never heard from again. Dozens of people went missing from cruises. *If you want to kill someone,* Uncle Thomas had said, *do it on the high seas.* Under maritime law, he explained to Paul, you're not required to report a murder you witness aboard a ship. Turns out, prosecuting crimes committed at sea is extremely difficult. It's often unclear who has jurisdiction when you're in international waters. Governments may occasionally attempt to investigate, but their chief motivation is always to clear their names. That's why bodies tend to disappear at sea.

"Yes?" Addison said.

There was a long pause while Paul's mind revved with paranoia. But this line of thinking seemed so farfetched, so implausible and fantastical, that he decided to keep it to himself. "Nothing. Never mind," he said.

81

Paul and Tatyana boarded a Bell 430 helicopter at the East Thirty-Fourth Street Heliport. They landed at Teterboro a few feet from the Gulfstream.

Four other people were already on board the jet, two couples who appeared to be old friends of the Galkin family. They spoke to Tatyana in rapid-fire Russian, and she didn't bother translating for him. He found out that they were bound for Bermuda. The yacht was sailing from Bermuda to St. Lucia, where the two couples would remain on the yacht. Paul and Tatyana would fly back, commercial, to New York.

"Where's your father?" Paul asked Tatyana during a break in the conversation.

"He's already on the boat."

Tatyana, for her part, had brought Pushkin with her in his plaid carrier. He mostly slept: she had given him a sedative.

The flight to St. George's, on the east end of Bermuda, took a little over two hours. The six of them plus Pushkin got onto another helicopter, which flew them over rows of neat pastel cottages and then to what looked like a cruise ship that was docked in the harbor.

This was Galkin's private yacht, the *Pechorin*. One of the Russian men, Leonid something—he had to get the man's last name—explained on the flight that the yacht was named after the protagonist of a novel by Mikhail Lermontov called A *Hero of Our Time*. Pechorin, a young czarist officer, is handsome, brave, and strong. A hero. But he is also, apparently, sort of a jerk, an asshole to women, prone to duels and playing Russian roulette.

Leonid was an accountant of some sort and apparently knew Galkin from the old country. He made the point that owning a yacht was the ultimate status symbol. "I mean, everyone flies private and has a car and driver, but not everyone has a mega-yacht."

"Not everyone does," Paul replied. "That's true."

"Moscow is crawling with Porsches and Aston Martins and Bentleys and Lamborghinis. But how many have boats like that one?"

"True."

The helicopter hovered above the yacht and then landed on one of her two visible helipads, this one on the foredeck, right atop a big brown *H*.

Paul had been on a yacht once before, Bernie Kovan's, which was quite spacious and elegant but less than a quarter the size of this one. He had been brought up to Bernie's yacht, anchored offshore, on a small boat, a yacht tender. Galkin must have thought that landing by helicopter would be more impressive.

He was right. It was.

Tatyana did not seem impressed, but then, she was used to it all. As they clambered out of the chopper, Paul noticed that the brown *H* was made of stained teak.

The *Pechorin* was built by the German shipbuilders Blohm and Voss. She was enormous—164 meters long, or 540 feet, yet she was not the largest yacht in the world. A few other oligarchs and sheiks, competitively inclined, had recently commissioned larger ones. This one had seven decks. Two helipads. There were berths for seventy crew, forty staff, and twenty guest cabins. Paul knew the *Pechorin* had two swimming pools, a steam room, a library for the guests, an IMAX movie theater, a submarine, an underwater observation deck, and a lot of toys like jet skis and speedboats. And a *banya*, a traditional Russian sauna stocked with birch twigs and eucalyptus. She was a floating palace.

They were greeted by a uniformed server bearing a tray of champagne flutes. Paul took a sip and was pretty sure it was Dom. Maybe Krug. Something expensive, anyway.

THEY HADN'T GIVEN A SINGLE thought to their luggage. It had been taken care of, shuttled from helicopter to plane to helicopter to their room on the yacht. A security guard, a male in his thirties who looked Russian, escorted them and the two other couples into a saloon, where they were asked to sit down before a machine of some sort that Paul didn't recognize.

"What's this for?"

The guard replied in a bored voice, "Security."

Paul looked at Tatyana, who said, "Your palm print. Mine's already in the system."

"For what?"

She said something to the guard, who answered with a chuckle. She laughed, then said, "They used to use fingerprint readers to open doors on the *Pechorin*. But he says the fingerprint reader is bullshit—an intruder can cut off your finger and use it to open any door."

"Hadn't thought of that."

"This system scans the veins in your palm. So it can only open the door while you're alive, because your veins are readable only when you're alive."

The guard pantomimed chopping into his arm.

"Right," she went on, "once someone cuts off your arm, it's useless."

Then they were led to their stateroom. Only, it wasn't a room. It was a suite of several rooms on an upper deck. A sign on the door read, MARK ROTHKO. It was the Rothko Suite. All the rooms were named after modernist painters. Paul was expecting gold-encrusted everything aboard the yacht, like Galkin's East Side town house, but the *Pechorin* was both extravagant and tasteful. And she still had plenty of gold.

"The yacht's interior was designed by François Zuretti," Tatyana said.

Paul shrugged. The name meant nothing to him.

"He's the hot designer among the Russians." The oligarchs, she meant.

Everywhere in the Rothko Suite was marble and onyx and mahogany and teak and custom-made carpeting. Subtle LED lighting. A walk-in closet about the size of Tatyana's old apartment. The bedsheets were Frette. There was a six-foot-wide movie screen in one of the sitting rooms and one almost as big in the master bedroom. That one was hidden behind a huge painting. You pushed a button, and the painting slid down to reveal the TV screen. The painting, of orange and yellow rectangles, was by Mark Rothko.

Perched on the front table was a bottle of Dom Perignon on ice and an arrangement of orchids. Paul realized that a mega-yacht like the *Pechorin* was meant never to be seen by the general public, yet her art and design features were recognizable to her owner's very wealthy private guests, who would appreciate the value of these details.

"I'm going to take a shower," Tatyana said. "Care to join me?"

"We'd better not," he said. "I don't think we have time for that. We have to dress for dinner." The truth was, ever since he'd agreed to cooperate with the FBI, his and Tatyana's sex had been almost nonexistent. And he knew it was all on him: the guilt had dampened his ardor. To make love to her felt somehow dishonest. Traitorous.

While she showered, Paul wrote down the names of the Russian couples they'd met on the Gulfstream, as best as he could remember them. (He'd brought along a little black Moleskine.) Then he inspected the suite more closely. Its walls were paneled in mahogany. The bathroom had a floor made of onyx and a vanity, counter, and walls made of marble. The fixtures were gold. Gold-plated? He wondered. Maybe. Probably. The hand towels were all monogrammed with a capital G intertwined with a Russian one, a Г.

"Who else is on board?" he called to Tatyana as she stood under the rain-head shower. "Besides the folks I met on the jet."

A long pause. Paul was about to repeat his question when she replied, "Papa has invited some rich, important people, and Polina will be here."

"Isn't she always?"

"Not always. She doesn't like to be in the sun. It ages your skin. You'll be delighted to hear that Niko's coming, too. With the latest in his parade of beautiful bimbos. A couple other people I don't know. And of course, Berzin and the security guards."

She emerged from the shower, dried herself with one of the big Turkish cotton bath towels, wrapped her hair with another, smaller towel.

"Pasha, is everything okay with you?"

"Me? Sure, what do you mean?" What was she picking up from him? She did know how to read him pretty well.

"Us, I mean. There's, like, this distance. Or, it feels cooler between us. And not in a good way."

He drew closer, put his arms around her. Was she sensing the guilt that seeped from his every pore?

"You're not cheating on me, are you?"

Softly, he said, "Come on."

After a moment, she said, "Well, something's changed. Anyway, I have to do my hair before it dries." She pulled away.

She blow-dried her hair, applied her makeup. They dressed for dinner.

Tatyana looked amazing; she wore a silky white maxi dress that was extremely sexy. He'd brought his blue blazer and a light-blue linen shirt.

Tatyana brought Pushkin to dinner in his little plaid carrier. "Pushok gets nervous if I leave him alone anywhere that's not home," she explained. She had once told Paul that "Pushok," her nickname for her dog, meant "Fluff Ball."

Paul put the DO NOT DISTURB sign on the suite door. It was in English and Russian.

"Why?" she said.

"We don't need turndown service." He was leaving his laptop in there, and he didn't want their suite searched.

Like that was going to stop anyone.

82

Dinner was to be served in an outdoor dining area on the aft deck, which was beautifully illuminated. With them so far away from the lights of the shore, the sky was black, crowded with stars. The yacht's railings were glass. Several bodyguards, in their gray suits, stood around awkwardly, a couple of them leaning against the bulkhead. That meant the boss was nearby.

Sure enough, Paul spotted Galkin sitting at a small table by a full bar, talking quietly to someone, a younger man with a mop of gray hair. Galkin was wearing a blue blazer and an ascot, like someone out of an Edith Wharton novel. When he saw his daughter entering with Paul, he stood up and extended his arms. He greeted them in Russian and hugged and kissed Tatyana and then, to Paul's surprise, hugged him. In English, he said to Paul, "Welcome to the *Pechorin*. You know who is Pechorin?"

"He's the hero of our time," Paul said.

"*Prekrasno!*" Galkin said. Terrific. "You understand?"

Paul nodded. "Yes."

"You read this book?"

Paul shook his head. "But I will."

"Pechorin is brave and lives his life fully. 'To the hilt,' you say, yes? He doesn't care about society. He never needs to impress people." Then Arkady changed the subject. "How is your room? Is okay?"

"It's great," Paul said. "Amazing. What a beautiful boat."

"Thank you," he said, nodding. "Not bad for half a billion dollars, yes?"

"Not bad at all."

"We talk later, yes?"

Paul, even though he'd been expecting this, felt a jolt in his gut. He said, "Sure," but Galkin had already turned to hug Polina, who was wearing a shimmering gold strapless gown that grazed the floor and looked dazzling. Polina hugged and kissed Tatyana, then Paul, while Galkin greeted the latest arrivals: the two couples from the jet, his old friends. Both the men wore blue blazers. They'd gotten the memo.

Then Niko arrived, wearing a blue blazer and white pants and Gucci loafers with no socks. He gave his sister a peck on the cheek and gave Paul a perfunctory nod. But at least no poisonous look this time. Niko was accompanied by a new girlfriend. He was constantly bringing a different girl around. Then he turned and gave his father a hug and a kiss on the cheek as well.

Dinner was served at one long table. The dining chairs looked like they were covered in gold leaf. There were place cards with the hosts' and guests' names in calligraphy. The stewards and stewardesses all wore white gloves. They were serving flutes of champagne, and vodka for whoever preferred it. The table was set with gleaming silverware and water and crystal wineglasses. On each plate, a white napkin was neatly folded and in a silver ring, in the shape of a fleur-de-lis. There were white floral centerpieces.

At one end of the table, presumably the head, sat Arkady Galkin. Polina sat at the other end. Tatyana was seated near her father. Paul was quite a ways from her. The place card next to his read, ILYA BONDARENKO. Paul committed the name to memory.

A moment later, Bondarenko arrived. He spoke fluent English with the flat accent of a Russian trying to imitate American and maybe overshooting. He didn't wear a blue blazer but a suit jacket and an open shirt. He had thick glasses and a pudgy face, a sallow complexion. He looked about Paul's age, maybe a little older.

"So how are you connected to this gathering?" Ilya asked as he sat.

"I work for Galkin," Paul replied.

"Oh, yeah? I used to, too. What do you do?"

"I manage U.S. equities."

"So you've got my old job," Ilya said. "If you don't mind my saying, I'm surprised he hired an American."

Paul didn't want to explain that he was married to Galkin's daughter.

"Where'd you come from?" Ilya asked.

"Bernard Kovan's fund, Aquinnah. Where do you work now?"

Ilya gave the name of a well-known U.S. hedge fund.

"Why'd you leave Galkin's firm?" Paul asked.

"Rather not say. Sorry. We didn't exactly part on good terms."

"No," Paul said. "I get it." He knew better than to probe. It couldn't be an accident that this guy had been seated next to him.

"Actually, I'm kinda surprised he invited me," Ilya added. "I've been on his yacht only once before. I figured once I was out of his orbit, I was dead to him. But I guess not." He picked up his large white cloth napkin and mopped sweat from his brow.

"You okay?" Paul asked. It was a cool night.

"Yeah, I'm fine. Just hot. Have you walked around this boat yet?"

"Not yet. Just got in."

"Pretty fucking amazing. You know what it's called, right?"

"Sure, *Pechorin*."

"You know who Pechorin is, right?"

"Hero of our times," Paul said, almost by rote. "Lermontov."

"You should read the book. Pechorin is arrogant and cynical. A destroyer of lives. A shithead. A moral cripple."

"Oh."

"It's a weird name for a boat. It's really a statement. Sorta like, I don't give a shit what you think of me. You do you. I do me."

Food was served by two stewards wearing white shirts, gray vests, and black pants. They placed down, from silver platters, some kind of chilled soup served in shot glasses, then a Thai green mango salad. The wines included a Lafite Rothschild as well as a Romanée-Conti. Paul was not a wine guy, but he knew these were very expensive wines. Galkin was showing off.

The main courses were grilled lobster on a bed of peas and rice in the Caribbean style and porcini-crusted filet mignon on a bed of roasted garlic mashed potatoes. You could choose one or have both. Go crazy.

Paul noticed that Ilya Bondarenko wasn't eating or drinking anything. His filet lay untouched. "Everything okay?" he asked.

"Not hungry," Ilya said. "Also a little queasy. Will you excuse me?" He got up and left the table.

Paul decided it was a good moment to take a break, so he got up from the table and looked for the bathroom. The day head, the bathroom, was inside the deck they were on, conveniently located close by. But he bypassed it and kept going down the corridor to the elevator. He took that up two floors to where Tatyana's and his suite was located. As he walked down the wide hall, which was paneled in a light tropical wood, he saw the door to their suite suddenly swing open and several men emerge from it. Two of the men were wearing the gray suits that all Galkin's security seemed to be wearing.

Paul froze. The third man was Berzin, and he was carrying a brown leather briefcase. Up close, Paul could see that the ginger-and-gray-haired Berzin's face was lined with wrinkles. Prematurely: the man was said to be only in his forties. Then there was that scar.

As he approached, and before Paul could say anything, Berzin spoke: "Apologies. I thought it was the WC." He gave Paul a thin, taunting smile and walked away.

83

Paul's immediate thought was that Berzin had seized his laptop to search it while he was at dinner. But it was still there on the mahogany desk in the room he was using as an office. Paul had left it closed and turned off. Now it was open and on.

So Berzin and his crew had at least tried to search it, he assumed. It was password-protected. Maybe that had defeated them. What else was there to search? Not Tatyana's stuff, certainly. The boss's daughter.

Paul returned to the dinner table just as dessert was being served. It was something made of molten chocolate. Everyone was conversing normally and laughing. The wine and vodka flowed freely.

After dinner, Paul and Tatyana returned to their suite. "For some reason, being at sea always makes me sleepy," she said. "I'm going to bed early. What happened to that guy sitting next to you?"

"He said he wasn't feeling well."

"Seasick, maybe?"

"On this boat?" Paul said. "You don't even feel the swells."

She shrugged again. She didn't appear truly interested. "I don't even know why he's on board. Papa normally likes to keep business and social life separate." She yawned. "I need to sleep."

BUT PAUL WAS TOO WIRED to go to sleep. He wanted to explore the yacht. He loved boats and knew them, thanks to Uncle Thomas, and he wondered if he would ever see this one again. Maybe not.

With dread, he reminded himself that he had a job to do: he had to look for the ship's manifest. The passenger list.

The corridors, he noticed, were wider than in most yachts, with higher deck head heights, nearly eight feet. He noticed concealed watertight doors, behind panels in the halls, as well as fire doors. He passed the central stair-case, which wound around the stainless-steel-and-glass elevator. He took the stairs down two floors to the main deck, where a couple of glass doors slid open, and he found himself outside, on the foredeck. There was a full moon, meaning great visibility, and the seas were calm. He saw the polished chrome anchoring mechanism. It was spotless. The crew worked hard.

He passed a couple of security guards strolling along the railing. He heard them speaking English, with English accents, and realized that a fair number of the guards onboard were probably British. The Russians liked to hire British bodyguards. Most of them had done time in the Sandbox, as they called Afghanistan and Iraq, and later went into close-protection work.

One of the guards glanced at him, then looked at the other guard. A paranoid thought occurred to Paul: what if they were to grab him and just toss him over the side of the ship?

No one would know what had happened to him. The guards didn't need a weapon.

He knew that, on most ships, if someone witnessed a passenger or crew member going overboard, there was a whole elaborate drill required by maritime law. The captain had to put out emergency radio calls to nearby vessels, reporting a man overboard. They had to send a digital alert to all ships in the area via the Global Maritime Distress and Safety System. Then all vessels in the region were required to assist in a search.

He thought of Uncle Thomas, lying in a nursing home, and the remark he'd made years ago: *If you want to kill someone, do it on the high seas.*

He turned around and returned to the ship's interior, where he saw, coming toward him, Leonid, the Russian he'd met on the flight over.

Leonid's eyes lit up. "Nice, eh? What I tell you?"

"Sort of mind-blowing, actually."

"There's a freezer just for ice cream. And a mini-submersible on the lowest level—a submarine!"

"That right?"

"What room are you in? We're in the de Kooning Suite."

"I'm in the Rothko."

"Hey, what happened to that guy who was sitting next to you? Ilya, I think his name was."

"I don't know. He wasn't hungry; he said that much."

"Well, Arkady always has a doctor on board. I'm sure he's getting good medical care." He turned, smiled. "I'm heading to the bar. Join me?"

"Another time. I'm off to explore."

84

He started with the bridge, the wheelhouse, where the ship was helmed. In order to enter the bridge, you had to put your palm up to a reader. He wondered if his palm would open the door, so he tried. The doors slid open. This surprised him. He must have been on a VIP list along with Tatyana and other family.

He passed down a narrow corridor and saw a large diagram on the wall, the general arrangement, which was sort of like the floor plan for each deck. He studied it closely. He saw "Massage Room," "Sauna," "Hammam," and one room labeled "Chromo-Therapy." He saw "Owner's Deck," with its private gym (probably used only by Polina, with her trainer), the "Owner's Dressing Room," "Owner's Beauty Center," and "Degustation Area."

As he stood in front of the general arrangement, his eyes searched the corridor. He spotted a door marked, CAPTAIN.

But was the captain in there? He decided first to look into the control room, which was spacious and almost futuristic. The steel walls were painted hospital white. The captain and the first officer sat at what looked like a carbon-fiber countertop, behind a massive control panel with an array of screens, including the green concentric circles of a radar screen and closed-circuit video screens.

The first officer, a woman, turned around and gave Paul a wave. Paul introduced himself. The captain was a very fit, tanned Australian in his fifties, and the first officer was a good-looking Frenchwoman. He idly wondered what their relationship was all about. They chatted a bit, and then Paul excused himself.

Returning to the narrow corridor, he tried the lever on the captain's office door. It came right open.

There was not much here, a steel desk and an office chair, a steel credenza. The desk was piled with papers, in neat stacks. The captain, probably like most seagoing officers, was organized and tidy.

It did not take Paul long to find what he was looking for.

On top of one of the neatly squared piles was a document stamped with the yacht's name, *Pechorin*, the registry (Cayman Islands), and the seven-digit International Maritime Organization number. It was the ship's manifest. It listed the crew by name, and then the passengers, alphabetically by name, passport number, and so on.

He didn't hesitate. He took a picture of the form with his phone, and then, just to be thorough, he took a second picture.

He scanned his eyes over the document, his heart thumping wildly, registering the names of the passengers. When he was done, he replaced the document on the pile, squaring it neatly, and left the small office.

No one was in the corridor, and from this angle, he didn't think he could be seen from the bridge.

Now he descended the winding staircase to the galley, which was also huge, as big as a decent-size hotel's kitchen. It was also immaculate. It had stainless-steel counters, several dumbwaiters, and a giant tank swarming with lobsters.

It took several minutes for his heart rate to return to normal.

He continued his tour, knowing that if anyone asked what he was doing, he had a ready-made, acceptable alibi.

Outside, on the aft deck near a helipad, was a jacuzzi. It was switched on, and in it were two nude figures. He recognized Tatyana's brother, Niko, and his latest girlfriend.

Paul turned around quickly and headed back to the ship's interior.

The yacht was too big to explore in one evening. But in a half hour of climbing stairs and passing through corridors that got narrower as he descended, he managed to see a wine cellar, a cinema, a walk-in freezer, and a very well-equipped gym for the guests. The water makers, which produced fifty or sixty tons of fresh water every day, were, like the pump rooms and the engine room, made of stainless steel or chrome, gleaming and spotless. He saw concealed doors that led to hallways for the crew. Even the crew quarters weren't too grim, from what he could see.

Finally, he circled around to the main saloon, where a big bar was located. He wanted a Scotch or bourbon. There were a few people seated near the bar. The guy from the plane, Leonid, was just leaving. They exchanged waves. Then only two people were left, the other couple from the plane.

Given a choice from among a vast array of single malts, he chose a Macallan 25, because he knew it would be reliably excellent, and of course it was. He also knew it cost thousands of dollars a bottle. He sat down by himself at a table far removed from anyone else, signaling unmistakably that he wanted to be alone. He wanted to enjoy his Scotch and think for a bit, be in his own head, think about what he was doing, try to calm himself. He thought about Phantom, about Galkin running money for the Kremlin. Paul wondered when Moscow would catch up with him.

He had barely taken three sips when he smelled Polina Galkina's perfume. He turned and didn't see anyone. Then he felt her hand touch his back.

"You're all alone?" she said. "Where is Tatyana? Tatyana is asleep?"

Paul nodded.

"Poor dear. She looked very tired at dinner. She was yawning."

"A long day."

"Yet you are Superman."

She sank into a leather club chair next to his. "I didn't have a chance to talk to you at dinner," she said. "You were so far away. Arkady never seats me near you." The night veiled her face.

"It's a long table."

"Are you enjoying yourself?"

"Very much."

"Tatyana gets seasick sometimes. Is she seasick?"

"I doubt it. I imagine there's an excellent stabilization system on this boat."

"I think she gets seasick smelling salt water. Or looking at the sea." She touched his thigh.

Was she putting the moves on him?

"That poor man next to you at dinner," she said, shaking her head.

"What happened to him?" Paul asked.

"In the infirmary, is what Arkady says."

"Does anyone know what's wrong with him?"

She shrugged. "Like they say, shit happens." She smiled uneasily, uncomfortable with the profanity.

He heard the faint chuffing of a helicopter overhead.

"Do you know why he was invited?" he asked.

"Who Arkady invites or won't invite, he doesn't share this with me. You are enjoying the yacht, yes?"

"Very much."

"And you are impressed with the yacht, of course."

"How could you not be?"

"It's all theater, you know." A smile.

Paul looked at her, said nothing.

"We all have roles to play on the stage. And we are the outrageously rich. People want us to be larger than life. This is something I found out about America when I moved here. People want you to be bigger than them or smaller than them but never their size. You are salt of earth or you are crème de la crème."

Paul nodded.

"You know people say Arkady is down to earth, yes? You have heard this?"

"Yes."

"Nobody says an Uber driver is down to earth, yes?"

Paul chuckled. "You have a point."

"You know, Tatyana's photographs intrigue me."

"Me, too."

"Her people, her . . . subjects? Their faces are all so blank. They're perfect screens."

"In a way."

"We want them to have the aura of authenticity, you would say?"

"Yes."

"But they're too perfect. Everything is too posed, too machined, too . . . perfect. You know?"

"I can't agree with you there."

"Tatyana has a way of seeing people that's also a way of seeing past people."

She placed her hand on his thigh again and, this time, let it linger there.

She was indeed putting the moves on him. *You wouldn't even call her a cougar*, Paul thought. *She's around my age.*

With a finger, she traced a design on his inner thigh.

"Polina . . ." he began. Arkady Galkin was probably a very jealous man.

"My husband is a very interesting, very deep character. He is playing multiple games, but I know this. He is . . . You know what is matryoshka?" She gestured with her hands, the figure of a roundish doll, and Paul got it at once.

"Is that what you call those Russian nesting dolls? One inside the other?"

"Exactly."

"Arkady is a matryoshka."

She was by now tracing higher up his inner thigh.

The whirring and whapping and whumping overhead grew suddenly louder, and Paul saw a white-and-red medevac helicopter touch down on the foredeck helipad, illuminated by bright lights from around the landing pad.

Polina withdrew her hand. At that moment, the doors from the yacht's interior slid open and a couple of white-uniformed officers, a man and a woman, sped through carrying a stretcher.

85

Sunshine flooded the suite the next morning. They had left the drapes open. The light glinted on the ocean waves. The light was different at sea. The water looked dark blue.

Paul kept thinking of Ilya Bondarenko's gray face as they loaded him onto the chopper, and he wanted to obliterate the image. He looked to see if Tatyana was awake. In the old days, they would have made love. But he couldn't imagine doing that right now.

She opened her eyes, smiled at him. "Is this whole thing just crazy to you?"

"This . . . ?"

"This . . . What can I say? This boat, this food, this suite . . . this luxury . . . ?"

"It's crazy, yes. It's very alien to me."

"You could get used to this, no?"

"No, I don't think so. I don't think I could ever get used to this."

She kissed him. "And this is why I love you. Mmm. I want some coffee." She picked up the phone on her side table. "Yes," she said, "coffee for me, black." She looked at Paul. "And you, darling?"

Paul was hungry. He ordered an omelet, bacon, multigrain toast, orange juice, and coffee. "You're not eating?" he said to her.

"I'm going to work out first. What did you do last night? Where'd you go? You weren't in bed."

"I went exploring," he said. "Wanted to see the yacht."

"So what ever happened to that guy who sat next to you at dinner? 'Bondarenko' I think his name was."

"Last night they took him away in a medevac helicopter. Probably taking him to the nearest hospital, which must be on Bermuda."

She looked suddenly concerned. "How do you know this?"

"I saw the helicopter land." He decided to be selectively honest. "I had a drink with Polina," he said. He wasn't going to tell her what Polina had been up to.

"And Papa, too?"

"No."

A bell rang, and Tatyana pressed a button on the bedside table. Paul heard the door to the suite open. Tatyana called out, "In here, please."

There was a knock on their open bedroom door. Tatyana said, "Come."

An older Black steward, wearing a blue uniform, entered wheeling a silver cart. "Good morning, ma'am, sir," he said with a Caribbean accent. "Would you like a bed tray?"

"Yes, thank you, Simon."

The steward opened a concealed compartment in the room's paneling and withdrew a silver tray, unfolded its legs, and placed it on the bed. Tatyana had pulled the sheets up to cover herself. The steward set up Paul's breakfast on the silver tray, poured coffee for both of them. "Would you like anything else?"

"We're fine, Simon, thank you," Tatyana said, and with a nod, he left the room.

The coffee was amazing, and the orange juice was freshly squeezed and delicious. The cloth napkins were monogrammed with Galkin's intertwined English and Cyrillic G.

Paul held the napkin up. "Funny your father goes with G for himself instead of a P for *Pechorin*."

Tatyana took a careful sip of the hot coffee. She set the cup down, sighed. "Not so long ago, this yacht was named for his wife, Galina, my mother, so all the towels and everything had a G on them. For 'Galina,' not for 'Galkin.' Or maybe both. Then they divorced, and he married Irina, and everything was monogrammed with a capital *I*. And after *they* divorced, he had to order a whole new set of towels, for the third time, and he must have decided to stop naming his yacht after his wives."

"Makes sense."

She took a few more sips of her coffee and then got out of bed to put on her workout togs, Lululemon yoga pants and a black T-shirt. She left for the gym, and Paul had a leisurely breakfast. He pressed the button for the TV; the Rothko descended, and the TV screen appeared. He watched CNN for a while, then CNBC, as he ate his breakfast. Everything was surpassingly delicious. He felt strangely calm.

After an hour, Tatyana still wasn't back, and he decided to get dressed and work out, too. But when he got to the gym, three floors down, he found it was empty. No Tatyana.

He went back upstairs and made a detour on the main deck, walked to the outdoor seating area, which was also deserted. Where had she gone?

On his way back to their suite, he heard Tatyana's voice. She was standing outside the door to someone's cabin, talking with a man whose voice Paul recognized. Then the man emerged from the room, and he saw the gray-and-ginger head of Andrei Berzin.

For a moment, he considered walking down the corridor and greeting Tatyana. Then he thought better of it and took the stairs up to their suite.

He was washing his hands in the bathroom when Tatyana returned.

"Did you work out?" he asked. Normally, her face was flushed and she glowed with perspiration after a workout. But not now.

"Yeah."

"Why were you talking to Berzin?"

"What? When?"

"A few minutes ago. I saw you coming out of his room."

A strange expression crossed her face and just as quickly vanished. "Oh, Berzin, he has a one-track mind," she said. "He's obsessed with threats to the family, and he wanted to talk about my personal security." She didn't sound very convincing.

"What *about* your security?"

"Oh . . ." she faltered. She fluttered her hands. "Everything. It's so boring. Do we have to talk about this?"

"I think I'm going to finish my tour of the yacht. Want to come with me?"

"I'm starving," she said. "I'm going to take a shower and order my breakfast."

The suite phone rang, startling him. He picked it up.

"Is this Mr. Brightman?" An Englishwoman's voice, crisp and efficient.

"Yes?"

"Mr. Galkin would like to see you, please," she said.

"Sure. When?"

"Right now, if you could. Do you know where the owner's suite is?"

86

Why did Galkin want to see him now? His late night in the office? Polina running her hand along his thigh? His rooting through the firm's old files stored in that defunct limestone mine, discovering a flash drive labeled "Phantom"—and taking it?

Or Moscow?

Or had he been seen photographing the ship's manifest?

There were any number of possibilities, none of them good.

In the elevator, he pressed 03, but the button didn't light up. Then, realizing that Galkin's floor was probably protected, he held his palm up to the black circle, the sensor of the palm-vein scanner device mounted above the number panel. It beeped, a light turned green, and the elevator started to move.

When it stopped, the doors slid open on a narrow corridor and an unmarked set of double doors. Security precautions, maybe. He rang the doorbell.

He waited a full minute—he smelled cigar smoke—and then the door came open. Galkin was resplendent in his blue blazer and open white shirt, no ascot.

"Ah, Paul," Galkin said, escorting him in.

The décor here was similar to their suite's, only the place was even larger. A leather couch, several groups of chairs, a massive slab of stone for a coffee table, and a lot of gold leaf everywhere.

Sitting in one of the club chairs was Andrei Berzin.

Paul's throat tightened.

Galkin pointed to the couch as if Paul were a well-trained dog. Paul sat at one end of it. The leather was buttery soft.

Galkin sat in a high-backed chair across from him, Berzin off to the side. A half-smoked cigar sat in an ashtray on a small, round side table next to Galkin. Berzin didn't appear to have one.

"You know Andrei Dmitrovich, I assume," Galkin said, turning toward Berzin.

"We haven't properly met," Paul said coldly, looking at Berzin. *I know who you are,* he thought. They'd exchanged words outside Paul's suite. And a few words in Moscow. After an awkward pause, Paul stood up and shook hands with Galkin's security director. Berzin's hand was dry and rough.

"Andrei Dmitrovich takes care of my security," Galkin said.

"Yes, I know," Paul said.

Berzin nodded.

"You are having good time, I trust," Galkin said.

"I am, thank you. You have a beautiful boat. But isn't she a bad investment, in purely financial terms?"

Galkin scoffed. "Oh, Paul, my friend, you have imagination of accountant. I will tell you this: one deal signed on *Pechorin* pays back many times over."

Paul nodded. "A good point."

"You like cigar?" Galkin said.

Paul shook his head. "No, thanks."

Galkin leaned back in his chair, crossed his legs. "You take something from me," he said, looking at Paul. He picked up his cigar and drew it back to life, expelling a cloud of bluish-gray smoke.

Paul's insides froze. Galkin had to be talking about the Phantom drive.

"Excuse me?"

More slowly now, enunciating clearly, Galkin said, "You take something from me."

"Did I?"

"Yes," Galkin said gravely. "My daughter."

Paul smiled, but Galkin wasn't smiling.

"Not really," Paul said. "She's still her daddy's girl."

"So I want you to accept my wedding gift, for Tatyana's sake. Do not deprive my daughter."

"Thank you so much for the apartment," Paul said. "It was extremely generous of you. But I need you to understand something. I need to build my own thing. You weren't born with a silver spoon in your mouth, either. I'm sure you understand."

Galkin tipped his head to one side, eyes squinting in the wreathing smoke: maybe he didn't know the expression.

"You came from nothing, got help from no one, and you built this empire," Paul explained. He knew that wasn't true. Galkin had been funded by the Kremlin. That's why he got so rich. "So I'm sure you understand why I want to do my own thing."

"Listen, Paul. I like you. You're not like these coked-up party boys Tatyana used to waste her time with. You have ambition. Zhenya Frost says you are good worker. But I want you accept my wedding present."

A long pause, and then Paul said, "Okay. We will, if Tatyana agrees. And thank you again." He and Tatyana had already agreed they'd accept it. He looked around the suite, at Berzin and then at Arkady. Galkin nodded as if a deal had been struck. "How is Ilya Bondarenko, do you know?" he asked.

"Recovering. He has terrible walnut allergy. Had severe allergic reaction to walnut oil in salad. But this is not why I ask you here. Andrei Dmitrovich has couple questions for you."

"Sure," Paul said, feeling his stomach contort.

Berzin cleared his throat. "You know Volodymyr Shevchenko, our IT specialist."

This wasn't a question. Paul said, "Yes. Vova worked on my computer last week."

"Someone using Vova's credentials signed into the system late one evening last week, and it wasn't Vova."

"Yes? Is that a question?"

"Was it you?"

"How in the *world* would I—"

"Just answer the question."

"Of course it wasn't me," Paul said hotly.

Berzin continued in his icily calm tone. "Vova thought he saw you leaving the building at two in the morning."

Thought he saw you. They didn't know. Paul had badged out using the credentials the FBI had provided, of course, not his own.

"Well, he's wrong. I was at home in bed."

"But when you—"

"*Khvatit!*" Galkin told his security director abruptly. "*Dostatochno!*" "That's enough," he was saying. Then, in English, he said, "Andrei Dmitrovich, this is my son-in-law. My daughter's husband."

"Of course," Berzin said hastily.

"There will be time for investigation." Turning to Paul, his eyes dead, Galkin said, "Are you a spy, Paul?"

"A spy?" Paul said. He felt a freeze creep up his spine. His mind was careening; he was unable to think clearly. Had they found the tracker in Galkin's briefcase and somehow figured out he'd planted it? "Come on, Arkady, that's ridiculous."

"Ah," Galkin said, raising both hands like a benediction. His small eyes glittered. "My security director says you are. I want to believe *you*. Because if you are lying to me"—he wiped his hands together as if he were ridding them of dirt—"I will not care if you are married to my daughter. Is all clear?"

87

Heart galloping, short of breath, Paul returned to the Rothko Suite, found Tatyana sitting in a chair, her little dog on her lap. His crazed thoughts had begun to organize themselves, form patterns. He had been sloppy in his search of AGF's network. He must have set off some kind of silent software alarm. A thorough investigation would indeed incriminate him. What if they pulled the CCTV for the building lobby that night and saw him leaving?

"What's wrong?" Tatyana said, reading his expression.

"Your father doesn't trust me."

"No? What do you mean?"

"He thinks I'm a spy. It's his Stalinist security thug, Berzin. He's got it in for me for some reason."

"Did my father say he doesn't trust you? In those words?"

"Not in so many words. He asked me if I'm a spy."

"Just like that?"

"Right."

"And what did you say?"

"I said no, of course not. I said that was a ridiculous accusation."

"Why did he even ask?"

Paul shook his head. "The details aren't important. One night, someone accessed parts of the company network that are sealed off from most employees."

"Vova saw you," she said, "coming out of the building in the middle of the night."

It was like a cold breeze had suddenly rippled the air. "Where did you hear that from?"

"From Berzin."

"Is that why you were talking to him outside his suite?"

She shrugged. She wasn't going to answer.

"So you already know all this?"

"Yes."

"And are you taking my side?"

"I don't know the facts," she said. Her voice was flat, matter-of-fact, but her expression had clouded.

"Do you believe me or do you believe Berzin?"

"You mean, do I believe you or do I believe my father?"

He felt his chest hollow out. There was a gnawing feeling in the pit of his stomach. "Exactly," he said.

"Pasha," she said after a long pause, "you know me by now. I am a Galkin."

88

The rest of the weekend passed quickly, a succession of meals ever grander and more impressive, costly wines and champagnes. Paul and Tatyana didn't talk much, and when they did, she felt far away. By the time they got out of the helicopter at the East Thirty-Fourth Street Heliport, he was ready to come home.

They arrived at Tatyana's old apartment, and Paul knew at once that something was wrong. To begin with, their welcome mat had been turned upside down.

"What is this?" Tatyana said.

"Strange," Paul said but didn't elaborate. Maybe it was nothing. Kids in the neighborhood pulled random pranks. People stole Amazon packages from people's front doors.

He keyed open the door, and Tatyana entered. Meanwhile, Paul felt on top of the door for the little strand of dental floss he'd left there.

It was gone.

Before leaving, without telling her, he'd put a few little telltale items in various places. Like spies do in the movies. So he would know if someone had been there while they were gone. Their lock was easy to pick.

He hoisted their suitcases and brought them into the foyer. She carried Pushkin in his carry case.

"Did you leave the lights on?" he asked her.

"Definitely not. I remember turning them off. You must have."

He didn't reply. He knew he hadn't left the lights on. Someone had been here and wanted him to know it.

His heartbeat thumped in his ears.

He went into the bathroom next to their bedroom and noticed right away that his razor blade had changed places with his shaving cream. The intruders had deliberately made their work obvious.

He emerged from the bathroom and went to the kitchen while Tatyana wheeled her suitcase into the bedroom. He pulled out a screwdriver from the junk drawer, returned to the bathroom, and locked the door behind him. He switched off the wall sconce to the left of the mirror.

Holding his breath, he unscrewed the backplate. He found the thumb drive still taped inside the plate. Still there.

He let out a breath. He'd successfully hidden it from them. They hadn't found it. He congratulated himself: not a bad hiding place after all.

He removed the little device and slipped it into his pocket, then screwed the sconce backplate back on.

Tatyana knocked on the bathroom door. "Can I come in to take a shower?"

"Sure," he said.

While she took her shower, he opened his laptop and inserted the thumb drive. Only a white X over a red circle appeared on the screen, and a few lines of text:

OSError: The volume does not contain a recognized file system. Please make sure that all required file system drivers are loaded and the volume is not corrupted.

The flash drive had been wiped clean. Before, it had been gobbledygook. Now even the nonsense text was gone.

He suddenly felt short of breath. Someone had indeed found the concealed drive, and they'd erased it.

And put it back.

He texted Special Agent Addison and asked to meet him as soon as possible.

WHILE THEY WERE GETTING READY for bed, and Tatyana was removing her makeup, she said, "When do you want to move?"

Her question caught him by surprise: he'd been lost in thought about how this might be one of the last times he'd watch her remove her makeup. About how he'd probably never live with her anymore. He had no choice about this, he was sure. Galkin's people would get him unless he took off before they had a chance. "Move what?" he said distractedly.

"To the new apartment, silly. Should we wait until this weekend, when you're free?"

"Yeah," he said.

"Of course, it might take a while to get a moving truck—I don't know if anyone's going to be free this weekend, last minute."

"We don't have that much to move," he said, deciding to play along. If he did decide to leave, it was crucial that it be a surprise to her father.

"What do you mean?"

"Well, what are we moving? I've got maybe two suitcases' worth of clothes in my apartment, and you—you might need a wardrobe trunk for your nicer clothes and that's it."

"What about my couch and dining table and chairs?"

"Why don't we sell them? The new place is already furnished, and your furniture might look funny there."

He knew he would never live with her in their enormous new apartment.

IN THE MIDDLE OF THE night, his cell phone rang, but he'd left it charging in the living room and didn't hear it.

IN THE MORNING, ON HIS way to the bathroom, he snatched his phone from the coffee table and checked it. One missed call. It was from Chad Forrester. He'd left a voice memo.

While he made coffee, he listened to Chad's message. As he listened, his stomach grew tauter and tauter, and he suddenly didn't want coffee anymore, didn't want or need the jolt:

Brightman, I'm so fucked. I'm, like, a dead man. They think I downloaded some top-secret files from, like, the inner sanctum or something, which I definitely did not do. I have no fucking idea what they're talking about. And, like, they say they have me on video leaving the office at two in the morning last week. Which is bullshit—I was home asleep! And they have audio recordings of me bitching about the firm.

I don't know what's going to happen to me, man. I mean, look what they did to Larsen, and if I die of an overdose, you know it's not true. And you're next, man. Don't come into work, man. I saw the security people coming out of your office, and you know what that means, right? I saw them going into Larsen's office right before they killed him. So, call me, man. Now.

Chad had called at 3:10 a.m.

When Paul called him back, the phone rang and rang and rang.

89

While Paul was in the shower, he thought about what Chad had said. *They say they have me on video leaving the office at two in the morning last week.*

Paul had deliberately worn the standard-issue young-investment-professional uniform: the quilted Orvis vest, the Yankees cap, the Stan Smiths. He'd meant to look like anyone in the firm. Plenty of guys wore Yankees caps, though not Paul. But maybe the Stan Smiths were a mistake—Chad wore them.

He felt queasy with guilt. He didn't know what to do.

He heard his phone ring. Dripping wet from the shower, he grabbed it off the bathroom vanity, saw that the caller was Mr. Frost.

"Yes?"

"When you come into work this morning, please come directly to my office," Frost said, and the line went dead.

At about the same time, his phone plinked with an incoming Signal text notification. That could be only one person: Special Agent Addison. They were already scheduled to meet at noon; was Addison canceling for some reason?

The phone slipped out of Paul's wet hand and hit the tile floor. "Shit," he said. He leaned over, picked it up. The screen wasn't cracked; the phone looked okay. He clicked on the FBI man's text message:

Do NOT go into work, leave the apartment immediately, meet now.

He felt his heart whumping in his ear. Maybe they had found the tracker in Galkin's briefcase after all. Oh, Jesus.

He dressed quickly, throwing on jeans and sneakers and a sweatshirt.

Tatyana, who was just waking up, saw him and said, "Where are you going?"

"Casual day at work," he lied. He kissed her, wondered if this was the last time he'd ever do so.

Then he walked quickly downtown to East Houston Street and

entered one of the few remaining old-style delicatessens in New York City. Addison was sitting at a table, a bagel and lox and cream cheese half-eaten on the table before him. Next to him sat a slightly pudgy young woman with short dark hair.

"Glad you made it," Addison said. "This is Special Agent Stephanie Trombley. She's just joined our team."

"Hi, nice to meet you," Paul said. Turning to Addison, he said, "What's going on?"

"One of your colleagues, Chad Forrester?"

"Yeah?"

"Forrester was hit by a car early this morning. He's dead, Paul."

90

Paul's heart juddered. "Were you in touch with him?" he asked Addison. "Or can't you say?"

Trombley looked at Addison, who said, "We were not in touch with him."

That could mean only one thing: Chad was killed because they, Galkin's people, thought he was spying on the firm. In trying to disguise himself as a generic investment guy for the CCTV, had he accidentally implicated Chad? Paul's chest felt hollow and his stomach roiled with acid.

"The situation has escalated," Addison said. "We'll talk across the street."

"Across the street?"

"You asked why I haven't taken you to our office. Well, our unit is based across the street, and you're going to be meeting with someone quite high up."

They crossed East Houston Street to a narrow white-brick building that had a tourist shop on the street level. The window was filled with I ♥ NEW YORK T-shirts and Yankees mugs and snow globes. Next to it was an unmarked door. They pressed through that door and entered a small, dusty lobby with a sign on the wall listing the building's tenants. Without speaking, they took the elevator to the fourth floor. Right where they got off the elevator was a door with a large inset glass panel on which was stenciled, in gold leaf lettering, KNIGHT & HAWLEY ACTUARIAL CONSULTING.

Through the glass, Paul saw a bland, plain-looking office, metal desks and metal chairs, some cubicles. Glaring fluorescent lighting. It could have been a small insurance firm stuck in the nineteen seventies. Maybe four or five employees. Agent Addison stood at the door, and it buzzed open. He put out his hand, and Paul obligingly handed over his phone. An ordinary-looking office that took extraordinary precautions. There were to be no covert recordings.

Looking around the office, Paul said, "What is this place?"

"The offsite unit for certain financial crimes investigations."

"Undercover?"

"Basically."

They were standing in a conference room off the main area, a sparsely furnished room whose walls were glass down to about waist level, an old-fashioned design. As soon as they'd entered, Paul noticed the outside noise diminish to nothing. The glass walls were clearly soundproof. Maybe bulletproof, too.

"Why did you warn me not to go into work?"

"Because our intel suggests you're about to be taken in by Galkin's security and questioned and then . . . well, who knows?"

"Yeah, I have a pretty good idea what happens to me next. So I need to disappear." Paul said. He then told the two FBI agents about how Tatyana's apartment had obviously been searched and how whoever'd searched it had found the thumb drive and erased it and then left the blank drive there for him to find.

"Disappear? You're talking about WITSEC?" Trombley said.

Paul knew that was what the FBI called the Witness Protection Program. He nodded.

"You want to go into witness protection. I understand. But it's a big decision. You'll have to leave your life behind, your name, your family. Are you really ready for that? And what about your wife? Are you prepared to leave her behind, too?"

"I don't know. I haven't decided. I don't think she'd go with me, to be honest." Her words—*Pasha, you know me by now. I am a Galkin*—echoed in his head.

"Here's the thing," Addison said. "There's a whole process to determine if you get admitted into Witness Protection. You've got to be vetted by my higher-ups, including the woman you're about to meet. Also, the U.S. Attorney General's Office, the U.S. Marshals Service, the Office of Enforcement Operations. It's a long, arduous process."

"Okay, you can get me through—"

"But it's only for witnesses whose testimony is crucial for the successful prosecution of a case. And we're not at that stage yet. I don't even know if we have a case."

"Does that mean I have to testify against Galkin?"

"It does. Without testimony, no witness protection, simple as that."

Paul felt a jolt of fear shoot through him. He imagined himself in a courtroom facing down Galkin, with Tatyana in the gallery, and it felt horrible. "If you don't get me in, I'm screwed. I'm dead meat. I'll have to do it myself. My own Witness Protection Program."

I'll need to disappear myself, he thought.

At that point, there was a knock on the door. Outside, visible through the glass, loomed a stout, squarish woman with blonde hair cut in a Diana, Princess of Wales, style. She was dressed in a navy suit with big shoulders. She was making a summoning sign with her index finger, palm up. A sign that meant she wanted someone to come out.

Special Agent Addison opened the door for her. She entered, and Addison and Trombley both immediately left the room. It was evident that this woman was their superior.

"I'm Geraldine Dempsey," the woman said, clasping Paul's hand. Her eyes twinkled. "It's so nice to know you." Her voice was surprisingly deep and pleasant. Then her eyebrows tented in a look of great concern. "You must be scared half to death."

91

Geraldine Dempsey—she introduced herself by name and not by title, which was interesting—had a thick twang. Texan, Paul decided.

"Scared? You could say that." He wondered why she was here, what she wanted from him. "I assume you're FBI, right?" he said. "What's your title?"

"I'm not FBI," she said. "CIA, actually."

"But . . ."

"You could call me a Russia expert, I suppose, though maybe the 'expert' part is in doubt these days. I mean, is *anyone* an expert on Russia? Who knows what's really going on over there?"

Paul nodded. He still wondered why she was here. She seemed to have juice. Maybe she was the emergency exit he needed.

"I don't understand," he said. "This is an FBI office, right?"

"We do cooperate from time to time, you know. Anyway, first I want to thank you so much for your contribution. You are a cooperating witness, is that right?"

"Yes."

"How long have you been providing information to the Bureau?"

"Several months."

"Wonderful. Well, as you might imagine, I'm very much interested in Arkady Galkin. And the fact that one of your colleagues at Galkin's firm is dead under suspicious circumstances."

"Two."

She arched an eyebrow.

"Jake Larsen died of, presumably, an overdose. And Chad Forrester was killed this morning."

She shook her head as if this were news to her. "So I'd like to get to the bottom of this." Her accent was *West* Texan, Paul deduced. He had a friend from El Paso who sounded just like her. "We think the killers are from one of the Russian intelligence services, probably GRU."

"Working together with Galkin?"

She nodded. "Let's sit down." She gestured toward the conference table, motioned for Paul to sit at its head, and she sat on his right side. "Tell me everything you know about Arkady Galkin, from the beginning. From the first time you met him. Actually, why don't you start with how you first met his daughter."

"Why?" Paul said. "What's the point? I've already told Special Agent Addison everything I know. Don't you guys talk to each other?"

"If you'll indulge me. I'm told you're a first-class noticer, and I want to hear everything from your own mouth, including all the nuances. So much gets lost in interoffice memos."

He took her through how he'd met Tatyana, at the charity function, how they started going out, how he'd had no idea who she really was, no idea that she was an oligarch's daughter. The ridiculously over-the-top anniversary party at Galkin's town house. How he and Galkin had bonded right away. How Galkin had lured him with a huge salary and bonuses. His growing suspicions that Galkin's firm was engaged in insider trading, how Galkin clearly had sources inside the U.S. government. And how he was probably working for Moscow.

She nodded. "Whom did you tell your suspicions to?"

"Special Agent Addison."

"I mean, apart from him."

"Nobody."

"Not even your friend Rick Jacobson?"

He momentarily startled. He'd never mentioned Rick to the FBI. She'd evidently done some background investigation.

"No, not Rick."

"You drove to the offsite storage facility where Galkin's firm keeps old records," she prompted. "Is that where you found that flash drive that was labeled 'Phantom'?"

He nodded.

"How did you know it would be there?"

"I didn't," Paul confessed. "It was just a lucky guess."

"No grass grows under your feet. What did you do with it?"

"Eventually, I gave it to Special Agent Addison."

"And did you keep a copy?"

Paul hesitated a beat. "Yes, I made a copy."

"Can I ask you why?"

"Why I made a copy?" He thought for a moment. Why had he? "In case anything happened to it," he said, which he knew wasn't an adequate explanation.

"You hid a copy in your—in your wife's apartment," she said.

"I did."

"Why?"

"It was the best place I could think of to hide it."

"But they found it anyway."

"Right."

"So you don't have a copy anymore, is that right?"

Paul hesitated, thinking of the copy he'd put up on SoundCloud. "Right," he said, though he didn't sound convincing.

An expression of distrust flickered across her face. "Do you know what's on that drive?"

"No. It's encrypted. It looks like garbage."

"And you didn't try to get it decrypted?"

"How the hell could I do that? That's way beyond my skill set."

"Now, tell me about how you found the secret files on your firm's server."

Paul told her about the night he hacked into AGF's network using the IT guy's credentials.

"Ingenious," she said. "You've got more guts than you can hang on a fence."

"Not really."

"What did you learn from those documents?"

"That Galkin's fortune all came from the Kremlin. That he's secretly managing the Kremlin's money."

Her expression didn't waver. Her features showed no surprise. "Did you keep a copy of those files?"

"No."

"Why not?"

"I don't know. There wasn't time."

A long pause. "And did you tell your wife about what you found?"

"Tatyana? No way."

"Or your friend Rick?"

"No."

"Or any other friends?"

"No."

"What did you learn on Galkin's yacht?"

"I got the passenger list. The manifest. I gave that to Addison."

"And I assume you made a copy of that, too."

Paul didn't answer her implied question. "Before we go any farther, let me ask you: does the CIA have a witness protection program?"

"Look, I like you," Dempsey said. "So I'm not going to bullshit you. The Agency is one giant bureaucracy. It's the worst bureaucracy in the entire U.S. government except for maybe the U.S. military. It's like the Department of Motor Vehicles on steroids. As they say in the mother country"—and then she said something quickly in Russian that Paul didn't get. Dempsey translated for him: "Anyone who served in the army doesn't laugh at the circus."

"What's your point?"

"We have a resettlement program for intelligence defectors. But that's not you. Alas. Why are you asking?"

"Because I think I'm next."

"Because . . . ?"

"Because I'm a cooperating witness for the FBI."

"But Galkin can't possibly know that."

"He knows I went into the firm's files, both at the office and in the storage place upstate. He may have found out that I was doing some investigation on him in Moscow. He may—it's possible, and good God, I hope not—they may have found the tracker in his suitcase and know it was me. They want me to come in, probably for questioning. And then I'm probably going to get hit by a car. Or die by poisoning."

"Well, Paul, we can protect you," Dempsey said. "As long as you remain a cooperating witness."

He felt a wriggle of some reptilian fear. "What does that mean?"

"I think you have copies of the manifest from Galkin's yacht on your phone. I'd like to see your phone, and I'd like to see you delete those photos. From the phone and from the cloud."

Paul just looked at her, didn't say anything.

"Same for any copies you have of files on Galkin. Those must be deleted as well."

"Why?"

"I'm afraid this is a matter of national security. It's a matter of compartmentation. We can't have those files floating around the internet, unsecured."

"They're quite safe."

"I'm sure you think so," she said with a smile, her eyebrows tented again, the way you'd speak to someone who was mentally deficient. "But they're not, and you need to hand them over or delete them right away."

Paul hesitated a long time while he thought. Then he said, "I'm willing to do that if you can guarantee me Witness Protection, WITSEC. Call it a deal."

She stared at him for a long moment.

Meanwhile, he examined the wooden tabletop, scratched and smudged. He examined the gray carpet, stained and grimy. There were fingerprints and smudges, too, on the glass walls.

He rewound Geraldine Dempsey's line of questioning. She hadn't seemed surprised by his conclusion that Galkin was underwritten by the Kremlin. In fact, nothing he told her had seemed to surprise her. And how did she know Rick Jacobson's name? Also, she was obsessed with whether he'd made and kept copies of the Phantom flash drive and the other files and whether he'd told anyone about them.

Over the last week, he had thought quite a bit about how to disappear himself, but he kept getting stuck on one thing: if he changed his name and vanished, he would be leaving Tatyana behind. She loved him, Paul believed, as much as she could, but her primary loyalty was to her family. She wouldn't leave with him.

But shouldn't he make sure?

Should he ask her outright? The problem was, if he asked her to go away with him, she would immediately tell her father. Of that he was certain. He'd have to take off as soon as she told him no.

Geraldine Dempsey was looking at him, her mouth a straight line, unreadable. Then she smacked the table gently and stood up.

"I'll see what we can do," she said at last.

92

When he was on East Houston Street, he called Tatyana, wondering if she was out taking pictures. She picked up on the second ring. "Hi," she said.

"Anything going on?" he asked.

"Going on?" she said lightly. "What do you mean?"

"Are you at home?"

"Yeah, why?"

"Are you there alone or . . . ?"

"Just me and little Pushok," she said. "Why?"

"We'll talk when I get back from work," he said.

"But . . . Zhenya Frost called me to ask where you were. He said you didn't come in."

"I had some errands to run," he said. "I'm on my way back into the office now."

He was lying to her.

But at least he had a plan.

THE IDEA HAD COME TO him a few weeks before, on one of his visits to his uncle's long-term care facility in New Rochelle.

The head nurse there was named Sheila Drake. She was a large woman with a great mane of auburn hair, in her thirties. Sheila was loquacious and not very discreet. She loved to talk about the son of a celebrity who was being taken care of here. She also often mentioned the young man who had been in a coma for nearly five years. She seemed to think that the more exotic her patients, the more qualified the nursing home.

"The young guy in a coma—what happened to him?" Paul asked.

"He was in a cycling accident and landed on his head."

"Five years ago?"

She nodded. "Hasn't spoken since. Hasn't opened his eyes. It's tragic. He's spent the end of his twenties in a coma. In a vegetative state."

Paul shook his head. "What a nightmare."

Even as he was speaking to his uncle, he was thinking about the young man in the coma. Does someone in a coma have dreams? Do they have nightmares? What did it mean, really, to be in a vegetative state? Did you not have thoughts?

He stopped for a moment outside the coma guy's room, next to Uncle Thomas's, and suddenly realized what he might be able to do.

PAUL HAD NOTICED THAT THE files on the patients were kept in black horizontal file cabinets against the wall behind the nurses' station. He'd also noticed that Nurse Sheila took her lunch break at 1:30 every afternoon.

On what would turn out to be his final visit to Uncle Thomas, he showed up at 1:30 and found the nurses' station unattended. The other two nurses were on their rounds. Looking from side to side, making sure no employee was in sight, he slipped behind the counter, found the right drawer, and pulled it open. Quickly, he found the folder tab labeled "ANDERSON, Grant."

Inside, he found what he needed right away: the man's Social Security number and most recent home address. He snapped a picture with his phone and then closed the drawer and was out of there before anyone appeared.

Grant Anderson was three years younger than him, which was close enough in age. That meant that Paul could borrow Grant's identity. After all, Grant wasn't using it. Taking—stealing—someone's identity turned out to be the easiest way to start a new life in the twenty-first century.

He rented a mailbox at a UPS Store on East Fifty-First Street. Using Grant Anderson's Social Security number and this new address, he was able to get a new Social Security card and a birth certificate, both sent to his UPS mailbox. It took about three weeks.

When the time was right, and if necessary, he was ready to become Grant Anderson.

93

Paul was now certain that he couldn't expect any help or protection from either of those two government agencies, the FBI or CIA.

He was on his own.

Returning to Tatyana's building on East Seventh Street, he took extra precautions. He watched the building's dilapidated brick entrance from across the street to see if anyone was loitering suspiciously. Any vehicles idling. He looked for a black Suburban, which seemed to be the Galkin team's SUV of choice, but saw none. Of course, if this was surveillance, or countersurveillance, he had no idea what he was doing. He'd been trained by spy novels and movies and TV shows, and that was all.

Finally, he crossed the street, entered the dim lobby without incident. Climbed up to the fourth floor, keyed the door open.

"Tatyana, you here?" he called out.

"Yes," she replied. He found her sitting on the couch chatting quietly with a graying ginger-haired man: Andrei Berzin.

Half an hour earlier, she'd said she was alone, with only her dog. Had she been lying then?

"Mr. Brightman," Berzin said.

"Just you and little Pushok, huh?" Paul said to his wife.

Tatyana opened her mouth but didn't say anything. She was vaping. She exhaled a curl of smoke. Her eyes searched him.

"It's just me here, no one else." Berzin said. "Tatyana and I were just catching up. But I came here primarily to speak with you. We need to have a talk, you and I."

The Russian security man wore an expensive-looking dark-gray suit with a crisp white shirt and a gold tie. His brown cordovan oxford shoes were polished to a glint. His hair, graying faded copper, was perfectly parted on his left side, neatly combed, gelled into place. Tatyana had said that Andrei Berzin had once worked for the KGB. Paul had never met any KGB agents, to his knowledge, but based on the thrillers he read and watched, he imagined them as silkily sinister, and Berzin fit the type. Who knew, maybe your average KGB agent was actually a thug and a brute; Berzin, in any case, was smooth.

Paul looked around the room, though what he was looking for, he didn't know. He looked at Tatyana. She put down her vape pen and said, rising from the couch, her dog in her arms, "Let me get us some tea. You men can talk." She left the room, with Pushkin over her left shoulder.

"All right," Paul said reluctantly, sinking into a chair facing the couch.

The two men looked at each other for a long time. Was Berzin here to take him prisoner for Galkin? And if so, why was he here alone, without thugs to help apprehend the boss's son-in-law?

"Tatyana and I have been talking about recent threats we've been receiving," Berzin said. "It's a strange time—there is so much antagonism in America against Russia and Russian people. All this American animosity we've been seeing recently."

"You're getting threats against Galkin?"

"There are crazy, unhinged people who call or email our company's offices all the time, making threats. Sometimes they even mention Mr. Galkin's children. We've increased security on his residences in the U.S., but that's not enough. We need to monitor the threats, know when they're being made."

"Okay."

"In a rational world, I would pass these threats on to the FBI, but we've had no luck there. They're as anti-Russian as anyone."

"Really?"

"I would call them Russophobes. So it falls to me to investigate and follow up."

"I see," Paul said, though he didn't.

"Ah, thank you, Tatyana," Berzin said.

She had arrived with a melamine tray on which were arranged a teapot with a chipped spout and teacups and pots of jam and sugar and milk. A plate of cookies. She handed each man a cup and saucer. The tea had already been poured. Pushkin skittered around her feet. Paul found it a bit odd that she had poured the tea beforehand, in the kitchen, rather than doing it the Russian way and filling their cups right in front of them.

He set the saucer and cup down on the table next to him without taking a sip. He could smell the smoky aroma of the Russian Caravan tea her father always served at home.

"Oh, Paul, I have those biscuits you like, from Fortnum and Mason." She handed him the plate of cookies, and he took one. He noticed that she didn't offer the plate to Berzin.

"Great, thanks," Paul told her.

Berzin took a sip of tea, and so did Tatyana. Paul did not. His paranoia had shifted into high gear.

"My father always drank his tea the old-fashioned way, with a sugar cube between his front teeth," Berzin said, turning to Paul. "I like it the modern Russian way, with a little jam stirred in." He reached over to the pot of jam and spooned a couple of teaspoons into his tea, then took another sip. "Would you like some jam, or do you have it like an American?"

"No, thanks," Paul said.

Berzin crossed his legs. He bounced one foot in the air with a steady beat. He took another sip of tea.

"You should have your tea before it gets cold," Tatyana said. She picked up Pushkin and cuddled him. Paul noticed that her face was flushed and damp. He could see beads of perspiration forming on her forehead and chin. He said nothing. She picked up her vape pen and inhaled.

"I think there have been misunderstandings," Berzin said calmly. "We have reason to believe you were taking things from the firm that don't belong to you, that you're not authorized to see or download."

"Not true," Paul said.

"If we are misunderstanding, we are open to talking."

Paul nodded. "Am I being fired?" he said.

Berzin smiled. He was not a man who smiled much, and this effort at one carved deep lines into his cheeks. "No, of course not, Mr. Brightman."

Tatyana dabbed at her face with a napkin.

"Are you okay?" Paul asked her. "Is it too hot in here?"

"No, maybe from the tea, I don't know." She laughed weakly. "Am I too young for hot flashes? I should have made *iced* tea, I guess."

Paul picked up his cup, then took one of the Piccadilly butter biscuits and dipped it into his tea. Then, leaning forward, he offered it to Tatyana's little dog, who licked his chops.

Tatyana let out a sudden screech and yanked Pushkin away from him, from the biscuit. Cradling her dog, she ran out of the room, and Paul got to his feet, his nerves jangling, his heart ricocheting.

94

Berzin watched the scene with visible alarm.

"Excuse me a moment," Paul said to Berzin. He didn't follow Tatyana into the bedroom. Instead, he turned and left the apartment, his heart hammering. He was in a state of shock as he descended the stairwell.

Tatyana knew something was in the tea and had gone along with it. There was no other explanation. His own wife had betrayed him—worse, had cooperated with Berzin to . . . what? Poison him?

Tatyana had known what Berzin wanted to do.

She had warned him: When it came down to it, she was a Galkin.

Nobody was lurking on East Seventh Street, no vehicles idling, no one apparently waiting for him. He walked down the block to St. Mark's Place. Maybe Berzin had been telling the truth that he'd come alone. But Paul didn't believe that. He had to have reinforcements in place, people who were ready to grab Paul if the poisoning scheme didn't work.

Earlier that day, Paul had bought a disposable phone at a bodega. It took a few minutes to download WhatsApp to the phone and set it up.

Now he turned off his iPhone. He had to assume that Berzin's people had cloned his phone, that they knew his whereabouts at every moment, from the phone's GPS. He'd read once about some kind of Israeli software that allowed governments to secretly install spyware on your phone, remotely, enabling them to monitor your calls and track your location.

Yes: he couldn't use his iPhone anymore.

Then he called Special Agent Addison on WhatsApp. He let it ring and ring until the call went to voicemail. Paul left a message, telling Addison to call back immediately, that it was an emergency.

A few blocks out of St. Mark's Place, he came to Third Avenue and walked to the Bleecker Street station, where he caught the 6 train and took it to Spring Street. A Black man sitting across the car glanced at him and looked away, the way you try not to look at crazy people on your train who might be provoked by your glance.

Adrenaline was flooding Paul's system. His heart was knocking. He walked down Lafayette Street a couple of blocks. He looked around, didn't see anyone obviously following him, but if they were good at what they did, wouldn't he not see them anyway?

He tried Addison again on his cell phone. It rang five times and then went to voicemail once again.

When he arrived at East Houston Street, he found the narrow white-brick building across from the great deli, the one with the tourist souvenir shop on the street level. The door to the lobby was open. He took the elevator to the fourth floor.

When the elevator stopped and the door opened, he saw the door with the curved retro gold lettering that read KNIGHT & HAWLEY ACTUARIAL CONSULTING. The window in the door was dark. The venetian blinds were closed.

But why was the FBI office closed, in the middle of a workday? The blinds were closed for some reason.

He found a doorbell button to the right of the doorframe and pushed it.

Nothing happened.

About to push the button again, he instead decided to knock on the door. As he knocked, the door came open.

The first clue that something was off was the smell in the air: sharp and familiar and coppery.

It was dark in there—all the window blinds were closed, and the fluorescent lights were off. In a moment, his eyes adjusted to the darkness, and he saw a sight that didn't register at first. It looked like the assistants at the front counter were napping, their heads down. He knew what he saw a moment before it made any sense to him.

Blood everywhere.

It was nearly kaleidoscopic and vaguely unreal, that first image, the colors. Dark red blood under the glaring overhead light. It looked like several of the victims—who, he now saw, included Special Agent Mark Addison—had pulled out their weapons, but clearly not in time. A few of the agents had tried to run but had been cut down. He didn't stay long enough to count the victims, but it looked like six. He was pretty sure he didn't see Special Agent Stephanie Trombley. All around the room, cell phones were ringing.

The image was too real to be real. At first, it reminded him of a scene from the kind of horror film he'd always hated, with gruesome deaths and blood and disfigurement.

He looked back at Addison. His head was lolling forward on his chest. In his outstretched hand was a black Glock. Blood was pooling on the wall-to-wall carpet, seeping into it; blood spattered the walls and the desks, and then there was that terrible smell, the acrid smell of gunfire and the dry, sweet, metallic tang of blood, like a copper penny in your mouth.

He heard sirens.

95

The blood looked fresh. It glistened; it hadn't dried yet.

His head was spinning. The terrible odor stayed in his nose, the horror of the gruesome images imprinted on his mind's eye. He looked around again. The hallway was dark and empty.

The sirens were closer, louder. Now he heard shouts: "FBI!"

They were entering the building. Vehicle doors slammed. He heard the crackle of walkie-talkie transmission. Feet thundered up the stairwell.

He knew he had to run, to get away from this nightmarish scene, or he might somehow be implicated, be questioned, be detained—and that couldn't happen. He ran down the stairs to the rear exit, so he wouldn't encounter law enforcement.

Where, he wondered, was Trombley? She was safe, unharmed. Maybe she knew what had happened. Maybe she'd know what to do. He had to trust her. Addison had trusted her, after all. He remembered, briefly, Geraldine Dempsey, the CIA woman from Texas, but he instinctively didn't trust her.

The building was narrow but deep. He finally found the back exit, a steel door with a crash bar and a sign warning that an alarm would sound if the door were opened. He decided to chance it. Sirens were going off everywhere; who would notice? He pushed the door open and nothing happened. The exit gave onto a small alley that led him to Avenue A.

Standing on the street, he pulled out the business card Trombley had given him and called the number using the burner phone he'd bought that morning. It was her direct line at the FBI office at 26 Federal Plaza in Manhattan. A male voice came on the line and said that Agent Trombley had been transferred to FBI Headquarters in D.C. Paul asked to be connected to her new office. The phone rang five times and went to voicemail. He called the number she'd jotted down on the back of her business card, her cell phone, and that line rang and rang as well and then went to voicemail.

About a minute later, his own phone rang. An unfamiliar number. He picked it up, said, "Yes?"

A woman's voice, loud. "Brightman?"

"Yes, is this Trombley?"

"Where are you?"

He stumbled on the words. "Near the office—East Houston Street and Avenue A—"

"Get out of there."

"You know about—?"

"A goddamn massacre!" Trombley rasped. "I just saw the flash. My God. Jesus!"

"Who did it?" Paul asked.

"I—I can't tell you anything. Right now, I can only speculate— probably GRU."

"In *America?*" Was it possible, he wondered, that agents of Russian intelligence had just wiped out an FBI office in order to keep them from uncovering Arkady Galkin as a Kremlin agent? Did that kind of thing actually happen within the borders of the United States?

"Who the hell knows? Just—get the hell out of there, Brightman."

"I need protection," Paul said.

She sounded nearly hysterical. "You want protection? *I* want protection."

Paul felt a chill as he ended the call.

He hailed a passing cab. The cab swerved over to the side of the street, and Paul hustled into it.

"Where to?" the driver said.

For a moment, Paul didn't know what to say. He cleared his throat. "Port Authority, please."

96

As the taxicab barreled down FDR Drive, Paul wedged his iPhone into the horizontal crease in the seat cushion. He couldn't shove it all the way in and out of sight, so part of it stuck out. But that was okay. The phone was black and the seat cushion was black. You had to really look to notice it. And maybe someone would steal it. That would be okay, too.

Let Berzin's guys ping the phone and think he was traveling all around the streets of Manhattan, wherever the cab went.

He was laying down a false trail. Just as he'd googled real estate in Ecuador, in the capital city of Quito, on his home laptop—which he assumed was also bugged. He'd even bought a book on Ecuador and left it in a desk drawer in his office, where it could be quickly found.

He'd also bought a plane ticket from Chicago to Quito, business class, one way.

Paul had the cab drop him on Forty-Second Street, and he entered Port Authority, New York's main bus terminal. It was said to be the busiest bus terminal in the world, and he believed it. In the mental state he was in, adrenaline-frazzled and scared, it seemed nearly postapocalyptic.

He found a ticket vending machine and bought a one-way bus ticket to Chicago with his Paul Brightman Visa card. It cost over two hundred dollars. The bus trip sounded like a grueling ride, over twenty-five hours. He had done a fair amount of googling on his laptop on extended-stay hotels in Chicago. He had no doubt that Berzin's crew kept track of his credit card payments. That wasn't hard to do. It was also likely that once Tatyana realized her husband had disappeared, she would call NYPD. They would probably investigate. They had access to credit card charges and the camera in this vending machine that was pointed at him. Once they found that he'd bought the plane ticket from Chicago to Quito, they'd begin to put together a theory.

At least, that was what Paul hoped.

He exited the terminal at Forty-Second Street, and very close to the entrance, he saw a homeless guy sitting on the sidewalk with a sign that read, TOO UGLY TO PROSTITUTE, TOO HONEST TO STEAL!

He dropped a buck into the guy's Starbucks coffee cup. "I like your sign."

"Well, all right." The man smiled a gap-toothed smile. He appeared to be in his sixties but probably was a lot younger; living on the streets or in homeless shelters will do that to you.

"Can I enlist you to help me with something?" Paul had taken a twenty from his wallet, and now he was waggling it.

"Hell yeah, you can. What you need help with?"

"Buy me a cell phone from that newsstand over there?" He tore the twenty in half and handed half to the man. Pointing at the newsstand, he said, "You get the other half when you come back with the phone. Cheapest one they have. The phone will cost you nineteen bucks." He handed him a twenty, this one intact. "Come back with the phone and keep the change. Then you get the other half of the twenty."

Paul half-expected the man to disappear with the twenty bucks. But he stopped at the newsstand and returned with a Nokia TracFone in a plastic blister pack.

"Wanna make another twenty?" Paul asked.

"You want another phone?"

"How about buying me a bus ticket to Albany? You know how to do that?"

"Oh, sure."

"Here's fifty bucks for the ticket." He took out two fifty-dollar bills, handed the homeless guy one. "It should cost around forty. Keep the change." He tore the fifty in half and gave the guy one half. "When you give it to me, you get the other half of this."

"Albany? One way or round trip."

"One way."

"One way, huh? Ain't coming back?" the man said.

Paul hesitated. "'Fraid not."

PART ELEVEN

THE SAFE HOUSE

Present Day

97

For a long time, Paul stared at the Deacon.

Paul Brightman, he'd said, to which the Deacon had replied, *I thought so.* So who the hell was this Stephen Lucas, and how did he know Paul's name?

"Get in there, Brightman," Lucas said.

Paul scrambled into the shelter. Underneath the blanket of leaves was a ridgepole supported by a couple of sturdy branches lashed together with twine. Inside, the shelter was lined with pine needles and leaves and grasses as insulation. Looking up, he glimpsed the branches that formed the ribs of the structure. This was an ingenious cocoon. His father had once made one from forest debris, meant to look like a deadfall, a pile of fallen trees and brush. It was far more elaborate than the debris shelters he'd constructed.

It was cold in there, but he knew that his body heat would warm the space up quickly. It was designed for that.

He heard Lucas say, "Hal, Leon, would you set up a stakeout, make sure this gentleman is safe?" The other two grunted, and Paul heard the crackling of twigs on the ground as they departed.

"You okay in there?" Lucas said.

"I'm good."

"I gotta move," Lucas said, "but I'll be back. We've got our own shelters. Gotta hide, too."

"Okay. And—uh, thank you."

Paul listened for the FBI SWAT team, who would not be able to move silently through the forest. The Pemigewasset Wilderness was immense, nearly fifty thousand acres in the heart of the White Mountains. But that didn't mean the FBI team wouldn't be able to find him in this vast forest.

The Deacon and his men were obviously some kind of anarchists who rejected the government and its laws and modern society and lived in the woods, off the grid, in their own society. He remembered seeing a couple of bearded men in the woods a few days before who didn't look like hikers, and now he wondered if they were part of this clan.

Paul stuck his head out of the shelter and looked around, but saw nobody. Nor did he hear anybody. He clambered out of the shelter, relieved himself, went back inside. He listened, heard only the sounds of the forest. The sky was dimming, and the sun hung low over an orange and pink sky.

A little while later, he was startled by a voice, which he quickly recognized as the Deacon's.

"You okay in there?"

"I'm good," Paul replied, poking his head out.

Stephen Lucas, aka the Deacon, was standing there, the cheeks above his beard deeply tanned and deeply wrinkled. Paul had no idea how old he was.

"Hey. What did you mean, you thought I was Paul Brightman?"

"Well, I thought you were *a* Brightman. You look like your father. And you talk like him."

"You *know* him?"

"Long time ago. Served together in 'Nam. Then I got caught up in the Weather Underground, and a couple of explosions went sideways, and I found myself a wanted man."

"So you're a fugitive."

"Call me whatever, I don't care."

"You live here in the woods?"

"Not here. Not anywhere. We're always on the move. Like the Indians—the American Indians, the tribal nations. We don't build pyramids, and we don't keep slaves."

Astonished, Paul said, "Are you in touch with my father?"

"I know he lives in Quadrant Twenty-Eight."

"Where's that?"

"Northern Pennsylvania. The Hammersley Wild Area in the Susquehannock State Forest. Closest town is Austin."

"Austin . . . Pennsylvania?"

"Right. Not Texas."

Paul scrabbled out of the shelter. "How do you know that?"

"How do I know that? We have means of communication. Like the tribes, like the French Underground in World War Two. Only, we've got walkie-talkies."

"They work in the woods?"

"Not far. A mile, half a mile. Uses FRS."

"Which is . . . ?"

Lucas shook his head, unwilling to explain. "We've got repeaters. Human repeaters, just like the Afghanis. Extends across most of the country."

"Jesus, how many people are we talking?"

"Nearly fifty thousand, all told. Why you so interested?"

"I've just never heard—"

Lucas interrupted him. "You got a plan? Or are you just running?"

"I—I have someone I want to talk to."

"On the phone or—"

"Gotta be in person," Paul said.

"Where?"

"Western Mass. Near Lenox."

"And how you plan to get there?"

"Bus," Paul said. Trains were out: Amtrak required a government ID. He worried about buying another used car: too many cameras record your license plate.

"Bus terminals have cameras, you know, just like train stations and airports," Lucas said. "More and more places use facial recognition. You can bet the FBI has sent your picture to every bus terminal and train station and airport in the country."

"So you have a recommendation?"

"Freight trains. You want to move without Big Brother noticing, hop a freight train. I'll tell you how to do it when the time comes."

"Huh." That sounded like an easy way to get killed or dismembered.

"You thinking of going off grid? Not so easy, unless you do it the way we do it."

Paul thought for a moment. He'd come to trust this guy. "I changed my identity," he said. "Hid out for a long while."

"How long?"

"Five years."

Lucas whistled. "Ain't easy these days. Digital era. I'm guessing you couldn't use credit cards."

"I used Visa and Amex gift cards. Bought with cash."

"You had a job?"

"Built boats."

"Probably paid in cash, right?"

Paul nodded.

"Wore a disguise?"

"Not really. A beard, that's it, but lots of guys have beards these days."

"Gotta obey all the rules. Never break the law."

Paul shrugged.

"And you stay off Facebook and Twitter."

"Of course."

"You get lonely?"

Paul shook his head. "Not really. For a while, I had a girlfriend. Good person. I wasn't so lonely." He thought about Sarah with a pang. He knew things were over between them, but he hoped against hope that she was okay.

"Leaving her behind?"

"It's over. Not really leaving her behind."

"Miss your old life?"

"From five years ago? Not a bit."

The shadows had grown long, and daylight was disappearing. The Deacon seemed to trust him, too. "I suggest you spend the night here," he told Paul. "Tomorrow we can move down to Concord."

"Why Concord?"

"That's the closest freight train. Get you down to Lenox, Mass. We've got people in that area who can help you out, you need help. You should join us."

"Living in the woods? No, thanks. Not for me. I prefer a normal existence, sorry."

"All you people living in what you call your 'normal existence' and what I call the Matrix, your lives are regimented in ways you don't even see. Man, I mean, people wear T-shirts saying they're nonconformists, same shirt their friends wear. Same Sysco trucks service all the restaurants they eat in. All the bankers wearing the same suits and ties, made by one of seven manufacturers, spending their days in cubicles. They're all slaves of the state. I don't care whether you call it New York State or Goldman Sachs."

"You just have to obey the law and—"

"Sure," the Deacon said, "the state demands obedience in everything that matters. Nursery school on, we're taught compliance. Learn how to be a good pupil. Sit quietly in your chair! Do what teacher says. Fill out this spreadsheet, earn your wage. Well, that ain't freedom. That's slavery masquerading as emancipation. Back in the day, the tribal nations, they were invited to disappear into the dominant system of the colonizers—by which I mean America—and they said, 'Hell no.' Lots of them got killed rather than assimilate because they knew the price was too goddamned high."

"You all live in the woods?"

"We've taken to calling ourselves the 'woodsmen.' You know that nearly ninety percent of the U.S.A. is uninhabited? Undeveloped wilderness. Forested like it was a thousand years ago. You throw a dart at a map of the U.S., you're likely not hitting Sacramento or St. Louis. You're hitting a place that other people say is nowhere. That's our somewhere. There's more space in this country where nobody is than where anybody is."

"You're survivalists."

The Deacon shook his head. "Most survivalists build communities. Instead, we have an empire that's always on the move. Like the tribal nations."

"So you're like a tribal nation of your own."

"We recognize no management class, no rulers—"

"Except you—you seem to be the boss."

"One of many. Just here to coordinate. We've got no system of hierarchy. No one gets assigned a number."

Paul nodded and fell silent. Neither man spoke for a while. Finally, Paul said, "It's not for me."

"Maybe it will be," the Deacon said. "You never know what happens. Anyway, I'll send the word on ahead, tell them to be on the lookout for you."

98

Paul assumed that the Deacon was right, that bus terminal employees around the country had probably been sent his photo. But he wasn't going to hop a freight train. He had a better, simpler plan.

Stephen Lucas had offered to accompany him to Concord, New Hampshire, the nearest big city, a distance of around sixty miles. That would be a journey of several days on foot, though, and Paul didn't want to delay any further.

He had to reach Ambassador John Robinson Gillette as soon as possible. Ambassador Gillette was the only person who could help, Paul believed. He was intricately connected to some highly placed people in government. And because of his son, J.R., he owed Paul a favor.

By midday, he and the Deacon had arrived at a "welcome center," a rest stop on I-93 South. There Paul saw several trucks parked outside the main building, sort of a tourist information center combined with a deli and a pizza place. When one of the drivers returned to his truck bearing a tall cup of coffee and a sandwich wrapped in white paper, Paul intercepted him. He offered to pay the truck driver fifty dollars for a lift to Boston. Boston was where the driver was headed anyway, so he gladly took the fifty bucks.

IN BOSTON, WHERE THE BUS terminal was crowded, Paul asked a homeless man to buy him a bus ticket to Lenox, Mass. He tipped the man twenty bucks.

On the bus, he thought about Ambassador Gillette.

The ambassador was the father of his college classmate J.R. Gillette, a friend whom Paul had sung with. Paul had met the father a few times, when he came to visit his son at Reed and once for drinks after an a cappella concert in D.C.

In their junior year of college, J.R. Gillette had what used to be called a "nervous breakdown." He was suddenly paralyzed with depression, stayed in bed all the time, sleeping or trying to sleep. He stopped going to classes, didn't do any of the reading. Paul dragged him, almost literally, to Health and Counseling Services. He secured a same-day appointment, waited with him until the appointment, and waited for him to be finished. J.R. was diagnosed as bipolar and given a prescription, which Paul made him take. Within a week, J.R. was partway to normal. Within two weeks, he was himself again. Paul went with him to see the associate dean of students and got J.R. an incomplete for the semester so he wouldn't fail all his classes.

J.R.'s high-powered father was grateful to Paul for taking care of his son. Gillette Senior had once been the director of the FBI, after serving as a judge on the U.S. Court of Appeals for the Eighth Circuit. He'd also served for a few years as CIA director. Earlier, he'd been ambassador to the Netherlands. He was the most connected person Paul knew. Deeply versed in international relations, Ambassador Gillette was a highly intelligent, gentle, and soft-spoken man. A legendary D.C. power player, he was an advisor to six presidents. The ultimate insider's insider.

And given Paul's connection to his son, he'd help. Paul was sure of it.

The ambassador had retired to a big old house in or near Lenox, in the western part of the state. He'd retired there because he loved Tanglewood, the summer home of the Boston Symphony Orchestra. Having grown up on Beacon Hill, in Boston, Gillette had gone to concerts at Tanglewood most of his life.

Paul had Gillette's address but not his telephone number. But that was fine. He wanted to surprise the man and not give him the chance to set him up the way Lou Westing had.

He was learning as he went along.

The ride took about three hours. He got off the bus at the Village Pharmacy in Lenox and proceeded on foot to Ambassador Gillette's house.

IN THE LATE NINETEENTH CENTURY, the area around Lenox, Massachusetts, had been the summer home for the rich from Boston and New York who wanted someplace quieter than Newport. There in Lenox and Great Barrington and Stockbridge they built great, lavish country mansions they called "cottages." Many of the houses had names. Most of these estates had long ago been turned into spas or museums or performing arts summer camps or headquarters for think tanks. But a few of the Gilded Age estates had remained in private hands, including Ambassador Gillette's home, Colworth Hall. It was an English manor house with twenty-two rooms, set on forty acres. It had been in the Gillette family since the ambassador's industrialist father bought it from the original owner's descendants in the nineteen fifties. Paul had visited it once, during college, with J.R.

The entrance to Colworth Hall was a wrought-iron gate flanked by stone pillars. Mounted to the right-hand pillar was a security camera and a call box. Paul considered his options. Press the button and maybe, if he was lucky, talk via video link with the ambassador.

And say what? "I'm a friend of your son's, and I need to talk with you"? The ambassador would surely say, "Hold on," then right away call his son and ask about someone named Paul Brightman, and the son would say, Paul Brightman disappeared five years ago, probably killed on orders of a Russian oligarch in the years before the war in Ukraine, when New York was still one of their playgrounds. Because that was the prevailing theory. Paul knew this because he had googled himself.

And maybe the ambassador would invite him in, keep him occupied while the FBI scrambled a team from Albany to arrest him. That was a risk he didn't want to take. So he had to surprise the man, assuming the ambassador wasn't afflicted with senility. And ask his help, his advice.

He moved away from the security camera and walked down the road, along the fenced border of Colworth Hall's grounds. He was fairly sure there would be a service entrance, which might not be covered by a security camera. Maybe that was a way to get in without being detected.

It was late afternoon, around five, and the sun hadn't yet set. He walked the length of a city block, turned a corner, and saw an entrance . . . with its own security camera in place.

There was another option.

He would ring the house on the call box, and if he was able to speak directly to the ambassador, he would introduce himself and see how the man reacted. If there was anything suspicious in his behavior, Paul would simply get the hell out of there.

He returned to the front entrance. There, he rang the call bell. Half a minute went by, and then a video image appeared on the intercom. It was a red-haired woman in her fifties dressed in a black housekeeping dress with white collar. "May I help you?"

"I need to see Ambassador Gillette," he said. "I'm a friend of his son's."

"I see. Will you wait a moment?"

"Of course."

The video screen went gray blue. He'd been put on hold.

When an image came back on, it was of Ambassador Gillette's face. He looked much older than the vigorous, seventy-something man Paul had met during college. He'd been notably older than most other fathers of his classmates. The years had taken their toll. "Uh, who's there?" the ambassador said. "You're a friend of J.R.'s?"

"Yes. From Reed. We've actually met a few times, you and I."

"I'm sorry, and you are . . . ?"

"Paul Brightman."

"The hell you are. Paul Brightman is dead." So he already knew about him.

"Not yet, I'm not," Paul said. "That's what I need to talk to you about."

"What—what's my son's favorite sport?"

"Favorite sport?" Paul was stumped. "He hates sports."

"Where did he live freshman year?"

"McKinley." The ambassador's eyes widened.

"Good Lord! I thought you'd been killed by Arkady Galkin's goons. Come in, come in."

The screen went blue again, and the cast-iron gate swung inward. Paul heard the electric swing gate operator's motor hum.

He walked up a long white flagstone driveway toward the mansion. Colworth Hall was spectacularly beautiful, built entirely of stone with chimney stacks and high-pitched gable rooflines. It was surrounded by an immense green lawn like a golf course, and in front of the house burbled a marble fountain.

By the time he arrived at the portico, the double entrance doors were coming open, antique dark-brown walnut, beautifully carved. Standing there when the doors opened fully was the uniformed housekeeper.

"Welcome," she said. "The ambassador is in his library. May I get you a drink?"

"No, I'm fine, thanks," Paul said, though he needed one.

Ambassador John Robinson Gillette was wheelchair-bound now, Paul saw. "Paul Brightman?" he said.

"Yes."

"Come on in. Take a seat. Did Noreen take your drink order? I'm having a martini. Noreen makes excellent martinis. Can I offer you one as well?"

"Scotch rocks would be excellent," Paul said.

The ambassador's wheelchair was parked before a big, roaring fire in a fireplace with carved stone surrounds. The floor was a highly polished mahogany. The walls were wood-paneled. Exposed beams crisscrossed the ceiling.

At ninety, Ambassador Gillette was a patrician figure who spoke with a precise mid-Atlantic accent. His silver hair and eyebrows contrasted dramatically with his dark-brown skin.

"You are indeed Paul Brightman?" he said.

"I am." Was the ambassador senile, or was he still testing him?

"Sang with J.R., too, as I recall."

"That's right."

"What's the name of the a cappella singing group you both sang in?"

"The Herodotones."

Gillette grinned. That was another test. "How *Reed* is that? From Herodotus, of course. Mr. Brightman, I can't tell you how grateful I am to you for helping out J.R. in college."

"He was my friend," Paul said. "But I'm ashamed I haven't been in touch." For the last five years, of course, it had been dangerous for him to reach out to any college friend. "How is he?"

Gillette shrugged. "He's been better. He's been able to keep a job, but I still worry about him."

"I'm sorry to hear that. Please give him all my best."

"You were a wonderful friend to him. So I imagine you have a story to tell."

"Yes, sir."

"Well, I don't know what I can do to help. I've been retired for quite some time. But anything I can do, I'm here for you."

Paul knew it wasn't quite true that Gillette was retired. He continued to serve as an emeritus advisor to presidents. He didn't fly to Washington, D.C. They called him in Lenox.

Noreen entered the study bearing a tray holding two full cocktail glasses. The ambassador preferred his martini in a highball glass.

Paul took the Scotch and thanked Noreen.

Then he told the ambassador his story.

99

The old man's eyes looked haunted. "You're asking why the FBI is after you," he said. "I couldn't tell you. I'm out of the swim."

"You know the FBI."

"Yes, yes, but . . . Look, taking someone's Social Security number, as you did, is identity theft, and that's either a misdemeanor or a felony, depending on where you live, where it's prosecuted. It's a wobbler. And it's never going to require a field team to bring you in. If what you're telling me is accurate, and there was a team waiting to grab you in New Hampshire, that doesn't sound right. That's way too overblown an operation for identity theft. And you're not a fugitive from justice. When I was director, I never would have approved an arrest in your case. No, there's obviously something else going on."

"Like what?"

"It might well be your connection to a Russian oligarch and your subsequent disappearance."

It also might be that I'm wanted for murder, Paul thought. *For the murder of a man who came to kill me.*

"Look," Paul began again, "five years ago, I found an entire FBI office massacred by *Russian* agents. Probably to protect an oligarch. Now it looks like the FBI is after *me!* I want to know what the hell is going on. I mean, I suppose I could turn myself in, but not before knowing what they want me for."

"Well, I don't have the slightest . . ."

"Can you make some phone calls?"

"I suppose I could, yes."

The fire crackled much like the one in the woods the night before, but this was much bigger, and the flames painted Gillette's face in shades of orange. The room smelled, comfortingly, of woodsmoke. Like a badly needed fire on a cold night in the wilderness.

"Does the name 'Phantom' mean anything to you?" Paul said.

The ambassador shook his head. "Besides what it usually means, no. Not that I can recall."

Paul was disappointed but he persisted. "That thumb drive I just showed you—what do *you* think's on it?" A few minutes ago, he'd plugged the drive into the ambassador's computer, showed him the junk that came up on the screen, explained where he'd found it.

"You're asking for a guess."

"Correct."

Gillette smiled. "Obviously, I have no idea. I'm not very tech savvy, as you might imagine. But I have a hypothesis. You know how the Mafia always keeps ledgers detailing whom they've paid off and how much?"

"You think it may be financial records of who Arkady Galkin owns and how much he's paid them?"

"Perhaps. That would be useful as kompromat—that's Russian for 'compromising information used to blackmail or control people.'"

"I know." It was getting hot sitting in front of the fire, and Paul felt a rivulet of perspiration course down his neck and then his back.

"Which is how Galkin controls people. My hypothesis is that this thumb drive you have—is that what you called that thing, a 'thumb drive'?—holds evidence that Galkin has paid off high-ranking agents in the FBI. Names of FBI special agents or directors he has on his payroll. In his pocket. Bank account numbers. And somebody wants it back. Someone whose name may be in those files."

"And the corruption may extend farther than the FBI?" Paul said. "Other intelligence agencies, maybe?"

"Quite possibly. Why not? CIA officers can be corrupted just as easily as FBI agents."

"And politicians?"

"Absolutely. Just as the oligarchs have done in England."

Ambassador Gillette shifted in his wheelchair. "The Russian oligarchs in Great Britain own so much of London, it's now called 'Londongrad.' They own most of Knightsbridge. So many oligarchs own property in Eaton Square, they call it 'Red Square.' These Russian billionaires give millions of pounds to the Tory Party. I mean, my God, the son of a *KGB spy* sits in the *House of Lords!*"

He continued: "Before the war in Ukraine, these oligarchs used to arrive from Russia carrying bags of cash and plunk them down to buy a fancy house, and then they'd hire attorneys to launder their billions, and they'd hire a British PR firm to launder their reputation and buy them friends in Parliament. They'd give huge gifts to universities and charities. Or set up a foundation. They still own some of England's biggest newspapers. And they own some of London's most prominent political figures. That's how they gain access to the ruling class. Even to Buckingham Palace. Their children are admitted to the most prestigious private schools. Put down ten million pounds, and you're a permanent resident. They dazzle us with their mansions and their superyachts, but look closely, and you'll see marionette strings."

"That go right to the Kremlin."

The ambassador nodded. "If they dare to speak out against Moscow, they'll be assassinated. And Number Ten Downing Street does nothing about it. Did you know that fourteen Russians have been assassinated on British soil so far? And more to come. The oligarchs also provided the funding that made Brexit happen, severing the U.K. from Europe. A disaster for England."

Paul watched the ambassador, impressed. He was as sharp as a man half his age. "They own politicians in London and Paris and Berlin and, my God, everywhere."

"Here, too, I bet."

Gillette nodded. "Oh, God, yes. Using dark money, they secretly own a number of U.S. senators and congressmen." He named a few names, and Paul's jaw jutted open.

"But since the war in Ukraine started," Paul said, "I thought most of the oligarchs were sanctioned. Their mega-yachts seized and all that."

"True."

"So what am I supposed to do? Let the FBI arrest me? I guess that would probably be better than being found by one of Galkin's agents."

"Neither a happy outcome."

"Who else can help me, do you know? Is there anyone who might know about what's going on?"

Ambassador Gillette was silent for a long moment. "Do you know the name Philip Horgan?"

"Sounds familiar."

"I think you should talk to him. If he'll talk. No guarantee he will. Philip Horgan is an ex-CIA officer who was fired for attempting to leak classified information. He's sort of a renegade. A bit of an oddball. Lot of ink on him in the *Washington Post*. He lives in Manassas, Virginia, and he's kind of a kook, but he knows a lot. Up to the highest levels. Which is why it worried so many people when he quit and started speaking out."

"Can I use your name?

Gillette chuckled. "Better not. He probably considers me part of the deep state that fired him. Probably hates me on general principle."

"Well, can you talk to someone inside the Bureau and call them off?"

"Oh, I can talk to 'someone,' all right," he said with a crooked smile, making air quotes with two fingers on each gnarled hand. "Hold on."

Gillette wheeled his chair over to his desk, a massive hulk of oak, and picked up a landline phone. He punched in a series of numbers. Then he said into the phone, "Tell the director that it's John Gillette."

A few seconds went by, and then Gillette said, "As well as can be expected, Bill, thank you for asking. I'm here with a gentleman who says he's wanted by the FBI, and we're trying to determine the best course of action." He paused to listen. "Uh-huh. Uh-huh. The name is Paul Brightman. I know him and can vouch for him."

Paul was immediately filled with alarm. Why was the old man saying this to whoever was on the other end of the line? Why was he giving out his name? Was it deliberate; was it merely sloppy?

"Yes, he's right here with me. He—is that right? Is that right? . . . And who's running the unit? . . . Ah. And she is . . . ? Aha. Aha. CIA, you say?" He jotted something down on a yellow pad. "Yes, that was a word he mentioned. All right, talk to you soon. Aha." He hung up the phone and wheeled back to Paul, his yellow pad in one hand.

"Strangest thing," the old man said, shaking his head. "Normally if I ask Bill for help, he'll fall all over himself to help me . . . Not that I call him often. He tells me you're a cunning fraudster and a danger to national security. There's an arrest warrant out for you."

Paul laughed incredulously. "Me? Seriously?"

"I'm afraid so. I don't believe a word of it, but that's the official word from the Bureau. Obviously, something's rotten in the state of Denmark. The director's clearly been misinformed by someone. Unless you're bull-dozing me right now."

Paul shook his head. "What's the arrest warrant for?"

"Alleged theft of classified national defense information."

"*What?* And how did I allegedly gain access to classified information?"

"I have absolutely no idea." The ambassador held the yellow pad up, at a distance in front of his rheumy eyes, and read it silently.

"So you're not able to call off the dogs?" Paul said.

"Afraid not. You obviously have something they want."

"The Phantom flash drive."

"Apparently."

"Why?"

There was a long silence. Paul heard the ticking of a clock.

Ambassador Gillette seemed to be debating what to say next. Finally, he said, "'Phantom' is the name of a secret project at CIA."

"Then why did *Galkin* have this thing?"

The old man exhaled, shook his head. "Why don't you leave it with me, and I'll make sure it's safe and it gets to the right people?"

Paul looked at Gillette for a long moment. He had once trusted the man, but certainly no longer. "No, I'm sorry. I can't."

"I have a terribly good safe. A Class-Six, GSA-approved. A Mosler, er, SecureSafe Five Thousand. You don't get more secure than that, I'm told."

"I can't. I'm sorry."

"You see, the director of the FBI now has to answer to the DNI, the director of national intelligence. Been that way ever since 9/11. That's the level this is at. I don't think Bill could call it off if he *wanted* to."

"You gave him my name."

"I'm not as quick-thinking as I once was. Age will do that to you."

But Paul didn't think the ambassador had slipped. He'd known what he was doing. The man was still sharp after all these years. He just felt bad about it.

The exterior lights of Colworth Hall started snapping on, blazingly bright.

The ambassador looked ill at ease. He gave Paul an apologetic glance. "You really should leave now. I—they'll be flying in a SWAT team from FBI Springfield as we speak. And they know they can land on my property. Plenty of room."

"Okay," Paul said. Ambassador Gillette had revealed his whereabouts but seemed conscience-stricken about what he'd done. He appreciated the warning. "Goodbye."

"Paul," the old man cried out.

"What?"

The ambassador was about to say something, but instead he looked anguished. "Just—just go."

Paul hurried out of the house, down the stone steps, onto the path, and then out the service entrance gate. In the distance, he heard the chopping of an approaching helicopter.

He kept walking, as much as he wanted to run.

100

Paul's father had a saying he often repeated when he was teaching his son forestry skills. "A thousand days of evasion is better than one day of captivity." Stan Brightman had learned that wisdom in Vietnam. And it always struck Paul as ridiculous. Evasion? From whom? Captivity? By whom? The Vietcong? A ten-year-old didn't imagine he'd ever be in danger of being kidnapped by anyone. But now Paul recalled the saying bitterly as he sat on a bus that reeked like a toilet bowl.

Most of the buses that went from Boston to Manassas, Virginia, transferred at the Port Authority bus terminal in Manhattan. But he didn't dare return to New York City, not now. They would be looking for him there.

When he got to the bus terminal near South Station, in Boston, he had discovered that there was exactly one bus that went to D.C. without changing at Port Authority. That bus took over nine hours and drove through the night, arriving early in the morning.

Paul had paid another homeless person to buy him a ticket. Paid generously, in fact.

At five fifty-three in the morning, when it was still dark, the bus pulled into Union Station in Washington. Paul found a Blue Bottle Coffee that was open, bought a coffee and a hot breakfast sandwich. Then he spotted an office for an off-brand car rental agency, but the place didn't open until eight. He tanked up on coffee—he'd slept badly on the bus—and waited. At eight, he rented a Jeep Compass, using a couple of prepaid debit cards—being sure to include a five-hundred-dollar cash deposit in case of damages—and drove to Manassas.

The ambassador had probably done him harm, but at least he'd given him a name of someone who might be helpful.

PHILIP HORGAN'S HOUSE WAS MODEST but set on a large lot, far apart from its neighbors. A squat brick structure with small windows, it looked like a miniature fortress. The blinds and curtains were all shut. The lawn badly needed mowing. The place looked abandoned. Or maybe the ex-CIA officer didn't do yard work.

Paul pulled into the long asphalt driveway, which was cracked and pitted. He noticed security cameras mounted on every corner of the house he could see, and another mounted above the closed garage door. And when he reached the small porch, he glimpsed a motion-sensor dome camera mounted to its ceiling. In fact, there wasn't a way to approach the house that wasn't covered by security cameras.

As he climbed the three brick steps to the front door, he heard a voice crackling over an intercom installed next to the door.

"Get the hell off my property," the voice said. In the background Paul heard what sounded like low canine growling.

"Mr. Horgan? My name is Paul Brightman. I need to talk with—"

The front door swung open and something large hurtled out in a blur, an immense black-and-brown dog with a blocky head, muscular body, vicious teeth, and a deep, ferocious bark. Paul saw its ears prick up, a big chain around the dog's neck.

There was no time to run. He knew there were things you were supposed to do when attacked by a dog. You were supposed to stand still, never run. You were supposed to break eye contact. But all rational thought had deserted him in an instant. The dog was on him so close he could smell the animal's foul breath.

Paul found himself pinned up against the garage door, the Dobermann growling and barking and lunging at him.

Its owner stood behind the dog, pointing a gun. "By the laws of the Commonwealth of Virginia," the man said, "I have the right to use deadly force. Now, what the hell are you doing on my property?" The man was balding on top with long gray hair below that touched his shoulders.

"Jesus, call off your dog! I'm not here to harm you. I need your help."

"Who the hell are you?"

"Like I said, my name is Paul Brightman, and—"

"Brutus, *off.*" The dog immediately sat on its haunches but continued growling. "Prove you are who you say you are. Let me see your driver's license."

"I . . . don't have one." He had gotten rid of all his Paul Brightman documents. Left them all—his passport, his driver's license, his Social Security card, his credit cards—in a safe-deposit box at a Citizens bank branch in Derryfield. Hoping never to have to use them again.

He should have introduced himself as Grant Anderson. At least he had a driver's license in that name.

"You don't drive?"

"I don't have any of my documents with me. If I were some kind of spy or something, wouldn't I have my fake documents at hand?"

Philip Horgan paused, tilted his head. "You might have a point."

"I want to ask you about Phantom."

Horgan's eyes widened. "Who the hell are you?"

101

The interior of the ex-CIA man's small house was even grimmer than the exterior. It smelled like stale cigarettes and old beer and mold. Magazines and newspapers were stacked haphazardly everywhere, empty Coke and beer cans littered the floor and the tops of the piles, and ashtrays overflowed with cigarette butts. Horgan had cleared off a chair for Paul by excavating a pile of newspapers and tossing them onto the floor. He insisted that Paul put his phone in a black sleeve that he said was a Faraday bag. It blocked all signals emanating to and from the device, he explained.

While Paul answered Horgan's questions, the Dobermann sat contentedly at Horgan's feet making a low rumble, a quiet growl, almost a purring sound. Meanwhile, Horgan chain-smoked Camel Straights.

Horgan got up and found in a steel file cabinet a printout that he said was from the CIA's internal employee newsletter, *What's News*. It was a photograph of a senior CIA official, identified as Geraldine Dempsey, receiving an award from the CIA director. A middle-aged woman with a thin mouth, a short, perky blonde Princess Diana haircut, and a navy suit with big padded shoulders.

"This is the woman at CIA whom I worked for. Geraldine Dempsey," Horgan said.

"West Texas?" Paul remembered Dempsey from the FBI office in New York.

"Exactly. Very good. She runs an off-the-books unit known informally by its cryp, Phantom."

"Cryp?"

"Cryptonym. Code name." Horgan lit another Camel. "Phantom. Known on the inside as F-A-N. For the Russian translation, *Fantom*."

"Wait, so . . . Phantom is the unit?"

Horgan exhaled a long plume of smoke. "You know the cryp. You must know something about this."

"I've put some things together, yeah. You tell me."

"An off-the-books operation."

"That does what? Targets Russian oligarchs or something, like Galkin?"

Horgan shrugged. "Phantom did black ops within the U.S., I know that much. I hear it's shut down."

"Black ops? What does that mean, exactly?"

Horgan seemed to have a nervous habit of jiggling his right knee up and down, Paul noticed, and now he was doing it again. "Clandestine activities. Given the way these things are compartmented, I only knew a fragment."

"But what *kind* of black ops?"

Horgan shrugged.

Paul decided to take a different tack: "And that woman, Geraldine Dempsey, fired you?"

"Right."

"What for?"

"Attempting to leak classified information."

"Did you?"

"I tried. God, did I try."

"About Phantom."

"You got it. Proof that CIA was using foreign talent to carry out black ops within the United States."

"I didn't see anything on the internet about a CIA leak."

"That's because nothing appeared. The Agency applied pressure, pulled strings. Both the *Times* and the *Post* spiked stories. As detrimental to our national security or some bullshit like that."

"What did you try to get printed? The identity of a CIA agent?"

"I would never do that." More knee spindling.

"Then what?"

"How the Phantom unit hired talent within the U.S. to do black ops. Wet work. Whatever you want to call it. It's all illegal, according to U.S. law. It's an outrage."

"'Talent'? For what?"

"You ever read about the killing of some FBI agents in New York?"

"I was there. Right afterward. I saw the bodies. I was told the Russians did it."

"Oh, the guys who did the dirty work were Russians, all right. I know. But they were hired by Geraldine Dempsey. By the CIA."

"*What?*"

"Light dawns on Marblehead," Horgan said with a peculiar smile. "Hired by a unit of the CIA. The Phantom unit. Dempsey hired a crew of ex-GRU goons, so it would point to Moscow. An old CIA trick. False-flagging."

"The CIA hired Russians to kill FBI agents in New York?"

Horgan just looked at him with an odd, knowing smile on his face, nearly a smirk.

"Hold on—so, it wasn't *Moscow* that was behind the murder of those FBI agents, it was . . . *us*? It was the goddamned CIA? The CIA killed FBI agents? That's incredible."

"To be precise, not CIA. The Phantom unit. A special unit within CIA kept secret even from the spooks."

"That massacre was officially sanctioned?"

Horgan nodded.

"I never saw that anywhere—never heard it was CIA."

"That's because the story was buried. Or it never came out. One thing my old agency is good at is keeping secrets."

"The CIA . . ." Paul said. "I thought they don't do that kind of thing anymore. Not for years. And even when they did . . . You're talking about killing FBI agents?"

Horgan laughed dryly. "Well . . . not till Geraldine Dempsey was named to head the Phantom unit."

"How could she—I mean, the director of the CIA must have known, right?"

"The goddamned *White House* had to approve it! That high up."

"This is a huge story."

"And of course it's totally illegal. Violates CIA's charter, U.S. laws. Man, I was expecting a front-page exposé. But not a single publisher in the U.S. would touch it. They couldn't face the legal pressure. You know, when I first heard about this, I spoke out in-house. I was a good boy. I went through channels, I lodged complaints with the inspector general, and . . . crickets. They just reassigned me. So in a moment of frustration and weakness, I called a *Washington Post* reporter. And then she had me fired."

"Who did?"

"Geraldine!"

"Couldn't you just self-publish?"

"Doesn't work that way. It's still breaking the goddamned law. And I don't have deep pockets. They were going to sue the shit out of me, shut me down, and I couldn't afford to fight them."

"And yet . . . you're alive."

"That wet work, that's the past. Not since Phantom was shut down. New leadership forbids any kind of lethal action like that anymore. They say the Russians may do it, but we don't. Besides, there's too many eyes on me."

"I don't—" Paul faltered a moment. "I don't get how Dempsey hasn't been arrested by FBI for what she's done."

"Because nothing's on paper. They don't have her dead to rights. They don't have proof. If you can get that, you'll get an FBI arrest pronto, no problem."

"She must have good contacts at the FBI," Paul suggested. "Don't you think?"

"Look, whenever she finds herself in a dangerous situation, she's always accompanied by SPS officers, and they—"

"SPS officers?"

"Sorry. That's the CIA's Security Protective Service. Draws from cops or FBI. The best of them are former FBI SWAT officers. So she knows how capable FBI agents can be. She uses them."

The dog got up and trotted over to Paul, nudging his knee. Then he sat down on top of his feet. Paul was careful not to shift his feet and antagonize the creature.

"Don't worry about Brutus. He's actually a big old softie," Horgan said. "A sweetie."

"Yeah, so I've seen." Paul said. "So it wasn't Russian government intelligence operatives doing the killings in the U.S. It was Russians hired by the U.S. To make it *look* like Moscow was doing them."

"Precisely."

"But why? Why did the CIA do something so . . . evil?"

"To protect Phantom."

"Phantom being . . . what?"

"Like I said, it's the code name for an operation."

"Which does *what*? Black ops for *what* exactly?"

"For Christ's sake, I don't know." Horgan's knee spindled.

"So why is the FBI coming after me?"

Horgan shook his head. "What do they say you did wrong?"

A long pause. "They're calling it theft of intelligence."

"Did you?"

"Steal intelligence? No. I took a flash drive labeled 'Phantom.' From a Russian oligarch, Arkady Galkin."

"And what's on that flash drive?"

"It's encrypted. So I don't know. At first I thought it was Arkady Galkin's kompromat on politicians or government officials he'd paid off. Like a Mafia ledger. But now I can only guess. Maybe it's proof of a CIA black-ops unit. Maybe Galkin knows what's going on at the CIA."

Horgan lit another cigarette. "Look, way back in the day, when Harry Truman founded CIA, he was afraid he might be creating some kind of super Gestapo agency, so he laid down the law: no domestic spying. And then, twenty years later, in the Nixon administration, the Agency was caught spying on American citizens. Which resulted in a huge outcry, Senate hearings. CIA promised to stop."

"Did it?"

Horgan smirked, shook his head, snorted. "A couple of years ago, it was revealed that CIA has been conducting what they call 'bulk collection' in America. Gaining access to millions of Americans' private data, their emails and text messages and phone calls. So, no, it doesn't stop, hasn't stopped, won't stop."

Paul watched Horgan, nodded.

"You have no idea how rotten the CIA is, do you? Your whole generation, you don't give a shit. When the Cold War ended, the U.S. and Russia could have been allies. You know that? But we tricked Gorbachev. We promised him that if he agreed to unify Germany, NATO wouldn't expand *one inch* east. Then, a few years later, NATO starts adding members. Oh, sorry about that little promise we made! You believed us? You poor schmucks. You second-rate country, you. Then, a few years later, we have the corrupt, alcoholic Boris Yeltsin—reviled by his people—running for reelection against a real, live Russian nationalist communist who's about to win, right? But we can't have that! The return of communism? No way! So what do we do? Lots of cold, hard U.S. cash gets dispensed liberally in Moscow to pay off whoever needs to be paid off. Whoever needs to dip their beaks. You probably never heard that two of Yeltsin's aides were arrested with shoeboxes full of hundred-dollar bills, did you?"

Paul shook his head.

"We did whatever it took, sloshed around whatever dirty money it took, to ensure *democracy* would live on in Russia. We swung the election. The vote was rigged. Maybe a little bit ironic, huh? Then we forced Yeltsin to choose a successor, and who might that be? The guy who became the czar and still rules Russia with an iron hand. Russia today wouldn't be so fucked up if we hadn't stuck our hand in and manipulated things the way we did. Thank the CIA for the fucked-up hand we now have." He shook his head and, for a long moment, didn't speak. Finally, he said, "Let me see it."

"See what?"

"The memory stick. Where is it now?"

"In my possession."

"Let me have a look."

"It's not with me," Paul said.

"Back in your hotel room?"

Paul wished he had a hotel room. Maybe later. He was exhausted and needed a good night's sleep.

"Why don't you go get it? I may be able to figure something out about it."

Paul shook his head slowly. "Can't do that. It's in a safe-deposit box," he lied. In fact, it was in his backpack on the floor next to him. "Does anyone know I'm meeting with you?"

"How do I know? They tap phones. Maybe you talked on a mobile phone. That's easy—"

"I've got to go," Paul said, and as he shifted his legs to stand up, the dog uttered a throaty warning growl.

102

On his way out of Horgan's house, he noticed a D.C. police car parked on the street near the end of the driveway.

For a moment he had no idea what to do.

Why a D.C. car? he wondered at first. He was in Virginia, not in the District of Columbia. He looked again and saw that there was only one policeman in the car, not the usual two. Why?

The cop was very likely there to arrest him. Perhaps working with Geraldine Dempsey and her team, he thought. Then he reconsidered. If the joint CIA-FBI team had truly tracked him here, or deduced that he would come here, there would be a lot of law enforcement officers. Not one person.

Something was off.

Paul descended the brick steps of the porch and limped to his rented Jeep, parked in Horgan's driveway. At that moment, the cop opened the driver's-side door of the patrol cruiser and got out. He was a muscular young man with a shiny bald head.

Paul thought of Berzin and the man with him who'd killed Alec Wood. The man accompanying Berzin had been bald and bullnecked, in his twenties.

This was the same person.

As Paul jumped into the Jeep, the side-view mirror next to his head exploded. The phony cop—because that was what he had to be—must have fired a silenced pistol; Paul had heard a loud snap, followed immediately by the hollow pop of the mirror shattering.

He switched on the ignition and slammed the car into Reverse. Backing up, he was moving closer to the fake cop, but he had no choice, he had to get off the driveway and into the street. The bald man jumped out of the way of the Jeep—his pistol, with a long silencer attached, momentarily at his side—but as soon as he recovered, he aimed with both hands and fired another shot. There was a loud snap again and the sound of metal against metal, a screech like a bullet creasing the roof of the Jeep.

Paul braked, shifted into Drive, and in that instant, he heard another shot and experienced what felt like a bee sting in his left shoulder. His shoulder and arm went numb, and for a moment, he felt nothing—as if a piece of glass had lodged itself in his arm and, for some reason, his pain sensors hadn't been triggered.

Another bullet shattered the Jeep's rear window. Adrenaline surged in Paul's body. His heart raced.

He thought for an instant about running back to Horgan's house, trying to get shelter, but then thought better of it. He didn't have time. And if he got out of the Jeep, he would be even more exposed.

Instead, he floored it. The Jeep lurched ahead, and he aimed it, a four-thousand-pound steel-and-aluminum weapon, at the false cop—who leaped to one side as he saw the vehicle coming straight at him. But the Jeep was faster, and an instant later, Paul felt a thud as it struck the man.

The bald man lay sprawled on the pavement, his limbs a tangle. Was he dead? Just badly injured? Paul didn't stop to check. He spun the steering wheel and accelerated down the street. Houses passed by in a blur. He made a right turn onto a wide avenue.

Then, abruptly, he felt an excruciating, burning sensation, like someone had pulled an iron poker out of a fire and plunged it into his shoulder, as the bald man's bullet had been deflected off the Jeep's tempered glass and penetrated his left shoulder. The hot pain radiated down his arm, down his biceps. His shirt was soaked with blood.

He didn't know where to go, but he had to decide quickly, because his attacker might have recovered, might be following him.

He couldn't go to a hospital. There was a law, he was sure, that required all hospitals to report any gunshot wound to the police. That would draw the immediate attention of the FBI. What the hell could he do? The pain was, if anything, growing in strength, a fireball inside his left shoulder, an unbearable starburst. Somehow, he had to get the bullet out, and he didn't think he could do it himself. He could hardly perform surgery on himself, one-handed. He would need a doctor.

But the most pressing thing was to get the hell out of there.

103

His left arm was stiff and painful, meaning he had to steer with just his right hand, and the shoulder pain was getting worse. But he had to keep going. He had to try to find his father, who might be able to help, if anyone could. He headed west on 28 to the Prince William Parkway and then to Route 66 West, passing through verdant countryside. After an hour and a quarter, when he was as certain as he could be that no one was following him, he stopped in the town of Winchester, Virginia. Looking for a CVS or other pharmacy, he passed a sign for a family practice physician and decided to go in and see if he could wangle an emergency appointment.

The doctor was booked all day, his receptionist said. You should go to the emergency room. Paul thanked her and went to a CVS, where he bought peroxide, SteriStrips, gauze bandages, tape, Neosporin, and Advil. He was covered in blood, but the cashier barely seemed to notice.

He returned to the Jeep, dry-swallowed a handful of Advil. He pulled off his shirt, poured peroxide on his wound, and yowled in pain. He daubed the wound with antibiotic. Then, though it was still weeping blood, he covered it with a large bandage and taped that into place.

A few minutes later, he continued driving. In short order, he was in West Virginia, then out of it. He was in Maryland briefly, until he crossed into Pennsylvania on the Dwight D. Eisenhower Highway. He was headed for northern Pennsylvania.

The Hammersley Wild Area in the Susquehannock State Forest.

Quadrant Twenty-Eight.

The pain in his shoulder was getting worse. It was on fire.

The last part of the journey, which took five and a half hours, was a straight line north, to northern Pennsylvania, close to the border with New York State. It was a monotonous drive, and at times, his head swam with the pain. He stopped just once, for gas and to change the dressing on his wound.

Austin was a tiny town in southwestern Potter County, Pennsylvania. He'd done his research on his phone. Population 482. Made Derryfield look like a booming metropolis. On the Freeman Run, a river powering paper mills and sawmills back in the day. The town was washed away when the big dam failed, a hundred some years ago, and then rebuilt. Its motto, he'd read on Wikipedia, was "The town too tough to die." He liked the sound of it.

He passed a campground where several RVs were parked. He looked for a downtown, but there really wasn't one to speak of. He passed several inns, a few restaurants, a gas station. A handful of brick buildings that looked like they'd been built at the beginning of the twentieth century or earlier. A pretty little town.

He was hungry, but the pain was calling. The wound kept seeping blood. He pulled over when he spotted a sign for an internal medicine practice. The office was on the second floor of a three-story wooden building. This doctor was booked all day, too, but his nurse-receptionist took one look at the bandages on Paul's shoulder and said with a professional scowl, "When did this happen?"

"A few hours ago."

"What is it?"

"A bullet wound. Hunting accident."

"You need antibiotics. Is the bullet in you, do you know?"

"Yes, I think so."

"Well, you need to get it out, like now. You need to go to the ER."

He shook his head. "I need to see Doctor Lichtenberg." He'd seen the name on the sign. Maybe a small-town doctor would make an exception and not report the gunshot.

She called the doctor in his treatment room, and he emerged in the reception area, a man in his fifties with a close-shaved gray beard. He stood, arms folded, and looked at Paul's bloodstained shirt. "What happened to you?"

"I got shot. Hunting accident. But I don't want this reported to the authorities."

"Where's the guy who shot you? He took off?"

"It's complicated. You don't have to report this, do you?"

"I do. I have to. If I don't, I could lose my license."

Paul nodded. The doctor was not persuadable, he could see that. "Could you at least prescribe me some antibiotics?"

"Same problem. If I don't report that I saw and treated a gunshot victim, I could lose my license. Can't take that chance. I'm sorry."

Paul left the doctor's office and found the town's only gas station, bought a map, some water, and some energy bars.

He had to enter the woods and try to find his father. Austin was very close to the remotest part of the state, the Hammersley Wild Area. Which, he read in the brochure, was over thirty thousand acres of wilderness. The brochure warned about bears ("Do not store food or any scented items like toothpaste and deodorant in a tent, including clothing with food residues.")

There was a small parking area off a dirt road called Gravel Lick Run. No one else was parked there. It was a cold, overcast day. The sky was steel gray. There was a faint drizzle. He parked the car, found a poncho in his now-loaded backpack, and put it on. He needed to cover up the blood. Then he set off.

He was following the Deacon's explicit instructions, but they struck him as crazy. Did he hope to run into his father just by walking the trails? What did the Deacon mean when he said that he'd tell his fellow off-gridders to be "on the lookout" for Stan? What exactly was Paul looking for in these thirty thousand acres? He wondered if he could really count on these eccentric men—but what choice did he have?

Once you get to Quadrant Twenty-Eight, the Deacon had told him, *find a clearing, a prominent landmark, and there I want you to build a cairn, a stack of stones. And wait there. Someone will find you.*

Paul walked on—his limp was no longer so bad, though his shoulder was on fire—and after a few minutes, he saw a couple of men carrying backpacks and wearing L.L.Bean attire. "Excuse me," Paul said. "Did you guys see anyone on your hike who looked like they've been living in the woods? Probably pretty disheveled?"

The guys both shook their heads, while exchanging a *What's up with this dude?* glance. Paul looked pretty damned disheveled himself.

He continued walking. About ten minutes later, he saw a couple coming toward him—in their thirties, athletic. He smiled and said,

"Quick question—did you guys run into anyone on your hike who looked like he may actually live in the woods? Someone sort of rough looking?"

The couple looked at each other and laughed. "There were several," the guy said. "Last one was—do you remember where?"

"Yeah," the woman said. "There was a guy we passed a couple of miles back."

"Oh, yeah? What'd he look like?" Paul asked the woman.

"Untrimmed beard, long hair. Clothes kind of tatty."

"Where was this?"

"Where Hammersley Fork meets Bunnell Ridge Trail," the guy said. "It's where the two mountain streams converge. This guy was filling his water bottle."

"But as soon as he saw us, he scurried off," his partner added.

"Thank you," Paul said. He waved goodbye and resumed walking through the woods. Forty-five minutes later, he found the intersection with Bunnell Ridge Trail, saw a campsite with a few tents pitched. Nearby, two streams converged. No one else was there. The Deacon had told him to build a cairn at a prominent landmark, and since the couple had described a bearded guy getting water here, Paul hoped he was in a fairly good location.

He put down his backpack and started collecting stones. It was painful, lifting stones with his shoulder in such agony. But he persisted, and after fifteen minutes, he'd assembled a stack of stones about three feet high. Sort of a New Age-y thing to build. Very Sedona. A prayer stone stack: a marker that told others you'd been there. But he was following the Deacon's strange instructions.

Then, not knowing what else to do, he waited. He sat on the ground on a tarp and waited.

After a while—an hour? Two?—someone emerged from the woods, a young-looking guy with a full beard and long hair, like his fellow off-gridders, in a dirty, ripped jacket. He was holding a CB radio handset.

The young guy approached, and Paul said what he'd been told to say. "Catch any muskie?"

"Got some frying up right now," the bearded guy promptly replied.

And that was the coded exchange, confirmation that this guy had been in touch with the Deacon.

"Thank you," Paul said.

The bearded young man pulled out the radio's long black antenna. "You want to see the Professor?"

Is that what they call him? Paul smiled. "Yes. The Professor."

The younger guy clicked a button on his handheld and then disappeared back into the trees.

Ten minutes later, an old man with stooped shoulders, long gray hair, and a full gray beard emerged from the forest.

Stanley Brightman stood for a minute and looked at Paul.

Paul looked back. Saw the bags under his father's eyes, the deep lines that scored his forehead and cheeks.

"You look like shit," his father said.

"Just about to say the same to you," Paul replied.

104

"First thing we're doing is fixing up that wound," his father said. "Before I look at that flash drive. What did you do? Tape it up without removing the bullet?"

Paul followed his father through the woods to a lean-to where he said he'd been living for the last month or more. It was a modest shelter made of branches and sticks with one tarp for the ceiling and another for the floor. It squeezed Paul's heart to see his father living this way. That someone who lurked so big in his imagination—whatever he thought of him—could fit into a space so small. He was undone by the stooped, creaky gait and unwashed countenance of a man who had once seemed so powerful, so important.

The space inside the lean-to was just big enough for Stan to lie down, with room left over, just barely, for a few items. Stan picked up one of them. It was his old M3 medic kit from Vietnam, which he used to refill and update when Paul was a kid. A CB radio on a charger base. Paul wondered how it was charged.

"Are you in pain?" his father asked him.

"A hell of a lot, actually."

"But you're breathing and talking, which is a good sign. Rules out a lot."

"Like?"

"You weren't shot through the lung. And you weren't hit in a major artery, obviously. You wouldn't be here."

He reached into a pocket and handed Paul a couple of capsules, which he said were ibuprofen. "Take these," he said. They sat down on the tarp, the ground hard beneath them. Paul figured his father must have gotten used to it by now. He was startled to notice a pistol lying on the tarp. What was his father doing with this Vietnam War–era weapon?

Father and son hadn't hugged each other, hadn't even shaken hands. Nor did either of them mention their long separation. His father asked him to tell him what he'd been up to; his tone was matter-of-fact, even brusque. Paul gave his father a quick account of the last six years of his life, starting with meeting Tatyana, how he'd changed his identity and disappeared, and ending with Horgan, the fired CIA officer. His Deep Throat. Stan barely showed any reaction. "How do you know they haven't followed you here?" he asked when Paul was finished.

"I wouldn't be here if they'd followed me," he said.

"They want to kill you or arrest you?"

"Kill me, I think," he said, remembering the Russian who shot at him in Virginia.

"Well, you ain't dead yet," Stan said with just a hint of a smile. "Let me take a look at those dressings."

His father opened up the olive-drab cotton duck kit, unfolding it two ways. Meanwhile, Paul took off his shirt. Stanley shone a flashlight on the wound. The opening was fairly large, ragged, bloody. There was also a lump a few inches away. Paul's skin was caked with dried blood.

With his finger, Stan pressed down on the top of Paul's shoulder.

The pain was incredible. Paul gritted his teeth.

"I feel the bullet right there. Hold on." Stan got up, left the lean-to. Paul heard rustling. In thirty seconds, his father returned with a small branch from an oak. "Bite on this stick. That'll get you through. I've got a Z-Pak here," he said, handing Paul some Zithromax.

His father had put on a pair of nitrile gloves and had taken various tools out of his medic kit: a scalpel; a straight hemostat, which looked like a roach clip; a gauze pad; surgical bandages; antibiotic cream; alcohol wipes; a curved needle; some fishing line.

"You're right-handed, aren't you?" he asked his son.

"Yes."

"Good. Bullet's lodged in the dome of the deltoid. Right on top of the AC joint."

When he had cleaned the wound area with an alcohol wipe, he picked up the scalpel and sliced into the top of Paul's shoulder.

It was painful, but Paul bit the stick and held still as his father removed the bullet—"Nine-millimeter, low-velocity projectile," he explained clinically—with the forceps. "The bullet isn't deformed, but there may still be fragments in there. A jacketed bullet would have gone through and through. This is messier."

Stan threaded the surgical needle with the fishing line. Using the hemostat, he sutured closed the wound he'd cut. "Got to leave it slightly open. For drainage. Same with the entry wound. Loose approximation of the wound edges."

"Okay," Paul said. He was surprised, even touched, by the unexpected tenderness of his father's care.

"By the way, I noticed you're limping. Something wrong with your left foot?"

"Ankle thing I'm recovering from."

"Shot there, too?"

"Nah. Just twisted it."

"When you were running from the law, huh? Well, you made it, anyway."

Stanley picked up the bullet, inspected its base. It had mushroomed a bit but was largely intact. "The flex tip and the crimped band; it's distinctive. Looks like a Hornady round."

"What's that?"

"It's what the FBI uses. Whoever shot you is probably with the FBI. Or was supplied with FBI ordnance." He picked up the pistol from the floor of his lean-to and shoved it into the pocket of his long army-surplus camouflage fatigue coat. "What have you gotten yourself into?" Stanley said. "Do you have anything to defend yourself with?"

105

The two walked toward town. As darkness fell, Paul rented a motel room in town with cash. Two double beds. He invited his father to spend the night in his room and was surprised when he agreed. A night in a warm bed or a night in a cold lean-to in the forest? Not a tough choice.

The room smelled stuffy, as if it hadn't been used for a while. The beds were covered in worn burgundy coverlets. An old TV set, a telephone, a Keurig coffee maker. The place wasn't seedy, but it was tired. Paul plugged his laptop into an outlet above the counter that ran around the perimeter of half the room. He turned on the antique Comfort-Aire air conditioner/heater, switched it to Heat, and it rattled to life.

His father, who'd always objected to modern conveniences, went over and shut the thing off.

Paul looked over. He thought, *Fuck you. I paid for this room; you don't get to dictate the terms.* But instead of flaring up, he said gently, "Hey, Pop, I know you don't like these things, but I'm in physical distress, and I need the comfort right now, and I'm going to turn this back on."

His father said, "You bet. Okay, let me see this thumb drive."

From his pocket, Paul drew the flash drive and inserted it into his laptop.

The screen filled with gibberish, as it had the last time he tried it, years before.

His father looked at the screen for a long time.

"Well, your hunch is right. This is indeed encrypted. But how old is this thing?"

"This flash drive is new. But I copied it from an old one, five years ago, and it had been in storage before that. Who knows how long it was there."

"That explains it . . . This code uses an old version of the Diffie-Hellman algorithm, one that contains an unintentional backdoor."

"In English, please?"

"It's encrypted; lucky for us, the encryption was cracked some years ago. Thanks to the leak of NSA hacking tools. As I'm constantly telling you, think of how much better off we'd all be if the NSA didn't exist. All these government intelligence agencies—"

"*Constantly telling me*? I haven't seen you in almost twenty years!"

"Well, I used to—only, you never listened."

Paul stared at him, infuriated and maddened, all the old feelings returning. He shook his head, sighed with frustration.

"It's probably hackable using EternalBlue," his father said.

"Which is?"

"A hacking tool created by the NSA. Leaked by the Shadow Brokers, an infamous group of hackers, seven or eight years ago. The people's crowbar, they call it."

"Does that mean you can decrypt this?"

"With the right software and a better computer than this, I could. And my computer science skills are rusty and way out of date."

"So now what?"

"A student of mine from Caltech teaches at CMU."

"Carnegie Mellon?"

"Right. He's brilliant. A genius of mathematical cryptography."

"That's codes, right?"

His father gave a skyward glance, nearly rolled his eyes. His standard response to something he considered dopey. "Uh, do you have one of those portable phones?"

THEY SPENT THE NIGHT IN the seedy motel, each of them exhausted. Paul wondered if he was spending his last night in relative comfort. The next morning, they picked up take-out coffee at a diner and hit the road. It was three and a half hours by car to Pittsburgh, via the PA 28, a boring drive, and for a long time they drove in silence.

Paul found himself thinking that there was something very American about what his father had become. The American isolato had a lot of company, from *Walden Pond* to the Westerns. Difficult men intoxicated by their own sense of integrity, cuddly as porcupines and supreme in self-reliance. Americans have always loved the archetype, whether frontiersman or fugitive or Jeremiah Johnson–style mountain man. Easy to heroize. But self-reliance could be self-centeredness, too. A retreat from the ties meant to bind. It took a toll on the people you were supposed to love and nurture. The creed hardened your skin but shrank your soul.

After half an hour, increasingly aware of the tense silence between the two of them, Paul said, "Thank you, by the way."

"For what?"

"Well, for taking out the bullet."

"Haven't had to do that since Vietnam."

"Huh."

"Coulda been a lot worse. Bullet coulda struck an artery. You woulda bled out." He shook his head. "Gunshot wounds are bad, especially if you're shot in the thorax."

Another long silence. Finally, Paul said quietly, "I just wish you'd shown Mom this level of care." The words had just come out of him.

A long pause. "The hell's that supposed to mean?"

"You didn't want to support Big Medicine, or whatever you called it. So you let her die." Paul's heart was hammering rapidly. It had come out, and he hadn't meant it to.

"Is that what you think?"

Paul didn't reply.

"Your mother went in and got checked out, and they told her it was inoperable and she had ten months to live. So she refused to take any medication. I argued with her, but that was totally her call. Her decision."

Paul was stunned into silence.

"She didn't want you to know," his father went on.

"Why—why not?"

"She didn't want you to know that she was refusing medical care, because she thought you'd try to talk her out of it."

"And she refused even palliative care, too?"

"Everything."

Dumbfounded, Paul said, "And—why didn't you ever tell me any of this?"

"Would you have listened?" Stan said.

A long silence. Paul didn't know what to say. Yes, he would have tried to talk her out of it. Guilty as charged. His father, not exactly the most psychological of men, was probably equally hamstrung.

He wondered why his father had never tried to establish a détente.

Then again, neither had he.

"You have a point," Paul said. "I wish—"

What to say? *I wish you'd told me this twenty years ago? I wouldn't have cut you off for all these years?* But that was too painful to admit.

"Yes?"

"I'm sorry," Paul said. He left it vague, unspecified. Sorry for what? He didn't say.

His father didn't ask.

Stanley put his hand on top of Paul's knee. "Water under the bridge," he said.

106

Carnegie Mellon University was located in the Oakland section of Pittsburgh, next to a large park. They parked on Forbes Avenue and walked to the Gates Hillman Complex. His father moved stiffly, as if he had arthritis. Along the way, Paul noticed a camera mounted to a streetlamp pole and wondered if it was the university's or the government's. He pulled the visor of his Mets cap lower over his brow. His father, he noticed, had done the same with his filthy fishing cap.

The Bill and Melinda Gates Building was a funky-looking structure rising from a ravine on the west side of the campus. Most of the buildings on the campus were classical looking, yellow brick with copper roofs that had turned green. But the Gates Building was modern, ten levels, each seemingly placed haphazardly atop the other, cantilevered, with black zinc shingles in a diamond pattern.

Inside, a long spiral walkway dominated the lobby.

"Stanley Brightman, in the actual flesh!" cried Professor Moss Sweetwater when they arrived. "Never thought I'd see you again!"

Professor Sweetwater was clearly a proud eccentric. For one thing, he wore turquoise-aqua socks. His office contained a big rolling whiteboard covered with numbers and strange characters and a standing desk.

The two men hugged each other.

"You're absolutely right, Stan," the professor said after Paul and his father had recounted their story. "This uses backdooring primes in the Diffie-Hellman key exchange algorithm. Like the backdoor discovered in the Dual EC DRBG."

"Sorry—what's that?" Paul asked, trying valiantly to keep up.

"The Dual Elliptic Curve Deterministic Random Bit Generator."

"Ah, *I* see," Paul said dryly.

"It's a bug in the Diffie-Hellman algorithm introduced by the NSA," Professor Sweetwater said. "See, they put out a crypto algorithm that contained a backdoor known only to them. I mean, they bribed RSA Security to put the backdoor in their software."

"Much clearer," Paul said, smiling faintly.

"Wow, what is this?" Stan said, tapping the front of a large computer standing on the floor in a rack five feet high with cables snaking out of it and coiling on the floor.

"It's got eight Nvidia Hopper GPUs," Professor Sweetwater said.

"I've only *heard* of that," Stan said, marveling.

Sweetwater turned to Paul. "Whatever's on this drive, it's a fossil. Seven years ago, this might have been unbreakable."

"But now?"

"A breeze. First thing we do is run a virus check on this thing." The professor's high-performance computer was buzzing and whirring and whining.

Apparently, the USB stick passed his test, because the next thing Paul saw was Sweetwater's computer screen filling up with neat rows of green and red numbers like soldiers on parade. The professor said something about hexadecimal numbers and complex numbers.

Paul said, "Uh-huh."

Professor Sweetwater said something about a lattice and elliptic curves and modular exponentiation.

Paul said, "Uh-huh."

Yet his father was following along avidly. "That's a defective crypto system," he said.

Sweetwater said to Stan, "If I had a quantum computer, I'd try to factor them using Peter Shor's algorithm."

As both men chortled quietly, Paul surveyed the office. He saw a framed photo on the wall of Moss Sweetwater with a handsome black Labrador, a red bandana around its neck.

"That your Lab?" Paul asked.

"Yup. That's Évariste."

Paul nodded, continued scanning. He saw a silver-framed citation, the Presidential Early Career Award for Scientists and Engineers. Framed covers of journal articles. On a regular steel desk were a vintage robot from RadioShack; a toy light saber with signatures all over it in Sharpie marker; a well-worn paperback copy of *Pnin*, by Vladimir Nabokov; a Japanese tea set. Next to the desk, shelves of yellow math books and the *Yale Banner* yearbook for 2015. A photograph of Professor Sweetwater at the White House; another of the professor, this time with Paul's father, a younger, happier Stan Brightman—both accepting some kind of award.

Stan and his old student chatted far more and more easily than Stan had ever chatted with his son. Some twenty minutes later, the professor said, "Anyone here read Russian?"

Paul circled back to the computer screen. "I do, a little."

He stared at the screen. It appeared to be an archive of emails, mostly in Russian, going back decades. He skimmed the emails, clicking and clacking and scrolling. He understood very little of it. The Cyrillic characters were interrupted occasionally, here and there, by stock symbols in English and occasional dollar signs. The emails were between two people: Arkady Galkin and Geraldine Dempsey. Both had Proton Mail accounts. Dempsey writing in Russian. Signing her emails "GP" in Cyrillic letters. Galkin signed his notes "AG."

No wonder Dempsey was so desperate to retrieve the thumb drive, this secret cache of messages.

Arkady Galkin had Geraldine Dempsey, a top-ranking CIA officer, on his payroll.

"Who or what is Phantom?" the professor asked.

"It's an operation," Paul said. "A CIA operation."

Then Professor Sweetwater's landline phone rang, jarringly. He picked up the handset and pushed the button to answer. "Marge." He listened for ten seconds. "Okay. . . . How many? . . . How do you know?" He listened, inhaled and exhaled, then hung up the phone.

He turned around to face Paul and his father. "The FBI called Marge to ask where my office was."

"They're coming here?" Paul asked.

"Apparently. But I think we've still got a little time before they get here."

There was a loud pounding at the door. A booming male voice: "Professor Sweetwater?"

The professor turned his head. Without opening the door, he called out, "Yeah, who's there?"

A long pause. "FBI," the man's voice said. "Please open the door, professor."

107

Professor Sweetwater's eyes widened. Paul shook his head.

"I'm sorry, I'm in conference and can't be disturbed," said Sweetwater. "Can you come back in half an hour, please?"

"We just have a few questions for Mr. Brightman—"

"Half an hour," Sweetwater said in a louder, more imperious voice. He ejected the flash drive and handed it to Paul, looking at him questioningly and speaking in a soft voice: "Which Brightman are they after?"

"Me," Paul said.

"What did you do?"

"It would take too long to tell you."

"You didn't kill anyone, right?" the professor said with a half smile.

Paul shook his head. He immediately flashed on the man who called himself Frederick Newman, back in New Hampshire, who'd gotten killed in their struggle over the speargun. Did the FBI want him for that murder, too, along with his theft of the Phantom drive? Not only was Newman a hired killer, but he'd gotten himself killed while Paul was defending himself.

"How the hell they know you're here?" his father whispered.

Paul thought of the surveillance camera he'd noticed on the edge of the Carnegie Mellon campus on the way over. "Facial recognition," he said without explaining. "Now what do we do?"

Sweetwater pointed to a second door in the office that Paul had barely taken notice of before, because it was covered with framed things and didn't look like it was used very often. "This opens to a conference room I never use," Sweetwater said, "and the door at the other end leads to an internal corridor near the elevator. But don't take the elevator. Keep going past the elevators, down that hallway, past the stairs, then hang an immediate right. That will take you to the Pausch Bridge, a pedestrian walkway that connects this building with the Purnell building, the Purnell Center for the Arts. Go. I'll keep them at bay while you guys go."

"Thank you," Paul and his father said at the same time.

Sweetwater opened the second door. The two Brightman men rushed into the dark conference room. Paul spotted the door to the corridor. There was a glass panel inset in it. He peered through it, saw nobody, then slowly opened the door. The elevator was fifty feet away. No one around. Maybe the FBI didn't know about this rear exit.

Then a woman came down the hallway, and Paul broke out in a cold sweat.

The woman came toward them, smiled, and passed by.

Paul and his father kept walking. Paul's heart was clattering. "If we get lucky, we won't have to do anything. Just walk out of here. *Slowly.*"

"How'd they know we were here?" Stan asked again.

"That camera on Forbes Avenue, maybe. Or maybe there's something in the flash drive that sent out an alarm. I don't know. They must have scrambled a local FBI team. They must have an APB out for me." He used the jargon for "all-points bulletin" from cop shows he'd watched.

"So you think they have a picture of you on some national database?"

"Probably." He swallowed. "You trust Sweetwater, don't you?"

"Completely."

Paul nodded. "Me, too, actually."

They saw the exit to the footbridge connecting this building with an older one, which the professor had said was the college's drama department, the Purnell Center. The bridge seemed to be suspended over a grassy area, some two hundred feet in length. Lit up blue. The side walls of the bridge were opaque but not tall enough to block a view from the ground. In case someone on the FBI team was watching—which was unlikely, he thought—the two men walked separately, Paul in front and his father twenty feet behind. They walked, didn't run.

"They don't want to shoot you," Stanley said. "They want to arrest you, am I right?"

Paul didn't reply for a long moment. Then he said, "I guess we'll find out."

108

They emerged from the drama school building into a wide-open area with a large stretch of lawn. It was a sunny but chilly day, so no students were sitting there, but a few people were walking around it and across it. The Gates Building was behind them, where the FBI agents were. If there were others, Paul didn't see them.

He and his father resumed their walking pace: steady, unhurried, with one far ahead of the other, so it wouldn't look like they were walking together. The FBI was probably looking for the two of them.

Paul took the lead, heading left to Forbes Avenue, where his rented Jeep was parked. Once they'd made it to the car, they would leave Pittsburgh right away.

"FBI! Freeze!" came a man's voice.

Paul felt himself go cold, and prickles of sweat broke out on his forehead. But he continued walking. As if he didn't know the man was talking to him.

"I said *freeze!*" the man shouted again, sounding closer still.

Paul turned around and saw, a few hundred feet away, a solitary guy around his age in a navy-blue FBI windbreaker, a weapon at his side.

Then he noticed that his father had stopped walking. He'd turned to face the FBI man, while at the same time hissing to Paul, "Run! Right now, go! Get out of here!"

"What the hell are you doing?" Paul said.

"Run, goddamn it!" Stan said again. "They're not going to shoot us both."

Stunned, unsure what to do next, Paul began running, hoping his father would come to his senses. But he heard his father shout, "I'll surrender! I'm too old to run."

"Tell your son to stop running," the other man shouted. "You—put down that weapon! You're giving me no choice!"

Paul glanced quickly back, saw the FBI agent and his father both standing still, facing each other. But Stan Brightman was leveling his Vietnam War–era pistol at the FBI man.

Paul kept running.

"Put down your weapon!" the FBI agent repeated.

Then Paul heard two gunshots, loud and nearly simultaneous.

As he ran, he turned back to look again. His father was down, crumpled onto the grass.

Paul kept going. His adrenaline was pumping wildly, his head was spinning. He couldn't think about what had just happened.

Had his father just been killed? Had Stanley Brightman sacrificed himself for his son?

The building on the other side of the lawn was some sort of student union. He headed straight for it, saw students going in and coming out, could tell it was probably crowded inside. Perfect.

Paul didn't dare look behind him. As he entered the building, he removed his sunglasses and his cap and slowed his pace. A crowd of students was heading upstairs, so he joined the flow, moving at their pace. The destination was a large student dining room.

He tried to keep a neutral facial expression, tried not to think about what he'd just seen. But he couldn't help it: Was his father indeed dead? Or could he be saved with medical intervention? And would the FBI bother to intervene?

Inside the dining hall, long lines of students shoveled food onto plates on trays from steel pans along a steam table. He spotted the entrance to the kitchen and knew that was the best way out. He slowed his pace and entered the kitchen, felt the steamy heat of dishwashers running and water boiling. No one turned to look at him. He moved to the back of the kitchen, saw the exit to some service stairs, kept going.

A minute later, he was on Forbes Avenue, where he spotted the Jeep. Two FBI agents were standing next to it, waiting for him.

He turned, reversed direction down Forbes, kept going until he reached a cross street, Morewood Avenue. A loud vehicle was coming down the street toward him, a rust-covered turquoise car, 1970s vintage. The car pulled to the side of the road, parking sloppily, and a young guy who looked like a student got out, slamming the door and leaving the car unlocked with the confidence of someone who knows no one is going to steal his heap of junk.

As Paul walked closer, he saw that it was an old Chevy Nova, probably around 1975. A compact muscle car. A car that was old enough to be hot-wired. He knew how to do that.

His father had taught him how.

HE MADE SEVERAL WRONG TURNS trying to get out of Pittsburgh and on to the interstate. The Chevy Nova was loud, sounded like there was a hole in the muffler. It was also an amazing gas guzzler; he could almost see the needle on the gas gauge drop before his eyes.

He was in a strange, thunderstruck state. In his mind, he kept seeing his father's crumpled body.

He knew that if you pointed a weapon at a U.S. law enforcement officer, and they decided they were in imminent danger, they had the right to use deadly force. He had no doubt his father had known it, too.

Stanley had stood, feigned surrendering, and then pointed his gun, knowing that it would slow the FBI agent down, allow Paul to escape.

His father, who had been gone for most of Paul's life, only to reappear so briefly. Paul didn't like him, but maybe he had loved him. No, he didn't love the guy, yet he mourned him.

He didn't know how to feel.

He was angry, he was grieving, he was in shock.

Yes, his father shouldn't have been so stupid as to pull a gun on an FBI agent. But he didn't deserve to be killed. Tears welled up in Paul's eyes. He felt something he hadn't felt since his mother's death, a stab of anguish.

109

As Paul passed through the tollgate, he noticed the camera photographing his license plate. Probably the student hadn't yet reported his car missing. Even if he had, Paul assumed it would take a while before the stolen license plate number went online.

And what if there were an APB out on him? Wasn't there a way to find out? There had to be.

He saw a sign for the town of Somerset and pulled to the side of the road. All he knew about Somerset was that it was a town in Pennsylvania. He called the Somerset Police Department. It had to be a small department, Paul thought. Where people were friendly, neighborly. Unlike a big-city police department.

The phone on the other end rang and rang, ten rings. He hung up and hit Redial. On the second try, someone answered. It sounded like a woman with a deep voice, but he wasn't sure it wasn't a man.

"Somerset Police. Is this an emergency?"

"Um, I know this guy, I overheard him talking, and he may be wanted by the police or the FBI or something. And I want to see if there's a reward if I turn him in."

"Who is 'this guy'?" the person said.

"I'm not sure, but I heard the name 'Brightman'?"

He was obviously fishing, but the clerk said, "Hold on."

The clerk got back on the line thirty seconds later. "There's a reward of half a million dollars," the person said in a louder voice. "If they apprehend him based on the information you provide, you get five hundred thousand dollars. You can give me the information, or else you can call the anonymous tip line."

"I'll do that," Paul said and disconnected the call.

The FBI was offering half a million dollars for information leading to his arrest. *Half a million dollars.* Once it was put up on the internet, that information would motivate a lot of people.

Instead of taking a bus, he would continue on to D.C. He found the nearest gas station and filled up.

Back behind the wheel, he observed the speed limit, stayed in the right lane as long as he could stand it.

He knew only one way out of the situation he was in. One way forward, and that way was littered with obstacles and filled with risks.

He called the only person in the FBI he knew he could trust.

110

Special Agent Stephanie Trombley's hair had gone gray since Paul last saw her in New York City five years ago, with Special Agent Addison, just before the massacre at the FBI office. Her hair was longer than it had been last time. Her face had aged more than you'd expect. But she had been through a harrowing time, seeing her colleague and friend, Mark Addison, murdered along with the others at the satellite FBI office on the Lower East Side of Manhattan. The stress alone must have aged her more than five years.

They met at a Chipotle on Tenth Street, in D.C., across from the FBI headquarters. She came alone, as she promised she would.

She had wanted Paul to meet her in her office inside the FBI building, but he had refused. Too risky. Now she stared at him as she entered the restaurant. When she sat down at his table, she said, "So you *are* alive."

"For now, anyway."

"I wondered. The best law enforcement agents in the country couldn't find you. What happened?"

"Some bad luck."

"Explain."

For a moment, he hesitated. How much could he tell her about how he'd killed an assassin, a man who'd come to kill him?

"I was spotted in a small town in New Hampshire," he said.

"How?" She tucked her hair behind her ears.

"I think a traffic camera captured my face."

She nodded. "So, that's how Dempsey and Berzin found you. And sent one of their killers after you. But you—"

"A little *good* luck. Killed him first." He explained about the speargun. "I wondered at first if it was Galkin who was after me. For running out on his daughter. But I guess his investment firm is shuttered." Paul had googled "Galkin" and read that he, like all the other Russian oligarchs, had been sanctioned after the Ukraine invasion. His yacht, his real estate around the world, his assets—everything confiscated. His firm dissolved. But after a few articles about Galkin's sanctioning, there was nothing further about him at all. Where he lived now, several years after the invasion; where he'd gone in the past year—a complete mystery.

"He's no longer a rich man. No longer in the position to offer a bounty on your head. Not that he would have. But you're still on the run."

"Right. And I need your help."

"I don't know what I can do for you, but go ahead and tell me what's on your mind."

"Who was after me in New Hampshire? I saw Berzin. Then I saw an FBI team."

"Well, it's complicated. Since the massacre of the FBI agents, Dempsey's unit was shut down, and an internal probe was launched inside CIA. Geraldine Dempsey and her team have methodically erased records of the operation, knowing that if the truth about the massacre came out, she'd be toast. There was just one dangling thread to be snipped off—and that was you. And when Berzin learned you were in New Hampshire—"

"But Berzin . . ."

"Berzin has been a longtime employee and asset controlled by Dempsey at CIA."

"Berzin! So he was working for *Dempsey* the whole time—not for Galkin?"

She nodded.

"Explain."

She did.

The pieces were coming together now. He listened impassively, not showing his surprise. Finally, he said, "She cooked up these intelligence charges against me. They're bogus. I want you to get your colleagues to drop the charges against me."

"That's not so easy. It's in fact incredibly complicated."

"Aren't you a supervisory special agent?"

"One of hundreds."

"I know you can do it. Did you guys ever figure out who this Natasha Obolensky is?"

Trombley smiled. "A closely held secret. Took us forever to crack it."

"But you did?"

"She doesn't exist. The CIA created her out of whole cloth, out of rumors and gossamer, and they used her to funnel billions into Galkin's fund when it was just starting. To the rest of the intelligence community, it looked like Natasha Obolensky was a wealthy, reclusive Russian living abroad, in Ireland. It looked like Kremlin money. But it was the CIA's."

"And all that insider trading at Galkin's firm?"

"All of it was based on top-secret defense-related government intelligence that Dempsey passed to Galkin. A major no-no."

Then Paul explained to her what he wanted to do.

Trombley looked around the shop, made sure no one was within earshot. "What you want to do is impossible."

"Impossible?"

"*Nearly* impossible."

"It will make your career."

"Undoubtedly. But do you think I can just snap my fingers, and—"

"I don't doubt it's complicated, that it'll require someone who's really good at working the law enforcement system. That's why I'm talking to you."

"I know damned well why you're talking to me. Because of what happened to Mark Addison."

Paul raised his eyebrows, then pulled a rueful smile. "Because I knew you'd care. And because you're the only FBI agent I know. There's that, too."

Trombley just looked at him, but in her eyes, he could see a world of hurt.

"Wait. If Dempsey's unit was shut down," he said, "how could she be sending people after me?"

She hesitated a long while. "That's a mystery, I'll admit. I'm in touch with the CIA's counterespionage unit—the mole hunters—which is a small, tightly compartmented group. We have an FBI officer embedded in that unit. We're taking the lead, but we have to coordinate with them. And they say we're going to need to get Dempsey on tape. And good luck with that. She's as smart as they come. Russian studies major at Swarthmore, PhD from Georgetown. Knows more than anyone—or so she believes. How do we get her to incriminate herself? Because until we do, we've got nothing. FBI won't do a thing."

"The Phantom memory stick isn't enough?"

"No. They need her on tape admitting responsibility for the FBI massacre."

A long pause, then Paul said, "I think I have a way."

"I'm all ears," said Stephanie Trombley.

111

The world's largest naval station, and the headquarters of the U.S. Navy's Fleet Forces Command, is NAVSTA NORVA, or Naval Station Norfolk, a giant base of over four thousand acres in the southeast corner of Virginia. Paul had driven the three hours from D.C. without a break. Now, just outside Gate 5, he stopped at the Pass and ID office to get the one-day visitor pass that was waiting for him. He used his Grant Anderson driver's license, praying they didn't check criminal databases. Clearly they didn't. The pass now hung from his rearview mirror. There was no way to get onto the base, he noted, not without handing over your ID. No one could sneak on. It was reasonably well protected.

The higher-ranking naval officers live in a neighborhood there called Breezy Point, in four-bedroom, pet-friendly single-family homes. The house he was looking for was located on Dillingham Boulevard. He found it, a handsome, if generic brick house with an attached garage and a good-size lawn. It looked like something you might see in a prosperous suburb. There were no armed guards circulating that he could see.

He parked his car in the driveway and rang the doorbell. He heard the familiar six chimes echoing throughout the house. A minute went by. He heard music thumping through the front door.

Tatyana Galkin answered the door.

He hadn't seen her in five years. Her hair was blonder than it used to be, and she'd styled it differently—up, in a messy bun. She was as pretty as ever, though the years had etched fine lines on her face, on her forehead and around her eyes. She'd gained a little weight, and it looked great on her. She wasn't wearing a wedding ring, neither his nor anyone else's. She was dressed in a plain white T-shirt and Paul's Reed College sweatpants, which he'd left behind. He wondered if that was a deliberate choice, knowing she was about to see him.

Her face, her eyes, were red, as if she'd been crying. He heard Taylor Swift singing something melancholy and bittersweet, probably "All Too Well." Sarah had liked Taylor Swift a lot, too.

"Pasha," she said, her voice hoarse.

She pushed open the screen door. He gave her a hug. She smelled the same. She hadn't changed her perfume.

He looked around. The front sitting room was furnished with institutional-looking furniture, as generic as the house. No gilt.

"Why are you crying?" he asked.

"It's difficult for me," she said. "Seeing you."

He nodded as they pulled apart. She shook her head. "I don't know," she said quietly. "I know you'll never forgive me, but I still want to say I'm sorry."

"For what?" he said softly.

She bowed her head, closed her eyes, shook her head again. "Don't make this hard for me. I chose my family. You know that. But you were my family, too. I just never really understood that."

After five years, he still felt guilty for having left her the way he had. He felt the pain of having once loved her and still loving her. He felt a swirl of emotions.

A long pause. He said, "Is your father—"

She interrupted him. "Berzin wasn't going to kill you. I would never have gone along with that. It was a sedative. A tranquilizer."

He shook his head. No need to revisit that day. "How—how've you been?" He wanted to ask if she was with someone else now, but this wasn't the time.

"Look at the way we live."

He looked around at the generic house with its generic furnishings and thought about what a comedown it was from Arkady Galkin's life of extraordinary luxury.

"But it's safe," Paul said. "You're protected."

"We're prisoners."

Behind her, Arkady Galkin loomed into view. "Music is too much," he told his daughter. "Turn off." He turned to Paul as Tatyana backed away. "Brightman," he said without a smile.

Galkin looked ten years older, not five. His potbelly was even larger. Now there were purplish circles under his eyes, which were dwarfed by his wild gray eyebrows. His face was scored with deep lines. His shoulders were stooped.

The music went quiet.

112

The two men sat in a screened-in gazebo behind the house. Galkin was smoking a cigar. The smoke filled the gazebo, burning Paul's eyes. Galkin was wearing the familiar blue-and-white-checked L.L.Bean fleece he liked to wear at home. His eyes were hooded and tired looking, bloodshot and sunken. His teeth were whiter, which might have been cosmetic dentistry, but he was a shell of his former boisterous self.

"Once I was one of richest men in world," Galkin said. "Now I am prisoner. Under house arrest. See, life unpredictable."

"'Man plans . . .'"

"'God laughs.' Yes. You are clever man." Galkin's head was wreathed in a low-hanging stratus cloud of gray smoke. "You disappear for five years. Can't be easy."

"Took some discipline," Paul said.

"You marry my daughter and then you disappear."

Paul said. "I think she knows why."

"I knew you are alive! I tell Berzin this all the time. You run out on my daughter. You steal from me. Take computer disk."

"Flash drive, maybe."

"Yes."

"Is causing me big *meegren* headache."

"I understand," Paul said. He had read some of the decrypted Phantom drive—certainly not all, since it was mostly in Russian, but enough to understand its staggering import. "I understand, too, that for the last two decades you've been a CIA asset. Controlled by Geraldine Dempsey."

There was a long silence. So long that Paul began to wonder if Galkin had heard him, had understood what he'd said.

"Was," said Galkin. "No longer."

"What happened?"

"War. Now nobody in Kremlin trust nobody."

"So you're useless to the CIA?"

"Correct. They say I am"—he smiled, said the words slowly—"'not *viable*' no more. So, for three, four years, we live as prisoners on naval base."

"All your money," Paul said carefully, "wasn't yours?"

"Wasn't mine? I invest! I build! I turn a few billion into many billions."

"But the original infusion of cash that set you up in business in the first place—"

"Ach." Galkin waved a hand in the air dismissively.

"That woman I met in Moscow—you know, the blind old woman, Ludmilla Zaitseva—was a CIA asset. She recruited you. She helped channel money from the CIA, is that right?" Paul flashed on Ludmilla's cryptic words: *The moment you think you have it all figured out is when you learn how dead wrong you are.* And then: *As for who pulling strings, that's where things get complicated.*

That had puzzled him, until now.

Galkin shrugged. "Who is CIA, who is KGB, all this I can't keep track."

"Okay." Paul thought for a moment. "But you still know how to reach your handler. Your case officer. You have her email."

He shook his head. "All channels closed. I am done now."

"What about in an emergency? Like if your life is threatened?"

"Yes, yes, there is way. I send up flare."

"Now, where did you used to meet with Dempsey?"

"Hotels, mostly. Sometimes safe house."

"Where?"

"New York, Washington."

"Safe house in D.C.?"

"Yes. Near. So?"

113

Brightman had had a thriller reader's notion of a CIA safe house, a capacious but discreet redbrick Georgian mansion in the tony Virginia suburbs with landscaped property. Instead, the safe house where Arkady Galkin had several times met Geraldine Dempsey was a humble single-story ranch-style house in the woods of Cabin John, Maryland. White-painted clapboard, faded red shutters, a set of gray-painted concrete steps in front. The cedar shingle roof was stained from the trees overhanging it. A couple of white concrete planters in front, with flowers that looked ignored. The house was surrounded by forest: a cabin in the woods, at the end of a long dirt road. It was entirely private, no neighbors, no one to observe the comings and goings.

Galkin showed up nearly half an hour late wearing a blue blazer and a tie. He'd dressed up for the occasion, Paul noticed.

"You sure this is it?" Paul asked.

"Absolutely. Is rented house. Government always cheap."

"How do you get in?"

"Is easy." Galkin found a lockbox hanging from the porch railing, pushed four buttons, and popped it open. Inside was the key. All very low-tech.

"The CIA must trust you," Paul said.

"Once they did."

"They didn't change the code."

"I tell you, government bureaucracy same everywhere. Never change." Galkin keyed open the front door lock, and the door came open, releasing a stuffy, mildewy odor. The house was rarely used, it seemed. But if Agent Trombley was as good as her word, the FBI had already been there earlier in the day, planting their clandestine recording devices. That was as far as they'd go. This entire meeting was Paul's initiative and his alone; the FBI would cooperate if and only if he were successful. So he was on his own.

Inside the house's cramped front room was beige wall-to-wall carpeting, a couple of red-upholstered lounge chairs, a big TV, cottage curtains. Down a little hallway off the living room was a bedroom and a bathroom.

An hour remained before Geraldine Dempsey had said she'd arrive at the safe house for an emergency consultation with Arkady Galkin. Paul looked around the small house, didn't see any obvious evidence of recording devices—then again, would he really know what to look for in the first place? Still, he did his due diligence, opening cabinets, pulling back the fringed chenille coverlet in the bedroom. Nothing that he could see.

Paul's plan was to get Geraldine Dempsey on tape, conversing with Galkin. Incriminating herself. The Phantom USB drive revealed her years-long relationship with her agent, Arkady Galkin, but it didn't connect her to the FBI massacre, and that they needed.

Paul rehearsed potential scenarios with Galkin, who was surprisingly avid. Dempsey's reluctance to meet—Galkin had had to cajole—had only confirmed that he'd been cut loose, that he was of no interest to the CIA any longer. This fact seemed to sharpen Galkin's resolve into obsession.

When they heard a car pull up, Paul immediately secreted himself in the bedroom. But he positioned himself so that he could see out the slats in the bedroom's venetian blinds, looking outside, at an angle so he wouldn't be spotted, as had been the plan. Paul watched as Dempsey's security guy entered the house, a tall, broad-shouldered man in a slightly oversize blazer that probably concealed a weapon. Paul had expected Dempsey to be accompanied by at least one officer from the CIA's Security Protective Service. The man opened the front door and poked his head in perfunctorily, for a beat, before Dempsey entered. She was wearing a belted trench coat and carrying a large black leather handbag.

"Arkady Viktorovich," she said in a booming voice. "You reached out using an emergency channel. This had better be a true emergency. You have disrupted a very busy day."

"We need to talk," Galkin said.

Paul had considered sitting on the bed in the very spare bedroom, but there was always the possibility that Dempsey would open the bedroom door just to check that there was no one else in the house. So he stood in the dank closet, through whose thin walls he could hear the conversation reasonably well.

"What exactly is going on, Arkady?" Dempsey asked, her voice slightly muffled. "Given that you no longer work for us."

"Brightman," he said. His voice was clearer, louder. "Paul Brightman is . . . at large. You must resolve this matter. He is threat to my family. He knows I used to work for you. If this gets out, Kremlin will come after me and my family and they will not rest until—"

A pause. "As long as your family stays on the base, you are protected."

"Which makes us prisoners," he said. "What life is this, after all I have done for you?"

"Phantom has been shut down. You know that full well."

"And you freeze my assets. My money is my safety. Nearly twenty years, I give intelligence to CIA. I invest. Make fortune. Now I want my money back. At least some money."

"You signed a waiver, years ago, agreeing to that stipulation. That money was never yours."

"I will make deal."

"That's off the table. Your signature's on the release. So if you're done complaining and trying to make *deals*, I would like to get back to my office. I have plenty of real work to do."

"If you release half billion dollars of my assets," Galkin said, "I give you Brightman."

"Brightman . . ." Dempsey paused. "That might be of interest. Tell me more."

Suddenly, a blaring noise came on—the TV, a news report, a cacophony. Dempsey had switched it on, Paul figured, to mask whatever she and Galkin were saying. To defeat any concealed recorders. Meaning she knew about them or expected them. For another minute or two, he listened, tried to make out the conversation, but couldn't.

He leaned over to retie his shoes. They were new and a little uncomfortable.

At that moment, without warning he heard the bedroom door abruptly swing open. "I know you're in there, Brightman," he heard the man say. "Step out with your hands up. *Now.*"

The closet door opened. There stood the security officer who'd accompanied Geraldine Dempsey, pointing a gun directly at him. The man was over six feet tall, in his late thirties, with a shaved head and a tightly clenched face full of premature wrinkles.

Behind him stood Geraldine Dempsey. Next to her stood Arkady Galkin.

"Mr. Brightman," Dempsey said, registering no surprise. "There you are. This is an unexpected pleasure. We have much to talk about."

"Like how you hired Russians to murder FBI employees who were about to discover your mole?"

"What in the world are you talking about, Brightman? You sound unhinged." She turned to the bald man, smiling exultantly. "Shawn? Please pat this fellow down." In a muttering aside, she added, "Let's make sure our conversation is between us only."

The security guard stepped forward, pistol clutched in his right hand and still aimed at Paul. Thrusting his left hand out, he patted Paul down, starting at his shoulders and working down his torso, back, and sides. He felt the reverse side of Paul's belt, searched his pockets, ran his hands down the backs and sides of Paul's legs. Triumphantly, he produced Paul's burner phone. He showed it to Dempsey, who shrugged. "Take it," she said.

When Shawn's fingers appeared to locate the tiny, concealed recorder-transmitter taped to the small of Paul's back, he stopped. "Shirt off," he said.

Paul hesitated but knew he had no choice. When he'd removed his shirt, Dempsey said, "Turn around." Paul turned, and Shawn ripped the device and its securing tape painfully off his lower back and handed the device to Dempsey.

"A transmitter, too?" she said. She shook her head. "The best-laid plans. Shawn, there's probably a pen in his breast pocket. Could I have that, too, please?"

Shawn snatched the backup recording device, the pen clipped to Paul's shirt pocket.

She seemed to miss nothing.

"How's this working out for you, Paul?" Dempsey said acidly.

"I'd say everything is going exactly according to plan," he replied.

"The hell you talking about?"

"You're predictable," Paul said to her, but explained no further. His plan was unfolding, if not in the way he'd anticipated.

"Outside," Dempsey said.

Her security man pushed Paul out of the room, down the hall, and opened the front door.

"You want to talk," Dempsey continued, "we'll go for a walk in the woods. Leave this . . . soundstage. Both of you." She waved her hand around dismissively at the house and all its concealed recording devices.

Paul knew what she intended to do to him, or have Shawn do to him, when he was outside of the house. He wasn't able to keep his heart from jackhammering. Because now everything had to work right, or else.

As the three of them—Galkin, Dempsey, and Paul—descended the front steps, Dempsey began to speak. "So, Mr. Brightman—"

Paul interrupted her. "If anything happens to me, an email goes out at midnight tonight sending the *decrypted* Phantom file to a carefully selected list of reporters and editors at the *Wall Street Journal*, the *Washington Post*, the *New York Times*, and a slew of networks and cable news outlets."

To his surprise, Dempsey said nothing. They walked into the woods, which were so thick that the house disappeared almost immediately. Might Paul have neutralized her? Setting up a digital dead man's switch these days was simple. He'd done as he'd said: composed a detailed email, set for a delayed auto-send. If he couldn't get to his Gmail account and delete the scheduled email, it would automatically go out. Only he could stop it. Killing him was therefore a bad idea.

"But I can stop it going out," he added. "Persuade me."

"Persuade you?" Dempsey gave a twist of a smile, looked at Galkin. "Arkady, your former employee apparently doesn't know about FISC."

Arkady looked at her, at Paul. He didn't look like he understood.

"FISC?" Paul said. Now they were walking along a narrow dirt path through the trees.

"The Foreign Intelligence Surveillance Court. Two hours ago, on my request—approved by the director of national intelligence, by the way—they ordered Google to comply with my request for access to your Gmail. Access granted, and your scheduled email has been deleted."

Paul found himself blinking, speechless, as he contemplated the

ramifications of this. Not just for his own safety: it meant that this con-
spiracy, this cover-up, went even higher than he'd anticipated.

"You see, Mr. Brightman, you're facing ten years in prison. For what's
called *willful retention* of national security information. So in case you
were hoping to try to negotiate with me, don't bother."

Paul was silent. They continued walking.

"You want to know what you're trying to sabotage? Only the most
successful espionage initiative since World War Two. One of the most
closely held secrets ever. A project at CIA so secret that it wasn't even
listed in the Agency's *classified* phone book. The most serious penetra-
tion of the Kremlin ever, do you understand?"

"To what end?" Paul said.

Dempsey sighed, shook her head at the futility. She shifted her
handbag, which was hooked over one shoulder. Her words dripped with
condescension. "As a young and perhaps overly ambitious CIA officer
assigned to Moscow at the end of the last century, Paul, I recruited an
equally ambitious young entrepreneur for a remarkable scheme. Made
him a deal. We'll make you rich, and in return, you'll spy for us. You'll be
an oligarch we *own*. An oligarch who'd have direct access to the Kremlin,
like all the other oligarchs. And I would be his case officer. At first, we
channeled CIA money into his fund. But we made it back quickly.
Arkady Galkin eventually became the most prized intelligence asset in
U.S. history. A periscope into the Kremlin! We were instantly aware of
everything the Russian leadership had decided. How do you think we
knew so far in advance that Moscow was going to invade Ukraine? We
were privy to all the twists and turns. We knew what they were going to
do before *anyone* else in the world knew it. And a whole secret unit of
the CIA grew up around him: Phantom. A small pod that brainstormed
new modalities in espionage. Siloed from the rest of the agency. And the
genius of the whole scheme? We didn't need funding. It self-financed!
So we didn't need congressional oversight. And now *you* want to make
the details *public*. Which would lay waste to decades worth of *invaluable*
intelligence. And one more thing. To reveal Arkady's role in betraying
the Kremlin would be to get his entire family killed. You want to do that
to Tatyana? Are you really that coldblooded, to put them all under a
death sentence?"

"He's protected," Paul said. "He's living on a goddamned naval base."

His thoughts spun furiously. He had a few more cards to play, but he had to time them exactly right.

Dempsey continued. "Remember that story in the news about the Russian mercenary who'd led a coup against the Kremlin—and whose plane exploded in the air north of Moscow a few weeks later? When it comes to disloyalty, the big man in Moscow doesn't screw around. So you can be sure your ex-wife and her father, among many others, would be obliterated if this information became public. They will find him, I promise you that. This does not end well for you, Paul. The fact is, your old boss Galkin is useless to us now. He began to believe his press clippings. Like Pinocchio, he began to imagine he was a real boy. Thought he was a real genius investor. I mean, look at his returns, right? Out of the kindness of our hearts, we're letting him and his family live on a naval base, protected from the machinations of the GRU. As best we can, anyway. And no, Arkady, you're not getting half a billion dollars back. You're not getting a cent. It's not your money. Never was."

Now Paul turned to Galkin, whose face was flushed. The former oligarch looked enraged. "You see, she's not your ally anymore," Paul said. "She's your enemy. She could put you and your whole family in peril. You really want to leave your fate in her hands? It's like you said, a puppet is free as long as he loves his strings! *This is your chance to cut your strings.*"

Paul looked at Dempsey, trying to gauge her reaction, then noticed, in his peripheral vision, a quick, dark furtive movement.

Galkin had pulled out a gun and was pointing it directly at Geraldine Dempsey. His case officer. His control. Where had Galkin gotten a weapon? He hadn't said anything about it.

"Don't be an idiot," Dempsey snapped. Paul could see the whites of her eyes in the twilight. She didn't know what her former asset might do now. "Put that down before you get yourself shot."

On cue, Shawn, the security agent, obediently raised his own weapon and leveled it at Galkin, and for a moment, there seemed to be a standoff. The man was doing his job, protecting his charge.

Galkin's gun wavered a bit in his grip. He was pointing it at Dempsey, then at Shawn. Back and forth, his expression fierce, perhaps a little frightened, too.

Paul recalled Agent Trombley's words: *That's the CIA's Security Protective Service . . . former FBI SWAT agents.* Maybe Shawn, too, was ex-FBI, he thought. Odds were he was.

So Paul tried again to provoke Dempsey. "How can you live with yourself?" he said to her. "You hired thugs to take out FBI agents. These were colleagues of yours, fighting the good fight, and you had them killed! How could you *do* that?"

Shawn, pointing his gun at Galkin, seemed to be listening.

"Oh, please," Dempsey said. "Spare me your nauseating self-righteousness. Yes, five years ago we had to cauterize a well-intentioned but potentially disastrous inquiry. And because the Phantom project survived, we were able to gain invaluable, policy-shaping intelligence. My colleagues and I send operatives into harm's way all the time. We never do it lightly. But you can't protect this country from danger without *accepting* danger. The men and women who volunteer to be this nation's sentinels accept that reality. In this case, the termination of this unit was an utterly tragic decision—and an utterly necessary one."

Shawn looked at Geraldine Dempsey, lowered his gun, his eyes narrowing. "Madam, what did you say?"

Dempsey's face flashed with annoyance. But had something just changed in the dynamic between her and her security guard? Galkin continued leveling his gun, now only at Dempsey.

Paul looked at the security officer, and their eyes locked. "Yeah," Paul said to him. "Extremists like her always imagine they're in the right. But as soon as human beings, good people, are considered pawns, we've lost our way."

"Shawn, I'm under attack here. Do your job—take them both down," Dempsey commanded.

The security officer shook his head ever so slightly.

Furiously, Dempsey shouted, "Shawn, take them *down*! And you, Galkin—do you think your family is *ever* going to be safe? I will cut you all off altogether! You will have *no* protection whatsoever!"

Paul was deafened by an explosion.

But it wasn't Shawn who had fired. It was Arkady Galkin. He looked stunned at what he'd just done. "I am not puppet!" he shouted.

Geraldine Dempsey's body twisted and collapsed to the ground, her handbag dropping a few feet away. "*God!*" she cried out, scrabbling at the earth.

Dempsey appeared to have been shot in the thigh. Galkin raised his gun again and pointed it at her.

Another ear-splitting explosion.

Arkady Galkin's chest had turned into a terrible bloodied mess. His gun dropped beside him as he crumpled to the ground. Shawn had taken him down.

Galkin was moaning. Paul turned. His former father-in-law was clearly in agony but hadn't yet died. He gasped, his mouth opening and closing like a fish's, and then Paul realized that Galkin was trying to say something, looking at Paul the whole time.

Suddenly a squad of FBI agents burst through the trees. A couple of them grabbed Geraldine Dempsey and handcuffed her. She was protesting loudly, indignantly. At the same time, though, she was seriously wounded, so she was placed on a folding stretcher, squawking.

Paul turned and knelt where Galkin lay dying, saw the grotesque slick red mess that was the oligarch's chest, nearly heard the faint words, barely audible, the whisper low and crackling. Rivulets of blood streaming from the corner of his mouth. He was trying desperately to tell Paul something.

Paul leaned down, his ear close to Galkin's head, straining to listen. But the oligarch's mouth had stopped moving. The mouth had gone slack, and it was pretty evident that he was dead. Paul couldn't help but think he looked at peace.

Epilogue

The cemetery was outside Derryfield, a nondenominational burial ground whose gravestones dated back to the eighteenth century. The funeral for Stanley Brightman was sparsely attended. He hadn't left many friends. Paul was apprehensive that no one would show up. He was pretty sure Sarah wouldn't. He didn't expect her to. That was over. Stan's body had finally been released by the FBI, after all this time. He was half-expecting the Deacon of the off-gridders, Stephen Lucas, but he didn't appear. Still, Professor Moss Sweetwater had come from Pittsburgh. So had a childhood friend of Paul's, a man named Walter Beckley, who'd flown all the way from Bellingham, Washington.

Stanley Brightman had left no instructions for his funeral, so Paul had improvised. He'd brought in a rabbi from Bethlehem, New Hampshire. A rabbi from Bethlehem seemed appropriately nondenominational. Paul's father had never practiced any religion. He didn't believe in it.

People were gathering before the ceremony in the small, plain cemetery surrounded by woods. Walter Beckley shook Paul's hand, gave him an awkward hug. "Boy, compared to the wild adventure your dad made of his life, yours must seem so bland and uneventful," he said.

"Yeah," Paul said, giving a thoughtful smile.

"I guess that's why people like us ski, you know? Life's not dangerous enough."

Paul chuckled politely, then said, "Well, something to be said for a quiet existence."

He noticed someone standing nearby, waiting to talk, saw that it was his father's old student Professor Sweetwater. "Excuse me," he said, and turned to the professor, who gestured for the two of them to walk a distance from the graveside. When they were a good fifty yards away from the gathering, Professor Sweetwater said in a low voice, "You know I still have those files on my computer."

"You do?"

"You want them sent to you?"

"No, thanks," Paul said. "I'm trying to get away from all that."

"Huh," the professor said with a half smile. "I get it. But if you ever change your mind, just let me know."

"Thanks."

"Whatever happened to the oligarch, anyway?"

Arkady Galkin had been buried in Mount Lebanon Cemetery in Adelphi, Maryland, in a small, private ceremony. Paul had heard about it only after the fact.

"He's dead," Paul said sadly. "A long story."

He saw someone approaching, gave his apologies to Professor Sweetwater, and turned to his cousin Jason Brightman.

"Jason," he said. "I didn't expect you."

"I know, I know," Jason said. "I never knew your dad. I knew he was a little—he kind of had a screw loose, right? But he was brilliant."

"Alex is okay?"

"Yeah, he had a family . . . thing, so he couldn't make it, but he sends his condolences."

"I'm so sorry I wasn't able to contact you these last few years."

"I understand. You were good to my dad, and I know he appreciated it even though he couldn't say it."

"I know. And your family saved my life, so there's that."

"Dude!" It was Rick Jacobson with Mary Louise. Rick approached, gave Paul a bear hug. "I'm so sorry," he said, and to Jason: "Pardon me."

"Thanks for coming." Paul kissed Mary Louise. "I appreciate it."

Rick placed both his hands on Paul's shoulders. "I think you owe me a long explanation and a couple of beers."

"Can you guys stay overnight in my house?" Paul asked. "Plenty of room, plus it's a long drive back to New Jersey."

The couple looked at each other. "That would be nice," Mary Louise said.

Over her shoulder, he saw a female figure walking slowly toward him. "Will you excuse me, guys?" he said.

With open arms he approached her. "*Dushen'kaya*. You came."

"I had to, Pasha. I know how important your father was to you."

Paul half smiled. "I guess, in some ways, yeah." He embraced her.

"You talked about him a lot."

She was wearing a long black dress fringed at the hem. He didn't know if it was vintage or just secondhand. Her situation had changed, but she hadn't, as far as he could tell. "Speaking of fathers and dying . . ."

There was a long pause. Tatyana took his hand in both of hers. "I think he knew when he pulled out a gun at the CIA safe house what would happen to him. I think he as good as committed suicide. Because the life he knew was gone. He was never going to get it back. He didn't want to live that way." Tears were streaming down her face.

"Where's your family? What's happening to them?"

"The government has been very good to us. Because of Papa's service all those years. They offered to resettle us all somewhere under another name in a foreign country, but it turned out to be Paraguay, and Polina put her foot down. That was out of the question. She's staying in the house on the base."

"And Niko?"

"He's here, Pasha. We drove together."

"What, you rented a car?" He was trying to get a handle on what their life without money looked like. He nodded. In the distance he saw Niko standing next to the handsome black-haired guy he'd noticed before driving Niko's car. *How the hell can he still afford a driver?* Paul wondered. Then he saw the man squeeze Niko's hand, and the penny dropped.

"That's not Niko's *driver*, is it?" Paul managed to say, astonished.

Tatyana smiled, closed her eyes, shook her head. "My father wasn't the only one playing a role. He's much easier to be around now."

A long pause as Paul processed what he'd just learned. Then he said, "Are you guys all safe? Do they think anyone's coming after you?"

"Not with Papa dead. That's who the Russians really cared about. The rest of us, not so much."

"And you? Where are you living?"

"For now, I'm living with Polina on the base. It's not ideal, but it's all I've got."

He looked at her a long time. "Do you like to sail?"

"You know I love the water, Pasha."

"I don't mean hanging around a yacht, Tatyana, I mean *sailing*."

As soon as he said it, he wondered if mentioning her lost world would upset her, but she was smiling at him.

"I know how to sail, Pasha, I had sailing lessons since I was six years old."

Of course she did, he thought. "Okay, good."

"Why do you ask?"

THREE MONTHS LATER

It had taken him nearly four hundred hours—ten weeks of working full time—but Paul finally built Tatyana the wooden sailboat she wanted, a Herreshoff twelve and a half. A Herreshoff twelve and a half was probably the finest, most elegant sailboat ever made. When she was first designed, by Captain Nathanael Herreshoff in 1914, she was built entirely of wood. Paul found the plans at MIT, including a modification with a centerboard, which would allow Tatyana to sail in shallower water. The boat was made in classic New England style, with oak framing, cedar planking, and teak trim. Sitka spruce for the mast and spars. All bronze fastenings and fittings and hardware, highly polished. A traditional laid-canvas deck. A most elegant boat.

He named her the *Tatyana*, a fact he'd managed to keep hidden from her till the boat's unveiling. She tried to play it off—she punched his shoulder, called him corny—but there were tears in her eyes. "You done good," she whispered.

He and Tatyana launched the boat two days later, from the Hamlin Pier, on a perfect spring day.

They checked that everything was secure, that there were no lines hanging off the boat in the water. He made sure the anchor line was nicely coiled, tied to its line well. That the bailing bucket was tied to the mast. He looked up to make sure the line wasn't tangled in the sail. The bow line and stern line were cleated to the pier. The sails were stiff, new; they'd have to be worked a while.

Paul was checking the lines again when he heard somebody approach.

He looked up and saw Special Agent Stephanie Trombley standing on the pier. She was wearing jeans and sneakers and a blue dress shirt rolled up at the sleeves. He'd never seen her looking so informal.

He felt a pulse of apprehension. "Agent Trombley, what a surprise."

She nodded and smiled. "Actually, it's Deputy Assistant Director Trombley now, partly thanks to you."

"Happy to hear it. Congratulations."

"Thank you. Nice little rig you've got there—did you build it yourself?"

Paul nodded. "So, you found us."

"That's what we FBI agents are supposed to be good at," she said.

"I guess that's right. To what do I owe the pleasure?"

"I thought you'd be interested to know that Geraldine Dempsey is on her way to prison for twenty-five years to life, depending on the judge. Since you last saw her, she's been living in the Washington, D.C., Correctional Treatment Facility."

"For what?"

"She's going away for the massacre of Mark Addison and five other FBI employees."

Paul nodded, busy checking the lines.

"All thanks to the fact that you got her to finally incriminate herself with her own words."

Tatyana peeked out from behind the jib. "Paul, we good to go?" she said. "Don't forget to make sure our phones are set."

He nodded. "We're good," he said. He'd secured their cell phones in Ziploc bags down below, so they'd stay dry. There was also a cooler down there filled with sandwiches and beer.

"The shoes, Paul," Trombley said. "I had to laugh. Very smooth move."

Paul smiled, remembering how he'd played it. He had expected

Dempsey to frisk him for recording devices at their meeting at the safe house, and had left her plenty to find—a transmitter taped to his lower back, a pen that recorded and transmitted, all the usual spy gadgets. But he guessed they wouldn't think to check his shoes, which were equipped with recording and transmitting devices—and which had broadcast Dempsey's entire confession to the waiting FBI team.

He'd been right.

Paul was watching Tatyana put the centerboard in the slip. She so clearly loved this boat.

"I know it's not exactly the *Pechorin*," Paul said.

"Oh, but isn't she yar?" Tatyana said to Paul in her best Hepburn imitation. That was from *The Philadelphia Story. Yar* was one of those old nautical terms that was hard to define. It meant fine, or ready to move, or shipshape.

Trombley wasn't finished. "The word from Langley is that Dempsey's excesses have been curbed and heads are going to roll."

"Let me guess," Paul said. "They're 'cleaning house.'"

Trombley smiled ruefully and nodded.

"And she got away with it all these years," Paul said, "because Phantom was self-financing and she didn't need budget approval from anyone. She ran the unit using the money Galkin made. She didn't need money from the intelligence budget to fund Phantom. It made its own money."

Trombley gave a slow smile. "Kind of genius, right?"

"So where's Andrei Berzin?"

"He's been arrested," Trombley said, fussing with her gray hair, which was blowing in the wind.

"But he was a CIA agent. I don't get it."

"He was arrested for the murder of a police officer in New Hampshire, Alec Wood. This is someone you know."

"He was a friend, yeah," Paul said. "But what I don't understand is why Dempsey was so determined to protect Arkady Galkin these last few years."

"She wasn't protecting *Galkin*. She no longer cared about Galkin. He was no longer of any operational significance. She was protecting herself. Covering her ass. The official story is that she went rogue."

"Went rogue?" Paul said. "What are you talking about? She reported to several layers of CIA executives and the director of national intelligence. They *all* must have known what she was doing."

"We just go with it, okay?" Trombley said. "For every single event, there's a hundred narratives. I suggest you climb aboard mine." She looked right at him, her tone direct. Not confrontational, but blunt. She wasn't joking around.

"Fine," Paul said, happy to leave all that bureaucratic bullshit behind.

"And that's where it ends," she said. "But you know . . . Look, I'm sorry to say this, but if you ever say a word of this—either one of you—we're going to come after you." Now she was looking at Tatyana, who was close enough to overhear everything she said.

"'Come after us'?" Paul glanced briefly at Tatyana, then turned back to Trombley. "I know you're just crossing your *t*'s, so I'll try not to take offense at your hard-ass tone. If your message here is that this time capsule needs to be buried, and deep? I get it."

"Appreciate that, obviously," Trombley said. "As to all your other stuff?" She was referring to the willful retention of national security information charges as well as the identity theft charges arising from Paul's using Grant Anderson's Social Security number for five years. "Those charges have all been dismissed. You should be fine now."

He nodded his head to acknowledge his gratitude.

"So—what's next, Paul?" Trombley asked. "You going back to your old life, make a bundle on Wall Street? You can do it."

"No, I don't think so," he said. "Tatyana and I prefer a simpler life. Turns out I'm happiest when I'm working with my hands."

Tatyana smiled at his last remark. She took his arm, held his hand. "By which he means, building boats for rich people." Tatyana had moved into Paul's farmhouse in Derryfield. "I don't have any money, really, anymore," he'd told her one evening around the kitchen table. "Neither do I" was all she'd said.

"So you guys setting sail?" Trombley asked.

"This very minute—in fact, could you help out and uncleat the bow line?" Paul said, untying the line at the stern of the boat and tossing it onto the dock.

"I don't know what you're talking about," Trombley said.

Paul pointed. She untied the line and threw it onto the bow.

They pulled away from the pier, sails luffing, until Tatyana turned the boat to windward and the sails filled, not a wrinkle. The boat heeled, leaned over into the water, and they were under way. She was a good sailor. Trombley waved goodbye from the pier.

Tatyana was sitting on the leeward side, her hand on the tiller. She was watching the sails, gauging the wind. "Man the sheet, Paul, okay?" she said.

He pulled the sail in, and they heeled a bit, but not uncomfortably.

She patted the deck. "Come sit next to me," she said. This was her boat, and she was in charge.

Now they were cruising. Paul felt the breeze at his back, the sunlight on his face. They were going the same speed as the wind. The sunlight sparkled on the water. Everything had gone wonderfully silent. There was a stillness, being in nature and being one with it. They were cooperating with the wind, they were one with the wind, and it was blissful and quiet.

"Where are we going, anyway, Pasha?"

Paul shrugged, smiled. "Wherever you want," he said.

ACKNOWLEDGMENTS

Several excellent books were particularly useful in illuminating the culture and role of Russian oligarchs, including Catherine Belton, *Putin's People*; Oliver Bullough, *Butler to the World* and *Moneyland*; and Elisabeth Schimpfössl, *Rich Russians: From Oligarchs to Bourgeoisie*.

In evoking Moscow circa 2019–2020, I was helped by Muscovites, visiting businessmen, and others, including Denis Morozov, Bernie Sucher, Josh Gelernter, John Freedman, John Kleinheinz, and a few who prefer not to be named. My good friend Steedman Hinckley, recently of the CIA, was a huge help on oligarchs and the "Kremlin" (which I use as a metaphor since, as he points out, the Kremlin is no longer the seat of the Russian government) but is not at all responsible for the malign schemes of Geraldine Dempsey. And speaking of CIA, big thanks to Ned Carmody and Gene Smith.

On Paul/Grant's disappearance and his new life, my thanks to Kelly Riddle of Kelmar Global Private Investigations; Nick Rosen, author of *Off the Grid*; Frank Ahearn, author of *How to Disappear*; Jay Groob of American Investigative Services; Skip Brandon of Smith Brandon; and Laurie Katz.

I'm grateful to my guides Dennis Haug and Chuck Johnson of the WIFM School of Survival in Barrington, New Hampshire, who took me into the Pemigewasset Wilderness on a bitterly cold January day, at my instigation; and to Chief George Joy and Dan Brooks of the Barrington Police Department. Thanks to Scott Trager of Northeast Off-Road Adventures, and David Gengenbach of Direct Action Driving.

My legal advisers included Peter R. V. Brown of Nutter McClennen & Fish; Jay Shapiro of White and Williams; and the money-laundering expert

Jack Blum. My medical adviser was, as always, my friend Dr. Mark Morocco. On Tatyana's photography: thanks to Cindy Kleine, and to Robert Klein of the Robert Klein Gallery in Boston.

On Paul's work life in New York City, my thanks to Chris Keller, Charlie Coglianese, Asher Carey, Hans Reuter, Jon Bassett, and especially David Weissbourd. My friend and unindicted co-conspirator, Giles McNamee, helped enormously and generously with Paul's career. I got some smart guidance from Seth Klarman of Baupost. Jenna Blum kindly devised Tatyana's wardrobe and style.

Paul's office espionage was assisted by some useful tips from Mark Spencer of Arsenal Consulting, Tom Hegel of SentinelLabs, Kevin Murray of Murray Associates, Jayson Street, and, once again, Jeff Fischbach. On encryption, my dear friend Bruce Donald of Duke University was a great help.

Thanks to my Reed College expert, the excellent novelist Alafair Burke. On the FBI's SWAT/HRT, I'm grateful to Dick Rogers, once again, and Danny Coulson. The rant by the "Deacon" (and also Stan Brightman) on governments as organized crime comes from the work of the political scientist Charles Tilly. My old friends from grad school days, Misha and Elena Tsypkin, checked on my rusty Russian.

Boats, from sailboats to yachts, figured large in this story, and I thank Becky Okrent, Nina Young, Allen Smith, Diane Byrne, Doug Reno, Samuel Blatchley, Captain Russell Zawaduk, and especially the superyacht captain Brendan O'Shannassy, founder of Katana Maritime. On wooden boats, thanks to Tom Sieniewicz, and Walter Baron of Old Wharf Dory Company in Wellfleet, Massachusetts.

My editor, Noah Eaker, improved the book immensely; I thank him and Edie Astley. Big thanks as well to Heather Drucker and Katie O'Callaghan at Harper. I'm grateful to Kate Miciak for a close read at an important point and to my wonderful UK agent, Clare Alexander. My brilliant brother, Henry Finder, was, as always, invaluable in numerous ways. My terrific agent, Dan Conaway (aka "Dr. Plot"), believed in this book from the beginning and gave it many helpful reads. Finally, I'm indebted to my wife, Michele Souda, for her steadfast support throughout my career, and our adored daughter, Emma Finder, my Taylor Swift consultant.

ABOUT THE AUTHOR

JOSEPH FINDER is the *New York Times* bestselling author of fifteen suspense novels, including *House on Fire*, *The Fixer*, and *Suspicion*. Two of his novels have been adapted as major motion pictures—*Paranoia* (starring Harrison Ford and Gary Oldman) and *High Crimes* (starring Ashley Judd and Morgan Freeman). Four more have won the industry's top best novel awards—*Killer Instinct* (the International Thriller Writers Award), *Buried Secrets* (the Strand Critics Award), *Guilty Minds* (the Barry Award), and *Company Man* (the Barry Award). Finder lives in Boston, Massachusetts.